BURIED
EVIDENCE

*Also by Nancy Taylor Rosenberg
in Large Print:*

Abuse of Power

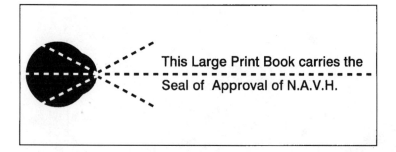

This Large Print Book carries the
Seal of Approval of N.A.V.H.

BURIED EVIDENCE

Nancy Taylor Rosenberg

Thorndike Press • Thorndike, Maine

Published in 2000 by arrangement with Hyperion.

Thorndike Press Large Print Americana Series.

The tree indicium is a trademark of Thorndike Press.

The text of this Large Print edition is unabridged.
Other aspects of the book may vary from the original edition.

Set in 16 pt. Plantin by Christina S. Huff.

Printed in the United States on permanent paper.

Library of Congress Cataloging-in-Publication Data

Rosenberg, Nancy Taylor.
    Buried evidence / Nancy Taylor Rosenberg.
        p.   cm.
    Sequel to: Mitigating circumstances.
    ISBN 0-7862-2924-1 (lg. print : hc : alk. paper)
    1. Public prosecutors — Fiction. 2. Women lawyers —
Fiction.   3. Santa Barbara (Calif.) — Fiction.   4. Large
type books.   I. Title.
PS3568.O7876 B8   2000b
    813´.54—dc21   00-061586

This book is for
my new granddaughter and angel:

Remy

1

"God, I want this maniac!" Lily Forrester said, her voice bouncing off the colorful tiled floors and decaying stucco walls. The Santa Barbara courthouse was a beautiful but ancient structure that would have served better as a museum than a processing house for justice.

"Why did you ask Judge Orso to meet with us this early?" Matt Kingsley asked his supervisor, a tall, lanky woman with freckles and curly red hair. Lily didn't look old enough to have a daughter in her second year of college. One of the most impassioned prosecutors in the county, she whipped around the office with nonstop energy, putting the younger attorneys to shame. In many ways, such intensity was frightening. Of course, anyone would get excited about the crime they were presently handling. The victim was an eight-year-old girl. Her father, Henry Middleton, had been arrested the day before on charges of attempted murder.

The crime had occurred on Halloween.

Betsy Louise Middleton, dressed in her pink satin ballerina costume, had consumed what easily could have amounted to a fatal dose of strychnine administered in a straw-shaped candy. The child's parents appeared to be upstanding citizens. The father owned a chain of furniture stores and served as a deacon in the First Baptist Church, one of the reasons the police had not immediately identified the couple as suspects. Instead, every person Betsy had visited while trick or treating that fatal night had been put through the wringer.

The investigation had been time-consuming and exhaustive. Only four days before, the break the authorities had been waiting for had finally arrived. While working a convenience store robbery, a police officer had stumbled across a Spanish-speaking witness in Ventura, a neighboring city located approximately twenty miles south of Santa Barbara. The woman had positively identified Henry Middleton from a photo lineup, stating that she remembered him purchasing that particular brand of candy the day before Halloween while his wife and children waited outside in their red Ford Explorer. The witness recognized the defendant, as she had purchased a mattress from his furniture company.

"Didn't you speak to Judge Orso yesterday?" Matt Kingsley's voice cut through the morning calm. His eyes were a muted shade of hazel, his blond hair stylishly long. His look was that of a former surfer without the charred skin. To add to his appeal, he drove a bright yellow Ferrari and purchased his clothes at Saks Fifth Avenue or Nordstrom.

"Yes," Lily said crisply. "I caught him on the golf course, though. He probably doesn't remember half of our conversation."

Santa Barbara was a small judicial district, and due to the early hour, the courthouse had yet to come alive. A bedraggled attorney was leaning against the wall, sipping a cup of coffee out of a Styrofoam cup. Kingsley, with his Brooks Brothers suit and squeaky new shoes, smirked as he took in the other man's morning stubble, wrinkled shirt, and dirty white sneakers. "Think this guy overestimated the travel time?" he said, spotting what looked like a garment bag on the floor next to the man's briefcase.

Lily's jaw dropped. For a few moments she just stared, unable to believe her eyes. She considered turning around, but there was no other way to reach their destination.

"Is something wrong?" Kingsley asked, noting how ashen her face had become.

She tilted her head so Kingsley would follow her instead of lingering. Once they were out of earshot, she stopped walking. "You're not sharp enough to lick that man's boots, let alone compete with him in the courtroom. You just walked past one of the finest legal minds in the state."

"Fine, whatever," Kingsley answered, straightening the knot on his tie. "Want to tell me why someone with one of the finest legal minds in the state is hanging around the courthouse like he lives here?"

Lily continued walking. "He doesn't want to take a chance on being late."

The young attorney snickered. "Hard to believe you'd worship this guy just because he always shows up on time."

"That's only one of his finer traits," Lily told him, flicking a piece of lint off her green linen jacket. Young guns like Kingsley always chased after the big case. When their heads hit the pillow at night, they dreamed of dynamite arguments, surprise witnesses, killer pieces of evidence, complex legal analyses. Only with maturity did they learn the truth — that many times the seemingly insignificant traits were what put a person in a league with the legends.

Matt Kingsley pulled his collar away from his neck, a stream of perspiration dotting his forehead. Only 8:00 a.m., and already the courthouse was steaming. By noon the place would be as hot as a boiler room. The building was not air-conditioned. Age alone precluded any attempt at modernization, and the historical society wouldn't allow them even window units. The only thing that made life tolerable was that everyone suffered: the judges, the prosecutors, the prisoners, even the jurors.

Once they reached Judge William Orso's chambers, Lily tried the outer door and found it locked. "Damn," she said, anxiously jiggling the handle, "don't tell me he forgot about our conference this morning. Someone's got to get this man to retire. I swear he's so senile he has trouble remembering his own name."

"How did Officer Stevens put this together?" Kingsley asked as they waited, reaching into his pocket for a package of chewing gum. He offered a stick to Lily, but she waved it away. "Certainly he didn't carry a mug shot of the father around with him. This wasn't even Ventura's homicide. The way I heard it, Stevens was at the store to investigate an unrelated robbery."

"I've known a lot of callous killers," Lily said, ignoring his question. "I honestly believe Middleton is the worst piece of human

11

garbage I've ever seen. He sat there and fed his own child strychnine for no other reason than greed."

"Maybe it was a mercy killing," he suggested. "The girl has a serious illness. Isn't that how they explained the million-dollar life insurance policy? I mean, no one insures their kid for that kind of money unless they think there's a chance they're going to die."

"Don't you know anything about this case?" Lily asked, appalled that he wasn't better informed. "Betsy suffers from a rare genetic disorder called Aicardi syndrome. She has a defect in the corpus callosum, the middle brain, which allows the right brain to communicate with the left brain. At the time Middleton had insured her, she hadn't been officially diagnosed. Her parents might have suspected that she had the disorder, however, because someone in their family could have died from it years before."

"Can't we find out?"

"Probably not," Lily told him. "These are the kinds of things families keep hidden, although they pass it along by word of mouth from one generation to the next. Aicardi syndrome was identified only in 1965. If one of the Middleton ancestors did die from complications from it, the correct cause of death was probably not listed."

"Hey, I'm not a doctor," Kingsley said. "I read something about right brain versus left brain when I was in college. That's about as far as I go."

"Just listen," she continued. "Children who suffer from Aicardi syndrome have seizures, some more frequently than others. Betsy also has a hole in the retina of her left eye and a small lesion on her right."

"Then she's blind?"

"Not blind," Lily corrected him. "Visually impaired."

Kingsley smacked his gum. "I thought she was retarded."

"Developmentally disabled."

"We're just talking," the young attorney said. "I wouldn't use the word *retarded* in the courtroom."

Lily gave him a look that would drop an elephant. "Then don't use it now."

Kingsley decided to shut his mouth.

"Okay," she said a few moments later, "here's how I see it. Middleton needed money. Because he had two normal children, he decided Betsy was expendable. Like a ripped sofa, you know. Except he didn't just toss her out, he cashed her in like a lottery ticket. Can you imagine holding your child in your arms and listening to her scream in agony?"

13

Kingsley's hand instinctively flew to his stomach. "Weren't the other children insured as well?"

"Not until Betsy was born," Lily said, chewing on a ragged fingernail. "To prove how diabolical Middleton is, we have to show the jury the years of preparation that went into this crime."

The picture she had painted was so evil the hairs were prickling on the back of his neck. "How could a person plot his daughter's death almost from the day she was born?" Kingsley asked. "You make it sound as if he was charting a long-term bailout plan for his company."

"Precisely," Lily said, her eyes expanding.

The young attorney could see the case unfolding on his supervisor's face, almost as if he were watching film footage of the actual crime. And what Lily visualized in her mind was generally accurate. She had a gift, an ability to take all the minute and disconnected pieces and fit them together like a puzzle. Up until a few days ago, when the Ventura police had handed them the goods, most of the prosecutors and investigators in the Santa Barbara office had decided the crime had been the result of a random act and would never be solved. Lily's conviction that Henry Middleton had poisoned his daughter had never wavered.

Lily fell deep in thought, her eyes trained on the floor. Suddenly she remembered something, jerking her head up. "You didn't tell me what the hospital said this morning."

"I told Mike Armstrong to call."

Lily's voice rose several octaves. "Did I tell you to have Armstrong check on Betsy's condition?"

"No, but —"

"But, my ass," she shouted. "What are we going to charge Middleton with?"

"Attempted murder, of course." A few sheets of paper fluttered in Kingsley's hands. "The complaint's right here. You don't have to go ballistic."

Lily snatched the papers from him, then darted around the corner. She tried to reach Armstrong on her cell phone, but the investigator's voice mail came on. Dropping down on a bench, she buried her head in her hands, asking herself why she had accepted another position as a prosecutor. Reviewing cases for the appellate court in Los Angeles might not have been as challenging, but the stress level was minimal. Since the events which had transpired in Ventura six years before, she had visited a shrink once a week. Therapy, however, was nothing more than a Band-Aid. Her sins were too serious to re-

15

veal to a priest, let alone a psychologist. Once she regained her composure, she returned to where Kingsley was waiting.

"You were right about that lawyer," he said, staring down the hallway. "He disappeared, then came back looking good enough to go on national TV. I swear. He wasn't gone longer than ten minutes max. He shaved, changed his clothes, combed his hair. The guy must carry everything he owns in that garment bag."

"Doubtful," Lily said, deciding to call the hospital herself. Each time she tried to punch in the numbers, though, her hands began shaking and she had to start over. How could she function when the only man she had ever loved was standing only a short distance away?

"You're probably right," Kingsley decided. "That's a Valentino he's wearing. I know, because I almost bought the same suit. What's his name, by the way? I think I might have seen him on *Rivera Live* the other day."

"Richard Fowler," Lily said, tossing the words over her shoulder as she ducked into the rest room.

2

Lily splashed cold water on her face, then finally managed to get through to Dr. Logan at the hospital. After she explained that the Middleton girl's father was about to be arraigned for attempted murder, the physician asked if he could speak to her in person. "I'm really on a tight schedule today," she told him. "Can't you give me an update of her condition over the phone?"

"Please, Ms. Forrester," Logan said. "Betsy's condition has deteriorated. We've been talking to her parents about removing her from life support."

"I'll be over as soon as possible," Lily told him, deciding she would have to postpone the arraignment. As soon as she disconnected, her daughter called.

"You left a message on my machine."

"Shana," she said, "I can't talk right now, sweetheart. Will you be home this afternoon?"

"Yeah," the girl mumbled. "Dad forwards the calls to his cell phone, though, so you probably won't be able to reach me.

17

What's going on?"

Shana was generally a positive, charismatic young lady. Most of their conversations were filled with gossip and laughter. Not only did she sound as if she were speaking through a pillow, there was something else that Lily couldn't quite put her finger on. "Are you okay?"

"I was up until three o'clock last night."

"Studying?"

"Of course," Shana said, sighing, "what else would I be doing on a Monday night? I certainly wasn't out partying. I was sick last week. I missed three days of classes."

"Did you see a doctor?"

"I'm fine, Mom," she told her. "I must have had a touch of the flu. What do you want to talk to me about? The message you left on my answering machine made it sound like it was something important."

Common sense told Lily to let it slide. She stared up at the overhead light fixture, a graveyard of dead flies. A public rest room wasn't a place to conduct a serious conversation, and running into Richard Fowler had left her unnerved. Had he even seen her? "I'll catch you later this evening."

"Tell me now," the girl insisted. "I won't be able to concentrate on my school work. You can't just dangle something in front of me, then make me wait. You know I'm curious by nature. You're the same way, Mom."

Lily poked her head out the door to the rest room. Kingsley was still standing in front of the judge's chambers. Damn Orso, she thought. They'd be lucky if he showed up for the hearing. "Is your father home?"

"I think he went out to get something to eat," Shana told her. "The car was gone when I woke up this morning."

"I know you can't transfer now," Lily said, deciding to speak her mind while her ex-husband was out of the house, "but I'd like you to reconsider attending the university here in Santa Barbara."

"Not this again," her daughter whined. "The fall semester just started. Why would you even mention me switching schools? I thought you were happy for me, that you weren't going to rag on me anymore."

"I *am* happy for you," Lily told her, leaning back against the sink. "Something's come up, that's all. If you were living in the dorm there wouldn't be a problem. Even sharing an apartment with a couple of girls might be an option. The rent on the duplex is almost two thousand a month."

"Why do you care?" Shana asked. "Dad pays for it."

"Not anymore."

"I don't understand."

"He called me yesterday," Lily explained. "I promised I wouldn't tell you —"

"Tell me what?"

"Your father's behind on the rent. He claims he hasn't sold a house in four months. I'm already paying for your tuition, food, clothing, even your car insurance."

"You're making this up," Shana said. "Dad sold a house last week. He has all kinds of big deals in the fire."

"I'm sorry, darling," Lily said, her chest constricting. John always managed to make her the bearer of bad news. He knew she would refuse to foot the bill for the duplex. He'd *had* to give it a stab, though, just like a gambler *had* to toss his last chip down on the table. "You know your father doesn't always tell the truth," she continued. "Even if he closed a deal tomorrow, Shana, it could be up to three months before he received a commission check."

"You're just saying these things because you're jealous," the girl argued. "You've always been jealous over my relationship with Dad. That's why you put him down all the time."

Lily suspected there was some degree of truth in her daughter's statement. She wouldn't call it jealousy, however. All the checks she sent to Shana were cashed by her ex-husband. With the exception of the rent, she had been supporting them both for over a year. "Your father made it sound like he doesn't anticipate being able to pay the rent for quite sometime," she went on. "I suggested he get a regular job, something that paid him an hourly wage. He hung up on me."

"But my friends are here," Shana cried. "I'll have to start over if you make me change schools. And you know Santa Barbara isn't ranked as high as UCLA. I want to go to a first-rate law school."

With her free hand, Lily opened the door to the rest room. She could already taste defeat. Her daughter had an emotional stranglehold on her. If she continued the discussion, she would be sucked dry. "I'll agree to allow you to continue at UCLA," she said, "but you'll have to move into the dorm by next semester. Otherwise, I might not be able to afford to send you to law school."

"Now you're threatening me!"

"I'm attempting to explain the facts of life to you," Lily said. "I earn a modest living, Shana. The price of education is astronomical. I've been saving for your future since the day you were born. I'd work a second job if necessary. I simply cannot support your father."

The line was silent.

"I love you," Lily told her, wishing such a negative discussion hadn't been necessary. "Everything will work out. It won't be so bad living in the dorm. You'll have fun, get to spend more time with your friends. Who knows? Maybe you won't need the added expense of keeping a car."

"Great," Shana snapped. "Thanks a lot, Mom. This is just what I needed to start my day. First I have to move. Now I have to give up my car. Everyone has a car in L.A. How will I get around?"

"You'll be living on campus." Lily paused. She should have never mentioned the car. The car was a sore spot. "Your father doesn't have a car, and he seems to be making out just fine."

Shana knew she was busted. When her mother had tapped into her savings to buy her a brand-new Mustang convertible for a high school graduation gift, she had made her promise that she wouldn't allow anyone else to drive it. "What am I supposed to do? Dad needs a car to sell real estate. Either he drives me where I want to go, or I catch a ride with one of my friends. What's the big deal?"

Negotiate, Lily told herself, taking in a

deep breath. Her daughter was a formidable young woman. Already she argued like an attorney. When given the chance, however, she could be as manipulative as her father. "I might be able to increase your allowance so you'll have more money to spend on entertainment and clothes."

A small voice said, "I have to go."

"Family problems?" Kingsley asked, overhearing the tail end of Lily's conversation.

She slipped her cell phone back into her purse, giving him a look that said he should mind his own business. No matter how attractive he was, the attorney annoyed her. Maybe he annoyed her because he was so good-looking. Just to prove her point, a couple walked by. The man glanced at Lily and immediately looked away. The woman smiled flirtatiously at Kingsley. He was used to women drooling over him. He loved it, encouraged it. "No sign of Orso yet?"

"Nope."

"As soon as he shows, ask him to postpone the arraignment until three o'clock this afternoon," Lily told him, her face locked in a grimace. "I need to go to the hospital."

The young prosecutor was bewildered. "Why can't we go ahead with the arraignment at ten like we planned? I go there at six

o'clock this morning to work on the complaint. I even had Brennan go over it with
me last night to make certain everything was
perfect."

Lily struck her forehead with the back of
her hand. "Think," she shot out. "Attempted murder is not first-degree murder.
We can plead special circumstances and ask
for the death penalty if Betsy died during
the night. Then Middleton might be looking
at something far more frightening than a
prison sentence."

3

Lily steered her black Audi into the parking lot of Saint Francis Hospital. She was thankful that the hospital was only a five-minute drive from the courthouse. Part of the luxury of living in a small city like Santa Barbara was the fact that everything was close, and, in most instances, a person didn't have to worry about getting stuck in traffic. Weekends were occasionally a problem, but most of the traffic snarled on the 101 Freeway or on State Street, the city's main drag. People from Los Angeles and the surrounding communities headed north during the summer months to escape the heat and enjoy the lovely beaches. When the mercury inched its way past eighty in Santa Barbara and people started perspiring and complaining, the temperature in Los Angeles and the San Fernando Valley generally rose over the hundred mark. On her drive to the office that morning, Lily had heard that it was supposed to hit 105 in downtown L.A.

"I'm here to see Dr. Logan," she told an elderly volunteer working the front desk.

"Is he expecting you?"

"Yes," Lily said, giving the woman her name.

When she stepped off the elevator onto the second floor, a handsome man in a white coat rushed over to greet her. "Christopher Logan," he said, shaking her hand. "You could have waited for me in the lobby. Didn't Mrs. McKinley tell you?"

"No," Lily said, her face flushing. They had talked on the phone at least a dozen times. His voice was familiar, yet she had not anticipated him being so small. Wearing a blue shirt under his starched white jacket, Dr. Logan had neatly trimmed dark hair, perfectly shaped facial features, and he possessed the kind of squeaky-clean look that one would expect for a person in his profession. Lily found herself checking her fingernails, fearful there might be a speck of dirt under them. When the doctor gazed up at her, he blinked several times. She wasn't the only one doing a double take. She doubted if the diminutive Dr. Logan had envisioned himself talking to a freckle-faced giraffe during their numerous phone conversations.

"Betsy isn't here," he told her. "She's been moved to the transitional care unit."

Middleton's arraignment had been postponed until three o'clock that afternoon, but Lily had two additional court appearances to make, one at ten-thirty and another at one. Her watch read nine forty-five. Logan motioned toward an unoccupied waiting room a few feet away, then waited until Lily dropped down on the edge of a chair.

"Before we go over there," Logan said, sitting across from her, "there's been a new development. Mr. Middleton's attorney called me ten minutes ago. He instructed me that Betsy was not to be removed from life support under any circumstances. I found this peculiar, as we've been working closely with the parents since the child was admitted last October. Only a few days ago Henry and Carolyn Middleton agreed that Betsy should be removed from the respirator. That's why I thought you should come here, since we were about to proceed with their request."

Lily's first assumption was that Logan and the hospital were eager to harvest the girl's organs. Then she changed her mind, doubting if a child whose body had been flooded with strychnine would have anything worth salvaging. "Can she breathe without the respirator?"

"No," he said, shaking his head.

"What about brain activity?"

"Slight," Logan said, clearing his throat.

They were staring directly into each other's eyes. Lily felt an urge to look away, but the nature of their conversation demanded a degree of intimacy. "How slight?"

"Almost nonexistent."

Logan was kind, intelligent, and, from Lily's previous contacts with him, highly cooperative. Extracting information from doctors, however, was never easy. She considered it along the lines of pulling teeth. "Is the child in pain?"

"I don't think so," he answered.

Generally when a patient was in the terminal stages of an illness, physicians attempted to comfort the family by convincing them their loved one could no longer experience pain. "How can you make such a vague statement?" Lily blurted out. "I'm not a family member, someone you have to placate. Is she in pain or not?"

Logan was a calm man, accustomed to dealing with difficult situations. His body language remained the same: his palms rested lightly on his knees, his forehead was unfurrowed, his voice low and steady. "I'd give you a definitive answer if I could," he said. "Betsy is in what we classify as a level six coma. She doesn't respond to external stimuli, so there's no reason to believe she's in pain."

Lily stood. "May I see her now?"

"Of course," Logan said, following her out of the waiting room.

They walked along a path to the rear of the hospital. Lily noticed several small ceramic statues of various animals positioned along the trail. Then they began climbing a steep series of concrete steps. Several times she had to stop and catch her breath. When they reached the top, she saw another structure located between the hospital and the extended-care facility. "What's in that building?"

"The nuns stay there."

"Is it a convent?"

"No," Logan replied. "It's just a place for them to rest." A question mark appeared on his face. "I guess a few of them might reside there."

Lily realized she was letting herself become sidetracked, possibly due to the hectic pace of the morning. "Is there any chance Betsy could recover?"

"Outside of a miracle," Logan answered, "I don't think it's possible."

Once they passed through the doors to the nursing facility, a middle-aged nun swished by wearing a white cotton habit. Lily glanced in a room and spotted another nun working over an elderly patient. The facility must be staffed by a specific religious order, she decided, probably one dedicated to the care of the terminally ill. No phones jangled, no televisions blasted, no orderlies pushed metal carts down the tiled corridors. The silence alone was ominous. The sisters seemed to drift from room to room on a cushion of air, their movements completely soundless. Patients were not moved to this transitional unit simply because their insurance would no longer pick up the tab.

Betsy Middleton had reached the last stop on the train.

The building was long and narrow, with the majority of the rooms on the ocean side. Even from the hallway Lily could see the entire coastline through one of the patients' windows. She had seen pictures of monasteries in Tibet perched on the edge of windswept cliffs. This particular facility might not be as removed from civilization, but she imagined there was a similar feeling of stillness and isolation. She felt as if she were floating just slightly below the clouds.

Dr. Logan reached over the counter and retrieved Betsy's chart, then motioned for Lily to follow him. "We don't usually admit children over here," he told her, stopping in front of a room. "In this instance our administrator made an exception."

Lily stared through the window at Betsy Middleton. The girl was in a crib, tubes and wires snaking out between the bars. A hard-ball of rage formed in her stomach. Because of the pending criminal charges, Henry Middleton would never allow his daughter to be removed from life support. He wasn't a stupid man. He knew they could charge him with murder. Far more was at stake than merely convicting a criminal. While the wheels of justice slowly turned, a precious soul was trapped in limbo.

The small mound beneath the covers no longer looked like an eight-year-old girl. Even though they were feeding her through a shunt in her abdomen, Betsy's body was wasted and her limbs had atrophied. She was curled up in the fetal position and couldn't weigh more than a large infant. Her hair was blonde with reddish highlights, almost the same color Shana's had been at that age.

"One of the saddest things about this case," Logan said, their shoulders touching, "is Betsy was only mildly impaired. I concur with the diagnosis of Aicardi syndrome, yet from all appearances, her corpus callosum is almost completely intact. The last test they gave her at the special school she attended listed her IQ in the mid-sixties."

31

"What you're saying, then," Lily said, acid bubbling back in her throat, "is she had a chance to live a fairly normal life?"

"More or less," he replied. "Don't get me wrong, I'm not saying she could have graduated from college. Before she developed the lesion on her right eye, however, her vision problems were minimal."

"I thought she had a hole in her retina."

"Left eye," he said, pointing at his own. "A person can manage fairly well with one eye."

When Lily faced the glass partition again, she saw a well-groomed woman in her late thirties leaning over the bed, tenderly stroking the girl's forehead. She must have been in the bathroom before. "You didn't tell me Mrs. Middleton was here."

"I didn't know," Logan said, shrugging.

Lily understood the sense of helplessness Betsy's mother must be experiencing. Six years ago she had stood over Shana, holding her hand and stroking her forehead. A mother's concern for her child was one of the most powerful forces in the universe. "You said her brain function was only moderately impaired. . . ."

"A lot of people have IQs in the sixties," he explained. "Many marry and have families. Since Betsy has a genetically inherited disorder, though, I doubt if I would have recommended that she have a child."

Just then Betsy began convulsing. Her mother shrieked, then frantically depressed the call button. Lily heard something drop on the floor, then realized it was the metal chart. Logan rushed inside the room, along with two nuns who seemed to have materialized out of nowhere. Never in her life had she seen people move that fast. One of the nuns handed the doctor a syringe. He instantly injected the medication into the intravenous tube already inserted into the girl's arm. As Carolyn Middleton cowered in the corner, the sisters fastened leather straps around the child's arms, legs, and torso. The seizure was so severe, the crib shook as if the building were collapsing. After five agonizing minutes, the girl's tortured body finally became still.

Dr. Logan found Lily with her hands pressed against the window, tears streaming down her cheeks. "It's over," he said, peeling off his rubber gloves and tossing them into a trash can.

"You mean she's dead?"

He reached in his pocket to hand her a tissue. "I was referring to the seizure."

"Bad choice of words," she told him, dabbing her eyes.

"I'm sorry," Logan said, bending over to pick up the girl's chart.

Mrs. Middleton lovingly rearranged her daughter's head on the pillow, then stepped out of the room. She was wearing black slacks and a white turtleneck sweater, and her brown hair was styled in soft curls around her face. Before the tragedy Lily would have pegged her as a superficial woman, the kind who spent her days shopping or playing tennis at the country club. One look in her eyes made it clear that those days were over.

Lily touched Logan's arm to let him know she was leaving. He must have misread her, however, thinking she wanted to speak to Betsy's mother. "This is Lily Forrester, Carolyn," he said. "She's the district attorney handling Henry's case."

Mrs. Middleton was stunned. "I have nothing to say to you," she said through gritted teeth. She took a step inside Betsy's room, then returned to where Lily and Logan were standing. "How could you possibly arrest my husband? Henry's a decent, God-fearing man. He adores Betsy, just like he does all of our children."

"I'm terribly sorry, Mrs. Middleton," Lily said. "I understand how difficult this must be for you. My daughter was the victim of a

34

violent crime several years back."

Carolyn Middleton refused to be consoled. "You don't understand anything," she said, her once lovely face twisted in a grimace. "What you just saw isn't new to me." She stopped and sucked in a breath. "I've had eight years of this hell. Betsy's been sick all her life."

Dr. Logan opened Betsy's chart to make the necessary notations. Lily shifted her weight but kept her eyes on Carolyn. "Why did you change your mind?"

"I don't know what you're talking about," the other woman said, fingering her pearl necklace.

"Dr. Logan indicated that both you and your husband were prepared to have Betsy removed from the respirator," Lily told her. "Then a few hours ago, your attorney called and rescinded that order. Was this a mutual decision?"

"I don't have to answer your questions," Mrs. Middleton said, dropping her hands to her sides. "Henry told me not to talk to anyone unless Mr. Fowler was present."

Lily thought she was hearing things. "Did you say Fowler? Richard Fowler?"

"Yes," she said, digging in her purse and handing her a business card.

How could Richard have agreed to represent someone as contemptible as Henry Middleton? Now she knew why she had seen him at the courthouse that morning.

Carolyn said, "Henry didn't do it."

"I appreciate how you must feel," Lily told her. "I'm only the prosecutor, Mrs. Middleton. Your husband's guilt or innocence will be determined by a jury." It was obvious that Carolyn Middleton needed Henry and was prepared to defend him. Without her husband the woman would disintegrate. The nice clothes, the carefully applied makeup, the regal way she carried herself. Henry had manufactured her just like he manufactured furniture.

Lily waited until she shuffled off down the corridor, then turned back to Logan. "How long can Betsy last this way?"

"She's been in a coma for almost a year. I've heard of patients who've survived for as long as ten years, even longer." He disappeared into the room, checking the flow on the IV, then quickly returned to conclude his conversation. "If there's anything I can do, please feel free to call me."

"Anything?" she asked, saying more with her eyes than she could with words. She watched as Logan's face paled, the meaning behind her statement striking home. "Do you have children, Dr. Logan?"

"Call me Chris," he said. "And to answer your question, I'm not married."

"Let's say you did have a child," Lily continued. "Would you want her to continue in this state? My office can file the necessary paperwork tomorrow, but for all I know, the court could take up to a year to render a ruling. Without the parents' cooperation, we may never get the authorities to step in and give us approval to remove her from life support."

Tearing off a piece of paper from Betsy's medical chart, the doctor scribbled something and then pressed it into Lily's hand. "This is my home phone number," he told her. "From now on, I think it might be better if we discussed Betsy's situation outside of the hospital. If you can't reach me at home, have the hospital page me."

4

At three o'clock Lily stood outside the dark wood doors of the courtroom, intentionally staging her entry. She had been late to her ten-thirty hearing. Knowing she wouldn't have the strength to face Richard Fowler on an empty stomach, she'd managed to choke down half of a tuna sandwich. Her eyes were swollen and irritated, her lipstick was gone, and her formerly crisp linen jacket hung limply on her shoulders. She anxiously checked her watch, wishing she had time to make herself look presentable. The corridors were empty, so she assumed Richard and his client were already inside. Finally she thrust her shoulders back, shoved open the doors, and strode straight to the counsel table.

Once she was seated, she retrieved Middleton's file from her briefcase, keeping her eyes trained on the front of the room. A distinctive scent drifted past her nostrils, a hint of lime. Even Richard's cologne was the same. Out of the corner of her eye she caught a glimpse of his profile. Being in the same room with him made it difficult to concentrate, let alone the fact that he was Middleton's attorney.

At forty-eight, Henry Middleton reminded Lily of a toad. She estimated his height at five-six, maybe an inch or two taller, but unlike the perfectly proportioned Dr. Logan, Middleton was almost as wide as he was tall. His hair was slicked back off his forehead, his neck almost nonexistent, his face small in comparison to his bulky torso, and his skin was oily and blotched. She signaled the bailiff so he could notify Judge Orso that she was ready to proceed.

Richard suddenly appeared beside her. "I didn't know until you walked in that you were assigned to this case."

"Bullshit," she said, refusing to look at him. "I've been involved since the onset."

Richard shook his head. "But I haven't," he told her. "Middleton hired me yesterday. That's why you saw me at such an ungodly hour this morning. I read about the crime in the papers, but since no arrests were ever made, I'd forgotten most of the particulars. I drove down here at five this morning to review the police reports and interview my client. I was hurt when you didn't stop and talk to me."

Lily started to mention his phone call to the hospital, then heard the bailiff calling the court to order. "All rise," he said. "Division Fourteen of the Superior Court is now in session, Judge William Orso presiding."

The judge swept into the room in a swirl of black robes. At seventy-three, Orso had beady black eyes, a hawkish nose, and a receding hairline. Seeing him glaring at them over the top of his bifocals, Richard returned to his position on the opposite side of the room.

The arraignment went swiftly. As soon as both parties agreed on a date for the preliminary hearing, Richard asked the judge to render a ruling regarding bail.

"The state's position, Ms. Forrester," Orso said, stifling a yawn.

"Your Honor," she said, "the defendant is charged with poisoning his daughter for monetary reward. Surely such a heinous crime merits that he be held without bail. Although the child is presently at Saint Francis Hospital, the court has an obligation to protect her from another attempt on her life."

"There's nothing to justify Ms. Forrester's position," Richard said, his words carefully enunciated. "My client is a highly respected member of the community. He has no prior criminal history. In addition, the crime occurred almost a year ago. Mr.

Middleton would have absconded by now if he possessed such intentions." He paused, then added, "For these reasons we respectfully ask the court to release the defendant on his own recognizance."

Lily rose to her feet, her voice booming out over the courtroom. "The defendant didn't flee immediately after the crime because he had no reason to flee," she said, gesturing toward Middleton. "Even though Mr. Fowler made it a point to emphasize that his client doesn't have a criminal record, this is not an ordinary crime and Mr. Middleton is far from the average offender."

Judge Orso addressed Lily directly. "Can you substantiate that the defendant poses a threat to the victim, Counselor?"

Richard had caused her to become so addled that she'd already tripped over her own feet. Any argument she made to convince the judge that Middleton might harm Betsy would be refuted by his phone call that morning insisting that she be kept on life support. All Middleton had to do was instruct the hospital to pull the plug if he wanted his daughter dead. "Can you answer the question, Ms. Forrester?"

"No, Your Honor," she said.

"Bail is set at five hundred thousand dollars," the judge said, tapping his gavel and disappearing from the bench.

Once the courtroom had cleared, an attractive, large-boned woman with rich mahogany skin and shoulder-length black hair slipped into the empty chair next to Lily. "How did it go?"

"Don't ask," Lily said, scowling. "Middleton's probably writing a check right now."

"You didn't think Orso was really going to hold him without bail, did you?"

Lily rolled her head around to release the tension. "We've got to find a way to have the IRS freeze his assets."

"Maybe you should have thought of that yesterday," Lenora Wells said, arching an eyebrow. Formerly a homicide detective with the Los Angeles police department, she was now the chief investigator for the Santa Barbara D.A.'s office. Due to the fact that they were close in age and both divorced, the two women had struck up a friendship.

"Weren't you scheduled to interview witnesses on that child-molest case this afternoon?"

"Done," Wells told her. "I just stopped by to see how things were going." She picked up a file folder and began fanning herself. "Everyone says you don't need air conditioning in this city. What's wrong

42

with these people? Are they nuts?"

"It's only a heat wave," Lily told her. "The weather report says it's supposed to cool down by tomorrow. Someone said it might even rain. Maybe that's why it's so humid."

"Where's Matt?"

Lily acted as if she hadn't heard the woman's question. Once she'd learned that Richard Fowler had signed on as Middleton's attorney, she'd stopped by the office of the elected D.A., Allan Brennan, telling him she couldn't work with an unreliable and incompetent attorney on such a complex case. Brennan had been thrilled to have her on board, but he refused to give her preferential treatment or allow her to think she could take over the agency. Either tolerate Kingsley, he'd told her, or she would have to try the Middleton case alone. Brennan had also pointed out that even though Kingsley was inexperienced, he was far from ignorant, since he held a law degree from Harvard.

"Hey," Wells said, "what's with you? Am I talking to myself? I just asked you a question. You act like you're in another world or something."

Lily rubbed her forehead. "Matt's going over some reports at the crime lab."

"I see," Wells answered, tilting her head to one side. "You two didn't butt heads again, did you? Usually one of my investigators does the legwork, not the trial attorney."

"Look," Lily said, grabbing her briefcase from the floor and slapping it down on top of the table, "when I ask a person to do something, I expect him to do it. This kid turns around and hands off everything to someone else."

Wells rubbed the side of her face. "Isn't there a word for what you just mentioned?" she said. "You know, like delegating authority."

"You're impossible," Lily told her. "And Kingsley's a spoiled brat."

"Oh, yeah," the other woman said, swinging a leg back and forth under the table. "Matt's not exactly a kid, you know. He's almost thirty. Are you certain you don't have a crush on him?"

"Don't be asinine," Lily said, annoyed that her friend would even mention something so ridiculous. "I'm forty-two, Lenora. When I start chasing young guys like Kingsley, do me a favor and shoot me. He still lives at home with his parents. He doesn't even write checks. He has an accountant who pays all his bills for him."

"My Julian might live at home until he's forty," Wells told her, tapping her fingernails on the table. "That wouldn't necessarily make him a spoiled brat. My sister still lives with my mother and she has three kids."

"We're not in the same ballpark," Lily told her. "Matt's parents own a seven-million-dollar estate. He only decided to enroll in law school after he was thrown from his horse and had to stop playing polo. One of these days I'm going to call Harvard and make certain he didn't print that diploma on his computer. Either that, or his daddy could have given it to him as a Christmas present. A big endowment goes a long way."

"Money talks."

"He hands off assignments like he hands over his dirty underwear to the maid," Lily continued. "Now, do you still feel sorry for him?"

"Humph," the investigator said. "Guess you won this argument hands down." She smiled, causing two deep dimples to appear in her cheeks. "Let's not call him a spoiled brat, though. I prefer the term 'rich little prick.' It's far more demeaning, don't you think?"

Lily felt the warmth of a person's hand on her shoulder. She knew instantly that it was Richard. She stood, then braced herself against the counsel table. Her friend waited for an introduction, then decided to handle the situation herself.

"Lenora Wells," she said, certain they'd met before. "I'm in charge of the investigative unit."

"Richard Fowler," he said, shaking her hand.

In heels, Lily stood almost six feet. Fowler had to be at least six-five, Wells decided, staring up at his face. But his height seemed incidental to his overall appeal. His dark eyes danced with mischief, a sharp contrast against his fair skin. Nice lips, she thought, not too thin. Although his hair was sprinkled with gray, he had a youthful physique and moved like a highly trained athlete. As an African American, Lenora found Santa Barbara slightly too vanilla. The majority of the men strutted around in moth-eaten cashmere sweaters or their ten-year-old Brooks Brothers suits. She appreciated a man who knew how to dress. Fowler's pinstripe suit was beautifully tailored, the cuffs of his shirt were emblazoned with his initials, and the leather on his belt was the same exact shade as his shoes. She placed her hand on the side of her neck. Kingsley might be good-looking enough to get her juices flowing, but this was a *man*. "Didn't you used to be a D.A. in Ventura several years back?"

"Yes," he said. "Lily and I used to work together."

Wells fell silent.

"Are you finished here?" Richard asked Lily. "I'd like to buy you a drink."

Lily checked the time. She'd told Kingsley to report to her office at five to brief him on the events of the day. "I can't," she said. "I have to meet someone in my office."

"I see," he said, disappointment etched on his face. "I could take a walk and come back. That is, if you're not going to be tied up that long."

Lily faced the table, tossing papers and files into her briefcase. Instead of jumping at the chance to be with him, part of her wished he would simply disappear.

"Tell me who you have to meet," Wells said. "I'll take care of it for you."

"No, no," Lily said, strands of hair tumbling onto her forehead. "I have to meet Matt."

"Excuse us," Wells told Richard. She cupped her hand over her mouth as she whispered to Lily. "Matt can wait until tomorrow, sugar. You can't let this man just stand here. I bet you haven't been out of the house in weeks."

Lily squeezed her forearm. Still, Leona didn't get the message. All she knew was a handsome man was offering to buy her friend a drink. She had no idea she was speaking with Henry Middleton's attorney, let alone Lily's former lover.

"Everything's under control," Wells said, her throaty voice echoing in the empty courtroom. When Lily glared at her, the woman placed her hand on her back and pushed her, almost causing her to fall into Richard's arms. "You guys go on now."

"Fine," Lily said, her teeth clenched. "I'll meet you in front of the building."

As soon as Richard left the courtroom, Lily opened her purse and pulled out her brush, running it quickly through her hair. Then she yanked out her lipstick, her car keys, a small container of breath spray.

"If you want to primp," her friend said, watching as Lily tried to apply lipstick without a mirror, "there's a bathroom right down the hall. And why is your hand shaking?"

"Tell Kingsley that Middleton made bail, okay?" she said. "I'll go over the lab reports with him in the morning. I've already read them anyway. I only wanted to get him out of my hair for a few hours." She jerked her head around. "I look awful, don't I?"

"Here," the investigator said, using her finger to wipe a smudge of lipstick off the

48

side of Lily's mouth. "What's the deal with this guy? I've never seen you so . . ."

Before Wells could finish her sentence, Lily had swept all her personal items back into her purse and raced out of the courtroom.

Richard Fowler stood on the sidewalk, inhaling the freshly mowed grass, the salty scent of the ocean, admiring the magnificent Spanish architecture of the historical courthouse. When Lily came bounding down the steps, the people milling around her disappeared. Time stood still for her, he told himself. Not everyone might agree, but in his eyes she was as lovely and captivating as ever. She reminded him of a female Einstein, not strictly on the merits of her intellect, but also due to her personality and mannerisms. She lived so completely inside her thoughts that it shouldn't have surprised him that she failed to notice him that morning. Her ability to focus on her work was mind-boggling, though, and he had been pleased when he'd heard she'd taken a position as a prosecutor again.

"Where are you parked?" she asked, shielding her eyes from the sun.

"Down the street," he said. "We could walk somewhere. There's a nice little bar about three blocks away. I haven't been there in a few years, but I'm certain it's still there."

"I don't want to go to a bar," Lily said crisply. "Get your car and follow me."

A troubled expression appeared on his face. "I don't have that much time. I'm supposed to see Greg tonight. And the traffic —"

Lily felt her stomach churning. Was she nothing more than an old acquaintance, someone to share a drink with before embarking on a long drive? "Maybe we should just forget it, then," she said, taking off down the sidewalk.

Richard was flabbergasted. How could she walk away twice in one day? He turned around in a small circle, trying to decide what to do, then had to jog to catch up with her. "You've been living in Santa Barbara for months now," he said. "If anyone should be hurt, it's me. Why haven't you called? It's not as if Ventura is in another state."

Lily stared down at the cracks in the sidewalk.

"When we last saw each other," he continued, "you said the door was open, that there was still a chance for us. Then you never returned my phone calls."

Lily slowly raised her head. "Why did you agree to represent Middleton?"

His voice was low, seductive. "Maybe because I knew it would give me a chance to see you."

"Then you did know I was prosecuting the case," she said, thinking he had lied to her. "You sandbagged me. You should be ashamed of yourself."

"Give me a chance to explain," he pleaded. "Just because I was aware you'd accepted a position here doesn't mean I knew you'd be prosecuting Middleton. It was a fluke, Lily. I have another case that falls in this jurisdiction. When Middleton started waving money in my face, it only made sense to take him on as a client."

"What kind of case?"

"Possession with intent to distribute."

"Now you're not only defending someone like Middleton," Lily said, incredulous, "you're representing drug dealers too. Weren't you planning to run for judge?"

"That was years ago," he said, frowning. "Things don't always turn out the way we want in life."

He was tossing the ball back in her court, making her feel guilty. She had enough guilt for the entire state. In addition, he was the one who had ended their relationship, abandoning her when she'd needed him the most. "You shouldn't have asked me to go for a drink if you were in such a hurry to get home. God, Richard, we haven't seen each other in years. You could have snagged Clinton Silverstein if you wanted a drinking partner. Haven't you heard? He transferred to our office seven months ago."

"I wasn't looking for a drinking partner," he said, pulling her onto the grass so people wouldn't overhear their conversation. "My associate could have handled both of these cases, Lily. I'm here because of you. It's the craziest thing. A few weeks ago I started having dreams about you. Since then I've been having trouble concentrating on my work."

"Really?" she said, smiling coyly. "Good dreams or bad?"

He laughed. "Would I stand here and let you rake me over the coals if they were bad?"

A pleased look appeared on her face. "We could take a walk on the beach. Since you're in a hurry, it's better if we go in separate cars."

"Sounds like a plan."

"I'll meet you in the parking lot of the Miramar Hotel," Lily tossed out over her shoulder. "You know, the place with the blue roof that runs parallel to the 101 freeway."

★ ★ ★

The sun was setting and the sky was awash with rainbow colors — blue, pink, rose, aqua. Richard and Lily left their cars in the parking lot of the hotel, then walked across the railroad tracks to the beach. Once they reached the sand, she removed her heels, carrying them as they walked. "The heat wave must have broken," she said, rubbing her arms. Several hundred yards off-shore, they could see a line of surfers waiting on their boards for the next big wave.

"You're chilled," Richard said, noticing her shivering. He removed his jacket and tried to hand it to her. "Put this on."

"I'm fine," she said, pulling her green linen blazer tightly around her body. "But it's nice of you to offer."

"I insist."

Lily smiled, slipping her arms into the sleeves. Now that he had removed his jacket, she spotted a small roll around his midsection. Instead of finding the extra weight unattractive, she thought it made him even more appealing. Men with bulging muscles and washboard stomachs might look good in magazines, but she'd never been attracted to them. Placing her hands in the pockets of his jacket, she touched his car keys, his wallet, his sunglasses case. Once again she inhaled the scent of lime. She felt momentarily secure, his jacket her cloak of protection.

They trudged through the sand in silence, then Lily suddenly stopped, gazing out at the frothy whitecaps. Her heart was pounding as hard as the waves. She wanted to feel his arms around her, run her hands through his hair. They shared too many painful memories, though, and she couldn't afford to get caught up in an emotional nightmare. When the judge had granted Middleton bail, she'd almost lost it. After all these years she was still battling. She wanted to believe that the system could dispense justice, that good would triumph over evil, that the innocent would no longer have to suffer. As long as a child like Betsy Middleton spent her days in the twilight zone of respirators, unable to communicate or experience even a brief moment of pleasure, her frail body wracked by seizures, Lily knew she could not rest. Richard may have dreamt about her, but instead of riding in on a white horse to rescue her, he'd shown up as her adversary.

"Do you remember the first night we were together?" he asked as a flock of seagulls swooped past them.

"How could I forget?" Lily's coworkers

had all gathered at the Elephant Bar in Ventura to celebrate her promotion to chief of the sex crimes division, a position Richard had held before her. "I don't know what possessed me to start chugging down shooters of tequila. I don't even like tequila."

"Maybe if you hadn't been intoxicated," he said, giving her a knowing glance, "you would have never gone home with me."

"True," Lily said, impressed with the simplicity of his analysis. In her opinion, Richard Fowler possessed two terrific attributes. He was a brilliant attorney, and he understood the opposite sex. Of course, this sounded strange for a man whose wife had left him for another woman.

"Weren't you celebrating something other than your promotion?" he asked, attempting to reconstruct the details of that night. "It was your birthday, right?"

"Yes," she answered. "No one remembered but my mother. Maybe that's why I decided to get smashed."

"I didn't know it was your birthday," Richard said wistfully. "If I had, I would have flown you to the moon."

Lily bent over and picked up a piece of driftwood. "You did fly me to the moon," she said, recalling their torrid lovemaking.

The alcohol had lowered her inhibitions, but it was Richard himself who had brought her out of her shell, taught her that sex could be a delightful experience. "The only problem is, John found out and asked me to move out. I would have never been in that house alone with Shana if —"

Richard's back stiffened. "What did he see? All we were doing was saying goodbye in the parking lot. Does that mean I'm responsible for what happened?"

"Of course not," she said, tossing the driftwood into the water, "but I'd never had an affair before. Actions have consequences. Maybe the terrible things that happened were a form of punishment."

"Your marriage was over, Lily," he said. "Your husband was already dipping his wand at the office."

"I guess having an affair could be classified as one of my lesser sins," she said, her voice low and pensive. "Some of the things I've done are so despicable I feel as if I can't stand up under the weight of them, like I'm carrying around this three-hundred-pound sack of bricks."

"Life has kicked us both below the belt," Richard said, his voice rising several octaves. "Because I accidentally walked in and caught Judge Fisher snorting cocaine in his chambers, Butler demoted me. The same week I came home and found half the furniture had been moved out of my house, along with a note from Claire that said she was divorcing me."

"Butler's a bastard," Lily said, referring to the Ventura County district attorney. "You should have gone public with the cocaine allegation. Then both Fisher and Butler could have flushed their careers down the toilet. No one who snorts cocaine should sit on the bench. To this day, I don't understand why you let them railroad you."

"I didn't stand a chance," Richard said. "It was Butler's word against mine."

She removed his jacket and handed it back to him. "You should have a fairly easy drive if you leave now."

When they reached her Audi, Lily discovered it had a flat tire. Richard offered to change it, but she didn't want to impose on him. "I'll call Triple A," she said. "I could even walk home and come back for the car tomorrow. My place is only a few blocks away."

"Don't be silly," he said, opening the door to his car for her. "I'll drive you home. Then I'll get a chance to see your new house."

Nestled in an area of exclusive estates, the house was a sprawling Tudor with magnificent grounds. Practically every specimen of tree, shrub, and flower had been artistically arranged around a manicured expanse of greenery. Orange, lime, and lemon trees, their leafy branches heavy with ripe fruit, filled the air with their fragrant aroma. A waterfall had been constructed adjacent to the backyard patio, and birds gathered daily to bathe in the reflecting pool.

Once they pulled into the driveway, Lily climbed out of the passenger seat of Richard's blue Lexus, then walked around to speak to him through the driver's window. "Thanks for the ride," she said. "I'm glad we got to talk. Since you're representing Middleton, we'll have to maintain our distance from now on."

"Who do you think you're talking to?" Richard said, opening the car door and forcing her to step aside. "I told you I only took his case so I could spend time with you. We'll just have to be careful, keep a low profile."

Before she knew it, he was standing at the door. She'd forgotten how strong-willed he was, how he couldn't take no for an answer.

"This place is fabulous," he said. "Aren't you going to invite me in for that drink?"

"Please, Richard," she said, her face flushing, "we're going to be seeing each other every day once the trial begins."

He extended his hand. "Give me the key."

"Damn you," she said, "don't you know how much an estate like this is worth? I'm only leasing the guest house. Even that's a stretch on my budget."

"Oh," he said, realizing he had embarrassed her. "Then let's go to the guest house."

Lily was too tired to resist. She led him down a winding path to a small stone cottage located on the back portion of the property, surrounded by rosebushes. Bugs swarmed around the exterior light fixture. Richard swatted them away as she dug in her purse for the key, finally unlocking the door and motioning for him to come inside. "I don't think you have to worry about anyone bothering you here," he said. "Looks like you've found yourself a nice little hideaway."

He pulled her into his arms as she was reaching for the light switch.

Lily twisted away. "I enjoyed seeing you, but I don't think we should take it any further."

Richard slapped his arms against his thighs in frustration. On the drive to Santa Barbara that morning, he had fantasized that they would pick up where they left off.

During the early days of their affair, Lily had been like a young girl experiencing sex for the first time. He could still hear her delightful giggle, feel her amazingly soft skin, imagine her breasts pressed against his naked chest. They'd made love on the sofa in his living room, their long legs sticking off the end. Their passion for each other had been insatiable; they'd even had sex at the D.A.'s office in an interview room, undaunted by the fact that they were placing both of their reputations on the line.

The guest cottage was charming, almost a scaled-down model of the main house. Spacious and tastefully decorated, the living room contained an overstuffed floral print sofa and two side chairs upholstered in a lime green fabric, one with a matching ottoman. Satin throw pillows were tossed here and there, and a crystal vase filled with fresh flowers was set on one of the end tables. An enormous carved bookcase with beveled glass doors took up an entire wall, and there was a small kitchen, large enough for a table and two chairs.

"I — I don't really need much," Lily stammered, her hands behind her back at the door.

Although the cottage was attractively decorated, Richard felt an overwhelming sense of despair. He spotted dozens of pictures of Shana on the walls, beginning at infancy and working their way to what must be a fairly recent shot. The image Lily presented in public differed greatly from the person who resided within these walls. She was still punishing herself, coming home alone every night, depriving herself of any chance of finding happiness.

"Can I use your bathroom?"

Lily pointed toward the door.

After he had relieved himself, Richard shook his fists in the air. He blamed himself for staying away this long, for not helping her. Now that he'd seen her, he realized he had to take action, but he also knew he had to do it without frightening her. When he exited the bathroom, she was standing in front of a mirror in the living area, staring at her reflection. "You're beautiful."

"Not hardly," Lily said, patting down her windblown hair. She hung up her jacket in the closet. Underneath, she was wearing a beige blouse and a matching skirt. The fabric of her blouse was thin, a silk and cotton blend. Without her jacket, her breasts were visible through her lightweight nylon bra. Because of her shape, finding clothes was difficult. If the skirt wasn't several inches too large in the waist, then it pulled across her hips. She solved the problem by wearing long jackets, unaware how provocative she looked without them.

"I wanted to buy a house," she told him, "but the real estate is too expensive."

"I grew up here, remember?" Richard said. "Of course, the market has skyrocketed since those days. The beach you took me to tonight is where I taught Greg how to surf. My parents' house was over by the railroad tracks." He paused, fond memories surfacing. "The train used to wake me up every morning. Small price to pay for living near the beach, don't you think? I was never late to school."

"How is your mother?"

"She's gone, Lily," he replied. "Mother passed away around this time last year. I guess you could say both of my parents are still residents of Santa Barbara, though, for whatever that's worth."

"I don't understand."

"They're buried in that beautiful cemetery behind the music academy," Richard told her. "Before Middleton's arraignment I drove over and visited their graves. My father purchased the family plots twenty years ago, or I wouldn't have been able to bury my mother next to him. Trust me, even the underground real estate is expensive up here.

Of course, most cemeteries don't overlook the ocean."

"Your father was a doctor, wasn't he?"

"A surgeon," he said, rubbing his forehead.

"I'm sorry to hear about your mother."

"She had a good life, Lily."

"Have you ever thought of moving back?"

"Not really," Richard said. "I'm still living in the same house in Ventura. I added a second story, though. It came out pretty nice."

Lily felt some of her uneasiness abating. "I'd offer you a drink," she said, "but all I have is Diet Coke."

"I'm driving anyway," he said, trailing his fingers over the top of the sofa. "Where's Shana?"

"She moved back in with John."

"I thought you said she was in college."

"She is," Lily told him, walking over to the kitchen to prepare their drinks. "Most kids would give their right arm to attend the university here."

"And Shana?"

"She insisted on going to UCLA." She paused, the subject of her daughter obviously a painful one. "I might not be able to afford a house in Santa Barbara, but I could have bought something in Goleta,

Summerland, maybe even Carpenteria."

"What happened?"

"Once Shana was accepted at UCLA," Lily continued, "John talked her into sharing a duplex with him in North Hollywood. Don't get me wrong, I understand why she didn't want to go to college here. She wants to go to law school, so in that respect we both know UCLA is a better choice."

"Santa Barbara is a party school, Lily," Richard told her. "Not only that, kids are supposed to move out when they go to college. That's how they mature."

"Didn't you hear me?" she said, raising her voice. "She's living with John!"

"Well," he said, chuckling, "from what I know about the man, that's about the same as living with a bunch of college kids."

Lily stopped, sucking in a deep breath. John's irresponsibility might seem comical to Richard, but she certainly didn't think it was funny. "At the very least, I expected her to spend the weekend with me from time to time. She's only visited me once since the day I moved in."

Richard saw another photo of Shana on the end table. He picked it up, having forgotten how much the girl resembled her mother. Now that she was older, people might even mistake the two women for twins. "Wow," he said, "you've got so many pictures of Shana in this place, I bet I could swipe one for Greg and you wouldn't even notice."

"I guess I went overboard," Lily said, taking his remark as criticism. "I don't entertain here, Richard. Looking at her pictures makes feel good."

"I was just kidding," he said. "Setting aside her preference for universities," he said, "why would she decide to live with her father? I thought the two of you were inseparable."

Lily's shoulders dropped. "Same story, you know. John acts like her houseboy. Since I work long hours, she decided to move back in with old reliable." She paused, then changed the subject. "How's Greg? Is he going to be upset that you're late? Do you want to use my phone and call him?"

"Let's skip the kid talk for tonight," he said, focusing on a spot over her head. "We can always play catch-up another day."

They took a seat on the sofa, both dropping down in almost the same spot. Lily felt his thigh brush up against her own. The chemistry between them was so powerful, she found herself undressing him in her mind. She coughed a few times to cover her embarrassment, similar to the way a man occasionally tossed his jacket over his lap to conceal an unexpected erection. In her eyes, Richard was everything a woman could ever want. His shoulders were naturally broad, his legs long and muscular. His buttocks weren't flat like some men.

No matter how much she desired him, however, she couldn't forget all the years she had suffered alone. Pushing herself to her feet, she yawned, hoping he would take the hint and leave. She stood there waiting until he did.

"Well," he said, "I guess I'll hit the road."

As they walked to his car, Lily asked about his former spouse. He had listened to her rattle on about her problems with Shana and John; therefore, reciprocating seemed appropriate. "How's Claire?"

"Good."

"Is she still with the same person?"

"Yes," Richard told her, scratching the top of his head. "They've built a nice life for themselves. From what I can tell, Claire is genuinely happy."

Lily was impressed with how well he had come to terms with his ex-wife's sexual preference. "I'll see you at Middleton's preliminary hearing."

"I want you," he said, pulling her into his arms.

Lily felt dizzy, vulnerable. "I want you too," she told him, "but I'm not going to make an impulsive decision. Those days are over, Richard."

"I agree we have to be cautious," he said, cupping the side of her face with his hand, "but the Middleton trial isn't going to last forever. Don't tell me you're never going to sleep with me again."

She smiled. "That's not what I said."

"Oh," he said, "I thought you were issuing some kind of ultimatum."

Lily rested her head against his chest, but her sense of well-being was short-lived. The frightened little girl surfaced, and she was surrounded by an avalanche of terrifying images. "Why did it happen?" she said, tears pooling in her eyes. "Maybe I wouldn't have reacted the way I did if he had only raped me. But my daughter —"

"Don't think about it," he whispered. "Are you still in therapy?"

Angry, Lily pushed him away. "Just because I refuse to sleep with you, you have the gall to bring up my therapist. Are you implying that I'm sexually dysfunctional? I might have had a problem right after the rape. That's not abnormal, you know." Her words came in short bursts. "I'm fine now. Just fine. I've had a number of lovers. No one has complained."

"Stop it," he said, seizing her shoulders. "You don't have to prove yourself to me. I care about you, that's all. You're getting upset over nothing."

"It's been six years, Richard," Lily shouted. "Where the hell have you been?"

"I tried to get in touch with you," he protested. "You never returned my phone calls."

"How many times did you call me?" she said, flinging her arms around. "Once, twice? My ex-husband calls me. My stockbroker calls me. After everything we went through, couldn't you manage more than a few lousy phone calls?"

"Good grief, woman," Richard exclaimed, his brows furrowing. "Haven't you figured it out by now? You confessed to a police detective. They could have subpoenaed me as a material witness. I was terrified I might end up responsible for sending you to prison."

"Bruce Cunningham moved back to Omaha," Lily said, her anger subsiding at the thought of the big homicide detective with the scuffed shoes and worn suits. "No one else knows the truth."

"Have you talked to him?"

"I called the Omaha Police Department," she answered, tearing a leaf off a tree. "Cunningham retired three years ago. He's working for a company called Jineco Equipment Corporation. I pulled up their Web site the other day, thinking I'd e-mail him and say hello, then decided I'm probably the last person he wants to come crawling out of the woodwork."

Richard looked up at the sky, thinking she was probably right.

"Since you've made it a point to remind me that I'm a murderer," Lily went on, "maintaining our ethics regarding the Middleton case seems almost hypocritical. What do you think?"

"I think I love you," Richard said, a wild look in his eyes. "No matter what, I'll probably always love you. You know that, though, don't you?"

Lily held up a palm, warning him to back off. Unleashing their feelings for one another at this point was premature, particularly under the circumstances. "Was it Middleton's idea to keep Betsy on life support, or did you explain what kind of charges he would be facing if she died?"

Richard started to answer, then stopped himself. First she didn't want to see him because he was Middleton's attorney. Now she seemed to be heading in exactly the opposite direction, hinting that he should conspire against his own client.

"She has terrible seizures," Lily told him. "Her limbs have atrophied. How do we know she isn't experiencing pain during these convulsive episodes? It's almost as if they're keeping a corpse alive."

"Read my lips," he said, pointing at his face. "Betsy Middleton is not your daughter!"

"I'm going to petition the court in her behalf."

Richard stared at her in a renewed state of awe. When she became excited or angry, her eyes shifted from blue to green. This was the woman who haunted him, scared him, ignited his passion to the point where he felt totally alive. Not the rape victim but the storm trooper, the avenger, someone with enough courage to place her neck on the line for the benefit of others. "Do whatever you feel is right."

Lily remained standing in the driveway as he got in his car and sped off.

5

"Dad," Shana called out from her bedroom, "where's my ice cream?"

John Forrester was asleep in a brown leather recliner in the two-bedroom duplex he shared with his eighteen-year-old daughter. Located on a tree-lined street in North Hollywood, the exterior was constructed out of stucco, the pale pink paint cracked and faded. The yard consisted of a small patch of grass. Even though the living room was sparsely furnished, it appeared cramped and cluttered. A green velvet sofa was backed up to a large picture window overlooking the street. Shana had insisted that her father rent a place with a fireplace, therefore, their wall space was limited. If they hadn't placed the sofa in front of the window, they wouldn't have been able to see the television set. The only other furniture was an oak coffee table, the surface littered with glasses, newspapers, and stacks of unopened mail.

Dressed in jeans and a black tank top, Shana left her desk to see why her father had not answered. "Wake up," she said, standing over him. "You promised you'd go out for ice cream. That chicken you made tonight was awful. It tasted like an armadillo."

"What time is it?" John asked, looking at his watch. "Why didn't you wake me before now?"

"Because I was busy writing a paper," she said, shoving her glasses back on her nose. "Can't you get rid of all this trash? You know I can't concentrate when the house is a mess. A cluttered house is symbolic of a cluttered mind."

John stared up at her, his eyes groggy from sleep. Up until her first day in college Shana's room had been a pigsty. Now the pendulum had swung in the opposite direction. The duplex had to be kept in perfect order. Standing, he tucked his shirt in and stepped into his loafers. At five-nine, he wasn't a big man. His daughter stood five-ten, only an inch shorter than her mother. If she hadn't possessed Lily's intelligence and drive, she would have no difficulty earning her living as a fashion model. Her eyes were sapphire blue, her skin unblemished, her cheekbones beautifully sculptured. Her auburn hair fell to the center of her back, but tonight she had it tied up in a ponytail on the top of her head.

"Baskin-Robbins might be closed," he

told her, brushing his hand over the top of his head. The only hair he had left was basically a fringe around the base of his skull. To make matters worse, his hair had turned gray during the past year, and he now had to have it colored twice a month. "Don't worry," he added, picking up his car keys off the coffee table. "Ralph's is open all night. Peanut butter and chocolate, right?"

"I don't want ice cream from the grocery store," Shana protested. "I missed so many classes last week, I had to stay up until three o'clock last night. Please, Dad, don't go back on your word." She grabbed one of the glasses off the coffee table and brought it to her nose. "Were you drinking this afternoon? Is that why you burned our dinner?"

"Of course not," he said, snatching the empty glass out of her hand. "One of my deals fell through. I was trying to see if I could salvage it. I got busy on the phone and forgot to check the oven."

"Maybe you should get a regular job," Shana told him, picking up the remote to lower the volume. Her father watched television incessantly. She was beginning to suspect that he was losing his hearing. He kept the volume at such deafening levels, it made it almost impossible for her to study. "Mom says you're not cut out for sales. She thinks you'd be better off getting a job that pays you an hourly wage. You know, something you could count on every month."

John bristled. "When did you talk to your mother?"

"Yesterday." She scooped up the old newspapers and dumped them in the trash can in the kitchen, then walked the short distance back to the living room. "Mom's already paying my tuition. It isn't right for you to expect her to pay for everything. It's not like she's rich or anything. She's a district attorney, Dad. She works for the county."

"She has more money than I do," he said bitterly. "Why didn't she go into private practice? When she went to law school, that was her intention. I'll never understand why she wanted to become a district attorney."

Shana hated being trapped between two individuals who were continually arguing. People thought divorce affected only young children, but they were wrong. As much as she loved her parents, the situation was sometimes maddening. She felt like a lawyer forced to defend both the criminal as well as the victim. "Mom's worked hard all her life. I'm proud that she's a district attorney again. She didn't belong in some boring desk job. She's too good in the courtroom."

"She could have done the same thing in Los Angeles," John said, his jaw protruding like a petulant child. "You could have seen her more often. Then I wouldn't have to listen to her complaints that I monopolize all your time."

"Can you please stop it?" Shana shouted. "After the years she spent in L.A., Mom wanted to be near the beach. Not only that, she had to take whatever position was available. You're talking stupid, Dad. I'm too tired tonight to deal with this crap." She headed back to her room, then turned around. "Hurry and you can make it to Baskin-Robbins before they close. I went out and did the grocery shopping yesterday."

"Why didn't you buy ice cream?"

Shana flashed her dynamite smile, displaying a perfect row of white teeth. "Come on, Dad. You don't like ice cream from the supermarket anymore than I do. Most of the time it's burned from the freezer." She licked her lips. "I know what you want . . . a great big sundae with nuts and whipped cream. Doesn't that sound yummy?"

John lumbered out the front door, climbed into his daughter's Mustang, and backed out of the driveway. Making her happy was the focal point of his life, even if she did have a tendency to treat him like an errand boy. He'd given up on women years ago. Now that he was in his fifties, certain things weren't as important. After college Shana would be entering law school. He had no doubt that she would become a successful attorney. She certainly wouldn't follow in her mother's footsteps if he had anything to do with it, working for peanuts as a county prosecutor. He envisioned her in one of those skyscrapers down on Wilshire, where all the high-powered lawyers kept their offices. Those were the people who raked in the big bucks, made a real name for themselves. People were fascinated with the legal system. All Shana had to do was play her cards right, and she might even have her own television show someday.

Pulling up at a stop sign, John glanced over at one of his listings, a three-bedroom fixer-upper with a swimming pool. When he'd decided to get his real estate license, he'd anticipated earning a large income with a minimal amount of effort. Instead, he spent everyday jabbering on the phone or chauffeuring people around. Resigning his job with the government might have been a mistake, but there was nothing else he could have done. He'd run into some financial problems a few years back, and cashing out his retirement had been his only option.

Outside of his relationship with Shana, his future didn't hold a great deal of promise. He had to get his career as a real estate agent off the ground and manage to sock away some money, or he would end up living the remainder of his life on Social Security. His retirement money was gone. The day before, he'd suffered the embarrassment of having to call Lily and tell her the truth — that he couldn't afford to continue paying the rent on the duplex. The fact that she had immediately ratted him out to Shana made him furious. No man wanted to look like a failure in the eyes of his daughter.

A black Mercedes came from out of nowhere, causing John to swerve to avoid a collision. "Idiot," he yelled out the window. Behind the wheel of the Mercedes, a pretty blonde had a cell phone to her ear. "Try looking where you're going next time."

Before the divorce, John and Lily had owned their own home. Maybe it wasn't a palace, but it was certainly better than where he lived now. He missed his old yard, the backyard barbecues, chatting with his neighbors. While Lily had devoted herself to prosecuting criminals, he'd coached Shana's softball team, prepared their meals, dropped whatever he was doing to rush to her school whenever she was sick. Lily was responsible for what had happened to his daughter. She'd refused to listen to him. If she'd quit the county and opened her own law practice, she would have never lured a maniac home and thrown all of their lives into chaos.

Shana's face flashed in front of him, the disgusted manner in which she'd looked at him. So what if he'd suffered a financial setback, needed a little help making ends meet? Why hadn't Lily kept her mouth shut? He'd begged her not to tell Shana. But no, the woman had jumped on the opportunity to degrade him. And his ex-wife was far from perfect. He knew things about her that would make a person's hair stand on end. Unlike Lily, though, he didn't run around telling people. "Bitch," he mumbled, a trickle of saliva running down the side of his face.

When he reached the corner of Melrose and Santa Monica Boulevard, John spotted the pink neon sign for Baskin-Robbins. The clock on his dashboard read eight fifty-five. He punched the accelerator and careened into the parking lot, missing the driveway and running up over the curb. He couldn't continue driving forward as there was a large metal container in front of him, a receptacle for people to place items they wanted to donate to the Goodwill. Throwing the car into reverse, he revved the engine, wanting to make certain the Mustang cleared the curb.

"Shit," he said, hearing a loud thud.

Slamming on the brakes, he looked in the rearview mirror, certain he must have struck a tree. The area was so dark, though, all he could see were the lights in the office building across the street. He rubbed his neck, wondering if he could put in a claim for whiplash, then reminded himself that he was no longer insured. After his DWI arrest his premiums had skyrocketed, and he had been forced to sell his car.

He got out to survey the damage when he saw the body on the ground, the legs twisted at an unnatural angle.

A faint voice pleaded, "Help . . . me."

John stood frozen. He couldn't breathe, think, move. He watched in horror as the man's eyes closed and his head flopped to one side. "No," he shouted, falling to his knees. "Please, God, don't let him be dead."

There was no blood, at least none he could see. Positioning his face over the man's mouth, he felt a whisper of breath on his cheek. He reached toward his legs, certain they were broken, then yanked his hands back as if he were reaching into a flame. What if he regained consciousness? He couldn't let the man see his face. "Are you satisfied now?" he said, blaming Lily. "This would never have happened if you hadn't upset me."

He had to remain calm, figure out a game plan.

John decided the man must be a pedestrian, as there were no other cars in the parking lot. Dressed in beige khaki pants and a white T-shirt, the victim appeared to be in his late teens or early twenties. His dark hair was long and unkempt, but there was an incredible softness to his features, causing John to question if he might be a female. No, he told himself, the voice he had heard had sounded too masculine. To make certain, he bent down again. When he failed to detect breasts beneath the person's T-shirt, he decided his first assumption was correct and the person was male. Regardless, the young man was astonishingly beautiful. A light seemed to be emanating from his face.

John rocked back and forth on his knees, overwrought with emotion. He'd been driving too fast. He hadn't been paying attention. His daughter had been right when she had accused him of drinking. After losing the only real estate contract he'd written in three months, he had consoled himself with alcohol. "What have I done?"

He felt a powerful urge to pick the young man up in his arms, place him in his car, then rush him to the nearest hospital. His pants seemed several sizes too large, and his arms were like skinny twigs. Was he one of those street kids? John asked himself. Hollywood was full of them. Many of them were runaways who turned to prostitution to survive. Could that be why his features appeared so soft and feminine? Did he hustle men for sex?

John's eyes darted to the ice cream parlor, then quickly scanned the parking lot. He didn't see any customers inside the store, and the salesclerk looked as if he was tallying up the day's receipts. He wasn't wearing his wristwatch, and for all he knew, the clock in the car might be slow and the store had already been closed by the time he reached the parking lot. He took note of the other businesses in the strip shopping center. The anchor, as they called it in real estate terms, was obviously Baskin-Robbins, but there was also a dry cleaners, a sandwich shop, as well as a small boutique. Outside of the ice cream parlor, the other establishments would have closed hours before. He was certain no one had witnessed the accident. He'd been convicted of driving under the influence only the previous month. The consequences would be disastrous if he called the police.

Leaping back into the Mustang, he roared out the opposite entrance to the parking lot. At the first intersection he made a right turn into a residential neighborhood. His chances would be better if he stayed off the main thoroughfares. Picking up his cell phone, he started to dial 911, then quickly disconnected. A police officer might respond in a matter of minutes. Sometimes they were only a block or two away when the dispatcher advised them of an emergency call. He had to be safely out of the area before he did anything. The last thing he wanted was to drive right past the police car. Had the boy seen his face before he'd lost consciousness? Could he have possibly memorized his license plate? Even though he hadn't seen any blood, he could have suffered internal injuries.

Young people who sold their bodies were asking for trouble, John decided, practically flirting with death. One of his tricks could have killed him, or the kid could have contracted a sexually transmitted disease. If he did decide to own up to what he had done, the police might think he had paid the boy to have sex with him, maybe even intentionally harmed him. With all his other problems, the last thing he needed was to become caught up in an ugly scandal.

The fact that the kid was probably a runaway might work in his favor. That meant there would be no relatives looking for him, at least, not right away. For all he knew, the authorities might not even be able to make an identification. The guy had been walking, so maybe he didn't have a driver's license.

John decided he would place an anonymous call to the authorities as soon as he got home. No, he corrected himself, his mind racing in a dozen different directions. Shana would hear and ask questions. Besides, the police had equipment that could trace every call. He had almost made a mistake and used his cell phone.

The only solution was to find a pay phone.

His knuckles turned white as he gripped the steering wheel. Perspiration spread across his forehead. His shirt was so wet it felt as if he had just removed it from the washing machine. He tried to focus on the road, but his vision was distorted. Several times he passed over the line into the opposite lane, almost colliding with an oncoming vehicle.

He wasn't drunk, he told himself. His vision was blurred because Lily had made him crazy. He had been sober when he'd left the house. "You're lying," he said, wiping his mouth with the back of his hand. Alcohol was a demon drug, no different than cocaine, speed, even heroin. Once again it had seduced him, lured him into a false state of confidence. How many glasses of Jack Daniel's had he consumed? All he recalled was tossing an empty bottle into the trash can while he was cleaning up the kitchen.

The lights to the shopping center where Ralph's was located loomed in the near distance. Outside the grocery store was a phone booth. Squealing to a stop at the curb, he left the engine running in the Mustang as he raced toward the phone. After digging in his pocket for his wallet, he came up with only a few dimes and a five-dollar bill. In his rush to get to Baskin-Robbins, he must have left his wallet on the coffee table at the duplex.

A middle-aged woman with salt-and-pepper hair was exiting the market, her arms laden with groceries. He opened his mouth to ask her for change, then stopped himself. The police could easily dispatch a unit to the phone booth after he reported the accident. The woman must live in the neighborhood because she was walking in the direction of the sidewalk instead of the parking lot. Their eyes met and he quickly looked away. How could he call from here? The woman would remember him.

John peered inside the store. If he went inside to get change from one of the checkers, he would encounter the same problem. He had to make certain no one would be able to connect him to the crime. He wanted desperately to do the right thing, admit what he had done, get medical help for the boy. He knew he couldn't, however. It was a matter of survival. A person couldn't sell real estate without a driver's license. But that was the least of his concerns. Because of his DWI, they'd send him to jail this time. Since the boy had been injured and he'd fled the scene of the accident, he could easily be facing prison in lieu of a jail sentence. How could he suffer through the humiliation of a prison sentence? Lily would never let him live it down. Shana would be devastated. In addition, he wasn't a young man. He would never come out alive if they sent him to prison. The inmates would have a field day with him. He had never been a strong man, and the type of people who ended up in prison could smell weakness like a wolf could pick up the scent of an injured deer. Using the edge of his shirt, he wiped his fingerprints off the glass window.

Finally he formulated a plan. He'd get the change, then drive to another pay phone to notify the authorities. Stepping on the electronic mat for the door opener, he tried to appear calm as he entered the store and approached a heavy-set blonde woman working the express counter. "I'm closed," she said, pointing at another cashier a few rows over.

Standing behind a young couple, he felt a sharp pain in the center of his chest. Was he going to drop dead of a heart attack and never see his daughter again? The man and woman in front of him had a cart full of food; the husband was unloading items onto the counter. Thinking of Shana made him realize he couldn't go home empty-handed. "Where's the ice cream?"

The sleepy-eyed checker didn't answer him.

"Didn't you hear me?" he yelled, bumping into the woman. "Where's the damn ice cream?"

"Aisle seven," the male checker told him.

A few moments later, John was back in line with a pint of Ben & Jerry's chocolate chip ice cream. He'd grabbed the first carton he'd seen in the freezer.

"You must be a real ice cream freak," the husband said, glowering at him. He was a tall, muscular man, his hair cut short on the sides, then gelled to stand up on top. On his right forearm was a tattoo of an eagle. "You almost knocked my wife down. You could have said you were sorry. Can't you see that she's pregnant?"

"I'm sorry," John said, staring into the woman's eyes. Her face suddenly took on the features of the beautiful young man. He wished he could tell him that he was sorry, that if things had been different, he would have helped him and not run off like a coward. Tossing the five-dollar bill on the counter once the couple had left, he paid for the ice cream and hurried out of the store.

Intending to drive to another phone booth, he found himself back on Melrose Avenue. Only the outside lights were burning at Baskin-Robbins, so he assumed the clerk he had seen earlier had gone home. Where had his car been parked? When he had been there before, the parking lot had been empty. The clerk must be a teenager. That meant he could have ridden a bicycle to work, or one of his friends might have picked him up. Surely someone had discovered the injured boy by now and contacted the authorities.

Driving slowly, John steered to the south side of the parking lot, where the accident had occurred. When he didn't see anything, he let out a long sigh of relief. The man must have had the wind knocked out of him, then got up and went on his way. Placing his foot on the brakes, he rested his head against the back of the seat. His prayers had been answered. He swore he would never drink again. Now all he had to do was clear his mind. He shut his eyes, willing his body to stop trembling.

Just then his cell phone rang.

"Where are you?" Shana demanded, her voice shrill and grating.

"I'm on my way home, honey."

"I'm so tired I'm about to pass out. All I wanted was something sweet —"

John cut her off. "I didn't go to Baskin and Robbins."

"Why not?"

"It was too late by the time I left," he lied. "I didn't want to disappoint you, so I drove all the way over to Lucky's. They didn't have peanut butter and chocolate."

"Great," Shana said facetiously. "You got ice cream, though, right?"

"I got —" John was looking in his rearview

mirror to see if it was safe to make a U-turn when he spotted the outline of the boy's body on the ground. When the rear section of the Mustang had struck him, the boy must have fallen behind a large shrub. He'd been in such a panic before that he'd failed to notice. "I'll talk to you when I get home," he said, tossing the phone on the passenger seat.

He circled the block, then slowed to a stop on the opposite side of the street. Pitiful cries filtered in through the open window. Not only had he verified that the incident had not been an alcohol-induced delusion, the victim had regained consciousness and appeared to be in terrible pain. Clutching his cell phone, he tried to force himself to call the police. He knew the boy's tortured cries would haunt him the rest of his life.

John ran his tongue over his lips. His mouth was parched, his head throbbing. Another stab of pain entered his chest. His legs began to ache. He felt paralyzed, almost as if he had been hit by a car instead of the boy. Scenes from his life played out in his mind. He saw his high school graduation, the day he'd married Lily. He saw himself holding his baby daughter only moments after her birth. The pleasant images abruptly disappeared, replaced with a menacing cloud of darkness.

John's shoulders shook. He wasn't a callous individual. He knew right from wrong. All he asked was to be able to walk away from this one mistake. He would not only swear off booze, he'd work harder, sell more houses, never again interfere with Shana's relationship with her mother. Outside of his arrest for drunk driving, he had never committed a criminal act, never purposely harmed another human being.

His nose began running. Unable to find a tissue, he retrieved a napkin from the backseat and blew it. In three months his daughter would turn nineteen. For someone so young, she'd suffered more than her share of heartache. He stared at the clock on the dashboard. For over an hour he'd wrestled with his conscience. He tossed the napkin out the window. The battle was over. By not reporting the accident, he might be saving himself from a prison sentence, but he was also protecting his daughter. Seeing another car's headlights approaching behind him, he stepped on the gas and headed home.

6

Richard Fowler parked his Lexus in the Ventura High School parking lot, opening the trunk and removing a fresh shirt encased in plastic from the cleaners. After he changed, he dug inside his gym bag and pulled out a bottle of Bay Lime aftershave, pouring some on his hands and then splashing it on his face. Back in his car, he checked his image in the rearview mirror, making certain Lily had left no incriminating smudges of lipstick.

Located high in the foothills, his home offered a panoramic view of the Pacific Ocean. At night the glittering lights of the city replaced the beauty of the shoreline. As he navigated the narrow, winding roads, he reminded himself of the one major draw-back — mud slides. After living in California for over twenty years, however, a mud slide seemed insignificant next to the threat of another massive earthquake. He had long ago decided he'd rather ride his house to the bottom of the hill than find himself submerged beneath the swirling waters of a monster tidal wave.

Entering the kitchen through the garage, he opened the stainless steel refrigerator, gazing inside at the contents. Yogurt, tofu, bean sprouts. Couldn't the woman at least buy real food? Grabbing an apple and a fancy bottle of herbal tea, he slammed the door shut in disgust. He couldn't even have a beer anymore, maybe a sack of unsalted pretzels. He'd had to fight for the right to have an occasional soda. *Nothing but flavored chemicals*, she'd told him, chastising him like a child.

When Richard had added the second story a few years back, he'd also remodeled the thirty-year-old kitchen. The counters were now a rust-colored granite, the cabinets constructed out of the finest cherry. Although he had admired the Tudor mansion where Lily rented her guest house, he preferred the clean, uncluttered look of contemporary design.

He was about to take a bite out of his apple when an attractive blonde came sashaying into the room. She was dressed in her exercise clothes, a pair of black tights and a halter top; therefore, he assumed she'd been working out in the basement gym. Her body was one of her finest attributes, and she seized every opportunity to display it. She had large breasts, a tiny waist, long legs, and her buttocks felt like rolled-up balls of steel. She might visit a plastic surgeon once a year for what he classified as a tuneup, but she could certainly turn heads. They'd been living together for three years, and even today he couldn't say for certain how old she was. She told everyone she was thirty-five. Somehow she'd managed to get a driver's license using what he suspected was a phony birth certificate. He'd never pressured her for the truth. What did he care if she wanted to shave a few years off her age? When a single woman got close to turning forty, insecurity became a major problem.

"Where have you been?" Joyce Lansing said, snatching the apple out of his hand. "I was about to call the police."

Richard said, "I'm handling a serious case, Joyce. My client was accused of poisoning his daughter. I'm late, okay. Does that mean I don't get to eat? Shit, woman, it's only an apple. A man could starve with the stuff you buy at the grocery store. What happened to food? You know, steaks, chicken, apple pie, ice cream."

"Don't lie to me," she said, glaring at him. "People don't have meetings at this time of night."

"Good Lord," he said, "it's not even ten o'clock."

"You could have called," Joyce said, impulsively hurling the apple at him.

With the time she spent lifting weights, she could pitch like a man. If Richard hadn't ducked at just the right moment, she would have popped him one. "Are you having a PMS attack?" he asked, picking the apple up off the floor and rinsing it in the sink. "Or do you just want to make certain you have my undivided attention?"

"Not funny," she said, smacking a wad of gum. "Now will you answer my question?"

"The battery went dead on my phone." Standing over the sink until he finished eating, Richard decided that the worst invention in the universe had to be the cell phone. When the only means of tracking people had been a pager, a man could still manage to make himself scarce. Now a woman could call you in the men's room while you were taking a leak. And boy, did they get ticked off when you didn't answer. In addition, they demanded an hourly report on your whereabouts and activities. Joyce and her girlfriends called each other incessantly. Most of the phone calls he had overheard were inane. The latest rage was designer phones that allowed a person to snap on different-colored exteriors to match their clothing. When the silly phone rang, it sounded like a little girl's music box. He'd seen women call each other from the next aisle over at the department store. If they weren't calling each other on their cell phones, they were shopping or trading stocks over the Internet.

"Marty talked me into taking on a couple of cases in Santa Barbara," Richard said, drying his hands with a paper towel. "That's why I had to take off so early this morning. The arraignment took longer than I thought, then I got stuck in traffic. Is that enough to get me out of the doghouse? Maybe you'd prefer that I start at nine this morning and give you a blow-by-blow of my entire day."

"Stop talking ridiculous," Joyce said, taking a seat at the kitchen table.

Bone tired, Richard rubbed his eyes. He didn't mind arguing a case in court. At least in most instances, he could look forward to being compensated. Domestic squabbles were a waste of energy. Defending himself when he'd done nothing wrong was irritating enough. Tonight, however, he had something to feel guilty about. Joyce probably sensed it. He could douse himself with the most pungent cologne in the world and it wouldn't help. He might not have slept with Lily, but he had certainly thought about it. "I'm sorry," he said. "Did you whip up a special macrobiotic dish or something? Is that why you're so bent out of shape?"

"You could have called me from a regular phone."

"We discussed the case over drinks." Richard had been afraid the dead battery trick wouldn't pass muster. He momentarily turned his back on her, not wanting her to see the smile on his face. The majority of his tricks were dated. Old dog, he thought. "I tried to call you from the pay phone in the bar, but it was out of service."

Joyce let out a long sigh. "I understand about your work, Rich," she told him. "All I ever ask is that you call. I don't think that's an unreasonable demand, do you?"

"Not at all," he said, hanging his head. The fastest way to turn things around was to act contrite. Women loved it when a man groveled. As soon as they were certain you felt like hell, they were ready to jump in bed and console you.

"The least you could do is make up a decent excuse," she said, a smile lifting one corner of her mouth. "Don't tell me there isn't at least one phone that works somewhere between Santa Barbara and Ventura."

"I was preoccupied," he said. "You know how I am when I have something on my mind. I'm juggling eight cases right now." He paused, clutching the bottle of tea in his hand. "I thought I could plea-bargain this drug case and get it out of the way. How did I know the idiot had two priors?" She was flirting with him, leaning forward so he could see her breasts, purposely posing to make certain they looked even larger than they were. He was about to reach the finish line.

"Don't you check all that out?"

"Why would someone be stupid enough to lie to his own attorney?" Richard asked, walking over and kissing the top of her head. He gazed at her breasts. Even if they weren't real, they looked and felt real. In today's world, everything was an illusion anyway. Perhaps this was part of Lily's appeal. She didn't have Joyce's body, but it wasn't always a person's physical appearance. When you genuinely cared for someone, as he did for Lily, you connected on a much higher level.

Joyce gazed up into his eyes, trapping his hand and placing it over her breast. He had crawled in the door like a snake, and already he had his hands in the cookie jar. Now he realized why married men had affairs. Not only was it physically exciting, the planning alone was challenging. The beauty of his situation was the fact that Joyce was not his wife. She might act like his wife, but without a formal commitment, there was only so much guilt she could lay on him. By taking on the Middleton case, he had provided himself with a way to spend time with Lily. Now he considered taking it a step further, possibly convincing Joyce that he should stay in a hotel during the course of the trial rather than exhaust himself by making such a long drive.

What in the hell was he thinking?

Men went off their rockers when it came time to end a relationship. The worst experience of his life had been discovering that Claire was having an affair. The fact that she'd fallen in love with a woman had been a jolt to his masculinity, but the wound itself had turned out to be nothing more than a mosquito bite. What difference did it make who she'd been having an affair with? She'd violated the sanctity of their marriage vows. He might toy with the notion of becoming a contemporary Don Juan, leaping in and out of beds from Ventura to Santa Barbara, but underneath he was a die-hard traditionalist.

When you loved someone, you married them, remained faithful to them, devoted your life to them. If you didn't love them . . . well . . . this was the muddle he found himself in with Joyce. The sex was great. Everything else was mediocre.

Richard walked over to the small built-in desk in the corner of the kitchen, thumbing through a stack of mail. The envelope containing his American Express bill was over an inch thick, and the telephone bills were astronomical. Joyce might not be aware of it, but even before he had seen Lily today, he had been racking his brain trying to figure out a way to disentangle himself from their relationship. They'd been together for three years. This time he had let things rock along past the breaking point. He was a three-year man, particularly when the woman started throwing things at him. The next time he pissed Joyce off, she might pitch one of her multicolored weights at him and crack his skull open.

Joyce owned her own business, a small marketing and research firm. The past year or two had been difficult due to the massive amount of competition she'd encountered from similar companies on the Internet, some firms as far away as Alaska. Formerly, she had relied on her interpersonal skills, drawing most of her clients from the local community. Many of these accounts had fallen by the wayside, since the great majority of what she did could be handled remotely.

His friends thought he was a fool for setting up housekeeping, then insisting on paying the majority of his girlfriend's expenses. Most of his buddies had been married for years, though, and their wives ordered them around like drill sergeants. He certainly wasn't going to take their advice. In addition, his married friends had no concept of how much time, energy, and money were involved in the process of dating. His law practice was thriving. So what if he spent a few thousand extra each month? All he was doing was buying himself a companion. Overall, it wasn't such a bad situation, especially if a man had a tendency to get lonely. Slightly shallow perhaps, but since his relationship with Lily had ended, falling in love had not been at the top of his list of priorities.

"I wouldn't complain if I didn't care," Joyce said. "Linda and Bill were sweet enough to take me out for Chinese. I left some vegetable chow mein in the refrigerator for you. If you skipped dinner, eating an apple isn't enough."

"I'm fine," he said, wishing he could get in his car and drive back to Santa Barbara. Already he longed to hear Lily's voice, gaze at her enthralling face, feel the rush of emotion that only she could generate. He couldn't discuss his work with Joyce, reveal his innermost thoughts, banter back and forth without it turning into a full-scale screaming match. Even though he didn't see eye to eye with Lily on every issue, their disagreements had always fallen more along the lines of a debate than a full-fledged argument. Although she wasn't an ignorant woman, Joyce's intellect paled in comparison to that of his former lover. Even with Lily's girlish freckles, she was a lightning bolt, a roller-coaster ride, a rare combination of femininity and masculinity. She had not only been his lover, she had been his friend.

"Linda's trying to get pregnant."

"Really?" Now that Joyce was no longer angry, Richard would have to engage in mindless chitter-chatter. With Lily there was no such thing. The woman didn't open her mouth unless she had something meaningful to say. "How does Bill feel about having a kid?"

"He's thrilled."

"Are you sure about that?" Richard had

been friends with Bill Gordon for years. On at least a dozen occasions he had sworn he would never have children. Since he'd already made a fortune in the restaurant business, he intended to travel and enjoy his success rather than take on the rigors of parenting.

"Everyone wants a family, Rich," she said, stretching her arms over her head. "That's why people get married."

"Well," he answered, "don't forget that Bill was a late bloomer. He didn't get married until he was forty-five. Everyone isn't cut out to be a parent, you know. Isn't Linda too old to have a kid?" As soon as the words left his mouth, he regretted them. For all he knew, Joyce and Linda were the same age. Bill was certainly no youngster. His friend had already passed the half-century mark.

"Are you trying to tell me something?"

"Of course not," he said, fearing another fight brewing. "I'm just trying to have a conversation with you." Not once had Joyce expressed an interest in getting pregnant. For several months now, she'd been dropping all kinds of hints, not just about having a child, but subtly trying to manipulate him into marrying her. Greg was twenty-two and had received his degree in oceanography from the institute in San Diego the previous year.

Richard had no intention of starting a second family at this stage of his life.

Heading to the master bedroom, he entered the walk-in closet to hang up his jacket. Joyce stripped off her exercise clothes and tossed on a robe. Then she followed him into the closet, wrapping her arms around his waist from behind. "You've been ignoring me lately," she said. "I thought we were going to spend a romantic evening together. Remember? You promised me last week. That's why I was hurt when you came home so late."

"Tomorrow," he said. "Why don't you make reservations at that Indian restaurant you like? I should be home by seven at the latest." His conscience kicked in and he quickly added, "I'll be here by six, okay?"

She circled around in front of him, opening the front of her flimsy negligee and pressing her breasts against his chest. "We don't have to wait," she said, smiling suggestively. "It's not *that* late. Don't tell me you're turning into an old man on me."

Richard felt like he couldn't catch his breath. How could he have sex with Joyce? What if he couldn't perform? More important, he didn't want to have sex with Joyce. No matter how serious the problems surrounding Lily were, all the old feelings had returned. After only a few hours together he felt like a heroin addict in need of a fix. Now that he'd seen her again, he had to find out if there was a chance they could build a life together. Her winsome appearance, her angular yet feminine body, even her unpredictable outbursts — all were intriguing but they were not the fire that fueled him. Even her brilliance and unwavering dedication to her career were commendable yet unexceptional. The world was full of intelligent women, many who were far more accomplished than Lily. As fiercely as she upheld the law, one fact would always remain. Lily had killed a man and gotten away with it. Single-handedly she had tracked down and assassinated a hardened gangster, a man with no regard for human life. In addition, she hadn't committed her crime under the cover of darkness. She'd shot him with her father's shotgun in broad daylight on the sidewalk in front of his own home. Faced with the same circumstances, could he have done what Lily did? He hoped he would never have to find out the answer, but how could he not love a woman possessed of such amazing courage?

He decided he would tell Joyce their relationship was over at the restaurant. "I don't feel well," he said, more truth than fiction.

"It's probably because you didn't eat enough protein," she told him. "Why don't I heat up the takeout for you? Then after you eat, you can jump in the shower."

"I can't," he told her, holding his stomach. "My stomach's upset."

"We have some Tums," she offered. "Do you want me to get you one?"

His skin felt clammy. He brought his hand to his forehead, feeling the moisture. Was he on the verge of suffering a panic attack? He'd never had a panic attack in his life. Telling Joyce they were finished was not something he was looking forward to, but finding himself in the eye of the hurricane again with Lily was downright frightening.

"Please," he said, waving Joyce away. "It's nothing. I'm tired . . . just let me get some sleep."

"Whatever," she said, wandering out of the room.

7

Shana was curled up on the sofa watching television. Just as she was about to doze off, she heard what sounded like a pebble striking the window. Peering out through a crack in the drapes, she saw a man standing on the sidewalk, his face bathed in shadow. Hunching down on the sofa, she hit the redial button on the phone, listening to the series of mechanical clicks. A recording answered, stating that the cellular customer she was calling was not available.

"Damn," she exclaimed, kicking a throw pillow off the sofa. Her father must have turned his phone off accidentally after she spoke to him. How could he take over an hour to drive only a few blocks down the street? She decided her suspicions that he had been drinking earlier that evening had been accurate. He probably got lost. Now she had to feel responsible for sending him out in the car.

Dropping to the floor, she crawled around the sofa to the window, not wanting the man to see her through the curtains. They weren't even drapes, just cheap sheers left over from the previous tenants. Her eyes widened as she strained to make out his features. He was the same height and build as Marco Curazon. The week before, she'd lingered around the UCLA campus after an evening class, visiting with some of her friends. While she was walking to her car in the parking lot, a dark-skinned man wearing a red parka had followed her. He had looked almost identical to the man who had raped her. Instead of going directly to her car and taking a chance that he might follow her home, she'd been lucky enough to flag down a campus police officer. By the time she'd climbed inside his patrol car, however, the man had darted between one of the buildings and disappeared.

Shana kept her gaze pinned on the sidewalk as she frantically dialed her mother's number. "Are you asleep?"

"I was," Lily said, bolting upright in the bed. "What's wrong? You sound —"

"There's a man outside!" Shana said, cupping her hand over the phone. "I think it's him, Mom! He tried to follow me home last week."

"When you say *him,* who are you referring to?"

"You know," the girl answered, "Marco

Curazon. He's been out of prison for six months. Didn't I tell you he'd come looking for me? I should have told Dad to buy me a gun. What am I going to use to protect myself?"

"You know how I feel about guns, Shana," Lily said. "The majority of people who buy firearms either shoot themselves or one of their family members. And when someone does break into their home, nine times out of ten the perpetrator uses the gun against them."

"Please, Mom," the girl said, "don't lecture me now. I'm really scared. I wish I still had Princess. At least she barked when people came around."

"I know, sweetheart," her mother answered, realizing she was referring to the Italian greyhound dog she had given to her just after the rape. Sadly, the delicate little dog had died the same year Shana had graduated from high school. Her daughter had been so devastated, she had refused to let her mother buy her another pet. "I'm going to call the police from the other line," Lily told her. "Don't hang up."

"Hurry," her daughter pleaded.

Lily rushed to the kitchen, where she had a separate phone line installed. As soon as she got the dispatcher on the speaker phone, she reported a suspicious individual lurking around her daughter's residence. "Did you hear, Shana?" she said into the portable phone. "The police are on the way."

"What if they don't get here in time?"

"We've been through all of this before," her mother said. "You're getting hysterical."

"How could they release him after what he did to us?" Shana said, incensed. "Explain that to me, okay? What's he going to have to do before they lock him up for good? Kill me or something?"

"Take a few deep breaths," her mother said. "Is the man still there?"

Shana jerked her head around. "I can't tell," she said. "Someone just pulled up in front of the house across the street. He must be hiding behind the car now."

"A sidewalk is a public place," Lily told her. "Of course you're going to see people walking around outside at night, especially in an area as heavily populated as North Hollywood. You can't let your imagination run wild. Where's your father?"

"I don't know."

Lily was pacing back and forth in the living room of her cottage. "What do you mean you don't know?"

"He went out for ice cream," the girl said, yanking the rubber band out of her hair.

"He never came back. For all I know he's sitting in a bar somewhere."

Lily was more disturbed by the fact that her ex-husband was drinking than her daughter's belief that someone was going to harm her. This wasn't the first time the girl had panicked since she'd learned Curazon had been released on parole. According to his parole agent, the man didn't even own a car. Time was the key. Shana would eventually feel safe again, but it wasn't going to happen overnight. Lily only wished she'd been able to convince her to attend school in Santa Barbara. How could she protect her child from such a great distance? "Wasn't your father ordered to attend A.A. meetings after the DWI conviction?"

"I guess." Shana turned her attention back to the window. "I see him . . . I'm certain it's Curazon! He just walked under a streetlight. His head is shaped the same, even his nose. He's not wearing the same jacket as he was the other day. Still, I'm certain it's him."

"The police will be there any minute." Lily knew she had to keep her daughter talking. "How could he possibly know where you live? Try to be rational, Shana."

"Maybe he found me through the Internet or something," she said. "They say you can find anyone these days."

"That's ludicrous," her mother told her. "Don't you see how childish you sound?"

"Now you're calling me childish!" Shana shouted, ready to hang up the phone.

"Curazon could never afford a computer," Lily continued, "let alone learn how to use the Internet. Your address isn't listed, anyway."

"How do you know?" she countered. "I bought all my textbooks over the Internet. I buy CDs all the time. Once you order something, your address is stored in some big computer where everyone can get their hands on it. Dad says prisoners have access to all kinds of things, even computers."

Lily wondered if what her daughter was telling her was true. Law enforcement agencies were only beginning to expose the opportunities for criminal activity in cyberspace. Locating a victim's address was an area she'd never considered. If what her daughter said was possible, victims all over the country could be in danger. "When you order something with your credit card," she asked, "don't you use a secure site?"

"Yeah," her daughter said, "but one of my friends told me they sell your name and address to various businesses for their mailing lists. How would a person know if these other companies had secured sites? I mean, maybe they don't give out your credit card information, but I still think people can find out where you live. And a person doesn't have to know how to use the Internet," she added. "You can pay someone to get information for you. Kids at school pay people all the time."

"You're a smart girl," Lily said. "Perhaps by the time you get out of school, people will specialize in this particular type of law."

Shana saw the man walking down the opposite side of the street now. "He's going to break into someone's house," she told her mother. "He's walking up to their door right now."

"Can you make out the address?"

"No," Shana said, panting. "It's too dark."

"Describe the house."

"White with blue shutters," she said. "And there's a white Jeep in the driveway."

Lily called the police again on the other line, alerting them that they might be walking into a burglary in progress. The dispatcher advised her that the officers were already in the area. "Do you see a police car?"

"Yes," she said. "They just showed up."

A police unit squealed to a stop in front of the residence she had described. A spotlight illuminated the area. Shana watched as two uniformed officers leapt out with their guns drawn. She looked for the man, but all she saw was a large brown dog. After a short time, the officers holstered their weapons, then began walking in the direction of Shana's duplex.

" What's going on?"

"I'm fine," Shana said, stepping outside onto the porch. "Dad's here now. The man must have been visiting one of my neighbors or something."

John had just pulled into the driveway. People were standing outside on their lawns. Shana felt like an imbecile. Without saying goodbye, she hit the off button on the portable phone, rushing down the sidewalk to speak to the police officers.

John placed his forehead on the steering wheel of the Mustang. His first response when he'd turned onto his street and saw the police cars was to continue driving. But he was weary, and without his wallet, where would he go? It's probably better this way, he thought, knowing he could never live with himself after what he had done. He only wished that he'd reported the accident. Hitting the boy was bad enough, but leaving the scene had compounded the crime. Shana was talking to the police officers.

Every few moments she would look over her shoulder toward the car. The police were going to arrest him and handcuff him, all while his daughter stood by and watched.

"Dad," Shana yelled, beating on the closed window with her fist. "Can't you hear me? Open the door."

Her father slowly raised his head. The two officers who had been standing in his front yard were now walking toward their police cruisers. He hit the automatic button for the window, having no idea what was happening.

"I feel like the jerk of the month," Shana said, hanging onto the car door.

"Wh-what do you mean?" John stammered. "Why were the police here?"

She glanced back over her shoulder. "I saw this man lurking outside my window. I freaked and called the police. Well, actually, Mom called the police for me. They even dispatched the helicopter. Didn't you see it?"

John shook his head. He positioned his hand over his mouth, fearful she would be able to smell the alcohol on his breath. Out of the corner of his eye he watched the police car as it pulled into a driveway, then backed out and took off in the opposite direction. "Did the police arrest the man?"

"No." Shana searched the shadows again. "I guess it could have been a neighbor. The police tried to convince me it was only a dog." She laughed, an involuntary release of tension. "Cops can be real dickheads. I'm not so stupid I can't tell the difference between a dog and a human being."

Shana reached for the car door, leaving John no choice but to get out. "Why didn't you call me instead of your mother?"

"I did," she said. "You must have turned your cell phone off."

"Are you certain you're okay?" John said, crushing her to his chest. "Could you see the man's face? Did he try to get into the house? Did the police ask about me?"

"You're hurting me," she said, prying his arms off. "Why would the police ask about you?"

"You know," he said, "maybe they wanted to know who you lived with."

"I'm an adult, Dad," she said, noting the circles of perspiration under his arms. "Mom was probably right. I haven't been getting enough sleep. When you don't sleep, your mind plays tricks on you. Let's go inside and eat our ice cream."

John stared at her with vacant eyes.

"Duh," she said. "The ice cream, remember?"

Acting more on reflex than conscious thought, her father reached into the backseat and pulled out a soggy brown sack. Before he could hand it to her, the carton of ice cream broke through the paper, the contents splattering onto the sidewalk. He stared down at the dark stain, thinking it resembled a spreading puddle of blood. Was the young boy still lying there suffering, alone in the dark night, waiting for someone to come and rescue him?

"You *have* been drinking," Shana said, pointing an accusing finger at him. "How can I count on you for anything?"

John stumbled backward as if she had slapped him, then watched as she stomped into the house and slammed the door. He no longer cared if she went running back to Lily. All the love and concern he'd showered on her since childhood would mean nothing if he was apprehended. The lights went out in the house across the street; classical music played somewhere in the distance. He had to protect himself now, shift into a survival mode.

Opening the trunk of the car, he removed a flashlight. At least by striking a pedestrian, he had eliminated any possibility of a paint transfer from the other person's vehicle. He had to make certain, however, that there were no other incriminating marks or evidence. After checking the body of the car, all he spotted was a small dent on the left side above the wheel. He was certain he could knock it out with a rubber hammer. The last thing he wanted was to have to take the car to a garage for repairs. Tossing the flashlight into the front seat, he plodded up the walkway.

Seated on the edge of the couch, John turned on the television, flicking through the channels until he found the local news. Afraid he would fall asleep, he made a cup of instant coffee in the microwave, then rushed back to the living room, anxious to see if there was any report of the accident. After listening to a report of a fire in the downtown area near Grand Avenue, a private plane crash near the Burbank airport, and a baby rescued from a trash bin, a pretty blonde reporter smiled into the camera as the words *Breaking News* flashed across the bottom of the screen.

"Police are on the scene of a fatal hit-and-run accident which occurred a short time ago at the intersection of Lankershim and Victory Boulevard," the woman said. "The victim was found . . ."

The boy was dead!

John splashed the boiling coffee onto his pants, scalding his inner thigh and missing his groin by only a few inches. By the time he turned his attention back to the television, the weather report was on and the banner at the bottom of the screen was gone. He was a contemptible, worthless excuse for a human being. Had he thought of someone other than himself and notified the authorities, they might have rushed the boy to the hospital and saved him. "Too late," he mumbled, covering his face with his hands.

A horrifying thought passed through his mind. Like a man possessed, he started sorting through the clutter on the coffee table. When he didn't find his wallet, he checked his bedroom, the bathroom, the kitchen, even rifled through the trash. Then he returned to the living room and yanked all the pillows off the sofa, shoving his hand in the cracks on the chance that his wallet had become lodged inside. He was certain he'd had his wallet when he left the house that evening. Snatching the car keys off the coffee table, he flung open the door and headed for the car.

"What's going on?" Shana appeared in the front doorway in her pajamas. "I finally fell asleep, then I heard you banging around. The living room looks like a disaster."

"Please, please," John said, "go back to sleep."

"Why did you take the pillows off the sofa?"

"I was going to sleep on the floor tonight," he lied. "Keep a lookout in case the man you saw came back."

"You need help, Dad," she said. "You're going out to another bar, aren't you? Were you looking for money to buy booze?"

"No!" he shouted, spit flying from his mouth. "Leave me alone! You don't care what happens to me. No one cares what happens to me."

"I love you," she said, coming down the sidewalk toward him. "I can't let you drive my car, that's all. You don't want to go out now."

"Here," he said, pressing the keys into her hand. His heart swelled with heaviness, longing for the days when she'd looked up at him in childlike delight, back when he'd still been her hero. Tears welled up in her eyes. "Don't cry," he said, gently wiping her cheek with his finger. "I would have done anything to stop that man from hurting you. You're a woman now, though. I have to solve my own problems, and you have to go on with your own life."

Shana sniffed. "What are you saying, Dad?"

"Call your mother in the morning," he

told her. "Tell her to make arrangements for you to move into the dorm."

"Why? What's wrong?"

"Nothing's wrong, sweetheart," John said. "Nothing for you to worry about . . ."

"Where will you go?"

"I'll probably move to a place where the cost of living is less," John said. "You know, a small town or something."

Shana started to protest, but he stopped her. "Everything will work out, angel. Now, go inside and try to get some rest. I just need some time to myself right now."

Thirty minutes had passed.

John had searched the Mustang, but his wallet was nowhere to be found. How long did he have before the police came to arrest him? Would they come during the night, or would the incriminating evidence remain hidden until daybreak? His daughter was aware he'd been drinking. The police would have no trouble piecing the crime together. Nothing much was left to hide.

He removed a plank on the front porch, pulling out his stash of cigarettes and a paper-wrapped bottle of Jack Daniel's. Shana thought he had quit smoking years ago, but he still indulged in a cigarette when things became stressful. For a few moments he simply held the bottle against his chest, caressing it like a priceless statue. After his DWI conviction he had attended the mandatory number of A.A. meetings. He knew he was in the throes of addiction, that he possessed what people referred to as an addictive personality. If it wasn't cigarettes, it was booze. If it wasn't booze, it would probably be something worse. Shit, he thought, opening the bottle and taking a long swig, he was even addicted to television. Slice about six hours of TV out of his day, and he would have probably sold enough houses to cover his expenses.

Once the burning sensation passed, the alcohol began to warm his body. He pulled out a Camel and fired it up, the match creating an amber flash in the darkness. The smoke filled his lungs, the nicotine enabling him to comprehend the magnitude of his actions. Standing under a large sycamore tree, he reached up and grabbed onto a branch, puffing out a stream of cigarette smoke. For every problem there was a solution. In the garage was a heavy rope he'd used to strap last year's Christmas tree to the top of the car. He wouldn't do it here, of course. He wouldn't kill himself where Shana would be the one to find him. About two blocks away was a park with trees strong enough to support the weight of a man his size. When your child no longer respected you, your role as a father was over. Burying him would set her free. First, though, he'd finish off the bottle, allow himself this one last indulgence.

8

After the harried phone call from Shana, Lily tossed and turned all night, unable to sleep. Waking at five Wednesday morning, she dressed and headed downtown, hoping to get a head start on the day.

The district attorney's office was located in a newer building directly across the street from the old courthouse. In addition to the district attorneys and investigators, the building also housed what had formerly been the municipal court. Now that the county of Santa Barbara had its own court system, private attorneys found it difficult to tell if a case was a misdemeanor or a felony simply by the court where the hearing was scheduled.

Lily classified the architecture of the building where she worked as fifties tacky. It resembled her old elementary school with the blue aluminum trim around the windows, the center courtyard, the cheapness of the construction materials. The building was certainly a contrast to the beauty and history attached to the original courthouse.

She'd heard rumors that the city council members were considering taking people on guided tours, and that weekend they were having an art show on the front lawn.

Located at the end of a long corridor, her office was far from plush. Most janitors' closets were more spacious. Although the temperature was only in the high sixties, she cranked open the casement window behind her desk in anticipation of the midday heat. Once she began working, her surroundings disappeared.

Flopping down in a worn black vinyl chair, she placed both of her palms on top of her mahogany desk. In the past Lily could work in the midst of chaos. These days she relied on rituals and organization. She drank out of the same coffee cup bearing an FBI insignia, always placing it on a coaster next to her computer when she left at the end of the day. Every month or so she would carry the cup home and sterilize it in the dishwasher. The rest of the time she simply wiped the inside out with a damp paper towel. Since she hadn't been in the mood to put up a pot of coffee in the employee kitchen on the first floor, as she generally did when she arrived this early in the morning, she'd stopped at Starbucks on the way in and treated herself to an overpriced cup of mocha latte. Dumping the liquid into her FBI mug, she took a sip, deciding the brew smelled better than it tasted.

The walls of her office were painted institutional white. Due to the age of the underlying plaster and the building's close proximity to the ocean, several spots were already chipped and the office had only recently been repainted. Other than her certificates and diplomas, the available wall space would accommodate no more than two pictures. One was a Monet print she'd purchased at the Museum Store on State Street. The other depicted a forest, dense with trees, a graceful deer standing next to a stream of shimmering water. This was the image she gazed at when pondering a complex issue. The fact that she had painted the picture herself made it even more meaningful. In the first year after the rape, her therapist had suggested she use art as a means of relaxation.

Positioned in the front of the painting were two of the ugliest chairs Lily had ever seen, even if her coworkers swore they were genuine antiques. The wood was so hard, she was certain it must have petrified. Of course, everything in Santa Barbara was classified as an antique, including at least fifty percent of the residents. Ancient surfers staggered down the street with parched skin and stringy white hair. Scores of hippies and homeless people had migrated from San Francisco like birds flying south for the winter. The area was also home to hundreds of artists and craftsmen, many of them hawking their wares from concessions they were allowed to set up every Sunday on the sidewalk next to the beach. Then there were the retirees, dressed in their white linen suits, their bow ties, their straw hats, and carrying their walking canes. Mix in the college students with their tattoos, pierced body parts, and outlandishly colored hair, and a person might think they were on a lot inside a Hollywood film studio.

Lily glanced at her watch, wanting to catch Shana before she left for the day. It wasn't even seven o'clock yet, so she decided to dive into her work instead. After her daughter had hung up on her, she had attempted to reach her again, wanting to verify that she was okay. The answering machine had picked up, so she had to assume the girl had gone to bed. Lily had then called the police and learned that they had found nothing even slightly suspicious.

Her thoughts turned to her ex-husband. Perhaps she had been wrong to tell Shana that her father could no longer afford to pay the rent on the duplex. She had told her, however, as a form of payback. When Marco Curazon had been paroled, she'd informed John merely as a precaution. She had never intended for Shana to learn that the rapist had been released from prison. John had terrified his own daughter for no other reason than to serve his own selfish needs. The only way he could keep Shana under his thumb was to make certain she remained dependent. The more fearful she was, the easier it was to accomplish his goal.

Lily opened her purse and removed her checkbook. Staring at the meager balance, she knew she would have to transfer more money over from her savings account right away. As she had told Shana the day before, she would do whatever was necessary to take care of her needs, but it was insane for her ex-husband to demand that she support him as well. She'd been feeding him for the past year out of the allowance she sent to Shana. The girl denied it, but she knew it was true. In a way, she couldn't blame her. No matter what he was, the man was her father.

Now that it appeared that John was drinking again, Lily was determined to find a way to extricate him from their lives. He was clinging to Shana, turning her into a substitute wife, preventing her from forming bonds with people her own age. No decent man would purposely suck the life out of his daughter. Her own father would have jumped off a bridge before he dropped to such a disgusting level.

Lily shook her head as if to clear it, finishing off what was left of her coffee. It was cold now, but when she forked over three dollars and change for a cup of flavored coffee, she made certain she drank every drop.

Placing the cup next to her computer screen, she glanced at a white plastic laundry basket located to the left of her desk. When the clerk made her daily rounds with new case assignments, Lily would read through the particulars, make the appropriate notations on her computer, then toss the file into the basket on the floor. The way the Santa Barbara D.A.'s office operated differed greatly from Ventura. As their staff was limited, prosecutors were not assigned to specific divisions such as homicide, sex, crimes against property, or charged with prosecuting only career criminals. In Santa Barbara they handled every type of offense. If she were a doctor, it would be similar to being a general practitioner rather than specializing in a particular form of medicine. Attorneys like Matt Kingsley and Clinton Silverstein might refer to her as their supervisor, but in actuality she was only a senior prosecutor.

Her new case assignments included a fraud, a shooting, and an auto theft. In the Ventura office, any prosecutor experienced enough to handle a crime as serious as a shooting would not be assigned something as insignificant as an auto theft. Some of the attorneys in Santa Barbara considered Lily a prima donna since she'd formerly run an entire unit, certain she would balk at the thought of handling such minor cases. They were mistaken, however, as she enjoyed the variety. Prosecutors who dealt strictly with violent crimes were more likely to suffer from burnout. Lightweight offenses could sometimes be fun. Due to her years of experience, she occasionally found a really big fish dangling at the end of a very small line. Individuals outside the profession didn't realize that the most sophisticated criminals were seldom apprehended. For every arrest listed on their rap sheet, they'd probably committed a hundred crimes that went undetected.

The last defendant Lily had prosecuted for auto theft had turned out to be wanted in the state of Washington for seven counts of armed robbery. The FBI agent who had driven down from Los Angeles to transport the prisoner had given Lily the coffee mug bearing the insignia of his agency. She'd teased him, telling him the FBI was turning into a commercial franchise. They sold T-shirts, caps, coffee cups, jackets, all kinds of merchandise. The agent had tossed back that at least most FBI agents didn't bring their laundry to the office. Lily had laughed. The item he was referring to might have been designed for the purpose he had mentioned, but it was now filled with files. It wasn't as if they didn't provide her with sufficient file space.

The laundry basket was symbolic. Everyone had to do their laundry, yet it was always a chore that could wait. Lily couldn't allow herself to dwell on the dozens of cases she had pending, knowing she would make herself a nervous wreck. Each morning she checked her computer to see if she needed to appear for an arraignment, file a discovery motion, schedule a witness interview, or request something from the crime lab related to her most recent assignments. As soon as she was certain she had covered all the bases, the cases in the plastic basket were temporarily forgotten. If someone asked her a question regarding them outside of the courtroom, all they would receive was a blank stare.

The five files Lily had to focus all her energy on were neatly stacked on the right side of her desk. These were the crimes she contemplated night and day. When she went to the bathroom, the details and images went with her. Even when she'd seen Richard for the first time in six years, her mind had not been completely free. Picking up the heavy Middleton file, she placed it in the center of her desk, then glanced at the names on the remaining four. The child-molest case would more than likely go to trial, she decided, reminding herself to speak to Lenora regarding the Bentley investigation later that day.

Lily's method of analyzing a crime was to place herself inside the mind of the offender. As she saw it, Arnold Bentley had no choice but to throw the dice. He had a beautiful wife, two adorable kids, a house, along with a fairly successful business. He owned a small store that specialized in children's clothing and unique toys, many items made by local craftsmen. Although the victim, a twelve-year-old female, was an articulate and convincing witness, the case was nonetheless circumstantial. Without penetration and ejaculation, it boiled down to who the jurors opted to believe — the victim or the defendant.

The victim, Deborah Saginaw, had babysat for Bentley's children on numerous occasions and never experienced a problem. On the night in question, Bentley had driven her home after attending a party with his wife. He turned down a dark street and forcefully groped her in the area of her breasts and genitals. As the girl was neither bruised nor injured during the assault, no physical evidence of a crime existed. According to the victim, she was certain Bentley had intended to rape her, and had stopped only when a car resembling her father's had driven by and spooked him. If the driver of the vehicle came forward, they might have a stronger chance of winning a conviction. With the trial date rapidly approaching, it was doubtful that such would occur.

What concerned Lily was the possibility that the defendant might be a pedophile who used his store to connect with children. Deborah fit the profile, as she was a prepubescent female. The girl was also too young to be looking after people's children, but that point appeared moot in light of the circumstances. There was also concern that

Bentley could be sexually abusing his own daughters; however, interviews with the girls had produced nothing to confirm such activity. Placing the Bentley file at the bottom of the stack, she feared the case might end in acquittal.

The third active case involved an assault with a deadly weapon. State Street, the main drag in Santa Barbara, had recently experienced a rash of violent crime, most of it related to the various nightclubs that had sprung up in recent years to cater to the large number of local college students. The problem was, the majority of the crime was not committed by students. The students were at the heart of the problem, however, as they were the consumers. Most of the perpetrators were gang members or drug peddlers from nearby cities. They shot and stabbed each other in an attempt to weed out their competition and establish their turf in the highly lucrative drug trade. Friday and Saturday nights had turned into a carnival atmosphere, with young people hanging out until the wee hours of the morning on either State Street or congregating in the even more dangerous alleys and side streets.

The case in question was a slam dunk in Lily's opinion. The defendant had been captured following a foot pursuit by one of Santa Barbara's finest, the bloody knife still clutched in his hand. Boy, she thought, staring at the photo of the weapon. The idiot was lucky he hadn't tripped and fallen on his own knife. Stupid criminals were a prosecutor's delight. In addition, he had a prior conviction for an aggravated assault in Los Angeles. Next week she would meet with his public defender and offer him two years in prison in exchange for a guilty plea. Mervin Hatteras, or the "Bug," as he was called, would jump on her offer in an instant. If not, he would be staring down six years for the aggravated term as to the stabbing, and another two years as an enhancement for what they called GBI, or great bodily injury. With this guy, throwing the dice would amount to placing four years of his life on the come line. As long as the knife didn't mysteriously disappear from the property room, Lily wouldn't lose any sleep over Hatteras. By this time next week another cell at the cramped Santa Barbara jail would be available, its former occupant en route to his new home at the California Department of Corrections.

Outside of Middleton, the only additional case Lily was concerned with at that moment was a homicide at an upscale nursing home. The victim had been a healthy seventy-three-year-old woman until she was diagnosed as suffering from lung cancer. After treatment with chemotherapy and radiation, Cottage Hospital had transferred her to Viewpoint, a skilled nursing facility. The day after her son had started making the necessary arrangements for her release, having been told his mother's cancer had been completely cured, the woman had died. If not for the son's persistence, the cause of death would have been classified as natural causes. Because he insisted on an autopsy, the coroner had discovered that not only had the woman never had cancer, she had died from a dose of morphine strong enough to kill seven people. No one felt stronger regarding the treatment of the ill or elderly, but as far as Brennan's decision to try the woman's death as a homicide, Lily was not in agreement.

First, the lab which had rendered the faulty diagnoses could not be held criminally liable. The woman's son could file a civil lawsuit, however, and would more than likely win a sizable monetary award. Establishing the elements required to make his mother's death a crime, particularly a homicide, would be next to impossible. These were the type of cases that ended up on a prosecutor's desk because the district attorney was a politician and the victim's son was what Lily classified as a door knocker, someone who kept at it until they got what they wanted. There was no notation inside the woman's chart indicating that she had been given morphine in the days prior to her death, and the four nurses who had been on duty that day claimed they knew nothing about it. From the evidence, there was no doubt that the woman's death had been caused by a series of tragic errors. For Lily to treat this as a homicide, the first step was to identify the suspect or suspects. Was she going to ask the court to issue an arrest warrant for the four nurses, along with the woman's physician and all the other employees who had had contact with her the day of her death? What possible motive would the nurses have to intentionally take this woman's life? Even the lab hadn't been made aware of their mistake until the autopsy was performed.

She set this file aside to discuss with Allan Brennan later in the week.

Lily had just stepped out of the ladies' room when Matt Kingsley cornered her. "Why did you ask Brennan to take me off the Middleton case? All I did was forget to make one lousy phone call."

"It was more than that," she said. "You weren't prepared. You thought you could wing it. Every time I told you to do something, you handed it off to someone else."

"You're crazy," he exploded, his blond hair tumbling onto his forehead. "People told me about you. I don't know why I didn't listen."

"Exactly what did they tell you?" Lily said, her hands closing into fists.

"They said you left Ventura because you had some kind of mental breakdown. You were handling a big case." He paused, searching his memory. "McDonald-Lopez . . . yeah, that was the name. The person I talked to said you got too involved and went off the deep end. I heard you were even nominated for a judgeship, but you were so out of it, you had to turn it down."

"I see," she answered, her facial muscles twitching. "And did this person advise you of the details of the case you just mentioned?"

"A young couple was murdered," he told her. "A gang rape, right? The girl was mutilated. One of the gang members killed someone else as well. A prostitute, I believe."

Lily fixed him with a steely gaze. He was too smug, too confident. Inside, she was seething. She glanced down the corridor, seeing if anyone was around. Once she was certain they were alone, she continued, "How does the McDonald-Lopez homicide and this alleged breakdown I suffered relate to you and your job performance?"

"I'm trying to remain detached," Kingsley explained, adjusting his jacket on his shoulders. "When Brennan told me I was going to be working on the Middleton case, he called me into his office and had a long talk with me. He told me this was a job, not a crusade. He said I wouldn't last if I became too sympathetic toward the victims. Brennan thinks that's one of your only weaknesses."

"Let me ask you something," Lily snarled. "Did this person who knows so much about me happen to mention what else occurred during the McDonald-Lopez trial?" Before he had a chance to respond, she impulsively stomped on his foot.

"What the hell —" he said, wincing in pain. "You almost broke my toe."

"Since you're determined to pry into my affairs," she said, lowering her voice, "my daughter and I were raped. A man broke into my home and held a knife to my throat, then made me watch as he ravaged my child. She was only thirteen years old, Kingsley.

My daughter's in college now. Last night I had to spend almost an hour on the phone attempting to reassure her that the man who raped her wasn't hiding outside in the bushes."

Kingsley was aghast. "I'm sorry," he said. "Didn't they apprehend the rapist?"

"They caught him," Lily said, clearing her throat. "Six months ago he was paroled."

The attorney leaned back against the wall, removing his shoe and massaging his toe.

"If Brennan wants you to consider this as nothing more than a regular job," she continued, "then tell him I said he should go fuck himself. And if he wants to get rid of me, I can have my office packed by tomorrow."

Lily marched past him. "Please," Kingsley said, limping after her, "I was wrong to say those things. Brennan will fire me before he'll let you go."

Once Lily reached her office, she tried to shut the door, but the young attorney edged inside. He pulled the door closed, then stood in front of it with his hands behind his back. "My ego was crushed when I heard you wanted me off the case," he told her, breathing heavily. "Brennan didn't say those things to me. I just made them up."

"Get out of my office," she said, glowering

at him. "Now you're not only incompetent, you've just admitted that you're a liar." She paused, tapping her pen on her desk. "I guess when you look like a movie star, have a Harvard degree, and can buy and sell most of the people you work with, it's hard to accept things not going your way."

"Listen," he said, opening his briefcase and removing what appeared to be a photograph, "I think I've stumbled across something important. Whether you realize it or not, I've been putting in at least ten hours a day on the Middleton case. That's in addition to my other case assignments."

Lily was standing behind her desk, annoyed that she had allowed him to irritate her. Even after six years of therapy, controlling her anger was still a problem. Her eyes roamed around the room. As far as the rape was concerned, he would have heard about it eventually. Most of the people in the office knew, they simply kept their mouths shut. Starting a war was foolish. She sat down, slipping on her reading glasses.

"Okay," Kingsley said, moving one of the chairs closer to her desk. "Middleton owned a chain of low-end furniture stores. The majority of his customers are Hispanic immigrants who work the fields in Camarillo, Oxnard, and the surrounding farming communities. Most of the people were unable to obtain credit. Middleton sells them cheap furnishings at inflated prices, forcing them to pay cash in weekly installments and refusing to allow them to pick up their merchandise until their bill is paid in full."

"I already know how he operates," Lily said, examining the picture he had handed her. "What bearing does this have on the case?"

"What you're looking at is a photo I took of one of Middleton's furniture warehouses in Van Nuys. Do you see what business is located next door?"

"I don't see the name," she said. "All they have on the doors are numbers."

"I didn't make the connection right away, either," he said, his speech rapid-fire now. "Look at the trucks parked in front."

Lily saw a row of white vans. On the sides were large plastic bugs, and the words SOS PEST CONTROL. "Do they use —"

Kingsley smiled. "Strychnine? You bet. They use it to poison gophers, mice, all kinds of things."

"Like a disabled daughter?"

The smile slid off his face. "I had a friend of mine who lives in the San Fernando Valley drive over to SOS and pretend he was applying for a job. He said they had tons of that stuff inside their warehouse."

Lily came alive. "So this is where Middleton got the poison?"

"It has to be," the young attorney said, leaning forward. "We knew he was too smart to just stroll in somewhere and buy strychnine, particularly since he planned to use it to kill his daughter."

Lily's opinion of the young attorney had skyrocketed. "What put you on to this?"

"I decided to pay a visit to all of Middleton's warehouse locations and see if I could come up with something we might have overlooked," he explained. "When I discovered the pest-control company, I suspected Middleton might be on friendly terms with these people since they'd been in the same location for almost as long as he had. Since his friends said he was a hands-on type of businessman, it made sense that he would stop by his various warehouses from time to time, if for nothing more than to keep his employees on their toes. Then I took it a step further, deciding it was feasible that he might have walked next door to SOS. When no one was looking, he swiped a bottle of strychnine."

"You might be right," she said, setting the photo aside. "We're still not any closer than we were before, though. Showing that

Middleton may have had access to strychnine isn't going to make a major difference. We need concrete proof that he had the poison in his possession at the time of the crime."

Again, Kingsley reached into his briefcase. "On October 29, two days before Halloween, Henry Middleton made a trip to his Van Nuys warehouse. Because he had an audit pending, he decided to do a little housecleaning."

Lily leaned back in her chair, her hands behind her neck. "Elaborate, please."

"He fired three of his top people."

"How did you determine this?"

"Well," Kingsley said, fingering the paper, "since you think I'm such a lousy prosecutor, maybe I won't tell you. Besides, my toe hurts like a bitch. I don't think the board of supervisors would think very highly of you if they found out you were physically abusing your coworkers."

Lily blinked several times. Henry Middleton was the embodiment of evil. She was determined to see him behind bars. But kissing Kingsley's ass was a big price to pay for a few morsels of information. For all she knew, the young attorney had nothing more than he had already shown her. Betsy's face appeared in her mind, however, and she knew she couldn't take a chance. "Do you think you can get me in trouble just because I accidentally stepped on your toe?" she told him. "If you want people to treat you like a professional, acting like a crybaby isn't going to earn you any respect. Run to the board of supervisors with something as trivial as this, and I guarantee you'll become the laughingstock of the agency."

"Touché," he said, knowing they were wasting valuable time sparring with one another. Besides, if he went head to head with her, he had no doubt who would come out the victor. "Okay, here's how I put it together. My father is pretty successful." He paused, his cheeks turning a bright pink. "Of course, I'm not telling you something you don't know, since you ridiculed me only five minutes ago for precisely the same reason."

"Go on," Lily said, sitting at rapt attention.

"I don't intend to reveal any family secrets, but when my dad was audited a few years back, his tax attorney suggested that he might be better off without a few of his employees. Get the picture?"

"I'm following you," she said, snapping her chair back into an upright position. "You decided Middleton might have received the same kind of advice. Correct?"

"Exactly," he told her. "I contacted the state employment office and discovered that five of Middleton's employees were terminated two days before the crime. One of these men was the person in charge of the Van Nuys warehouse. We have verification because this individual filed for unemployment benefits." He pushed himself to his feet. "Mind if I use your phone?"

Lily picked it up and turned it around to make it more convenient. "Be my guest."

Kingsley glanced at the paper in his hands, then punched in a phone number. A gruff male voice came out over the speaker phone. "Is this Mr. Nash?"

"Maybe," the man said. "Who wants to know?"

"This is Matthew Kingsley with the Santa Barbara District Attorney's Office," he said, his tone crisp. "I spoke with you a few days ago about your termination from Middleton Furnishings. Do you remember?"

"Yeah, I remember."

"You were fired on October 29 of last year, is that correct?"

"That's the date," Jake Nash told him. "I've been unemployed ever since."

"Was Mr. Middleton on the premises on that date, the day you were dismissed?"

"He was there," the man said. "In addition to my regular severance pay, he gave me an envelope containing five one-hundred-dollar bills. He said he was sorry, but business was bad and he had to cut back on his employees."

"What else did he tell you?"

"Not to talk to nobody," Nash told him. "He said someone might come snooping around, asking lots of questions. Seems one of his competitors had put the Internal Revenue on his back. Guess they were trying to force him out of business, know what I mean?"

"I certainly do, Mr. Nash."

"If I stayed loyal and didn't talk to the tax people, Mr. Middleton promised he would hire me back once the dust settled. Then I read about the problem with his kid."

"Did Middleton ever attempt to rehire you?"

"Nah," Nash said. "I even had trouble collecting my unemployment."

"Why was that?"

"Well," he continued, "like I told you the other day, I had to resubmit my application three times. The unemployment people said there was no record that I had ever been employed at Middleton Furnishings. Since I kept my pay stubs, I was finally able to get things cleared up, but it was pretty strange. I worked there for over five years. You would have thought someone would have remembered me."

"On the day you were fired," Kingsley asked, "did Middleton go next door to the exterminating company?"

"Yeah."

"Are you certain?" the attorney continued. "When I ask you to testify in court, you'll have to swear that what you're telling me is the truth."

"I realize that," Nash said. "I don't lie, mister. If someone had come around asking me about Mr. Middleton's business, I would have told them the truth too. Just 'cause the boss gave me five hundred bucks don't mean nothing. Jake Nash can't be bought."

"When did Mr. Middleton go next door?"

"As soon as he got there," he said. "That would have been around lunchtime, because I saw him talking to one of the guys who worked at SOS when I ducked out to pick up some sandwiches for my crew."

"Who was he talking to?"

"Now that," Nash said, "I can't be entirely certain about. If my memory serves me correct, he was either talking to Danny Metz or Bob Sanders. Basically, he was just walking around. You know, looking things over, shooting the breeze."

Lily made the time-out sign with her hands. After Kingsley placed the call on hold, she said, "I'm impressed. You've established that Middleton had access to strychnine. This will help our case. Surely you realize by now that anyone can purchase strychnine. It still isn't enough, don't you see? We need someone who can testify that they saw Middleton take the poison from the exterminating company. What's the story on the two men he just mentioned?"

"Can I finish?" Kingsley asked, popping his knuckles.

Lily swept her hand toward the phone.

"Mr. Nash," he said, after tapping back into the line, "when Henry Middleton gave you the envelope with the five hundred dollars in it, did something else occur that you considered peculiar?"

"He had a bottle inside his jacket," he said. "It fell out, and I bent over to pick it up. Before I could get my hands on it, Mr. Middleton kicked it away. Then he snatched it up and ran out to his car, all worked up, as if he was about to have a stroke or something."

Lily leapt to her feet, too excited to remain seated.

Kingsley beamed in satisfaction. "Can

you describe this bottle?"

"It was nothing but a plastic Coke bottle," Nash explained. "That's why I thought the whole thing was screwy. Why would Mr. Middleton get so bent out of shape? All I did was pick up his soda after it fell out of his jacket. Thing is, I didn't think the liquid inside looked dark enough to be Coca-Cola. The boss also wore pretty expensive clothes to be stretching them out by carrying around his soft drinks inside his jacket pocket, know what I mean?"

"Did this bottle have a top that could be taken off, then replaced?"

"Yeah," he said. "Don't you know what kind of bottle I'm talking about? It was a Coke bottle, man. There's a zillion of them things out there. Surely you've seen one. That is, unless you live on Mars or something."

"I've seen a Coke bottle, Mr. Nash," Kingsley told him, giving Lily a look that said this was a strong witness, a man who wouldn't crack under cross-examination. "I'd like to ask you a few more questions. Is that okay?"

"Shoot."

"Can you tell me how I might get in touch with Danny Metz or Bob Sanders? I understand neither one of them are still employed at SOS."

"I can't help you there, pal," Nash told him. "Both Metz and Sanders were ex-cons. We used to hire those kind of guys at the furniture place now and then. Once they earn a few dollars, they tend to split. Killing bugs isn't much fun, not that I don't respect any man who puts in an honest day's work. I turned sixty this year, see, so I know how tough it can be to find a decent job. Some places would rather hire a jailbird than an old fart like me."

"Have you ever served time in prison?"

"Never," Nash barked, his deep voice booming out over the speaker phone. "And I've never been convicted of anything outside of a few parking tickets. You're talking to a stand-up guy. Didn't I already tell you that?"

"You certainly did," Kingsley answered, tossing another piece of paper on Lily's desk.

"Perfect," she whispered, using her finger to press her glasses back in place on her nose. Kingsley had checked Jack Winston Nash, a.k.a. Jake Nash, through every criminal record system in existence, even Interpol. Not even the parking tickets showed up. The man was so clean, he could have run for president.

"One more question," Kingsley said,

pacing back and forth in front of Lily's desk. "After you heard that Mr. Middleton's daughter had been poisoned, why didn't you call the police and tell them what you just told me?"

"Several reasons," he explained. "First, I would have never dreamed a rich guy like Middleton could do something so terrible to his own kid. I also didn't realize that he canned me only three days before his little girl was poisoned. When you called and started asking questions, I looked back over my paperwork and decided it might be worth mentioning. That's when everything began to click in my head. I usually make it a rule to mind my own business, but when someone hurts an innocent kid, then I guess you could say it's everyone's business."

"You're a good man," Kingsley told him. "We'll be in touch. If you can think of anything else that occurred that day, please jot it down and call us immediately."

Lily circled around to the front of her desk. "This is great news, Matt," she said, grabbing him by the shoulders. "Our entire case might turn on the testimony of this one witness, a man you flushed out on your own."

"Thanks," he said, his chest swelling with pride. "Does this mean you want me to remain on the case?"

"Without a doubt," she told him, glancing down at his feet. "How's your toe?"

"I'll live," he said, shrugging. "My dad used to beat the living daylights out of me. I'm here, so I guess I survived." He took a few steps toward the door, then paused and glanced back at her. "I'm sorry I acted like such a creep earlier. People prejudge me. Just because my family has money doesn't mean I'm a fool. I want to make my own way in life."

"Well," Lily said, already typing the details of their phone conversation with Jake Nash into her computer, "it looks as if you're going to get that chance."

9

"I'm in jail."

Lily picked up the phone in her office, expecting to hear her daughter's voice. She had left several messages on Shana's voice mail that morning, but she had as yet to return her call. "John?" she asked. Her ex-husband's voice was so strained it took her a few moments to recognize him.

"You have to help me," he pleaded. "They just arraigned me."

Lily's heart began pounding. "Where's Shana?"

"I guess she's in school."

"Good Lord," she said, concerned she might be responsible, "why didn't you speak to her? She called me last night in a panic. She was certain Marco Curazon was stalking her. That's why I called the police."

"You don't understand," he said, knowing she thought the police had mistaken him for Shana's prowler. "I went out to get ice cream. When I got back to the duplex around ten o'clock, the police were already leaving. The man Shana saw must have been a neighbor. Please, Lily, she's okay. I was arrested later . . . I don't know . . . shortly before midnight."

"But Shana doesn't know you're in jail?"

"She was asleep," John continued. "I decided it would be better if I didn't upset her. She's been under enough stress lately. I thought the police would release me last night after they booked me. I had no idea they were going to lock me up and haul me into court this morning."

Lily was appalled that the man she had once been married to was confined in a correctional facility like a common criminal. When she'd learned he was drinking again, though, she had feared another drunk-driving arrest. A DWI conviction wasn't such a lightweight offense these days, and John already had a prior conviction. "How high was your blood alcohol?"

"They didn't arrest me for drunk driving."

"Oh," she said, dismayed. "Then what —"

"Vehicular manslaughter."

Lily almost choked on her own saliva. "You killed someone?"

"Maybe I didn't do anything," he shot back. "Maybe I was just standing outside having a nightcap. You should talk. What happened to that guy? You know . . . what was his name? Hernandez, right?"

The receiver tumbled out of Lily's hands. The past six years disappeared and she was back in Ventura. Bobby Hernandez had first entered her life as a suspect in the rape and kidnapping of a prostitute. Lily was the supervisor over the sex crimes division at the time, and had assigned the case to Clinton Silverstein to prosecute. When the victim, Patricia Barnes, had failed to show up on three separate occasions, Silverstein asked Lily for permission to withdraw charges. Silverstein felt the case was what they called a "failure to pay," meaning due to her occupation, she agreed to have sex with Hernandez and cried rape only when he fled without paying her. Instances such as this were not unusual. Generally, the prostitute's pimp was behind the false accusation; the intent was to send a message to other tricks that they couldn't get away without paying. Therefore, it was Lily's signature on the release forms that became Bobby Hernandez's ticket to freedom.

She remembered having placed Hernandez's file in her briefcase, telling Silverstein she would make the proper notations regarding the dismissal at her home later that evening. John and Lily had separated the previous month, and twelve-year-old Shana had elected to live with her father, a decision that hurt her mother enormously.

Lily remembered leaving the office, eager to see Shana and show her the house she had rented and all the pretty things she had purchased for her new room. The evening had gone beautifully. Shana had loved her room. Lily had cooked her favorite meal — fried chicken and mashed potatoes. After dinner they had lounged on the sofa like sisters, thumbing through family albums and reminiscing. Not used to living alone, Lily had forgotten to lock the sliding glass door in the kitchen. Although she knew enough about criminals to realize the rapist would have still managed to find a way to break into the house, John had insisted the crime would have never occurred if not for her carelessness.

Lily could hear the rapist's sneakers squeaking on the linoleum floor, feel his fingers digging into her flesh as he dragged her down the hallway, her robe tossed over her head like a death shroud. She'd been certain she was going to suffocate. Not only was she thrashing about wildly, the terry-cloth robe was thick and her attacker had pulled it tightly over her nose and mouth. When Shana had heard the sound of a struggle and called out to her mother, all thoughts of her own danger had vanished.

"Is something wrong?" Susan Montgomery, Lily's assistant, had been standing quietly in the doorway. A quirky brunette, she wore her hair cropped short and she dressed like a college student, even though she was the mother of three small children. Today she was wearing a plaid miniskirt, a red sweater, and matching red leggings. As she tiptoed into the room, her concern for her supervisor intensified. Lily's forehead was damp with perspiration and her skin was ashen. "Are you sick?"

"I-I'm —" Lily tilted her head toward the woman's voice, but she couldn't force the words out of her mouth.

"Your ex-husband is on the phone. He says it's urgent . . . that he got disconnected during an important conversation. What do you want me to tell him? If you don't want to speak to him, I can —"

"No," Lily said, frantically retrieving the receiver off her desk. Hearing only a dial tone, she gave her assistant another blank stare.

"Mr. Forrester is on the other line."

"Thanks, Susan," she said, waving her out of the office.

Hernandez had been a dead ringer for the rapist. After the assault Lily had sent Shana home with John, then retrieved the Hernandez file from her briefcase. She remembered crawling across the floor on her hands and knees, her bathrobe reeking from her daughter's vomit. She not only had their attacker's mug shot, she had his address. She was certain he had followed her home from the government center in Ventura. From the day the county had erected the new complex, housing both the courts and the jail, Lily had been fearful something awful was going to happen. The windows of the jail overlooked the parking lot. Prisoners could watch victims, witnesses, even prosecutors as they got in and out of their cars each day.

In her frenzied state, all Lily recalled was the rapist's dark skin, his red sweatshirt, the gold crucifix dangling around his neck. Bobby Hernandez's facial features and body conformation not only looked exactly like the rapist's, he had been wearing a red sweatshirt and a crucifix in his mug shots. For years she had worked with victims, warning them not to make identifications based on such superficial details.

Susan Montgomery was standing beside her desk again, pointing at the blinking light on the telephone console. Deciding her supervisor must have had an argument with her former spouse, she handed her a cup of ice water. "Drink this," she said.

"You'll feel better."

Lily thanked the woman with her eyes. "Can you shut the door for me, Susan?"

"Sure," she said. "And if it will make you feel any better, whenever I get a call from my ex-husband, I start hyperventilating."

John was accusing, desperate. "You hung up on me. They don't allow you fifteen phone calls, you know. This is a damn jail, Lily! I called you for help."

"I didn't hang up on you," she said, knowing she had to defuse the situation immediately. "A judge called me regarding a case I'm handling. All I did was place you on hold until I answered his question."

"Don't shovel that shit at me," he said. "You're just stalling, trying to show me what a big shot you are, that even judges come running to you. I don't care who the hell calls you. If you know what's good for you, you'll get your ass down here."

Lily's right leg began jumping up and down. She had to place her hand on it to hold it in place. Was Bobby Hernandez stalking her from the grave? Until a person took a life, they could never understand the gravity of their actions. She was forever tied to a dead man. On the nights when sleep eluded her, she would spend all night pacing like a caged animal, feeling as if she were handcuffed to the rotting corpse of Bobby Hernandez. People in prison might envy her. She could come and go when she pleased, walk on the beach, get in her car and drive to work each day. But she was not free. Imprisoned by her own deeds, she lived in constant fear of exposure, locked in a macabre marriage to the man she had killed. After gulping down the whole glass of water, she asked, "Where are you calling me from?"

"Didn't you hear me?" John yelled. "How many times do I have to tell you? I'm in the Los Angeles County Jail."

"I understand you're in jail," she said, hissing the words at him. "Exactly *where* are you in the jail? Are you in booking? Are you in an interview room? I'm trying to determine if anyone can hear what you're saying."

The line fell silent. A short time later, a garbled male voice rang out in the background. "The only person who can hear me," John told her, "is this weirdo standing behind me. I tried to tell him to get lost. I think he's from Iran or somewhere."

"You're using a pay phone, then?" She wondered if Susan had accepted a collect call. How else would he have been able to call her long-distance from the jail?

"First the cops interrogate me," he said, "now you're giving me the third-degree. Trust me, this guy doesn't speak English. Even if he did, he wouldn't know what we're talking about."

Lily lowered her voice. "Why would you bring up Bobby Hernandez?"

"Because I know the truth," he said. "Shana and I both know you killed that man. You killed him because you mistook him for the rapist. You tracked him down and assassinated him. That's premeditated murder."

Lily's eyes glazed over. Instead of the nervous tremors she'd experienced earlier, her muscles locked into place. "Bobby Hernandez was a murderer," she said, the words erupting from deep inside her subconscious. "He was on his way to becoming a serial killer. Remember Peter McDonald and Carmen Lopez? Hernandez and four of his fellow gang members murdered them. They bashed the boy's head in, raped the girl repeatedly, then shoved a tree limb up her vagina, rupturing her abdominal wall."

"That's not the point."

"That's precisely the point," Lily said, slamming her fist down on the desk. "Hernandez developed a taste for killing.

161

He decided it was more exciting than taking drugs and robbing people. On his own, he kidnapped, raped, and murdered another woman."

John vaguely recalled the atrocities of the case she had mentioned, but at the time he'd been more concerned over what had happened to his daughter than the fate of strangers. "I didn't say the man deserved to live," he said. "Have I ever accused you or threatened to turn you in?"

Lily had no choice but to lie. "I didn't kill him."

"Hey," he said, "you scratch my back and I'll scratch yours. Isn't that the way the world works these days?"

She bit down on the inside of her mouth. Why had he waited six years to confront her? Knowing her ex-husband as well as she did, she had to consider that he might be bluffing. But John and Shana did know things that only Detective Cunningham had uncovered during his investigation. He knew she had stayed out until dawn the night following the rape. And Shana had walked into the garage, catching her mother squatting near the rear of her Honda as she wiped off the black magic marker she'd used to alter her license plate. In one particular instance, Lily had even blurted out the truth. John had been ranting and raving, saying he wanted to kill the man who had viciously raped his daughter. His wife told him that it wasn't necessary, that she had already killed him. When John had failed to take her seriously, she had recanted and told him her statement was only wishful thinking.

"What do you want from me, John?"

"You're an attorney," he said. "Do you want Shana to find out her father's in jail? She hasn't recovered from what that Curazon monster did to her. He raped my baby. She was just an innocent little girl."

"Calm down," Lily said, hearing him whimpering. "Did the judge set bail?"

"Yeah," he said. "A hundred thousand."

"A hundred thousand!" Lily exclaimed, expecting a lower amount. The offense of vehicular manslaughter carried the same weight as second-degree murder. Under those circumstances, bail in this range might be justified. Her original assumption, however, was that the district attorney in Los Angeles had arraigned John on a number of charges. Most defendants were either too frightened to hear half of what was said during their arraignment, or they had difficulty deciphering the legal jargon. And prosecutors frequently added more serious counts to the original pleading, hoping these charges could be used as leverage to get the defendant to enter into a plea agreement and avoid taking the case to trial. In order to charge John with vehicular manslaughter, though, he would have had to have killed someone with his car during the commission of a felony. "What exactly did you do?"

"You mean, what they said I did?"

Now they were going to play *this* game, Lily thought, having heard the same evasive tactics spewing out of the mouths of hundreds of criminals during the course of her career. She was tempted to bail him out of jail just so she could drive him to a dark alley and smash both his kneecaps with a baseball bat. He didn't mind accusing her of murder on a jailhouse phone, but he wasn't about to admit his own guilt. "Fine," she snapped. "Tell me what crimes the police are alleging that you've committed."

"There was an accident," he said. "The cops claim I left the scene. You know, a hit-and-run. When they arrested me, I was sitting on the front porch sipping on a bottle of Jack Daniel's."

"You're on probation, John," Lily said. "You swore you weren't going to drink."

"I know," he said, "but it breaks my heart

to see Shana scared. She thought she saw Curazon last night."

"I know," Lily said. "I called the police, remember? You certainly didn't do Shana any favors by getting yourself arrested."

John continued, "I wasn't behind the wheel when they arrested me. Having a drink isn't a crime."

Heaven help me, Lily thought, her thoughts racing. As soon as they concluded their conversation, she'd have to call and see if the court would allow him to post bail with a ten percent deposit. This was the general rule of thumb unless the judge specified that the defendant fork over the entire amount. Even then she didn't have ten thousand dollars in cash. She'd have to get a loan from the credit union. Loans took time. She had to shut John up, though, and the only way was to meet his demands. "Were there any witnesses to this *alleged* hit-and-run accident?"

"None that I know of," he answered. "I mean, you're the hotshot attorney. You know the cops never tell you these kind of things."

Lily massaged her forehead, attempting to analyze the situation objectively. When the evidence was weak, most prosecutors allowed the suspect to remain at large in the community until they had a chance to build an airtight case. Once they made an arrest, the clock began ticking, and if the case resulted in an acquittal, the suspect could never be tried for that particular crime again. Since Henry Middleton had been free for almost a year, Lily was baffled as to why they had locked up her ex-husband. "Why did they arrest you if they didn't have a witness, or some type of concrete proof? I don't even know how they identified you since the accident was a hit-and-run. Was there damage to your car?"

"They found my wallet," John said reluctantly. "I didn't even realize it was gone. The police said they found it in the grass a few feet from the guy's body. The public defender and I decided that whoever hit this person must have stolen my wallet, then dropped it at the scene of the accident."

Lily had a nasty taste in her mouth, as if she had just consumed a dozen rotten eggs. She knew John was guilty. He would have never called and threatened her if he was innocent. Now they were both murderers. "Let me go," she said. "I'll have to try to raise the money."

"I need money for an attorney as well."

"Didn't you just tell me you're being represented by the public defender?"

"I had no choice at the arraignment," John told her. "But even he told me I should hire someone else. He says he's got more cases than he can handle. You know, I need one of those fancy attorneys who specializes in this kind of thing."

Lily started to ask about the victim, then stopped herself. She didn't want to hear the details yet, not when she was being extorted to bail out the person who had killed him. "How can you do this to me?"

"What?" he asked. "Ask you to help me? I'm the father of your child."

"You didn't ask me, John," she said, scribbling notes to herself on a yellow pad. "You threatened me. Isn't that what we're talking about here?"

"If you'd killed the right guy," he said. "I'd have given you a medal and never mentioned it again. The bastard who raped my daughter is back on the street, Lily. Why don't you shoot him?"

"You're out of your mind," she said. "Keep talking this way, and I won't lift a finger to help you. And let's get something straight right now. No matter what kind of ridiculous accusations you hurl at me, I have no intention of paying for your attorney. The district attorney in Los Angeles may not be able to charge you with driving under the influence, but you and I both know that this person would be alive if you'd remained sober."

John's voice took on a sharper edge. "Oh, you'll help me. You can't afford not to help me. I know how much that job means to you, how scared you are of ending up in my situation. You know how dirty and cramped it is in prison. Just because you're a woman doesn't mean you'll have a smooth ride. You've put your share of women behind bars." He paused, then added, "Maybe a few of them would like to have a little talk with you, know what I mean?"

Lily knew when she was defeated. She picked up a file and hurled it across the room, watching as the papers struck the wall, then scattered all over her office floor. She felt like leaping through the phone and strangling him. Only in the past year had she started to put her life back together. And there was Shana to consider.

"I expect to be out of here by this evening," he told her. "Do we understand each other?"

Lily swallowed her pride. "I'll do the best I can."

"Just get the job done," John said. "After I begged you to keep it a secret, you called and told Shana I was broke, made her think her old man was nothing more than a burned-out loser. That's why I fell off the wagon."

"An innocent person is dead," Lily said. "I have to walk off my job, scrape together every penny I have, then run like a nut to Los Angeles to bail my ex-husband out of jail. All these years you've blamed me for the fact that Shana was raped; now you're trying to blame this on me as well?"

"Do you know what it feels like to be humiliated?" John said, his voice laced with venom. "You're the woman who swore she'd stand by me until I died. Are you proud of yourself, Lily? Once again you've managed to rip our family apart."

10

"How did I do?" John asked, his hands clasped tightly on the arms of his chair. "I'd make a pretty good actor, don't you think?" He was wearing the same clothes from the night before, and his face was covered with day-old stubble, his shirt wrinkled and stained. Seated at a table in an interview room at the Los Angeles Police Department, he had just concluded his phone call to Lily.

Detective Mark Osborne tipped his chair back on its hind legs, glancing over at his partner. A thirty-one-year-old Hispanic divorcée, Hope Carruthers was a striking brunette with enormous brown eyes and olive skin. Born Esperanza Maria Cortez, she had decided to use the name of Hope after joining the police department. Not only did she like the connotation, it simplified things. When she had gone by Esperanza, she wasted time spelling her name every time she made a phone call.

Mark Osborne, along with a slew of other officers in the department, thought Hope Carruthers was a dream walking. She could rebuild your carburetor, cook a better meal than your mother, possessed a beautiful, feminine, and shapely body, and no matter how much adversity life threw at her, she managed to show up every day with a smile on her face. Unfortunately, Hope had earned her detective shield the hard way. An unknown assailant had opened fire as she and several other officers were attempting to break up a fight in the South Central area of Los Angeles. The bullet had entered her back, barely missing her spinal cord, then zigzagged its way through the left side of her body. After five operations she still walked with a limp, but Osborne would hand over a year's salary for one night in bed with her. Twirling his wedding band on his finger, he cleared his throat and attempted to focus on the business at hand. "To be honest," he said, "I'm not certain what's going on here."

Carruthers took over. "Both your wife and daughter were raped, Mr. Forrester, is that correct?"

"Yes," John said, his eyes misting over again. "That's why I can't let this accident thing go any further, don't you see? My daughter needs me. She doesn't depend on her mother. Her mother lives too far away, and she's too caught up in her career."

"Maybe that's because of the line of work

she's in," Osborne said, wadding up a piece of paper and tossing it into the trash can.

"Oh, I see," John said, swiping his mouth with the back of his hand, "you guys don't believe me because Lily's a district attorney."

Osborne placed his arms on the table. "I don't know your ex-wife, pal. Just because you twisted her arm to bail you out of jail doesn't mean she's a murderer."

"Lily doesn't give a shit what happens to me," John said, panicked that his plan might be backfiring. "Do you think she'd come running down here if what I told you wasn't the truth? When she shows up, then you'll know. The guy in the jail told me you'd let me go if I helped you solve a murder, even set me up in one of those witness-protection programs where I get a new identity, a house, and enough money to get by on. All you've got against me is my wallet. I'm not as stupid as you people think. My wallet doesn't prove I killed that kid."

Osborne pressed his index finger and thumb together, then moved them across his lips to simulate a zipper, letting his partner know that she shouldn't respond to his statements. With a suspect as loose-lipped and desperate as Forrester, the best way to proceed was to keep them talking. The more they talked, the deeper the hole they dug. And the silent treatment would cause a guy like this to cough up even more information."

"I certainly don't want to be around when you arrest Lily," John told them. "I just told you she killed a man! Why do you think our daughter lives with me instead of her mother?"

During his twenty-three years on the force, Mark Osborne had seen just about everything. The man sitting in front of him could very well be presenting them with information on a serious crime, but nonetheless, he made his stomach turn. He despised cowards. He'd rather deal with a professional killer than a man who would rat out the mother of his child. Regarding the hit-and-run, they might not have the right driver, but there was no doubt as to the car. An hour after John Forrester's arraignment, the crime lab had reported finding pieces of the victim's flesh trapped in the undercarriage of the Mustang. Antonio Vasquez had been a nineteen-year-old student from Argentina. From what his parents had said when Hope notified them of their son's death, the young man had saved for years to come to the United States.

When Osborne nodded, Hope attempted to clarify the situation. "The rapist isn't the man your ex-wife killed, though, since I just heard you mention that he's been released on parole."

"She shot the wrong person," John said, using the edge of his shirt to blot the sweat on his face. "This guy she killed, Bobby Hernandez, looked exactly like the rapist."

Detective Carruthers heard someone knocking on the door. An officer whispered something to her, and she motioned for Osborne to step outside the room. "We managed to find a newspaper clipping in the on-line archives of a local Ventura county newspaper which confirms that an individual by the name of Bobby Hernandez was murdered six years ago in Oxnard on the date Forrester indicated." She stopped to cough, covering her mouth with her hand. "We'll have to get in touch with the police department in that area to verify all the particulars. From what we were able to determine, though, no one was ever charged or convicted of the crime. If they were, the victim wasn't important enough to merit a follow-up article."

Mark Osborne had the same stoic expression on his face as before. They both returned to the interview room.

John was squirming in his seat. "You're going to let me go, aren't you? I didn't do

anything wrong. Even if I was guilty of this
. . . this crime . . . it wasn't something intentional. I just handed you a murderer. People
get famous over this type of deal, especially
when the person is a public official like my
ex-wife."

Detective Osborne checked the tape recorder to make certain it was recording
properly. Now that they had confirmed that
Forrester wasn't simply talking out of his
asshole, and a homicide had actually been
committed, they had to proceed with
greater caution. "We want to make our-
selves perfectly clear here," he said. "We
never promised you anything. You requested that we monitor a phone call to
your ex-wife. All we did was comply with
your request."

John stared at the clock on the wall.
"You've got to give me the car back," he
said, acting as if he hadn't heard anything
the detective had told him. "My daughter
probably thinks someone stole it."

Osborne stood, shoving his chair back to
the table. An enormous man in his mid-
fifties, most of his muscles had turned to
flab, yet he still posed a menacing presence.
People at the department had given him the
moniker of "Bulldog." His face bore an almost permanent grimace, his eyes bulged in

their sockets, and for a man who stood six-three and weighed over two hundred pounds, his face looked as if it had been compressed in a trash compactor. "According to the vehicle registration," he said, "the Mustang we impounded is registered to Shana Forrester. Shana Forrester is your daughter, right? Does she still reside at 1145-B Maplewood Drive, the location where the patrol arrested you last night?"

John momentarily stopped breathing. "God, no," he exclaimed, gasping for air, "don't tell me you think Shana had anything to do with this boy's death. I told you a pick-pocket must have lifted my wallet. I wasn't even aware it was gone, or I would have called and canceled my credit cards. That's the person who should be locked up, not me."

Mark Osborne walked over and gazed out the window, then turned back around. "How old is your daughter?"

"Nineteen."

"Is she in college?"

"Yes," John told him, his hands locked between his thighs. "She goes to UCLA."

"Did she know the victim?"

"The victim?" John repeated. "Bobby Hernandez? I keep trying to explain to you people that Hernandez wasn't the rapist."

"We're referring to Antonio Vasquez," Osborne said, "the victim of the hit-and-run accident."

"How would Shana know this boy? Wasn't he a street person or something?" As soon as the words left his mouth, John wanted to retract them.

The detective removed his pocket knife, then began cleaning his fingernails. No information had been released at this point relating to the victim. "Vasquez was a freshman at UCLA, Forrester. That's how patrol identified him. They found his school ID in his pocket. What made you think he was a street person?"

John was momentarily speechless. They were tricking him, making things up, attempting to confuse him so he would confess. He'd been certain the young boy he'd struck had been a street person, possibly even a male prostitute. A muscle in his face twitched. He felt a sudden urge to urinate, as if an unseen force had punched him in his lower abdomen. "I don't know . . . something the cops said . . ." A student! He had killed a college student! His guilt had somehow been diluted by his assumption that the young man he had left to die had either been living in despair as a homeless

177

person or risking his life selling his body for sex.

Osborne continued, "Where was your daughter last night?"

"At home."

"With you, right?"

All the color drained from John's face. By the time the police had picked him up in front of the duplex, he'd consumed the entire pint of Jack Daniel's. He couldn't recall what he'd told the arresting officers regarding his whereabouts at the time of the crime. He couldn't even remember what he had said to the public defender that morning prior to the arraignment. The attorney had been in such a hurry, they had exchanged only a few words. "I — I want my attorney," he stammered. "I refuse to answer any more questions."

Hope depressed the stop button on the tape recorder, then left the room to arrange for the prisoner to be transported back to the jail. Detective Osborne turned back to the window. He'd interrogated fourteen-year-old gang members who were more sophisticated. Had John Forrester been behind the wheel of the Mustang? At this stage of the game, he couldn't be certain. A nineteen-year-old college student could easily have borrowed her father's wallet, then headed out for a night of partying. And a girl who had been viciously raped just might have grown hard enough to hit someone with her car, then flee the scene of the crime. The prisons were full of people who had been victimized during their childhood. This didn't mean they shouldn't be held accountable for their actions, but it did bear testament to the far-reaching consequences of crime.

Once their prisoner was handcuffed and escorted out of the interview room, Osborne told Carruthers, "We need to interview the girl right away. Call UCLA and find out what her last class was, then instruct dispatch to send a patrol unit to pick her up."

"God, Mark," she said, "after all this young woman has been through, don't you think we should wait a few days? The lab just got started on the car this morning. Once they sift through all the evidence, we may be able to exclude her as a suspect."

Osborne shook his head. These were the kind of days when he asked himself why he'd ever pursued a career in law enforcement. "We know we're going to find the daughter's fingerprints because it's her car. And we know the father drove it as well. Any additional forensic evidence will be located on the exterior portion of the vehicle."

"You may be wrong," Hope countered, attempting to come up with an alternative scenario. "Whoever hit Vasquez could have placed him inside the car, thinking they'd drive him to the hospital. He wasn't that heavy, Mark. I think the coroner said he only weighed a hundred and twenty-three pounds. Also, they believe he was alive for at least an hour after he incurred the injuries. Perhaps when the driver realized that his victim had died and what type of charges he was facing, he dumped his body out near the shopping center. That means we might find more evidence inside the car."

"We have to talk to the girl," Mark Osborne said. "The only way we're going to find evidence inside that car would be if we're looking at something far more complex than a fatal hit-and-run."

"Just because the victim and Forrester's daughter both attend UCLA doesn't mean a great deal," she reasoned. "It's a big university, Mark. That's like saying there's a connection because they both lived in the same city."

"It's a close call, Hope," he said. "For all we know, Shana Forrester went out on a date with Vasquez. Since his family said he didn't own a car, she could have picked him up in the Mustang. What if he tried to force her to have sex with him? With her history, she could have easily gone berserk, pushing him out of the car and then running over him."

"But her father has a serious drinking problem," Hope said, disagreeing with him. "I don't even have to look at his blood alcohol to tell you Forrester was tanked to the gills last night. The damn stuff is oozing from his pores. Between that and his body odor, being in the same room with him made me feel like I was going to gag."

"I have two kids at home," he said, both of them exiting the interview room. "Trust me, if my daughter killed someone, I'd be sweating buckets. Nothing smells as bad as fear."

"What about the old homicide?" Hope asked, trailing behind him down the corridor. "How deep should we dig?"

"Make some phone calls," Osborne said, his footsteps clanking on the linoleum flooring. "A killing that occurred six years ago can't be classified as top priority right now. Besides, the crime didn't occur under our jurisdiction. Before you do anything, though, call both the coroner's office and the lab and read them the riot act. I expect the autopsy on Vasquez to be completed by tomorrow, the forensic work by the end of next week, so don't let them give you any bullshit about how backed up they are. Right now that boy's parents are about to board a plane from Argentina. I hate long plane rides, don't you?"

They took off in different directions. When Hope had first begun working with the detective, she'd had trouble deciphering some of his offhand comments. This time, however, she knew precisely what he meant. Spending hours inside a cramped airplane was never pleasant, even when a person was embarking on a vacation. Mr. and Mrs. Vasquez were traveling to the United States for one reason — to claim the body of their deceased son.

Richard Fowler's office was located in a two-story building on Victoria Boulevard across from the Ventura County government center. Although he owned both the building and the land, he leased out the top floor, providing him with an additional source of revenue. His associate, Martin Schwartz, walked over to him in the parking lot.

"I just got out of court," Schwartz said, shielding his eyes from the midday sun. At forty-five, he was a mellow man with bushy brown hair and a barrel-shaped body. "Want to have lunch?" he asked. "I was thinking of walking down to Marie Callender's for a bowl of soup."

"I'm going to have to catch a bite later," Richard told him. "I'm on my way to the P.D. to speak with Fred Jameson regarding the Pierson matter."

"The security guard who accidentally shot his wife?"

"You got it," Richard said, unlocking the door to his car. "Thanks for the invite, Marty." He turned the key in the ignition in order to bring the conversation to a close.

Approximately fifteen minutes later, Richard was sitting in a chair in the detective bay at the Ventura Police Department. Twenty detectives all worked in the same space, their offices consisting of small partitioned cubicles. He had no idea how they could concentrate. A cacophony of voices filled the air, phones jangled, and officers and support personnel roamed up and down the aisles. He was reminded of his days at the district attorney's office, but unlike the detectives, each of the prosecutors had their own private office.

With a thick head of silver hair and pale green eyes, Detective Jameson stood just under six feet. A ruggedly handsome man, he was dressed in a white shirt, a striped tie, and dark slacks, and the butt of his service revolver was protruding from his shoulder holster. The silver hair was deceptive, a genetically inherited characteristic passed down from his mother. At thirty-eight, Jameson had been with the department for five years, having transferred from the sheriff's office in San Francisco. He was a high-energy type of guy, likable, yet sometimes unpredictable when it came to temperament. Over the years he'd had several run-ins with the D.A.'s office, and had no qualms about speaking his mind. Now that Richard was on the opposite side of the fence, a diehard like Jameson considered him persona non grata.

"I filed a discovery motion thirty days ago," Richard said, studying crime-scene photographs of the Pierson shooting. "I should have received copies of these weeks ago."

Jameson put his feet on top of his desk. "Your client might skate," he told him, unconcerned with Richard's implication that he was in violation of a court order. He enjoyed his work, but he'd always rebelled against rules. Joining the police department fresh out of college, he'd been lured by the power of the badge. His career in law enforcement had not met his expectations, though. He possessed the education and drive to rise to the top, but a few years back someone had slammed him with a bad rap, and he was now bucking the stigma. "Too bad Pierson's wife wasn't able to verify his story. Then we wouldn't have wasted our time."

According to her physicians, Mrs. Pierson would eventually recover. It was doubtful, however, if she would ever remember the events of that evening. "Let's face it," Richard told him. "Kenny Pierson is a cop, or you wouldn't be talking to me."

The detective stuck a toothpick in his mouth, a sour look on his face. "Pierson is a rent-a-cop, Fowler. That's not the same as being a member of the force. What have you got to complain about, anyway? You should be thrilled that we would even make an attempt to prove this crime was an accident. Most men who shoot a woman in the head go to prison, regardless of the circumstances."

After replacing the crime-scene photos back in the file, Jameson stood to walk him out. "We're waiting for ballistics to officially confirm that the trigger mechanism was defective," he added as they were buzzed through the security doors into the lobby.

"As soon as we get their report in writing, I'll contact Paul Sullivan at the D.A.'s office and request that they drop the charges."

"Thanks," Richard told him, shaking his hand. "Oh, there's another matter I'd like to discuss with you if you have the time."

"I'm listening," Jameson said reluctantly. He was edgy and overloaded with work, to the point where he would have preferred putting an end to the conversation. His son had a baseball game that afternoon, and he had been planning on slipping out a few hours early.

"Does the name Marco Curazon ring a bell?"

Jameson rested his back against the wall. Above his head was a row of framed portraits of former police chiefs, along with several plaques honoring officers who had been injured or killed in the line of duty. "Wasn't he the guy who was convicted of raping Lily Forrester and her daughter?"

"Yes," Richard said. "He's been paroled."

"Hey," Jameson said, "we only arrest them. You got any complaints, take them up with the parole board."

"I've already spoken to his parole agent," Richard told him. "The man's dangerous, Fred. He's carrying what appear to be pictures of Shana Forrester in his wallet. Not only that, from what I hear, they could be recent."

Jameson's eyes flashed with interest. "How did this come to light?"

"One of my clients hung out with Curazon before he got busted again," the attorney said. "Curazon showed him pictures of an attractive redhead, claiming she was his girlfriend. I know you didn't handle the rape itself, so you've probably never seen Lily's daughter. You know Lily, though, and her daughter looks exactly like her."

"There's a lot of redheads, pal," Jameson said acerbically, walking over and spitting the toothpick out in a trash can. The most disturbing crime he had ever investigated had been overturned on appeal. Lily Forrester had been partially responsible; therefore she wasn't one of his favorite people. Several years back, Walter Evans, a retired city councilman, had been shot and killed during a car jacking. Evans' brother, Alan, was a prominent local judge. During her employment with the appellate court in Los Angeles, Lily had reviewed the case and arrived at the conclusion that Jameson might have falsified evidence to ensure a conviction. This, coupled with errors made by the presiding judge during the trial, had ultimately resulted in the reversal. Walter Evans had been a close friend of Jameson's father, a man the detective had known and admired. He felt bad that Forrester and her daughter had gone through such a terrible ordeal, but at least they had come out of it alive. He might have made a few mistakes in the Evans investigation due to his relationship with the victim, but the accusations that he had intentionally falsified evidence had been devastating. Allegations of this nature, even when unsubstantiated, seriously jeopardized a police officer's chance for advancement.

"It's more than just the fact that the girl in the photo was a redhead," Richard told him. "Curazon told him she went to college at UCLA, the same school Shana Forrester attends."

"What do you want us to do?" Jameson said, disgruntled. "Curazon's parole agent has the authority to search his property, his house, even ship his ass back to prison."

"He's absconded," Richard told him. "I've already contacted his parole agent. Curazon's been out of pocket for several months. His agent has a hearing scheduled next week to have his parole revoked. They have to find him, though, before they can send him back to prison."

"Now I know where you fit into this picture," Jameson said, a sly smile on his face. "You and Lily Forrester had something going on, right?"

Richard flushed, pulling his collar away from his neck. "We worked together. I consider her a friend, just like you do the officers in your department."

"That's not what I heard," Jameson said. "Rumor has it you guys were lovers."

"My relationship with Lily Forrester is none of your business," Richard barked, wishing he had approached someone else within the department. "I came here because I know how the system works, okay? Whether a person is wanted for a parole violation, a kidnapping, even a murder, unless the crime just occurred or the media jumps on it, they become nothing more than a set of statistics in a computer. I want your men to try and find this guy. He hasn't left the area. He just decided not to report to his parole officer. And you know why, Jameson?"

"Have you told Forrester that Curazon is carrying around pictures of her daughter?"

"How do I know the girl in these snapshots is really Shana Forrester?" Richard said. "The guy my client spoke to may not even be Marco Curazon. The man didn't show him a picture ID. Maybe his name just sounded similar. We're talking ex-cons,

Jameson, not brain surgeons. I refuse to panic Lily and her daughter until I have some kind of verification."

"I thought you said Curazon had absconded."

"He hasn't left the area," Richard told him. "He just decided not to report to his parole officer. And you know why, Jameson?"

Without realizing it, Richard had become so agitated he was standing only inches from the detective's face. In most instances Jameson would never tolerate someone encroaching on his personal space. He knew from experience, however, that it was sometimes the soft-spoken, controlled types like Fowler who could snap and do something crazy. Deciding not to antagonize him and end up in a fistfight, he took several steps backward.

"I'll tell you why," Richard said, jabbing his finger at him repeatedly. "Curazon is about to commit another crime, that's why. He's going to rape either Shana Forrester or her mother. I don't know when and I don't know how, but I want you to find this crazy fucker before he gets a chance to carry out his plan."

190

11

Richard walked out of the police department, heading to his car in the parking lot. As soon as he started the car, his cell phone rang. "Richard Fowler," he said into the microphone mounted above the visor.

"Where have you been?" June Overland asked in her nasal twang.

His office manager was either hyperactive or obsessive compulsive. Without her, his law practice would disintegrate. "Start acting like a wife, and I'll have to divorce you."

"Fine with me," she said. "Judge McKinley called regarding your lunch date next Thursday. Javal Thornton claims they're abusing him in jail. Seems he's developed an allergy to the meat loaf, or at least to the tomato sauce. He demanded that you file a grievance. I told him for the money he's paying us, he'll have to file his own grievances. Kenny Pierson's mother also called. She inquired about the lab reports on the gun. I told her we wouldn't know anything until the end of the week."

Richard felt a headache coming on. Talking to June was draining. He steered the Lexus out of the parking lot. Thus far he hadn't heard anything that couldn't have waited until he returned to the office. The woman had worked for attorneys for over twenty years. Her excess energy was generally channeled into the kind of tasks most employees avoided like a bad case of the flu. Wanting to bring her up to date on the latest computer technology, Richard had paid for her to take courses at the community college. She not only talked ninety words per minute, she typed just as fast, her fingers flying over the keyboard with the precision of a concert pianist. Now that the fifty-nine-year-old woman had mastered the computer, there was hardly a scrap of paper left in his office. June had scanned in every client file, then rushed out and purchased a CD-ROM that contained an entire law library. Finishing the paperwork by the time he arrived at the office, she spent the rest of the day collecting overdue bills, counseling clients and their families, even rearranging the office furniture.

"Is that all?"

"No," June continued. "A strange women called three times during the past hour. She refused to identify herself. You must know her, though, because she referred to you by your first name."

"Didn't you check the caller ID?"

"The call came through the main switchboard for the county of Santa Barbara."

Richard failed to notice that the BMW in front of him had stalled. He slammed on his brakes, narrowly avoiding a collision. He started to ask June to give him the number, then decided to wait and call from the privacy of his office. Although there was a small chance that the female caller was related to Rob Whittier, the man he'd represented on the drug case and the individual who had provided him with the information on Curazon, his gut instinct told him it was Lily. "I'll be back in the office in ten minutes," he said, hitting the off button on the phone.

Navigating around the stalled vehicle, he found it hard to stomach that a man like Curazon could be back on the street after only six years in prison. The criminal justice system had more than a few dirty secrets that it kept hidden from the general public. The fact that prisoners were released prior to completing their terms occurred as a result of overcrowding, yet in the majority of instances, prison officials were merely following the law. When a judge imposed a sentence, victims and their families left the courtroom believing that the offender would spend whatever term they were given behind bars. Sadly, this was seldom the case. The courts never mentioned the bonus points handed out for what was classified as good time and work time, cutting inmate sentences by almost fifty percent.

Richard parked his car in his designated parking spot, getting out and heading toward his office. The sun had been out when he'd left the police department. Now a dark cloud loomed directly over his head. Before he reached the front of the building, it began pouring. He stopped walking, tilting his face toward the sky. The drastic change in weather seemed symbolic, almost like an omen. For six years he had rocked along in a quasi state of normality. Joyce might not be the love of his life, but the problems she presented were minor. Had he made a mistake by contacting Lily? Was she the mystery woman who had called his office three times in less than an hour? He belched loudly, his stomach bubbling. Since he'd left the D.A.'s office, his stress level had dropped considerably. Representing criminals had its rewards. He didn't spend many sleepless nights worrying about the outcome of his cases.

June Overland burst out laughing when she looked up and saw him standing in front of the reception console. A short woman with large breasts, her hair was gray but tinted a golden blonde. "You look like a duck who forgot how to swim."

Soaked, hungry, and deeply concerned about Lily, Richard was not amused. "Are my messages on my desk?"

"Where else would they be?" she answered, bristling. "When you try to be funny, I'm supposed to crack up. Just because you're having a bad day, you bite my head off. Not only that, you're ruining our new carpeting. Haven't you ever heard of an umbrella?"

Richard entered his office and slammed the door. He grabbed a stack of pink message slips off his desk, setting them all aside except for the one where June had left the caller's name blank. Slipping his jacket off, he draped it over the back of his chair, then headed to his private bathroom to relieve himself and run a comb through his wet hair.

Richard stared at his image in the mirror. While he had been busy building his practice, and Lily had passed her days reviewing cases on appeal, Marco Curazon had been confined in a cramped cell, his days passing in agonizingly slow motion. What had he done to occupy his mind, to contain his hostilities, to pull himself from one day to the other? Read novels, obtain his GED, attend services in the prison chapel? "Right," he told himself, shouting for June to bring him a fresh shirt.

"I can hear you better when you leave your door open," the woman said, handing him one of the plastic-wrapped shirts she picked up every Wednesday at the cleaners.

"Thanks," he said, balling up his wet shirt and handing it to her.

"Poor baby," she said, gawking at him, "you're shivering."

"I'm fine, June."

She stood on her tiptoes and placed her hand on his forehead, checking to see if he was running a fever. "I'll make you a cup of hot tea," she told him, reaching over and fastening the buttons on his shirt. "You can't walk into an air-conditioned office looking like you just crawled out of a swimming pool. You'll catch your death."

Richard stuffed his shirt inside his pants. He appreciated her concern, but he wasn't in the mood to be mothered. "Forget about bringing me tea right now. I need to make some phone calls, so please, just close my door on your way out."

He knew what men like Curazon did to pass the time in prison. They bonded with new crime partners, pumped iron to shape their bodies into powerful killing machines, planned who they were going to victimize or punish when the prison gates finally swung open.

He dialed the number on the message slip, ending up with a recording stating that he had reached the county of Santa Barbara. Since he didn't know Lily's extension, he had to wait for an operator to come on the line. "Lily Forrester, please."

"Hold on," a female voice said, the sound of computer keys tapping in the background. "Ms. Forrester is with the district attorney's office, extension 210. Do you want me to connect you?"

What else would he want? "Please," he said, impatient. Lily's voice came on and he began speaking, then realized he was talking to a recording. Waiting for the beep, he left a message for her to call him. A few moments later, he hit the redial button and again reached the main menu for the county offices. She had to have an assistant, someone who could give him the number to her cell phone or, at the very least, contact her and tell her he was back in his office so she could call him. He felt like kicking himself. When he'd seen her the day before, he'd failed to ask her for her home number.

After fifteen minutes of irritation, he placed his hands on top of his desk and stared at the adjacent wall. He had shouted at the operator when she'd claimed she didn't have a listing of employee positions, only their names and extensions. Picking up a case file off his credenza, he tried to concentrate but he was too distracted. He didn't want his stomach to gurgle with acid. He detested the fact that he'd become unglued and cursed at an operator who was only attempting to earn a living. Only twenty-four hours after he'd seen Lily and he was already suffering the consequences.

"I'm going to lunch, June," he said, striding into the outer office. "If the same woman calls again, give her the number to my cell phone."

She looked shocked. "But you never give your cell phone number to clients. Maybe she's a nutcase or something. What kind of person refuses to leave their name?"

"A person who's in trouble," Richard told her, grabbing an umbrella out of the stand by the front door before he stepped outside into the rain again.

12

By three o'clock that afternoon Lily had scraped together the ten thousand she needed to post John's bail. She had emptied out her checking account, dipped into her savings, and still come up short. The remaining two thousand she had obtained by taking cash advances on her credit cards. When the first of the month rolled around, she wouldn't be able to pay her bills. That was two weeks away, however, and she hoped to have arranged a loan through the credit union by then. Steering the car onto the 101 Freeway headed to Los Angeles, she dialed Richard's office, then finally connected with him on his cell phone. "I need to see you right away."

Richard was eating lunch. "Is something wrong? Why didn't you leave your name when you called the office this morning?"

"I didn't think it was a good idea," she said. "Where are you?"

"At Madeline's Restaurant in Ventura."

"I've never heard of it," Lily said, afraid she'd get lost. "How about the Elephant

Bar? We both know where that place is."

"Of course," he said, even though he would have to call June and ask her to re-arrange his afternoon schedule. "Can't you tell me what this is about?"

"Not over the phone." Lily depressed the gas pedal but tried to stay within the speed limit. The last thing she wanted was to cause an accident. "I'm on the outskirts of Camarillo right now. I think I can be there in fifteen minutes."

As soon as she disconnected, Shana called. "I just got out of class and I don't have a way to get home. When I got up this morning, my car was gone. I caught a ride with Jennifer."

"Why don't you see if she can pick you up?"

"I can't find her," her daughter told her. "Look, Dad and I had an argument last night. I took the keys to my car away from him. He must have found the spare set and taken the car anyway. He's acting like such a jerk right now, Mom. You can't imagine."

The understatement of the year, Lily thought. "Can't you take a bus?" She re-fused to tell her daughter over the phone that her father was in jail on charges of ve-hicular manslaughter.

"It's raining. I've been sick, remember?

That's why I wanted to cut class and go home early today." Shana stopped and blew her nose. "The last time Dad forgot to pick me up, I had to take the bus and then walk seven blocks."

"What about a cab?" her mother suggested. "I'd come and get you, but I'm too far away. Do you have any money on you?"

"Only a few dollars," Shana said pensively. "I didn't expect you to come and get me, Mother. I only called because I thought you might have spoken to Dad today. I feel bad that I've been bugging you so much lately. It was silly for me to call you last night. I should have called the police myself."

Lily searched her mind, trying to come up with a believable story. "Your father is probably in the middle of a real estate transaction," she said. "Business has been slow lately. I'm sure you wouldn't want him to miss out on an opportunity. I could be at the school in a few hours. Then we could have dinner together. Can't you hang out in the library until I get there?"

They made arrangements to meet at the UCLA cafeteria at six o'clock that evening. "I don't want Dad to drive my car anymore."

The fact that John had been driving

201

Shana's Mustang at the time of the accident could cause enormous problems. Overnight, their lives had become a sham. John was lying to her. She had lied to him when confronted about the Hernandez homicide. Now she was lying to her daughter.

"We'll discuss the car when I see you tonight."

Lily could post John's bail, but she knew the police wouldn't release the car until the trial was over. Problems seemed to be rushing toward her like a freight train. Her mind was too weary to assimilate them, let alone come up with solutions. A car wasn't like replacing your child's goldfish when it died, then convincing her nothing had happened. How could she prevent Shana from learning the truth? The situation was too serious, and as usual, John had managed to make her the bearer of bad news. Her lips compressed in bitterness. She picked up the envelope containing the ten thousand dollars and clutched it in her hand, thinking of how long she had scrimped and saved, determined that Shana's future would be secure. She decided her son of a bitch ex-husband would just have to cool his heels in jail.

On the outskirts of Ventura, she drove into what appeared to be the center of the thunderstorm. She flicked her windshield wipers on high, their clacking sound making her even more jittery. The heavy rain made it difficult to see where she was going, but luckily, the Elephant Bar was located on the access road to the freeway and its sign was large and distinctive. Lily saw Richard's Lexus and pulled into the adjacent parking spot. She motioned to him, then leaned over and opened the passenger door to her Audi. Other than a battered pickup truck, the parking lot was empty. The bar didn't open until four o'clock, one of the reasons she had thought it would be a good place for them to meet. "What's going on?"

Lily explained the situation as calmly as possible. Having him near her made her feel stronger, less panicked. "I can't take a chance on discussing this with anyone else," she said. "I was going to bail John out, then I changed my mind on the drive down. Even if he suspects the truth, he doesn't have proof."

A tense silence ensued. "You might be making a mistake," Richard said quietly. He saw the look on her face and quickly interjected, "Please, Lily, let me finish. I doubt if anyone really gives a damn who killed Hernandez. The only way the police will re-open the investigation is if someone higher up the ladder pressures them, maybe due to complaints from the victim's family. Force John's hand, and you have no idea what kind of can of worms you might be opening."

Lily placed her head down on the steering wheel. The windows were fogged up, rain was beating down on the roof of the car, and Richard's presence was no longer comforting. Her childhood had been difficult, if not abysmal. Her marriage to John had been good in only one aspect — Shana. She had struggled to obtain her law degree, tried her best to be a loving parent, worked diligently in her career.

Richard lightly touched her arm. "Manny Hernandez saw you, Lily. He was the primary witness to his brother's murder. He's the one who helped the Oxnard PD put together that composite drawing of you."

Instead of her earlier state of agitation, Lily suddenly felt like she had entered into another dimension, as if the past had overlapped the present. "Is that composite still floating around?"

"I have no idea," he said. "Manny told Cunningham there was something peculiar about the person who murdered his brother, remember? I think he used the word *spook*, if I'm not mistaken. You know, like he thought you were a ghost. Your skin tone is extremely fair, and whether you realize it or not, you have distinctive features. Your high cheekbones, the shape of your eyes, your long neck, your height. Even under the duress of seeing his brother killed, Manny knew the shooter wasn't another gang member."

Scenes from the night of the rape played over in Lily's mind. In addition to altering her license plate, she had attempted to disguise her appearance. At the time she'd shot Hernandez, her hair had been stuffed inside a blue knit ski cap, and she had been dressed in Levi's and hiking boots. No one would ever imagine that a female district attorney would travel to one of the most dangerous neighborhoods in Oxnard, leap out of her red Honda Civic, slam a shotgun down on the roof of the car, then proceed to blow a man away. For all practical purposes, Lily had committed what most experts would consider the perfect murder. Shana and John had stumbled across a few pieces of the puzzle, but Detective Cunningham had come the closest to putting together the entire picture even before she had broken down and confessed to him. Although he had let her go in what she viewed was an act of compassion, she suspected the detective might have fallen in love with her.

"Are you following me, Lily?"

"Yes," she said, a glassy look in her eyes. "But the police killed Manny Hernandez. A dead witness isn't very effective."

"I know," Richard said tensely. "That's not the point. The composite drawing was in all the newspapers. We have to find out what Bruce Cunningham did with the evidence."

She glanced at her watch. "I promised Shana I would pick her up at six. We don't have much longer. Do you know who took over Cunningham's caseload?"

"Fred Jameson."

Lily jerked her head around. The Oxnard Police Department, where Detective Cunningham had worked, no longer existed. A few years back it had merged with Ventura. "Are you certain? I mean, with the merger and all —"

"Yes," Richard said, "I work with these guys all the time."

"That settles it," Lily said, telling him the details of the Evans case and what role she had played in overturning the conviction. "Jameson hates me. I'll have to give in to John's demands."

"Post the idiot's bail," Richard told her, his teeth clenched. "If he continues to pressure you into giving him money for an attorney, I'll arrange to have a friend of mine represent him. Then you won't have to worry about the financial end of this mess, and we'll have some control over the situation."

"I can't ask you to do that," she said. "You'll have to pay this man."

"Money is the least of my concerns," he said. "I care about you, Lily."

"Hold me." Once his arms were around her, she could feel his heart pounding. A few moments later she pulled back, fearful she was going to cry. "Maybe it's time you stopped caring about me, Richard."

He reached for the door handle. "I tried that, remember?" he said, stepping out into the rain. "You've got my cell phone number. Call me later tonight."

13

Lily posted John's bail at the Los Angeles County Jail shortly after five o'clock Wednesday evening. She had no intention of waiting for his paperwork to be processed, knowing it could be hours before he was released. As far as she was concerned, he could walk home.

After she parked in the visitors lot on the UCLA campus, she stopped in a rest room and washed her face, smeared on some lipstick, wiped the smudges of mascara from underneath her eyes, then secured her hair in a heart-shaped barrette at the base of her neck.

The cafeteria was located almost a mile from the parking lot. Lily was wearing a mustard-colored suit and high heels. Although the rain had finally stopped, the air was heavy and humid. She smoothed down her skirt, wrinkled from the hours she'd spent in the car. Shana was seated alone, staring at the screen on her laptop computer. "Hi, sweetheart," Lily said, slipping into the chair across from her.

Her daughter closed the lid on her computer, then shoved it in her backpack. "Thanks for coming, Mom," she said, standing and hugging her. "I have no idea what happened to Dad. I've been trying to reach him ever since I called you."

"Let's not worry about that right now," Lily told her. "Are you hungry?"

The cafeteria was noisy and crowded. On the side where they served espresso, there was a long line. The food section consisted of primarily salads and sandwiches. "The food sucks in this place," Shana told her. "Don't you want to eat somewhere else?"

Even as tired as she was, Lily didn't want to talk to her daughter in a restaurant. They could pick up something and eat at the duplex, but then she would have to risk running into John. There was also the problem of the car. "When is your first class tomorrow?"

"I only have one class on Thursdays."

"When?"

"From seven to nine at night."

"Great," Lily said, standing to leave. "Let's get going."

Shana slipped her arms into her backpack, then followed Lily out of the cafeteria. "Why did you want to know when my next class is scheduled? Where are we going?"

"Santa Barbara."

"I've had it," Shana said, as exhausted and frustrated as her mother. "I was planning on coming up next weekend. Don't you have to go to work in the morning? It doesn't make sense for me to travel all the way up there for one night."

"Please, Shana," Lily said, deciding to take her shoes off and walk the rest of the way in her stockings. She'd rather ruin a cheap pair of nylons than end up with blisters on her feet. Outside of the courtroom she favored sneakers or sandals. "I'll explain everything in the car."

"How are you going to drive me back?" She stopped and stared at her mother's feet. "Why aren't you wearing your shoes? Is there a full moon or something? Everyone seems to have gone nuts today."

"The parking lot is a long walk," Lily told her. "I have tender skin, remember?" She placed her arm around the girl's waist. The sky quickly darkened, almost as if the sun had dived into a murky black lake. Even on a clear night the frenetic pace of Los Angeles kept most of its residents from stopping long enough to appreciate the beauty of a sunset. Of course, the smog didn't help. The campus itself was lovely, however, with an abundance of mature trees and a large expanse of greenery. "I'm sorry

I upset you the other day."

"It's okay," Shana said, keeping in step with her mother. "Are we at least going to stop by the house so I can pick up a change of clothes?"

"I'd rather we didn't," Lily told her. "We're the same size. I've got plenty of things you can wear at my place."

For sometime they walked in silence, both of them deep in thought. Shana saw a bench and pointed at it. "Let's sit," she said, dropping down as if she were about to collapse. "I know something is wrong, Mother. Did Dad have a heart attack and die? Is that why you're here, why you want me to go to Santa Barbara with you?"

"Of course not, honey," her mother said, tenderly brushing her hair off her forehead.

"Then what —"

"I should have never told you about your father's financial problems," Lily said. "I suspected he was drinking again, so I got angry."

"You were right," Shana said. "He *is* drinking again."

Lily sighed. "Regardless, it wasn't right for me to tell you something he told me in confidence. Why do you think I've been pressuring you to live with someone other than your father?"

"You don't want to support Dad."

Lily's voice took on a more authoritative tone. "I might have been concerned about making ends meet the other day, but something else related to your father has developed. I don't want you involved, do you understand?"

"But I am involved."

"I know you love him," Lily said, looking down at her hands. "He'll always be your father. But situations develop where you have to temporarily disconnect, even from someone as close as a parent."

"I love you more than anything in the world," Shana said. "You think Dad's the reason I don't spend more time with you." She watched in envy as several students walked by, laughing and talking, wishing her own life were as carefree. "I have trouble staying with you," she continued, sucking in a deep breath. "Please don't take this wrong . . . but we were together that night . . . in that house you rented in Ventura."

Lily said, "You don't have to explain."

"No," she protested, her voice rising, then cracking. "I should have told you these things a long time ago. When I first saw your place in Santa Barbara, I wanted to scream. It's surrounded by rosebushes, Mom!"

Lily opened her mouth, but her daughter cut her off. "Don't interrupt me," she said, tossing her backpack onto the ground. "That's another thing you do that annoys me. When we're together, you talk incessantly. You seem to think you have to entertain me, like you're afraid of just *being* with me." She removed a bottle of water from her backpack and took a swallow, then handed it to Lily. "The reason I don't come up and see you isn't because Santa Barbara bores me. I can't sleep when I'm at your place. I'm afraid someone will climb through the window and either rape us or kill us."

Similar to how Lily imagined herself chained to Bobby Hernandez, her daughter associated her with the most devastating experience of her life. Why couldn't the men who committed these atrocities realize the trauma they were inflicting? She took a sip of Shana's water, then handed it back to her. "I don't understand the significance of the rosebushes."

Shana leaned forward, her elbows on her knees, rubbing her palms over her face. "The windows were open that night," she told her. "I remember how his body stank, then I must have blocked everything else out." She turned to face her mother. "While he was doing those awful things to me, all I remember is the smell of roses."

★ ★ ★

Lily pulled into the driveway of her daughter's North Hollywood duplex at eight-thirty that evening. After Shana's emotional revelation, pressuring her to return to Santa Barbara was out of the question. They stopped at a café and had dinner, most of the meal passing in silence. As soon as she got up the courage to tell Shana about her father's arrest, Lily decided the best way to proceed was to rent her a car.

"Why isn't Dad home by now?" the girl said. "Now I'm really worried."

Lily saw a light burning in the living room. "Did you leave the lights on this morning?"

"I don't remember." Shana started to get out of the car.

"Don't go in yet," her mother said, catching her by the hand.

Shana's eyes widened. "Do you think that guy I saw last night came back and broke in?"

"No, no," Lily said, clearing her throat to cover her uncertainty. "It's probably only your father."

Shana stared at the empty driveway. "If Dad came home, where's my car?"

"The police impounded it," Lily told her, shifting sideways in her seat. "Your father was arrested last night. That's why I wanted you to go back with me. I knew you'd have no way to get around without your car. Don't worry, though, I'll make arrangements to rent you one."

"Shit," Shana said, kicking the panel underneath the dashboard. "Another drunk-driving arrest. I knew it, Mom. I even took my car keys away from him last night. He still went out, damn him."

As calmly as she could, Lily related what had occurred. When Shana heard her father had not only been arrested but had struck and killed a pedestrian, she broke down and cried. "I don't want to see him," she spat out. "I'd claw his eyes out, the stupid jerk. Take me to Santa Barbara. Take me to China. Take me anywhere."

"Relax," Lily said, "I reacted the same way. Getting yourself all worked up isn't going to solve anything. Let me go inside first. More than likely, your father hasn't been released from jail yet and you just left the light on by accident. Once I'm certain he's not home, we'll collect some of your things and rent a hotel room. First thing in the morning, I'll see if I can get you a spot in the dorm. If nothing else, I'll throw your father out, and you can advertise for a roommate."

"What about that big case you're handling?" Shana asked, pulling out a Kleenex and blowing her nose. "You know, the one where the little girl was poisoned? I don't want this mess with Dad to interfere with your job. What you do is too important."

"I'd rather stay here and take care of things in the morning. Both of us need to get a decent night's sleep." Lily got out of the car, taking her cell phone as a precaution. Running into John would be unpleasant, but with Marco Curazon out of prison, far worse things could happen.

When she reached the porch, she discovered the extra key she kept to the duplex was missing. She started to return to the car to get Shana's key, then tentatively reached for the door handle, finding it unlocked. John must have found a ride home, she decided, stepping inside. The living room was empty, however, and the phone was ringing in the kitchen. The phone stopped ringing, but she didn't hear her husband's voice.

"John," she called out. "Are you here?"

Just then Lily heard noises in the back section of the duplex. "Now isn't the time to play foolish games, John. Let me know if you're in the house or I'm going to call the police."

Get out! a voice inside told her. Spinning

around, she almost tripped on the steps leading to the walkway. Back in the car, she fumbled with her keys, finally finding the ignition key and starting the car.

"What's going on?" Shana asked. "Why didn't we stay and get my things? Was Dad home or not?"

"I don't know," her mother said, speeding off down the street. "The door was unlocked. I heard strange noises."

"Maybe Dad was in the bathroom and he didn't hear you," Shana told her. "I think he's losing his hearing. Lately he plays the TV so loud, I have trouble studying."

"Remember what I'm telling you, Shana," Lily said, pulling over and parking a few blocks away. "When you sense something isn't right, always trust your instincts. As soon as I found out the door was unlocked, I should have left. I'm convinced someone was inside there, but I don't think it was your father."

Lily hit the preprogrammed 911 button on her phone, requesting that a police unit meet them at the duplex. "We were at that location twice last night," the female dispatcher said, the address flashing on her computer. When the patrol had been unable to locate Shana on the UCLA campus, Hope Carruthers had followed Detective

Osborne's instructions and issued an order for Shana to be picked up for questioning. As soon as the dispatcher shifted to another screen and read the alert bulletin, she asked, "Are you related to Shana Forrester?"

"Yes," Lily answered, thinking they were balking at sending another unit out. "I'm her mother. Last night when I called, I was in another city. Just a few minutes ago, I drove my daughter home and found the front door unlocked, the lights on, and I heard strange noises inside."

"Where are you now?"

Lily glanced at the street sign. "In the 1300 block of Cliff Road."

The dispatcher continued, "What kind of car are you driving?"

"A black 1996 Audi."

"Is your daughter with you?"

"Yes," Lily said, clasping Shana's hand.

"Wait for the officers at that location," the dispatcher advised. "They'll check the residence first before they contact you."

"Don't hang up," Lily told her. "There's a possibility my ex-husband is inside the house. I don't want the officers to mistake him for a burglar and shoot him."

Approximately twenty minutes later, a police unit pulled up behind the Audi, its headlights illuminating the interior of the car. Shana had dozed off, her head resting against the passenger window. Lily tried to slip out of the car without waking her. "Where am I?" the girl said, her eyes springing open as soon as her mother opened the car door. "I was having this terrible dream. A building had collapsed, and I was buried under all this rubble."

"Stay here," Lily told her. "I'll handle the police."

The two police officers separated, heading toward opposite sides of the vehicle. "Are you Lily Forrester?" Gary Stafford asked, a stout, blond-haired man in his late twenties.

"Yes," she said. "What did you find at the house?"

"We didn't spot any signs of a break-in," he said. "There's always the possibility that you might have surprised an intruder. When you return, check to see if any of your property is missing."

"It's my daughter's residence," Lily said, placing one foot inside the car. "Thanks, officer."

"Ah . . . Mrs. Forrester," Stafford said, holding onto the door. "I'm sorry, but we're going to have to take your daughter down to the police station. You can come along if you wish, but since she's an adult, you don't have to be present for us to interrogate her."

Lily was aghast. The word *interrogate* resounded in her ears. "What is this about, officer? My daughter hasn't committed a crime."

"No one said she did, ma'am." Officer Stafford glanced over the top of the patrol car. His female partner asked to see Shana's driver's license, wanting to verify they had the right individual. Shana retrieved her wallet out of her backpack, removed her license, then looked anxiously toward her mother. "John Forrester was arrested last night for vehicular homicide in front of the address we just cleared," the officer continued. "The car involved in the accident was registered in the name of Shana Forrester."

"This woman says I have to go with her," Shana cried, pressing her body against the car. "I don't understand. Are they going to arrest me? God . . . this can't be happening. Why would they think I killed that person?"

"Don't panic," Lily said, rushing to her side. "They only want to ask you some questions. No one is going to arrest you or hurt you."

Stafford joined them. "Can't this wait until tomorrow morning?" Lily asked him, holding Shana around the waist. "I just told her about her father's arrest, so you can imagine how stressful this has been. I promise I'll bring her down first thing in the morning. All you have to do is give me the address."

"I'm not the investigating officer," Stafford explained, taking in the dark circles under Lily's eyes and the panicked look on her daughter's face. "I can do a check with dispatch and see if they can track down the detectives who issued the bulletin for you, see what they say."

"I'd really appreciate it," Lily said. "It's almost ten o'clock. Both of us are exhausted."

Stafford returned to his unit, using his portable phone to bypass central dispatch and contact the investigative bureau. After being advised that the detectives had left for the day, he asked to be patched through to Hope Carruthers at her residence.

"You have both Lily and Shana Forrester?" Carruthers asked, turning off the television set in her apartment.

"Yeah," Stafford said, squinting at the two bedraggled women though the windshield. "They look like they've been through the wringer, to tell you the truth. Are you certain you want us to bring the girl in tonight? Isn't she only wanted for questioning? Her mother swears she'll bring her in to-morrow."

"No can do," Carruthers said, knowing how adamant Osborne had been about questioning Shana Forrester. Lily being present was an unexpected bonus. "Bring them to the Burbank station ASAP. I'm walking out the door right now."

"What about their car?"

"Let the mother drive," the detective told him, picking up her gun and badge off the coffee table. "Stay on their tail, though, Stafford. There's more going on here than you could ever imagine."

14

Henry Middleton walked into the master bedroom of his six-thousand-square-foot home in the foothills above Montecito. His wife, Carolyn, was sprawled out on the four-poster bed still dressed in her clothes. "You squandered over five hundred bucks on that cashmere sweater," he told her. "Sleeping in it seems ridiculous, particularly since we're on the verge of losing everything we have."

Without looking at him, she flopped over onto her side. "I didn't get home from the hospital until almost six. Maggie quit, so I had to rush back out and get the kids something to eat. I'm too exhausted to move, let alone take my clothes off."

Middleton kicked his shoe halfway across the room. "I spent last night in a frigging jail cell and you're tired because you had to visit your dying daughter? Give me a break, Carolyn."

"Shut up, Henry," Carolyn snapped. "Betsy had another seizure. Not only that, that lady district attorney showed up at the

223

hospital and started pumping me for information."

Henry's jaw went slack. "At the hospital? Lily Forrester was at the hospital?"

"Isn't that what I just said?" Carolyn glowered at her husband. "Did one night in jail cause you to lose your hearing?"

Henry dropped down on the bed beside her, his face twisted in concern. "What did Forrester ask you? Good Lord, my entire future is on the line. I told you not to speak to anyone unless my attorney was present."

With the heel of one foot, Carolyn pushed on his side until he had no choice but to return to a standing position. "I didn't tell her anything," she said. "Quit acting like a baby, Henry. You know they'll never convict you. They don't have enough evidence." She reached over and picked up a bottle off the nightstand, poured several pills into the palm of her hand, then washed them down with a glass of wine.

Her husband wrestled the bottle away from her, squinting as he read the label on the prescription. "This is Betsy's seizure medication. Why in God's name are you taking her pills?"

"Why not?" Carolyn said, a dull look on her face. "I've been taking them for months. In case you haven't noticed, my nerves are wrecked and my back is killing me from sitting in that awful metal chair all day."

"Why don't you ask them to bring in another chair?" he said, running his fingers through his hair.

"The place is run by nuns, dickhead," she barked. "There's not a comfortable chair in the entire place. Even the hospital equipment looks like it's a thousand years old."

"That's still not a reason to take Betsy's pills."

"They're muscle relaxers," she told him, gulping down the rest of the wine, then slapping the glass back down on the end table. "They help me to relax. The booze doesn't cut it anymore, even the strong stuff."

Henry paced back and forth in front of the bed, the pill bottle locked in his hand. "You're an idiot," he said. "You could overdose. I'm not a doctor, but I'm certain you shouldn't mix this type of medication with alcohol. If anything happens to you, the police will accuse me of trying to kill you as well as Betsy."

Carolyn's lips curled into a smile. "Maybe I will overdose."

"Why would you even say something like that?" Henry asked. "Haven't I been through enough? Do you want them to kill me?"

Carolyn sat up in the bed, a petulant look on her face. "I thought everything would be over by now."

"This is only the beginning," her husband told her, still attempting to absorb the enormity of the situation. "There's the preliminary hearing, selecting a jury, then the trial itself. According to what Fowler told me, we could be looking at a year, even longer."

"I wasn't talking about the trial," Carolyn said, glancing at a chip in her dark red fingernail polish. "I can't spend every day of my life at the hospital. You insist that I keep going so everyone will see what a devoted mother I am. Why should I have to prove myself? Betsy's a vegetable now."

Henry Middleton lunged at her, seizing her by the shoulders. "She's your daughter, for chrissakes."

"Get your hands off me," she snarled, throwing her arms out to break his grip. "We agreed to turn off the respirator. I was looking forward to taking a vacation, putting this behind us. Now I'm stuck here. I can't even go to the country club."

Henry was speechless. Had he really married this woman, had children with her, sworn undying love to her? Was it the pills and alcohol talking, or had she always been this way and he'd been too blind to notice?

"The kids are having trouble at school," she continued, placing another pillow behind her back. "Cathy came home crying yesterday. Jacob stays in his room all the time with the door closed. He doesn't even have his friends over anymore."

"At least you're not on trial for attempted murder," her husband told her. He was more than aware of the problems his children were encountering. It broke his heart, but for the moment there was little he could do to rectify the situation. "You know why we can't have Betsy removed from life support, Carolyn. I'd be facing life in prison or the death penalty."

Carolyn Middleton climbed off the bed, pointing her finger at him. "I've been in prison since the day that child was born. Don't forget that, Henry. You spent all your time at the business, building your empire, making yourself feel important."

"I was only trying to make a living," Henry said. "I did it for you, Carolyn. I did it for the children. You wanted them to go to the finest schools. You wanted this expensive house. We've always had help. You make it sound like you took care of Betsy single-handed."

"We don't have help now," she said. "No one wants to work in a house where someone is on trial for attempted murder, where every time they walk out the door, they have to worry that they'll be assaulted by a reporter. Find a way to make it go away, Henry."

He slumped into a chair, burying his head in his hands. A few moments later, he peered up at her. "How? Tell me how I can possibly make this go away. It's too late, don't you see? We have to ride it out, pray that you're right and they don't have enough evidence to convict me. Fowler thinks the D.A.'s office may have only filed to save face in the community."

Carolyn gave him an icy stare. "You're good at solving problems, Henry. Isn't that what you've always told me? Haven't you always bragged that you can fix anything? Find a way. If you don't, I will."

By nine-thirty that evening, Dr. Christopher Logan's impeccable appearance had wilted. Starting his day at four o'clock that morning, he had lost two patients in one day, both of them under the age of seven. His face was covered with day-old stubble, his white coat stained and wrinkled, his dark hair sticking up on top of his head. When he became overly tired, his speech became almost indecipherable. "I'm sorry," Sister

Mary Luke said, leaning over the nursing counter at Saint Francis Hospital. "What chart did you ask for?"

"Middleton," he muttered. "Betsy Middleton."

Sister Mary Luke appeared to be in her early forties, but having worked with nuns for a number of years, the doctor had long since stopped speculating when it came to age. Her face was round, her eyes clear, her skin unlined, her eyes a translucent shade of gray. "I checked on Betsy thirty minutes ago when we made our eleven o'clock rounds," she told him. "Why don't you go home, Dr. Logan? You've had a trying day."

"I thought I'd just look in on her."

"Her time is coming soon, isn't it?"

"With or without the respirator," the doctor said, quickly scanning the girl's chart.

"Is it the seizures?"

Logan flipped the metal file closed, the metallic ting echoing in the tiled corridor. "Seizures are inherent with patients who suffer from Aicardi syndrome," he explained. "The strychnine caused them to become more violent. Her body isn't strong enough."

The sister's voice was soft, consoling. "Perhaps God is calling her home."

"If God wanted to call someone home," Logan said bitterly, "why didn't he call the bastard who poisoned her?"

Instead of blistering at his use of profanity, her voice took on an even lighter tone. "The Lord works in mysterious ways."

Logan headed down the corridor, slipped into the darkened hospital room, and stood quietly beside Betsy Middleton's crib. After two years in the seminary, he had quit and entered medical school, believing he could serve God better saving lives than souls. After four years as a physician, however, he knew his faith was once again being tested. Signing a death certificate for a child who had only briefly tasted life left a wound so deep that it took months to heal. Lately, he found it almost impossible to worship a creator who allowed innocent children to suffer. In the beginning he had carried his pain to the altar. For a while his prayers and his belief in a higher power had provided him with the strength and acceptance to carry on. Similar to ingesting too many antibiotics, he had built up an immunity to the stock answers like Sister Mary Luke had just made. The Lord might work in mysterious ways, he told himself, but human beings performed untold evils. From his perspective, the Lord wasn't doing enough to stop them. It was bad enough to see a child die from illness. To watch them waste away due to an intentional act committed by the person who parented them was beyond comprehension.

He walked over and placed his hand on the respirator that kept Betsy Middleton alive, looking down at her gaunt face, her gaping mouth, her unseeing eyes. Several places on her body were badly bruised from today's seizure. A few months back the convulsions had been so severe and her bones so brittle, she had suffered hairline fractures in both her left arm and ankle. He had to resist the urge to scoop her up in his arms and carry her out of the hospital, maybe take her home and rock her in his arms until the sun came up and her body became still and silent, her soul finally released from its dark prison.

He didn't know Henry Middleton that well, certainly not enough to classify him as a killer. Before his arrest Betsy's father had visited her several times a week during the evening hours. On the occasions when he had spoken to him regarding her condition, the man had merely nodded and listened. But Carolyn was different. Even though she came to the hospital almost every day, there was something about her that disturbed him. She went through the motions, but he didn't get the sense that she was a genuinely compassionate person. He had seen this type of detachment with other parents, though, even among other members of the medical profession. When people were faced with an ongoing problem, they sometimes had to suppress their emotions in order to perform their duties as caretakers. Carolyn's demeanor was more along the lines of restless indifference, almost as if she was eager to wash her hands of anything related to her daughter.

He was not here to judge, he reminded himself. His role was to heal. The problem was, he no longer felt like a healer. He didn't know if Betsy was somehow drifting in a world he knew nothing about, a world that defied medical description, or if she was trapped in a place of unfathomable terror. Brain waves or no brain waves, he wondered if she longed to be held, to feel the sun on her face, to taste food, to feel particles of sand beneath her feet on a warm beach. Had her spirit already disconnected from her body? Was he looking at only the remains of a short and tragic life?

He started to leave when a more profound question passed through his mind. Did Betsy know the true identity of the person who had poisoned her? Such thoughts were moot, because no matter what she knew, she had no means of telling him.

Adjusting her covers and checking her IV, another thought surfaced. To his knowledge, Betsy had never experienced a seizure when her father was in the room, even in the early stages when her coma was nowhere near the level it was today. Removing his penlight from his pocket, he opened her chart and flipped through the thick stack of papers, noting a pattern that might or might not be significant. Over the past year Betsy Middleton had stolen his heart. He knew the time would come when he would sign her death certificate, just as he had for the two children who had died only hours apart that very day. His attempt to discover the person responsible would be his gift to her, he decided, however modest his findings might turn out to be. Of course, there was an additional reason he wanted to become more involved in the criminal case — the opportunity to get to know Lily Forrester.

Chris Logan was single and lonely, and the prosecutor was a beautiful, intelligent woman. As a young man he had bypassed the pleasures of a relationship with the opposite sex due to his decision to enter the priesthood. Then after leaving the seminary, medical school had consumed him, leaving him time for no more than an occasional date. His shyness and youthful appearance were deceptive. Three months back he had turned forty. Recently he had started to fantasize about getting married. It wasn't children he yearned for, as his patients more than filled that need. And he wasn't completely naive when it came to women. He'd had a number of love affairs over the years, but they had been awkward and unsatisfying. His past involvement with the church made it seemingly impossible for him to develop a lasting relationship with a woman. He not only thought Lily was attractive physically, he found her desirable in many ways.

Leaving the room, Logan handed Betsy's chart back to Sister Mary Luke. "Have someone copy her file for me, please. I want to work on some aspects of Betsy's case in my spare time."

"Don't you have enough work without taking things home with you?" she asked, writing a note and affixing it to the file for the morning shift to handle.

"There might be something there," he said, smiling spontaneously. "You know, something I've failed to see before related to the criminal side of the case."

"Humph," she said, her modest laughter rippling down the silent corridor. "It wouldn't have anything to do with that pretty redheaded attorney, would it?"

Dr. Logan's face flushed. "You never fail to amaze me. Can't a man have any secrets around this place?" He started to leave, then stopped and glanced back over his shoulder, a puzzled look on his face. "Were you on duty when Lily Forrester came to the hospital yesterday? I don't recall seeing you."

"No," she said, shaking her head. "We call it being one with God. Surely you remember a few things from your seminary days."

Logan held up a hand, chuckling under his breath as he took a few steps down the hallway. "You can call it anything you want," he said, "but I call it gossip." He playfully shook his finger at her. "That's a sin, you know, almost as bad as those occasional cigarettes you smoke."

Her hand flew to her chest. "I don't smoke. Why would you accuse me of such a thing?"

"Well, someone does," he replied smugly. "Every time I pass the house down below, I get a whiff of cigarette smoke. Who's the culprit?"

"My lips are sealed," Sister Mary Luke said, dropping her head to return to her paperwork.

15

Seated in an interview room at the Burbank Police Department, Shana Forrester was pale and drawn. Being in a police station brought back memories of the rape, and she found the big detective with the rugged face and stoic demeanor frightening. "Can I have a glass of water?" she asked the female detective, her throat parched.

Hope placed a hand on the girl's slender shoulder. "How about a soda?" she asked. "We have a vending machine in the building. Are you hungry? Would you like me to get you a candy bar or something else to eat?"

"Water is fine," Shana told her, linking eyes with her mother across the table. Mark Osborne hadn't said a word since they had entered the room. As he leaned against the back wall, the detective's gaze shifted back and forth from Lily to Shana, amazed at the uncanny resemblance between the two women.

"May we proceed?" Lily asked, crossing her arms over her chest.

Osborne circled the table as he spoke. "Just so we don't get confused, do you mind if I call you Shana?"

"No," she answered.

"Do you know a young man by the name of Antonio Vasquez?"

"The name doesn't sound familiar," Shana said. "Am I supposed to know him? What does this have to do with the accident?"

"Well," Osborne said, grabbing onto the back of a chair, "Vasquez attended UCLA."

"So do thousands of other people," she told him, tracking him with her eyes as he walked around inside the small room. "My classes are so large, I don't even know the names of half of the people who are in them."

"Where were you between eight and ten o'clock last night?"

"At home." She chewed on a ragged cuticle, then added, "Aren't you going to tell me who this Vasquez person is?"

"Antonio Vasquez is the young man who was killed."

Shana straightened up in her seat. "I'm sorry," she said. "Maybe if you show me a picture of him, I could tell you if I've seen him around campus. He's not one of my friends, if that's what you're asking."

"Let's go back to your whereabouts at the time of the accident," Osborne stated, knowing they could check with the school to verify if Shana Forrester and Antonio Vasquez had attended any of the same classes. "When you say you were at home, are you referring to the duplex on Maplewood Drive?"

"Yeah," Shana said, a hint of her mother's temper surfacing. "Don't tell me you don't know where I live. The police have been to my place three times in the past twenty-four hours. I wouldn't be sitting here if my mother hadn't called you guys again."

Feisty girl, Osborne thought, rubbing his finger across his chin and feeling the stubble. He'd always considered it a cliché when people described redheads as temperamental. From what John Forrester had revealed about Lily, though, and now discovering that her daughter had the balls to smart off to him during an interview, he decided the color of a person's hair might actually have some bearing on their disposition. Even though they had no intention of confronting Lily regarding the old homicide, it had been worth dragging his ass out of bed to see both her and her daughter and to attempt to get a handle on the overall situation. The two women's history was mind-boggling: both of them had been raped, the former husband was accusing his wife of killing a hardened gangster and somehow managing to get away with it, and now the father and daughter were linked to the death of an innocent young man. As he saw it, when the body count started adding up, it was time to put the entire family under the microscope. "Where was your Mustang during the time period I just mentioned?"

"My father had it," Shana told him, her blue eyes unflinching. "He drove it to the store to get ice cream. He got rid of his car a few months ago, so I've been letting him use mine."

"What time was this?"

"Before nine."

"Can you be more precise?"

Shana probed her memory. "We were worried that Baskin-Robbins might be closed," she told him. "I'm almost certain Dad left around eight-fifty. It might have been a few minutes earlier, though. Every clock in our house is different. The only clock that's fairly accurate is my watch. I wasn't wearing it last night because I was writing a paper. I don't like things on my wrists when I'm working at my computer."

"Don't you have a record of the time I called the police last night?" Lily interjected, hoping they could eliminate any possibility that Shana was behind the wheel of the car at the time of the accident. What better alibi could her daughter have than the police themselves?

Detective Osborne picked up a file folder off the table, opening it and checking the computer printout listing the times the officers had arrived and left Shana and John Forrester's residence on the prowler call. "The coroner hasn't officially set the time of death," he said, looking up as Hope Carruthers returned and placed a glass of water next to Shana. "Right now he's speculating that the victim's injuries were incurred somewhere between 9:00 and 9:20. The call you placed on behalf of your daughter from Santa Barbara, Mrs. Forrester, was recorded at 9:38. This would have given Shana more than enough time to drive back to the duplex from the location where the accident occurred, then call you claiming someone was lurking around outside of her house."

"But the car wasn't there when the police came," Shana protested. "Doesn't that prove I wasn't driving?"

"According to the patrol officers who responded," Osborne continued, "they saw a white Mustang pull into the driveway just as they were leaving at 10:03. Did you hit that boy, drive home, then send your father back to take care of it for you?"

"No way," Shana shouted, leaping to her feet. "I would never do something like that. And I resent the fact that you're accusing me of lying."

"Either you or your father killed that boy," the detective said, wanting to take advantage of the fact that he had unnerved her. "The crime lab found pieces of the victim's flesh trapped in the undercarriage of the Mustang."

The area around Shana's mouth turned white, and for a few moments she leaned forward as if she were about to vomit. Lily sprang to her feet. "This interview is over," she said, shoving her chair back to the table. "I brought my daughter down here to be questioned, not interrogated. You've already arraigned her father. I know because I posted his bail. I won't stand by and have you bully a young woman who's doing her best to cooperate. You're out of line, Osborne. Keep it up and I'll have your badge."

"Oh, really," he said, locking eyes with her.

"Why don't we all calm down," Hope said, the only person still seated at the table.

"We're only attempting to get to the truth, Mrs. Forrester. You're a district attorney. Surely you must understand the seriousness of this situation, the terrible crime that's been committed."

Shana shook her head in defiance. "When can I get my car back?"

"Let's go," Lily said, grabbing her handbag and Shana's backpack. "Your car is the last thing we need to be concerned about right now."

Instead of coming home early as he had promised, Richard Fowler had called Joyce from his office and asked her to meet him at the Anamaagh Indian restaurant on the corner of Collins Road in Ventura. Several emergencies had developed, however, and Joyce had been left waiting for almost an hour. Sitting alone in a red plastic upholstered booth, she had consumed four beers on an empty stomach and was clearly intoxicated.

"You're the one who insists everyone has to be on time," she told him, her speech slurred from the alcohol. "I guess it's okay for you to be late, though. You're an important attorney. Who am I, huh? Just a stupid woman trying to keep her business from going under."

"I had no intention of being late," Richard said, asking the waiter to bring him a glass of the house merlot. "Why didn't you order an appetizer or something?"

Joyce leaned forward, her breasts pressing against the table, angry and combative. "I should have left. That's what I should have done, okay? You know how foolish I felt sitting here by myself? I called your office seven times."

"You know I don't answer the phones after hours."

"Where were you?" she said, her voice booming out over the restaurant. "You were with another woman, weren't you? Why don't you tell me the truth? You haven't slept with me in over a week. You've got to be getting it somewhere."

Richard picked up the menu, ignoring her accusations. As soon as the waiter returned with his wine, he ordered several of Joyce's favorite dishes, then placed his napkin in his lap. The way she was acting, he decided this was as good a place as any to end their relationship. "It's obvious that you're not happy with me, Joyce," he said softly. "You're a wonderful woman, but perhaps it's time we went our separate ways."

"Are you saying what I think you're saying?" she asked, flopping back in her seat in shock. "You have the gall to make me wait over an hour just so you can tell me you don't want to be with me anymore."

Richard felt his armpits dampen with perspiration. He felt as if the temperature inside the restaurant had risen at least twenty degrees in the past five minutes. Pulling his collar away from his neck, he continued, "We can still see each other if you want. I just think it might be better if we don't live together anymore. I'm under a lot of pressure at the office."

"You contemptible piece of shit!" Joyce shouted, red-faced and furious. "I sold my house. Where am I supposed to go? You can't waltz in here and tell me to move out. I've lived with you for three years."

"It's not like you're going to be out on the street," Richard told her, realizing the breakup was going to be more difficult than he'd imagined. "You invested the equity from your house in the stock market. Your business might not be earning as much as it did in the past, but your investments have skyrocketed in the past year or so. If you don't want to buy another house right away, you can always lease something. I need my space right now, Joyce. I can't give you the kind of attention you want. Be reasonable."

"Reasonable, sure, right," she said,

sniffing back tears. "I thought you loved me, that we were going to get married, start a family. I wasted three years of my life on you. By the time I find someone else, I might be too old to have children. What you're doing to me isn't fair. You used me, and now you're throwing me out like I'm some kind of garbage."

Richard imagined another brick falling into his guilt basket. "I never said I wanted to get married," he told her, scowling. The waiter, dark and small in stature, unobtrusively placed the platters of food he had ordered on the table, then quickly disappeared. "One of our biggest problems is that you've never listened," he continued, toying with the stem of his wineglass. "I don't want to have another child. A few years from now Greg will get married and start a family of his own. Then I'll have grandchildren. If you wanted a more serious relationship, you should have moved on a long time ago. You knew where I stood on these issues. I've never deceived you."

Joyce was sobbing now, mascara streaming down her face, her legs splayed out underneath the table. People in the restaurant were staring at them. "But I thought —"

"I'm sorry," Richard said, letting out a long sigh. He glanced at the platters of food.

His stomach was rumbling with hunger, but he knew there was no way he could eat. He looked over his shoulder for the waiter, intending to have him box up the food, then get the check so they could leave before things got even more out of hand. "We're not in high school, Joyce," he told her. "You need to concentrate on your business right now. I have to put all my energy into my law practice. Do we really have to turn this into an emotional nightmare? Can't we end this like two civilized adults?"

Richard was reaching in his pocket for his wallet as Joyce stood. She picked up a platter of curried chicken and threw it at him, barely missing his head. The dish shattered on the floor behind him, but the brownish-yellow sauce splattered onto his suit, his hair, his tie, even his cell phone. He scooted his chair back and began picking pieces of sticky chicken out of his lap. Joyce circled the table, grabbed his wineglass, and dumped the dark red liquid over his head. Then she stomped out of the restaurant.

The owner, along with several waiters, rushed over, shouting at Richard in broken English. The only word he could make out was "police." He held his hands in the air. "I'll pay," he said. "Don't call the police, please." He pulled out two hundred-dollar bills and handed them to the owner. Removing his jacket, he draped it over one of the chairs, knowing it was ruined. "See," he said, pointing at his jacket, "I even left you a present."

The owner shook his fist, spouting out another stream of what had to be profanities. Richard ignored him, wrapping his cell phone in a napkin and beating a hasty exit out the rear door of the restaurant. So much for dinner, he decided, getting in his car and steering back in the direction of his office. He hadn't installed a shower and a convertible sofa in his office for nothing, just as his offer to foot all the bills during the time a woman lived with him reached beyond generosity. When you provided perks, there was less to complain about at the end of the line. Being afraid of returning to his own home was crazy, but when a relationship was over, things invariably got ugly. Tomorrow he would call Joyce and give her a week to move out. If she refused to comply, he'd get a court order.

16

Even though the drapes were drawn and the windows locked, the morning sun blazed into Lily's bedroom in Montecito Thursday morning. She had driven straight to Santa Barbara after they had left the police station, finding a blanket in the trunk and insisting that Shana curl up in the backseat during the long ride. Under the circumstances, seeing her father had been out of the question, and missing classes for a few days was unimportant compared to the problems they both were facing.

Tossing on a pink terry-cloth bathrobe, Lily peeked into the extra bedroom to make certain Shana was all right before heading to the kitchen to put on a pot of coffee. She had forgotten to set her alarm clock, and it was already past nine. Generally she was awake by sunrise, but the events of the night before would have drained anyone. Once the coffee was made, she poured herself a cup and went outside onto the small porch, using her portable phone to call Matt Kingsley and let him know that she would be taking the day off.

"Did you come down with the flu?" the young prosecutor asked. "It's already going around, you know. They say everyone should take a flu shot."

"I'm not sick," Lily said. "Something else has come up. Tell Brennan I'm taking a vacation day. You'll have to cover my calender."

"Is something wrong?"

"My daughter came into town unexpectedly," she told him. "I'd really appreciate it if you could take care of a few things for me. How does your day look?"

"Pretty light," he said, glancing at his computer screen. "I've got two appearances this morning. Since they're both arraignments, I should be able to get in and out fairly quick. I was going to spend the majority of the day on Middleton."

"Good," Lily said. "Here's what I'd like you to do. Are you ready?"

"Shoot."

"Call Ron Spencer and go over the details of the plea agreement we're offering his client, Mervin Hatteras, on the aggravated-assault charges. We have a settlement conference scheduled for next week. I want to make certain they're not going to pull something idiotic and force me to take the case to trial. You shouldn't have any trouble finding the file. It's somewhere on the top of my desk."

"I've never even heard of this Hatteras guy," Kingsley whined, anxious that she wanted him to go so far as to attempt to obtain a settlement on a case he knew nothing about.

"The guy they call the 'Bug,' remember?" Lily said. "He's the drug dealer with a prior, the one who wanted to eliminate his competition. Advise Spencer that I'm willing to commit to two years in prison in exchange for a guilty plea as to count one, the assault charge. If his client agrees, we'll drop the enhancement for GBI and put the case to bed. The man Mervin stabbed had a record a mile long, the majority of his previous offenses unbelievably violent."

"Fine," Kingsley said crisply. "Anything else?"

"Lenora interviewed Deborah Saginaw," she continued, "the victim in the Bentley child molest. I never got a chance to talk to her. Find out what additional information she might have obtained from the victim, then get her to e-mail me a copy of her report here at the house. I'm certain this case is going to trial, so we need to stay on top of it."

Kingsley was scribbling notes to himself as fast as he could, but when Lily shifted into high gear, it was hard to keep up with her. "Aren't you coming in tomorrow?"

"I'm not certain right now," she told him, glancing back at the door to the cottage. "What did you find out at the lab the other day regarding Middleton? Anything new?"

"Well," he said, on more familiar ground now, "I've been trying to learn everything I can about strychnine. Are you aware that dealers use it to cut cocaine, heroin, as well as amphetamines?"

"No," Lily said, wondering if this information would have any bearing on the case. "My expertise isn't that strong when it comes to narcotics cases. I've heard of them cutting drugs with baby laxatives, that type of thing."

"Adams over at the lab told me that tons of dealers use strychnine because it hypes people up, similar to what they expect from the illegal drugs they're used to taking. Strychnine exaggerates responses to visual, auditory, and tactile stimulation, meaning a person might think they're getting LSD or something similar." He paused, glancing at the paperwork the lab had given him. "Years ago hospitals also used strychnine as an antidote in instances of barbiturate overdose, in the treatment of an illness called sleep apnea, and a number of other medical problems."

"We're not concerned with antiquated forms of medical treatment, Matt."

"I know," he said. "I just thought you should know that all the dealer has to do is go into a hardware store and say he has a mouse problem. Certox, Kwik-kit, Mouse-Rid, Mouse-Tox, Pied Piper Mouse Seed, Ro-Dex . . . all these products contain highly concentrated amounts of strychnine."

"We've already covered this ground," Lily said, thinking he was wasting her time. "Most people use exterminators, anyway. You're the one who flushed out Jake Nash and the SOS people where Middleton supposedly got the strychnine."

"Hold on," Kingsley said, "I have to take this call."

While Lily was waiting, she contemplated what he had told her. Betsy Middleton had ingested what they assumed was sugar laced with strychnine. The lab had found traces of both substances on the straw-shaped candy the Middletons claimed she had been given at an unknown location while trick or treating on Halloween. Other than her regular prescription medications and the strychnine, no other drugs or chemicals had been discovered in the child's system. When Betsy had first been brought into the emergency room, however, the physicians had assumed that the seizures, along with the other symptoms she was exhibiting, were related to her illness. Three days had passed before a doctor had suspected something out of the ordinary and ordered a toxicology report. A drug such as cocaine, as well as most amphetamines, would have no longer been detectable after this period of time, since these forms of narcotics passed quickly through a person's system.

"Sorry," Kingsley said, coming back on the line. "That was the court, or I wouldn't have taken the call. Where were we?"

Lily's mind was spinning. "You might be on to something with this cocaine thing," she told him. "The only reason we arrived at the decision that the delivery system for the strychnine was that particular brand of candy was because the Middletons suggested it. They even provided the police with the empty straws to send to the crime lab."

"That's because they wanted the police to believe that some nutcase placed the strychnine in the Halloween candy," Kingsley quickly countered. "We know Henry did it, Lily. We have a witness who saw him purchasing that exact type of candy. Also, there have only been a few isolated cases of people tampering with Halloween candy over the past five or ten years. Most responsible parents monitor their kids' candy very closely."

"They claim Betsy grabbed it and ate it while they weren't looking," Lily told him. "Because she was mentally as well as physically handicapped, Middleton was probably proud of himself for coming up with such a believable story. I'm certain he remembered the days when people put razor blades and the like in Halloween candy. Remember, put yourself in the mind of the offender."

"I'm trying, Lily," Kingsley said, sighing from exhaustion. "You have no idea how many hours a day I've been devoting to this case."

"If you want to play with the big boys," she told him, "you might as well get used to it. By the time this thing gets close to going to trial, you'll be lucky to squeeze in two hours of sleep in a day."

"Jesus Christ," he said, falling back into his spoiled, you're-beating-me-to-death routine.

"Good call, Kingsley," Lily said. "But I suggest you do your own homework."

On the front section of the porch were plants in hanging baskets. Lily reached up and snapped off a dead leaf, then rested her back against one of the wooden pillars. "Before we can convict Henry Middleton," she explained, "we have to know precisely what happened, not only on the night the crime was allegedly committed, but in the days leading up to it. What if Henry or someone else in that household was using cocaine or some other drug cut with strychnine? I keep mentioning cocaine because the Middletons were successful, and that's the type of drug use you generally see with people who have money. What if Betsy got her hands on their stash accidentally? That means the whole thing could have been an elaborate cover-up."

"What about Jake Nash?" Kingsley asked. "Our primary motive centers on the fact that Middleton poisoned Betsy so he could collect on the insurance. The way you're talking, you're batting our motive right out of the ballpark."

"When you're desperate to convict some-one," Lily explained, "you jump on anything that makes sense. I'm not trying to undermine what you accomplished in finding Nash. But ask yourself what the man really saw. Middleton walking next door to the exterminating company, chatting with the people who worked there, then acting a little strange when a soda fell out of his pocket.

We're talking one humongous leap to convince a jury that Middleton stole liquid strychnine from these people in broad daylight, then stored it in a soft drink container, particularly since you just emphasized how easy it would have been for him to get it from another source."

"Slow down a minute," the attorney said, even more agitated than before. "I only mentioned that cocaine was used as a cutting agent because I thought it was an interesting fact. And don't forget that most people, even drug dealers, might not have a problem walking in and buying the products I just mentioned. But Middleton isn't a drug dealer, Lily, and he wasn't buying strychnine to kill gophers or mice. He was preparing to commit an atrocious crime against his own daughter."

"Don't you see?" Lily said, still excited about the unfolding possibilities the young attorney had brought to light. "We're going to have one hell of a hard time convincing a sophisticated Santa Barbara jury that a well-to-do, church-going member of their own tightly knit community possessed the degree of cruelty necessary to poison his handicapped daughter for profit. The straw factor may be more significant than you think. What do most people use to snort cocaine?"

"Rolled-up bills," Kingsley answered, remembering a report he had once read that claimed that half the paper money in circulation had trace elements of cocaine on it.

"They also use straws," Lily told him. Just then she saw Shana standing in the doorway rubbing her eyes. "We'll discuss this later. Just keep rolling it around in your mind, see how it fits into the picture. We can't merely concoct a motive that sounds good. We have to be able to prove it beyond a reasonable doubt. Don't forget that Betsy may not be alive by the time this goes to trial. When you ask a jury to put a man to death, you damn sure better have the truth in your hands."

Kingsley swallowed before speaking. "I hear you loud and clear."

Lily clicked off the phone and placed it on the round redwood table, walking over and embracing her daughter. "How did you sleep, sweetheart?"

"I slept," the girl said, glancing out over the yard. "I didn't smell any roses. What did you do? Come out here last night and cut them all down?"

Her mother smiled, recalling how chilled she had been the night before as she'd pruned the garden with a flashlight. "Pretty astute observation, kiddo," she said. "I think you might be sharper than the man I was just on the phone with, and *he* has a Harvard diploma. Maybe we'll have to open our own law practice one of these days."

Shana's face fell. "Right," she said bitterly. "As soon as I get out of prison for killing that poor guy. I can't believe he went to UCLA, Mom. What am I going to do when people find out?" Taking a seat in one of the chairs, she placed her head down on the table. "I guess you'll get your wish now. I'll have to change schools no matter how this turns out. I'm always running from one thing or the other. Sometimes I think it's going to be this way the rest of my life, almost as if I'm doing something to attract these awful things. You know, like bad karma or something."

Lily began massaging the tense muscles in her shoulders. "Why don't I make you some breakfast? Problems are magnified when you don't have any food in your stomach. I promise you're not going to go to prison, Shana. Your father is responsible, and he's the person who will have to pay the price. I'll make certain of that, even if it's the last thing I ever do."

Shana slowly raised her head. "I don't want to talk to Dad. I don't care how many times he calls, understand? This is the end of the line for me, even if he is my father. I put up with his laziness, the disgusting way he kept the house, even his drinking. I never thought it would come to this, though, that he'd go out and kill someone."

"You must stay strong," her mother said, outraged that her daughter had to be placed in this position. In a way, it was ironic. She had just been discussing how another father had destroyed his daughter's life. Due to the grace of God, Shana wasn't near death and comatose, but the man who had fathered her had placed her in serious jeopardy. Did the problem rest in a man's inability to accept failure? Both Henry Middleton and John had been experiencing financial problems, and from all appearances, they had skidded completely off track. "We'll figure out a game plan as soon as I make you something to eat."

"I'm not hungry."

"You'll get sick if you don't eat," Lily said, her brows furrowed with concern.

"My stomach's in knots," Shana told her. "If I eat, I'll throw up."

Lily hovered over her. "Will you at least drink a glass of milk?"

"Sure," she lashed out. "Put it in a baby bottle."

"What's that comment supposed to mean?" Lily said, crestfallen.

"I don't want you to treat me like a baby," Shana said. Seeing the hurt look on her mother's face, she added, "I'm sorry, Mom. I'm being a bitch. I usually have coffee and a slice of toast for breakfast. Since it's so late now, why don't you get me a cup of coffee? Then later on, maybe we can go out for lunch."

"Of course," Lily said, opening the screen door. "And you don't have to apologize, Shana. I understand how you feel right now. We're going to get through this. All you have to do is hang tight and trust me."

Lily left her sitting on the porch while she went inside to get her coffee. When she picked up the cup, however, her hands were trembling. It wasn't fair that her daughter had to face another problem of such mammoth proportions, not when she'd struggled so hard to put the rape behind her. And only recently her sense of security had been shattered with the knowledge that her attacker was no longer behind bars. On top of all that, the questions posed at the police station had convinced Lily that Shana needed legal representation. Her thoughts turned to Richard Fowler. Shana knew him, even though they hadn't seen each other for years. Back when Lily and Richard had been working together, Shana had even struck up a friendship with Richard's son.

By the time she returned with the coffee, Shana was in tears. Lily sat down next to her, holding onto her free hand as she sipped the steaming brew. "Do you remember Richard Fowler?"

"Of course," Shana said, releasing her mother's hand so she could wipe her eyes with the edge of her sweatshirt. "I tried to find Greg about a year ago. Did he graduate from college?"

"Yes," Lily said. "I saw his father recently. He's representing a client here in Santa Barbara."

"I thought he was a prosecutor like you."

"He's in private practice now in Ventura," Lily said. "I was thinking we should call him, maybe see if he can come up this afternoon."

Lily watched as her daughter's frustrations turned once more to fear. She locked her arms around her chest, almost as if she had to hold herself together. "Are you dating him?"

"We're friends, Shana," her mother told her. "We go back a long way together. He's a brilliant attorney. Sometimes when you have a problem, calling in a big gun right away isn't such a bad idea."

"I thought you just said that the police were going to prosecute Dad. Why do I need an attorney?"

"Like I just said," Lily answered, "it's always wise to be prepared. I didn't like the way the police treated you last night. But on the other hand, they have to do their job, which means they have to rule out any possibility that you were behind the wheel of your car. You haven't been charged with a crime. In reality, your father has been arraigned, so they've already begun the criminal proceedings."

"Why didn't you just let him stay in jail?"

"I was concerned about you," Lily lied, focusing on a spot over Shana's head. Would the truth eventually surface? That she had posted John's bail only after he'd threatened to expose her for the murder of Bobby Hernandez. She shuddered at the thought that Shana could have not only one but possibly both of her parents facing serious charges.

Shana pushed herself to her feet, pulling a strand of her tangled hair in front of her face. Even with the enormous stress she was under, her mother couldn't help but marvel at her remarkable beauty. The paleness of her skin made her eyes sparkle like priceless sapphires. The sun picked up the gold highlights in her vibrant red hair. While her mother watched her, she gracefully lifted her chin, staring up at the sky as if she wished she could somehow take flight, leaving the problems of the world behind her. "Call your friend," she said, her voice just above a whisper. "You know, Richard."

"Why don't you take a shower?" Lily suggested, choking up with emotion. "I put some fresh towels in the bathroom. I'm sure you can find something of mine to wear. Pick anything you want."

"Seems like old times, huh? You know, when we lived in Camarillo and I was always raiding your closet."

"Yes, it does," Lily answered. "I only wish you were here under different circumstances."

"It doesn't really matter why I'm here," Shana said, suddenly appearing older and wiser than her years. "The most important thing is that we're together, Mom. Maybe it takes something awful like this to make a person realize what's really important in life. We've always been strong when we're together. Marco Curazon might have hurt us, but we survived. I'm sure we'll survive this as well."

17

Fred Jameson barged through the doors to the detective bureau feeling energized and ready to take on the world. He cupped his hands together, then blew into them. "Can't anyone turn the frigging air down in this place?" he called out, his voice carrying throughout the partitioned offices. "I feel like I'm in a meat locker. It's colder in here than it is outside. Doesn't the city realize they're wasting the taxpayers' money?"

"Can it, Jameson," a male voice answered. "Some of us have to work for a living."

"Work, my ass," the detective continued. "What are you doing, Keith? Downloading porno off the Internet? Why don't you send the one with the girl and the dog to the captain? I'm sure he'd get a real bang out of it, even though I hear he favors sheep."

Keith Marconi poked his head over the top of the partition. "What got you so wound up this morning? Did you get laid last night or something?"

Jameson removed his jacket, draping it over the back of his chair. "You're close," he told the other man, pulling out his comb and running it through his prematurely gray hair. "What I stumbled across might turn out to be better than sex."

Settling in his chair, Jameson dialed the number for the personnel department. "Detective Jameson here," he said. "I need a number for a former employee from about six years back, a homicide detective named Bruce Cunningham. The last thing I heard, he was living in Omaha, Nebraska."

While he was on hold, Jameson leaned back in his chair and propped his feet up on the desk, picking up a yellow notepad as he stared at his computer screen. The call regarding Lily Forrester had come in the day before, but he'd been in the field working another homicide and had not taken the time to check his messages until he had arrived home later that evening.

"I'm sorry," Robbie Johnson said. "The only information I have on a Bruce Cunningham is that he transferred to the Omaha Police Department from Oxnard. Since he doesn't receive a pension check from the city of Ventura, we don't have a home address or phone number listed in his file. To be perfectly honest, we lost a great deal of data when the two departments merged. Oxnard has yet to put all their records into the computer system. You can't imagine how many boxes of paperwork got shipped over here."

"Thanks," Jameson said, deciding he'd heard more than he wanted to know. Just his luck to dial up a woman who had worked for the department for twenty years.

Rather than continue his efforts to track down Cunningham, he called the central property room. "Hey, Wayne," he said, recognizing the officer's voice, "I need you guys to tell me what we have down there on an unsolved murder. Occurred about six years ago in Oxnard. The victim's name was Bobby Hernandez."

"What's the case number?" a gruff voice replied. "You know how many evidence containers we have with the name Hernandez on them?"

"Damn," the detective said, "do I really have to come up with the case number? Come on, Wayne, cut me some slack. Your people know how to find this stuff on the computer in about five seconds."

"No can do," the property sergeant told him. "My staff is up to their eyeballs in work."

Once he was off the phone, the detective pushed his chair up to his desk and glared at the computer in front of him. He had as yet to jump on the technology bandwagon, even though he had finally admitted that he had no alternative. Regardless, he still wanted to take out his gun and shoot the thing just for the sheer satisfaction it would give him. First it was the Y2K problem, and everyone thought the world was going to end. Now people were so preoccupied playing on the Internet, no one got any work done. Pretty soon a man would need a computer to tell him when it was time to take a leak.

The information he was looking for might not even be in the Hernandez file, as the case had been closed for some time. For all he knew, the file clerks might not have downloaded the particulars into the computer. Before he let his imagination run wild thinking he was going to make it payback time for Lily Forrester, he had to be certain there was sufficient evidence to talk the brass into reopening such an old case. The situation was complicated by the merger between the two departments, just as good old Robbie Johnson had brought to his attention. Several active and viable cases had gone down the drain due to the fact that crucial evidence had been lost or damaged while in transit from the Oxnard facility to Ventura. He typed in the name Bobby

Hernandez for a record search, waiting until the computer returned with a message telling him there were 4,838 matches. Great, he thought facetiously. He had no choice now but to track down Cunningham. If nothing else, the former detective might recall enough of the particulars to allow him to at least narrow the parameters of his search.

"What's the name of the company again?" he asked the operator at the Omaha Police Department.

"Jineco Equipment Corporation," she said. "Their showroom is located on the corner of Eighty-fourth Street and L."

"Hey, lady," Jameson said, "I'm in California. I don't want to *go* to the place. All I want is their phone number."

The detective dialed the toll-free number she gave him, and within minutes he found himself speaking to Bruce Cunningham. Once he had explained that he had taken over Cunningham's caseload, he knew he had to be polite and ask him what he was now doing for a living. As notorious as Cunningham was in local law enforcement circles, the two men had never met. "We sell and service power washers, along with various agricultural equipment, most of it manufactured by a company called Karcher. Are you in the market for a power washer?"

Jameson was doodling on his notepad. "Why didn't you go into private security? People pay big bucks for your type of experience. Don't tell me you prefer sales over law enforcement?"

"You bet," Cunningham answered. "I enjoy what I do, Fred. You did say your name was Fred, didn't you?"

"Yeah," the other man said, thinking he could cut to the chase now. "I'm calling about an old murder case you handled. The victim's name was Bobby Hernandez. We've come across some new information that's pretty sensational. The problem is, I'm having trouble locating —"

Cunningham cut him off. "Exactly what information are you referring to?"

The line fell silent. Jameson needed his cooperation. He had to keep in mind that the other man was no longer a police officer, however. "Oh, you know how these kinds of things go, *Bruce*," he said, deciding if Cunningham could call him by his first name after exchanging only a few words with him, he could do the same. He suspected the former detective's reputation had not developed from myths and exaggerations, as was generally the case. Eliminating formalities was a clever way to instantly take a conversation to another level. "Most of the leads that come in this late in the game generally turn out to be a waste of time. I just thought I might be able to pick your brain, you know, see what you remembered."

"Didn't you mention something sensational?"

Jameson was blown away. He didn't recall making such a statement. He knew he had *thought* about how much publicity they would generate if they prosecuted Lily Forrester on murder charges. The words must have simply slipped out of his mouth. It was an eerie sensation to discover yourself making statements you had no intention of making. A number of years back he'd worked with a cop who possessed a rare talent for making people confess. Some of the old-timers had told him that this was one of Cunningham's primary claims to fame, that even the hardest criminals would break down and spill their guts to him. When a man possessed that kind of power, a person had to be extremely cautious. "Surely you must realize," he continued, intentionally pausing before each word, "that department regulations preclude me from releasing any details related to a criminal investigation."

"I have to take care of a customer,"

Cunningham said curtly. "Have a nice day, Fred."

When Jameson heard the dial tone, he tossed the receiver up in the air, then watched it fall onto the top of his desk with a loud thud. "That sneaky son of a bitch," he exclaimed, standing and turning in circles inside his cubicle.

"Stop talking to yourself, for heaven's sake," one of the female detectives said as she walked past.

"Wait, Sandy," he said, stepping outside into the hallway. "Are you headed in the direction of the kitchen? Grab a cup of coffee for me, will you?" Another boost of caffeine, he decided, might be what he needed to clear out the morning cobwebs and help him figure out how to get Cunningham into cooperating with him without the man ending up knowing more about his business than he did. He'd already consumed five cups, though, and everyone at the office insisted he was a caffeine junkie. Everyone had their demons. He'd rather drink coffee all day than slug down a case of beer every night.

Sandy Weinberg was a statuesque brunette, not what a man might consider pretty. After ten years on the job, she was highly respected. "Get it yourself, Fred."

"Thanks," he yelled, wanting everyone in the room to hear him. "What is this, anyway? Pick-on-Fred day?"

Grabbing his jacket off the back of the chair, Jameson decided it was time to hit the street. He had a fresh stiff in the morgue, and two additional homicides only weeks away from the trial date. For the time being, Lily Forrester and any connection she might have to the Hernandez killing would have to wait.

18

A little after three o'clock Shana went to the guest bedroom to take a nap. John called just as Lily was about to carry her portable computer outside to the porch to see if she could get some work done. She walked over and shut the door to her bedroom.

"Where's Shana?" John asked, beside himself with concern. "I thought she spent last night with one of her friends, then went to school today. I've called everywhere. No one has seen her. That girl Jennifer, the one she hangs out with all the time . . . she says Shana didn't even show up for her morning classes."

"She's with me."

"You bitch!" he shouted, furious. "You took her to Santa Barbara? You couldn't even call me —"

Lily started to hang up, then decided he would only call back. "You not only killed that kid, John, you killed him in your daughter's car."

"I didn't kill anyone."

"When are you going to stop lying?"

"And you don't lie?" he shot back. "Right, Lily. Tell me you haven't been lying about shooting that Hernandez guy. At least I don't put other people behind bars for doing the same thing I did. You're a hypocrite, Lily, a damn hypocrite."

"The crime lab found pieces of the victim's flesh trapped in the undercarriage of Shana's Mustang," she told him. "We spent hours at the police department last night. Since the car is registered in Shana's name and she was alone at the time of the accident, they have to consider her a valid suspect. They think she might have even known the boy because they both went to UCLA."

"Flesh? Did you say flesh?" John was mortified, unable to believe his ears. She was trying to torture him, punish him. "Why are you saying these things? Because I made you leave your precious job to post my bail? You couldn't even wait until they released me to give me a ride home. I had to use what little money I had on cab fare. Stop playing fucking mind games with me, Lily!" He paused and sucked in a breath. "The police don't have enough evidence to convict anyone, let alone Shana. They didn't say anything to me about finding pieces of flesh."

"It takes time for the lab to go over the

car," Lily told him. "I'm telling you the truth. The police know whoever killed that boy was driving the Mustang. They just don't know if it was you or Shana."

"You're going to make me lose my mind," John said. "God, tell me this isn't true."

Lily was standing over the bathroom sink now, staring at herself in the mirror. A fiery rage was building inside her. Seeing it on her face was terrifying. It was leaping from her eyes, a muscle in her forehead was twitching, her lips had compressed into an angry, narrow line. "You've already lost your mind," she lashed out. "Not only that, you've lost your daughter."

"Put her on the phone."

"She refuses to speak to you."

"You did this," John snarled. "This is just what you wanted, to drive us apart."

Lily remained silent, her back rigid.

"We used to have everything," he continued. "We had a nice house. I had a good job with the government. Shana was a cheerleader, the most popular girl at her school. You're the one who destroyed our lives. Why do you think I started drinking? Why do you think Shana didn't want to live with you?"

"You killed that boy," Lily said, her energy depleted to the point where she could barely speak. "He was a student at UCLA, John. I may have to hire an attorney now to represent Shana. She's afraid to go back to her classes because people are going to know what's going on."

"You're the cold-blooded killer," John said. "When you make a mistake, everyone is supposed to look the other way. Not with old John, huh? No, I lose everything. I go down for the big count. I'm the scum of the earth. Isn't that what you're telling Shana? You've been waiting for something like this so you could turn her against me."

"I want you out of the duplex," Lily told him, hissing the words out. "I'm not giving you another penny. You have three days to move out."

"I don't have any money," he pleaded. "I don't even have a car now. How can I find another place to live? You have to help me."

"You're on your own, John," she told him. "The only person I'm concerned about is Shana."

"I'm not going to let you get away with this," he shouted again. "You want to play dirty? Fine with me. See how you feel when you find your ass in the hot seat. You're going to be sorry."

"I'm already sorry," Lily said, sinking back against the bathroom wall.

★ ★ ★

"Was someone here?" Shana asked, walking out of the guest bedroom not long after Lily had received the phone call from John. "I was sleeping when I thought I heard someone arguing."

"No one was here." She headed to the living room, her daughter trailing behind her. Lily had to use every ounce of strength she possessed to regain her composure. "Richard will be up later this evening. We lucked out because he has a court appearance scheduled here tomorrow. He said he had already made reservations in a local hotel. This way, he won't have to rush home."

Dressed in a pair of her mother's tapered beige slacks and a brown sweater, Shana acted as if she hadn't heard a word Lily had said. "That was Dad on the phone, wasn't it?"

"I don't want to lie to you," her mother answered, shrugging. "You told me you didn't want to talk to him. All I did was deliver your message, adding a few words of my own."

Shana shook her head. "Have the police contacted him again?"

"No, darling," Lily told her, patting a spot on the floral print sofa. "Come, sit down with me. I doubt if anything will happen for a few days. That's the way most criminal investigations unfold. They wait for the forensic work to be completed, contact whatever witnesses they can find. Basically, they build their case the way a carpenter builds a house." She wondered how much Shana remembered about the months following the rape. Lily glanced over at her furtively. Did she recall the day they had gone to the Ventura police station to view a photo lineup of possible suspects?

Lily picked up a throw pillow and hugged it to her chest, praying her daughter had forgotten that day. Because of the blowup with John, the likelihood of him making good on his threats regarding her involvement in the Hernandez homicide had grown even stronger. Shana was occupying herself by reading an article from a recent journal published by the American Bar Association that she had picked up off the coffee table. As her mother stared at her profile, Shana's features became those of the thirteen-year-old girl she had been at the time of the rape. Before she knew it, Lily had dived back into time.

"Okay, this is what we're going to do today," said Margie Thomas, a detective with the Ventura police. *"I've prepared some pictures of men who resemble the man you and your mother described and have backgrounds that make them*

279

possible suspects. I'm going to let you sit at my desk, Shana, and look at half the pictures. Your mom will sit in the other room and look at the other half, and then you'll exchange. If you see someone that resembles the man who attacked you, write down the number by his name. You may see several faces and not be certain, but that's okay. Just be sure to write down all the numbers." She paused and focused on Shana only, aware that Lily was all too familiar with the routine. "If you do see someone, then we can try to get this man in for a real lineup so you can be absolutely certain." She stopped and stood, adding, "Any question and I will be right across the room."

Lily started thumbing through the photos, seeing a number of photos of men she'd prosecuted through the years, sometimes amazed that they were back on the street and trying to recall the exact particulars of each case. Looking at the photos the way they were presented made her think of the proofs professional photographers give their clients to make a selection, and she realized that it had been over a year since Shana's last portrait. She glanced through the glass and saw her daughter intently staring at each face on each page at Margie's desk.

If Hernandez had murdered Patricia Barnes in order to prevent her from testifying against him, merely fulfilling that first mission that Lily had suspected all along — to kill her — then he might have followed the same pattern with her and her daughter. Perhaps God had intervened and it was His hand that guided her that night.

Deep in thought, Lily jumped when the door to the small office opened. Shana was ashen and wide-eyed, her hands by her side, an excited expression on her face. Margie Thomas opened her mouth to speak, but Shana blurted out, "I found him. I know it's him. I'm certain. Show her," she urged. "She'll know it's him too."

Lily felt perspiration oozing from every pore in her body and knew that she would be drenched in seconds. Waiting for the heavy pressure in her chest signaling a heart attack, she felt blood rush from her face.

Margie saw her distress. "My God, you look ill," she said, turning to Shana with a degree of urgency. "Go and get your mother some cold water from the cooler — right at the back of the room you were in. And bring some paper towels from the bathroom and soak them in cold water. Hurry, now."

"Do you want me to call an ambulance?" the detective asked Lily, seeing the moisture darkening the pale green blouse she was wearing, watching as beads of sweat dropped from her forehead over her nose and down her chin. "Are you having chest pains?"

Lily tried to monitor her breathing and calm

herself. She felt like there was a tight band around her chest. She must be having a panic attack. Shana had seen a photo of someone who resembled Hernandez, and she would realize it was the wrong man as soon as she saw him in person. "I'm okay. Just too much pressure, I guess."

Shana returned, her mouth tight with concern, carrying the wet towels and a cup of ice water. She handed them to her mother and stood back, watching while Lily wiped her face and the back of her neck while she sipped water from the Styrofoam cup. "I'm fine," she said, reassuring Shana. "Just give me a minute and I'll look at the photo."

"Relax," Margie said. "You can even go home and come back in the morning. One more day —"

"No," Shana said, her voice louder than normal, insistent, "let her see it now. Then you can put him in jail."

The detective turned and took Shana's hand. "Just give your mom a minute, honey. This has been real hard on her too. Even if your mom agrees that this man resembles the man who attacked you, we can't just go out and arrest him. You'll have to see him in a real lineup, and we'll have to get an order from a judge to arrest him."

Shana stared impatiently at Lily, impervious to whatever was wrong with her, wanting her to *confirm her selection. Lily could see her chest rise and fall visibly with each breath.*

"Okay," Lily said. "Let's see the photo."

Asking Shana to return to the desk she had been at previously, the detective handed Lily a stack of pages with photos just like the ones she had been looking at before they entered.

"Go through each one slowly and don't respond just because she has told you she saw someone. I told her to remain outside, Lily, but she followed me in here. If you do select someone, it should be completely independent." Seeing that Lily appeared in control, she told them, "I'm going to step outside. Come out when you're through."

As she searched each page, Lily now was really looking, wanting to see the man Shana had seen, certain that he resembled Hernandez but knowing that half of Oxnard resembled Hernandez. She occasionally glanced out the window of the office, looking for her daughter. She was out of visual range. Margie had more than likely taken her to the vending machines for a soda or to the rest room. On about the twentieth page of photos, she saw him.

My God, a dead ringer, she thought, leaving no question as to why Shana had become so excited. Even if he was not the right man, simply seeing his face propelled her back to the fear and humiliation, the degradation of that night. Her pain for what her daughter had suffered was agonizing. The man had an almost identical shape to his face, his eyes, his nose, his mouth. Even the way his hair was cut was similar to Hernandez's. He looked younger, however, and Lily knew he was not the rapist. He couldn't be. The rapist was dead.

She took her time and studied his face closely. She recalled how photographs were sometimes miles apart from the actual person. They were one-dimensional, and this man in the flesh, in profile, in body conformation, could look entirely different. Removing the paper towels from her neck, she felt the crisis had passed. Just go through the motions, she told herself, and even agree he looks somewhat like the attacker. Once they saw him in person, the whole thing would be dropped. Lily would state that he wasn't the man and that would be it.

She picked up the package of photos and calmly left the office. Margie and Shana were walking through the doors to the detective bureau. Shana held a Coke in her hand and appeared subdued but anxious. Lily had her finger on the page containing the photo of the man she was certain Shana had picked.

The three of them met in the center of the room. "I admit, I have one that's real close, but I'm pretty sure it's not the man," Lily said without enthusiasm. Seeing the taut look of frustration in Shana's eyes, she quickly added, "But it's real close and worthy of additional investigation."

Setting the photos down on Margie's desk, she turned to the correct page and placed a finger on his face. "Number thirty-six is the one I picked." Her look was questioning, but she didn't have to wait long for a response.

"That's him," Shana said, turning to the detective eagerly. "Told you. That's him. Number thirty-six."

"Shana, I don't feel as positive as you. I want you to know that from the start, and remember, I got a better look at him when he was leaving. You were terribly distraught."

The visual image of him standing in the light from the bathroom appeared in Lily's mind: the red sweatshirt, the profile — she even recalled the top of his head as he bent down to snap his pants. She glanced back down at the photo, but also noticed the other men on the page. Out of six, two were wearing a red T-shirt or sweatshirt. She then started thumbing back through the pages and saw more red shirts. One man was wearing a gold chain with a crucifix. She turned the page and saw another man wearing a crucifix, only smaller. If she let her imagination go now, she might end up in a mental institution. The man she had shot was the man. It must end there and end now.

"Mom, you didn't even have your glasses on that night, and you don't have them on now," Shana snapped. "He raped me, remember, and I can see perfectly." She turned to Margie and said sarcastically, "She's supposed to wear them when she drives too, but she never does."

"I only need them to read — just a little far-sighted," Lily informed the detective. "Anyway, arguing over it right now is counterproductive. Can you pull him in for a lineup?"

"I'll get right on it and call you as soon as it can be arranged. Why don't you two go home now, get some rest and try to put this out of your mind?" As Shana walked past her mother, heading for the door, Margie gave Lily a look with those Liz Taylor eyes and shrugged her shoulders. "Life's a bitch, isn't it?"

"You got that right," Lily replied and started walking out, trying to catch Shana.

Margie's voice projected and echoed in the large room. "Oh, I'm sure I don't have to mention this, but it might not be a bad idea for you to wear those glasses when I can get this guy in here for the real thing."

By the time Lily made it out of the building, Shana was waiting by the passenger door of the Honda. As she started the car, Lily told her, "They'll get the lineup together and we'll go from there, okay?"

"He's still out there. I know it now. I thought

he'd run away. He didn't. He's still out there. You told me he'd go away and never come back so he wouldn't get caught."

Lily hesitated, torn now, not knowing exactly what to say and thinking she must call the psychologist and get Shana in to see her tomorrow. She felt that assuaging her rising fear was the right thing to do, even if she became angry. "I really feel he's long gone, honey, and like I said back there, I don't think it's him. I can see things faraway better than I can close up; that's what farsightedness means. When he was close, it was very dark, but when he was leaving, he was faraway and in the light." She reached for her hand, holding it tightly. "I don't think the man you saw was him. He's gone. You're a smart girl. You know a lot of people look alike. Even you and I look alike, but of course, I'm a lot older. If we were the same age, people could mistake us even. See?"

Shana reached out and turned on the radio, a rock station. She then said over the noise, "It was him, Mom. When you see him with your glasses, then you'll know."

19

Fortified with lunch and flying on a double espresso, Detective Jameson strode back into the detective bureau and picked up his messages, hoping Cunningham's curiosity had gotten the best of him and he'd called back. No such luck, he thought, taking his seat and dialing the toll free number again. "Bruce Cunningham, please," he said once a female voice came on the line.

"Is this in regard to an order?"

"Yeah," he lied, "I need about five hundred of those power washers shipped out to my plant today."

"What's the name of your company, sir?" the woman queried in a clear, professional tone.

"Oh, Bruce and I are old buddies," Jameson said, resuming his customary position with his legs tossed up on his desk. "I've been a customer of his for years. Since I'm giving you guys such a big order, maybe it would be fun if we surprised him."

Jameson expected to hear Cunningham's voice on the line immediately. Instead he found himself listening to a recording about all the various equipment the company supplied and the services they performed throughout the world. When the recording stated that they washed the statue of Christ in Rio de Janeiro, he thought he was hearing things. Where in God's name did this guy work? Omaha was a long way from Rio de Janeiro. He'd never been to Brazil, but he'd seen pictures of the landmark they mentioned. He assumed it took an awfully powerful piece of equipment to wash a statue that large. Finally the detective came on the line.

"This is Bruce Cunningham," he said. "Are you ready to fill me in on what's going on, or would you prefer that I send you a bill for the equipment you said you were ordering?"

"I guess you folks have caller ID, right?"

"Something like that," Cunningham answered, talking faster than he had during their earlier call. "Hernandez was a mass murderer, in case you aren't aware of it. He and his gang butchered two high school kids. Then Hernandez splintered off from the group, kidnapped a prostitute, raped her, then later murdered her to keep her from testifying. I was there when they exhumed the body, and trust me, it wasn't a pretty sight. Why would anyone in their right mind want to waste their time trying to prosecute his killer?"

Jameson ran his hands through his thick head of silver hair. "Bad guys get killed every day, Bruce. The laws wouldn't amount to a hill of beans if everyone just decided to look the other way. That prostitute you just mentioned was breaking the law. You still wanted to see someone pay for her death, right?"

"Prostitution and murder don't fall into the same category."

"Point well taken," Jameson said. "Look, there's no reason for you and I to beat around the bush. All I'm asking for is enough information for us to access the records on the case and determine if there's anything worth pursuing. The records from the department you used to work for didn't make it over here completely intact. Finding anything in this massive database we have now is something of a nightmare, if you know what I mean."

"I can't help you," Cunningham told him. "Besides, I was about to walk out the door." He paused and then added, "I only have one suggestion for you, Fred. Concentrate on the present. I'm certain you've got plenty of homicides to keep you busy. This Hernandez thing isn't worth either your time or mine."

Jameson once again found himself listening to a dial tone. The fact that Cunningham had reacted the way he had about the Hernandez case made him suspect that what John Forrester had told the Los Angeles authorities about his wife killing the man to avenge her and her daughter's rape was factual. He placed a call to Hope Carruthers, asking her if she could arrange for him to interview John Forrester at the jail.

"He's not in custody," she told him. "His ex-wife posted his bail."

"No shit," Jameson exclaimed. "Can you give me his home phone number?"

"No problem," she said, typing in John's name and pulling up his booking sheet on her computer screen.

"Thanks," the other detective told her. He was ready to hang up when another question popped into his mind. "How did you find out that this case had never been resolved so quick? I've been beating my head against the wall all morning, kicking this damn computer and getting nowhere. The name is too common, and we've got problems relating to our record files for those time periods."

"Check the newspaper archives under the date of the rape," she told him. "That's the way we found it. Then you should be

291

able to cross-reference, retrieve your file. Sometimes they're not lost. It just takes awhile to find them."

"Which rape are you referring to?" Jameson asked, thinking she meant the rape of Lily Forrester and her daughter. He wasn't certain if there were any newspaper articles on that crime, since the law precluded them from publishing rape victims' names back in those days.

"Try checking under the McDonald-Lopez killings," Hope advised. "According to John Forrester, Hernandez and his brother were both participants in those crimes, although Bobby had killed in addition to that. If I remember right, the Oxnard P.D. shot him before the remaining defendants went to trial."

"I know the guys in Oxnard killed Manny Hernandez," he said, deciding he had enough to find what he needed regarding Lily. "I wasn't working here at the time, but at least I've heard people mention it. How is your investigation going on the hit-and-run, by the way?"

"We're trying to patch together an airtight case," Detective Carruthers told him, still coughing from the same cold. "I'm convinced the father is our man, but my partner doesn't completely concur. He's got both experience and rank over me. I have no choice but to follow his instructions." She took a few moments to explain their problems with the case, essentially that they had to rule out any possibility that Shana had been driving at the time of the accident.

"Thanks for your help," Jameson said, slowly replacing the receiver. In his estimation, his dislike of Lily Forrester was justified. He admitted he might have been overzealous in his efforts to convict the man who had murdered his longtime friend, Walter Evans. But in his entire career he had never once tampered with a report or falsified evidence. No one was infallible, he realized, and he didn't doubt that he'd been responsible for arresting his share of innocent people during the course of his career. In that regard, perhaps Lily had simply made an error in judgment. His gut instinct, however, told him that she might very well have gunned down the man she thought had raped her daughter. Cunningham was probably right and Hernandez had deserved to die, but Lily Forrester had no right to make herself his executioner.

Jameson had to admit, though, that he felt sorry for at least one member of the Forrester family. He had never met Shana Forrester, and he wasn't about to speculate as to whether or not she had been involved in the death of the young man in Los Angeles. He did know one thing. This was one young lady who was no stranger to problems.

20

Shana shook her mother by the shoulder. "Wake up, Mom. It's getting late."

"Oh," Lily said, staring out over the room in a daze. "I guess I was exhausted. What time is it?"

"Almost five," she said. "I woke you because I wanted to know what we were going to do for dinner."

"Are you hungry now?"

"No," Shana said. "I can't find the TV remote, though."

Lily found the remote stuck between the cushions of the sofa, handing it to her and then excusing herself to go to the bathroom. She couldn't stop thinking about the events which had occurred in the days following the rape. She splashed water on her face, staring at her reflection in the mirror. Returning to the living room, she told Shana she was going to soak in a hot bath. "We'll figure out what to do about dinner when I get out, okay?"

"Take your time, Mom," she said. "We had a big lunch."

Lily filled the tub with water, then stripped her clothes off and climbed in, leaning back and closing her eyes again. After Shana had identified Marco Curazon from the photo lineup, Lily had taken the mug shot out of Hernandez and compared it to the one Margie Thomas had given her of Marco Curazon. With her glasses on, she'd noted a number of differences in the two men's appearances, yet she'd continued to refuse to believe that she'd killed the wrong person.

As she pressed on her eyelids with her fingers, another crucial incident appeared, the images and details so real, she felt as if she were watching them projected on a screen. They had tracked down Marco Curazon and brought him in to participate in an actual lineup. Shana had been the first to view the men.

"Mom, give me the car keys," Shana said. *"I'll waitthere. I can start working on some of my homework."*

Lily desperately wanted to know what had transpired inside that room, yet she knew she was forbidden to ask until it was over. She tried to read Shana's eyes when she came out, searching for something, but she appeared remarkably composed, calmer now than before. If she had just seen the man who had raped her, would she be this composed? It must have been exactly as she'd thought from the start — that once she saw him in person, she'd know it wasn't him. She started to follow Margie, who was already headed toward the room with the two-way glass where they conducted the lineups.

"Give me the keys, Mom," Shana asked again.

"Here," Lily said, handing over her purse. "They're in the bottom somewhere."

Once she looked at the men assembled, it took her only seconds before she saw him. Then she could look at no one else. The lights were low in the viewing room, and Margie sat without speaking. "Tell them to turn sideways," Lily told the detective, listening as she spoke to the men via a microphone. She walked to the window and placed her palms on it, staring at his profile. He looked older than in the mug shot. "Was the photo of number three that we saw the other day recent?"

"I thought it was because he was in jail on a parole violation, but it wasn't. It was five years old, from an old booking. Someone forgot to put the new one in the file."

"Tell them to bend down like they're tying their shoes or something," Lily asked, and the woman detective complied.

Finally she left the window and collapsed in the seat, her head in her hands. In the past, every time she'd recalled the rape, the face of Bobby Hernandez had appeared instantly. Her mind was reeling like a boat about to capsize. The man in the room was more than a face in a mug shot; he was a presence, and that presence reached through the glass and seized her with fear. Had she murdered the wrong man? She raised her eyes again and looked at him. She could taste the crusty knife in her mouth. It was him! Shana had been correct. Then the boat tipped again and she saw Hernandez. She was battling her own will. There was still a thread of doubt. If she could only see Hernandez again in person, then she might know. Bile rose in her throat and she swallowed it. Hernandez would never be seen in person again. She'd made sure of that.

Removing her glasses, she reached for her purse to look at the mug shot she'd brought from the office. Her fingers brushed against the carpet, then her palm. Shana had her purse. Inside was the mug shot of Hernandez. Leaping from the seat, she rushed to the door, Margie right on her heels.

"Come back," the detective yelled, thinking she was having another panic attack. "We have to finish this and then you can leave."

Lily was out the door and actually running through the squad room, passing the records bureau, where every head turned, as she slammed through the double doors to the lobby. Her breath coming hard and fast, she bent down and held her stomach just as Margie caught up with her before she was out of the building.

"Please," Margie Thomas said, also gasping from chasing Lily, "I have to know if you've seen enough." Her lavender eyes were full of annoyance. "My God, you're a D.A. Get a grip." Once she had said it, her eyes filled with regret. "I'm sorry, okay? That was a low-down thing to say, but I'm only trying to do my job."

"It's number three," Lily snapped at her, refusing her apology, knowing she was making her feel like shit. "I'm going to get Shana, and we'll come back and give you a statement." The woman had her hand on Lily's arm, and Lily jerked it away. "I'm only doing my job, too. It's my daughter." With that, Lily turned and walked out of the station.

She went directly to the passenger side of the Honda and tried to open the door. It was locked. Shana saw her and rolled down the window. In her hands was the small picture of Hernandez.

"Who is this?" she demanded, no longer composed, her eyes wild with confusion.

"It's just an old defendant in a case at the office. Someone gave it to me, thinking he looked like the man I described. It's nothing." Lily reached inside the car and tried to take the photo from Shana's hands. The girl held it

away where Lily couldn't reach it.

"No! It looks just like him. I want him brought in for a lineup. I thought it was the guy in there — number three — I was so sure. But now —"

"Shana, please give me the picture. You were right. I picked number three too. This other guy isn't the guy." Lily tried to still her racing heart by taking several slow, deep breaths, willing herself not to think of all the ramifications of what was happening. She had to stop it now. "He's dead. It was a mistake. I just found out."

"What do you mean, he's dead? Does Margie know about him?"

"The man who gave me the photo didn't know that he'd been killed. He was killed in a gang shooting or something a long time ago, months before the rape. He means nothing to Margie or anyone now. I told her we'd come right in and make a statement. She's waiting."

"Everyone looks alike. Maybe that guy isn't the one, either." Tears started falling from her eyes.

Lily pulled the latch on the door and opened it, reaching in to Shana, leaning down beside the car. "Honey, we're not the judge and jury. All we're doing is telling the truth — that the man in there appears to be the man who attacked us — nothing more. Once I learned this man in the picture was dead, I just forgot to put the picture back." Shana let her remove it from her hands. His name was printed at the bottom of the photo.

"Get my purse and we'll go in. Then we can go home and try to put this out of our minds. Okay?"

Once the photo was back in her purse and she and Shana were walking back to the building, she said, "Don't mention this to Margie. We'll all be confused, and it will be a waste of time. I wasn't supposed to take this photo from the office, and I'll get in trouble."

Shana looked at her mother only a moment, but her expression was one of disbelief. "I won't tell Margie," she said quietly. "It doesn't even look that much like him anyway. His face was thinner and he was uglier, meaner-looking. He had pimples like the man I saw in there. That's the man."

Lily surfaced from the past, getting out of the bathtub and drying herself off. When she returned to the living room, she saw Shana staring at her, almost as if she had been reliving the same events as her mother. The girl had to know the truth. Would she ever turn against her if John followed through on his threats to expose her? Lily couldn't believe she would ever do such a thing, especially not after her father's recent involvement in the hit-and-run. But what

301

would transpire if she was forced to testify? How could she allow her to perjure herself under oath? Just the thought of it made Lily's stomach roll over.

"Did you enjoy your bath?" Shana asked, using the remote to turn off the TV.

"Not really," Lily said, flopping down beside her again on the sofa. "I have a better understanding why you haven't spent more time with me. You're right when you say being together makes us strong. Unfortunately, it also makes it impossible not to think about the rape."

Shana remained silent for some time, a sullen expression on her face. "You're not going to keep paying Dad's rent, are you?" she said finally. "Unless the police blame me for what he did, he's going to end up in jail. At least he won't have to work or worry about a place to live."

"It sounds as if you really meant it when you said you were fed up with your dad," Lily said, testing the waters. "I'm in no way condoning what he did, but he didn't intentionally kill that young man. Alcoholism is an illness. John might have some serious faults, but he's not a criminal, nor is he in any way violent. I've prosecuted people who kill just for the thrill of it, Shana. I don't believe he falls into that category, do you?"

"No," she told her, removing her chewing gum and wrapping it up in a tissue. "But let's face it, Mom, if he had thought about someone other than himself, he would have notified the authorities right away. Then maybe that guy might have lived."

"You definitely possess the potential to go beyond the level of an attorney," Lily told her. Her wet hair was wrapped in a towel. She removed it so her hair would dry. Sunlight was still streaming in through the doorway. Even though Lily had trimmed the roses the night before, several of the gardenia bushes were still blooming, and their delicate scent was drifting in through the open screen door. "The points you just emphasized are the precise factors a judge will take under consideration when your father's case goes before the court. He's lucky they didn't charge him with murder."

"What did they charge him with?" Shana asked. "I thought you said it was vehicular homicide."

"The specific charge is gross vehicular manslaughter while intoxicated, which falls under section 191.5(c) of the penal code. They've also charged him with a separate count of felony hit-and-run. They can't try him for both. They only added the extra charge in case they decide to settle the case somewhere down the line."

Shana fished a brush out of her backpack. "Turn around," she told her mother, repositioning her by placing her hands on her shoulders. "I want to brush your hair while we talk. Remember how you used to brush my hair?"

Lily was touched. She was glad her back was turned. She didn't want Shana to see the tears in her eyes.

"Go on, Mother," she said, gently pulling the bristles through Lily's wavy hair. "You were explaining the charges to me. I enjoyed reading your law journals this afternoon."

"Well," Lily said, sniffling, "the way that section reads that I just mentioned, they could prosecute whoever committed this crime under section 188, which is homicide. In order to do so, though, they have to establish that his actions constituted wantonness and conscious disregard for human life."

"How long would he have to serve in prison?"

"On which term?" Lily asked. "The crime he's been charged with falls under one set of guidelines, while the other section I mentioned is considered an indeterminate term."

"Does that feel good?" Shana asked, continuing to brush her mother's long hair.

"Wonderful," Lily said, her scalp tingling. "What was I saying?"

"You were telling me how long Dad might have to go to prison."

"I'm not sure we should talk about this," Lily said, turning around to look at her.

Shana was emphatic. "I *want* to talk about it."

"Fine," Lily told her, taking a deep breath. "The aggravated term is ten years. He won't serve ten years, however. He'll only serve five, maybe six."

When Shana stopped brushing her hair and fell silent, Lily said, "Richard can explain a lot of things to you tonight at dinner. Why don't we take a walk? There's some beautiful trails around here, especially in the foothills. I hike almost every weekend."

"I don't want to go for a hike." Shana's face clouded over again with concern. "What are we going to do about Dad and the duplex?"

"We'll have to get a truck and move your belongings somewhere else," Lily said, turning around to face her. "I called the landlord today and told him we would be terminating our lease at the end of the month. It was up for renewal, anyway."

When she saw the girl's face fall, she added, "I didn't think you would want to continue living there under the circumstances. You'd be alone, honey, and I don't want you to be afraid."

"You said I could advertise for a room-mate."

"I'm not sure that would be the best course of action right now," Lily said, rolling her head around to release the tension. "If your dad can't find another place to live, he's going to end up on your doorstep. From the way it looks, he'll probably go to prison, but since he's out on bail, we're talking six or seven months from now. With the way the Los Angeles system is clogged, it might even be longer."

"What about my school?"

"That's a decision you're going to have to make on your own," she answered. "I called campus housing as soon as I woke up this morning. There's nothing available in the dorms right now. Someone could drop out, though."

Lily took a seat in the wooden rocking chair. Shana stretched out on her stomach on the sofa, staring at the framed photographs of herself on the end table. "Where's that picture of me you had taken last year? You know, the one we had made in that glamour photo place in the West Hills mall."

Lily knew precisely what picture was missing. Shana looked so gorgeous in it that her eyes were drawn to it all the time. She walked over, thinking the portrait was either hidden behind one of the others on the table, or she had accidentally knocked it to the floor. When she couldn't find it, she stared at the table, realizing something else was missing.

Shana occasionally received mail at her mother's post office box in Santa Barbara. Unless it was something urgent, Lily would store whatever arrived during the month inside the pre-addressed envelope she kept tucked under the edge of one of her pictures. This way she wouldn't forget to include it when she mailed out Shana's monthly check. Lily distinctly recalled placing a card from one of the girl's former camp buddies during the past two weeks. Yet the entire envelope was missing.

Although Lily was fearful someone might have been inside the cottage, she tried to remain calm, hoping the items would turn up somewhere. They both searched the cottage, even getting on their hands and knees, then finally gave up. "This isn't a very large place," Lily told her. "When I moved from the house, I might have put the picture you're talking about in storage with some of my other things."

"I've seen it here," Shana said, visibly shaken. "The last time I came to visit you it was here. That means you couldn't have stored it with your other things when you moved in. I'm not an idiot, Mother. I know what I saw. Stop trying to placate me."

Lily rubbed her sweaty hands on her jeans. "It's only a picture, honey."

"But it's gone! Someone must have taken it." She walked over and slammed the door, shoving the dead bolts into place, then leaning against it. "Marco Curazon was paroled to Camarillo," she said. "That's only a twenty-minute drive from here. What if the man outside the duplex really was him? And I told you the guy who was following me around campus a few days ago looked just like him."

Lily rushed over, pulling her into her arms, knowing Shana's fear would intensify if she knew the envelope with the address of the duplex was also missing. "You're panicking because of all the stress you've been under. I shouldn't have said anything about you being afraid to stay at your place. That was foolish of me. It's my fault for upsetting you."

"No," Shana shouted, wrenching away. "Why would you say it's your fault? I hate it when you do that, make yourself responsible for every thing that goes wrong." She flung her arms in the air. "It's his fault! Why did he have to rape us? And the stupid courts should have never let him out of prison. I don't care what the law says. People who do things like that should never get out of prison. Never! Did you hear me? Never!"

"Please, calm down," Lily said, cupping her hand over her mouth, then letting her arms fall limp at her sides.

"I don't want to calm down!" Shana shrieked, as if she had no choice but to release the pent up rage inside her. She walked over to her mother and seized a handful of her bathrobe in her hand, a wild, out-of-control look in her eyes. "I'd like to hurt someone right now, do you hear me? I'd like to break something, kick some guy in the balls, maybe smash something over his head!" Suddenly she started walking backward, the tempest past, appalled that such terrible words had poured out of her own mouth. "I'm sorry," she told Lily. "I don't know what made me say those things."

"I do," Lily answered, taking her hand.

"Where are we going?"

"For a really fast ride," her mother told her. "There's a place about fifteen minutes from here. Once you feel the speedometer hit a hundred, I guarantee you'll feel better."

Shana stared at her as if she were insane. "I can't believe you'd suggest something like this after what happened with Dad."

"Your father was drunk." Lily opened the screen door, stepping out into the fresh air. "About ten years ago the county sent me to a defensive driving school. I scored higher than all the men. This place I'm taking you to used to be a racetrack. A former investigator for the Santa Barbara D.A.'s office who races cars as a hobby told me about it. He gave me a special code to get inside the gate. When I occasionally feel like I'm going to explode, this is how I let off steam."

21

Not long after Lily and Shana returned from their drive, Richard called, inviting them to have dinner with him at the Plow & Angel restaurant, located at the San Ysidro Ranch in Montecito. Even though the establishment was referred to in local circles as simply the "Ranch," it had been in existence for over a hundred years and was considered one of the most elite resorts in the country. Since it had once been a working ranch, guests stayed in bungalows, each with its own distinctive decor. The bungalows also differed in size and amenities. Many had fenced-in backyards with Jacuzzi tubs and numerous bedrooms, and some of the newer bungalows were so elaborate, the guests even had the use of their own private swimming pool, making them feel as if they were staying in a luxurious home.

"I thought you said he wasn't coming up until eight."

"His last client of the day got sick and canceled," Lily told her, excited at the prospect of seeing Richard and hoping it would lift both of their spirits. She had to trust in

her belief that John would suffer the consequences of his actions, and that no matter
what he did or said, the police would never
reopen the Hernandez case. Shana might
have to transfer to U.C. Santa Barbara, yet
Lily didn't think it would have a serious im-
pact on her future. They could always make
arrangements for her to attend another university the following year. The only thing
that really mattered in the long run was her
name on a diploma. Of greater concern was
the fact that Shana would have to accept her
father going to prison. She was strong,
though, and Lily had faith in her ability to
once again overcome adversity and move
forward with her life.

"Do I have to get dressed up?"

"This is a *very* nice place," her mother
told her. "I've only been there one time
since I moved here because it's pricy. The
history is fascinating, though, and I feel certain you'll enjoy the meal."

"What do you mean by history?" Shana
asked, sorting through her mother's closet
for something to wear.

"I can't recall *all* the famous people who
they say have stayed there," Lily answered,
tossing her robe on the bed. "Let's see, John
and Jackie Kennedy spent part of their honeymoon at the ranch, all kinds of legendary

actors, musicians, writers, and artists. They have pictures on the walls in one of the buildings in case you're interested."

"Why do they call it the Plow & Angel?" Shana asked, pulling out a black knit dress and holding it up to her body, then glancing at herself in the dresser mirror. "That's kind of a peculiar name. I mean, I wouldn't associate the word *plow* with a fancy restaurant."

"If I remember correctly," Lily said, "the ranch was named after a Spanish farmhand who used to arrive late to work every day because he spent his mornings praying. I'll show you the statue when we get to the restaurant. The plaque claims he was able to plow as many fields during the afternoon as the rest of the workers could in an entire day. He told the owners of the ranch that he was able to accomplish so much because he had an angel on his shoulder. He was canonized by the Catholic Church."

"Does that mean he was made a saint?"

"Yes," Lily told her. "If I'm not mistaken, they made him the patron saint of husbandry."

"What does he do?" She laughed. "Find you a husband?"

"Not exactly," Lily answered. "Husbandry has something to do with agriculture. That's not a bad idea, though."

"What?"

"You know," Lily said, "a saint that finds single ladies husbands."

"Saints are dead people." Shana looked as if her mother had tipped over the edge.

Lily wanted to inquire if she ever went to church. Better to leave that conversation for another day, she decided. She'd been lax, however, when it came to insisting that her daughter be raised in the Catholic Church. John's family had been Presbyterian; therefore, like many couples who married outside their faith, they had reached an impasse, remaining detached from any specific religion for most of their married life. Lily had managed to convince John that her daughter should be baptized as a Catholic, but Shana had never gone through the confirmation process. "If you want," she added tentatively, "I can take you to visit the mission, or we can stop by the parish church I joined up the road."

Shana was surprised, as her mother had never mentioned anything along these lines. "You really joined a church?"

Lily felt her face flush in embarrassment. "Yeah," she said, placing her hands on her hips. "I don't go every Sunday, but when things get me down, I drop by the church or go to a service. Lately I've been trying to attend mass on important days. I guess when you get older, you get more serious. Either that, or I feel I have a lot of atoning to do."

"Wow," the girl said, her eyes widening. "I'm impressed."

Lily's wardrobe consisted mainly of suits, as she felt they suited her profession. Out of the few dresses she owned, one of her favorites was already in her daughter's hands. She settled for a black jacket with red velvet patches on the shoulders and a fairly short skirt to show off her long legs. Years before, Richard had remarked on numerous occasions that her legs were one of her more alluring features. "Do you need nylons? I have a new pair."

Shana was in the bathroom, fiddling with her mother's cosmetics. "We don't wear the same size shoes," she said, glancing down at her black flats. "Will I look out of place in these? Is the restaurant that fancy?"

"Not really," Lily said, joining her in the bathroom. "We're not eating in the main restaurant. The Plow & Angel is more casual. Those shoes will be fine, and you can forget about the nylons."

Richard had said he would meet them at the restaurant at seven o'clock. She assumed he felt uncomfortable coming to the house because of Shana, or maybe due to the fact that Lily had asked him to act as the girl's attorney if the police decided to question her again.

Once they were both dressed, they drove the short distance to the San Ysidro Ranch in Lily's black Audi, the engine sputtering a bit from their tension-relieving spin around the abandoned racetrack. They stopped a moment in front of the old stone structure. Lily showed Shana the bronze statue and plaque she had mentioned. The individual that the church had canonized was depicted hard at work behind a horse and plow, with what appeared to be a creature with wings sitting on his right shoulder.

Through the open doorway Lily saw a man with Richard's build and hair coloring sitting at the bar. He turned around, almost as if he could sense Lily's presence the moment she stepped into the room. Wearing a dark suit, white shirt, and a red tie with small yellow flowers on it, he looked incredibly handsome. Lily kissed him lightly on the cheek. "I really appreciate you driving up tonight, Richard. How was the traffic?"

"Not bad at all," he said, smiling. "I was happy to get away."

"Nice to see you again," Shana said, shaking his hand. "How's Greg?"

"Great," Richard said. "He was asking

about you just the other day. Your mother tells me you're going to UCLA."

Shana looked down at her shoes, sad that she might have to change schools. "Is Greg a marine biologist now?"

"Almost," he said, glancing over at Lily. "He works at Sea World in San Diego. He takes care of the dolphins."

Shana had first met Richard's son only a short time after the rape. Greg had taken on the role of an older brother, spending time with her, comforting her, trying to help her remain rational during a time when her world had crashed down around her. An avid surfer, she remembered how the young man had loved the ocean. His father had wanted him to become an attorney, and Shana sensed a lingering residue of disappointment. She couldn't recall when she had first decided to follow in her mother's footsteps. Being a victim and witnessing the criminal justice system firsthand had played a major part in her decision.

Not many of Shana's peers had realistic plans for their futures. Some of them hadn't even declared a major. She recalled how she'd once yearned to be a model, particularly since her mother had modeled when she was young. But Lily had been dead-set against Shana getting involved in the modeling profession, although everyone who saw her thought she possessed tremendous potential. Her height and willowy frame in itself could have taken her a long way, let alone her beautiful face and the fluid manner in which she moved her body. Thoughts about becoming a model had vanished after the rape, however, whisked away by the same wicked wind that had stolen her innocence.

Shana had long ago stopped confiding in John. Her father had disappeared into an alcohol-induced fantasy where he imagined her becoming a famous defense attorney who would support him in his old age. Any recent attempts to engage in serious discussions with him hadn't seemed worth the effort. She also knew John would never encourage her to become a prosecutor like her mother, which was the first step toward achieving her ultimate goal. Just as Lily had before the rape, Shana aspired to be a judge. She also fantasized about winning an appointment to the Supreme Court. Her dreams seemed so lofty and unobtainable that she'd been embarrassed to mention them even to her mother. "Tell Greg I'm happy for him," she said, a slight catch in her voice. "Not many people get the chance to do what they want in life."

"He's not quite where he wants to be *yet*," Richard told her, his eyes roaming around the room for the waiter. "He's still got another two years left."

"I don't understand," Shana said. "I thought he graduated last year."

"He did," Richard told her. "He's still working on his doctorate."

"So what does he do at Sea World? I thought you said he took care of the dolphins."

Seeing the waiter gesturing toward their table in a secluded section in the back of the restaurant, Richard placed a hand on Shana's back to guide her. "For the time being," he said, "Greg feeds the dolphins and cleans out their tank. He gets to use his scuba gear, though, so he enjoys that aspect of his job. His salary is a problem. I keep reminding him that eventually he'll be able to pull down a decent income."

"Everyone has to start somewhere," Lily interjected, stepping in front of them to take her seat at the table. She knew what Richard meant about kids wanting their lives to come together instantly, then becoming disenchanted when they realized they had a longer road ahead of them than they thought. During the time she had attended law school, she'd juggled a husband and a child in addition to a part-time job. Otherwise, they could have never survived, and even then they had lived from month to month. Even though Shana was determined and bright, Lily couldn't imagine her bearing up under the weight of so many responsibilities. Richard ordered a steak, Lily a Cornish hen with wild rice stuffing. Shana said she wanted only a salad, then picked at it most of the evening, telling them that she was saving her appetite for dessert. After they finished their main course, Shana leaned over and whispered in her mother's ear. "Aren't we going to talk to him about Dad and the accident?"

Lily cleared her throat before speaking and glanced around the restaurant. By this time most of the other diners had left, so she felt comfortable proceeding. "Shana is curious about how long her father might have to serve if he's sentenced to prison. We were going over the details this afternoon, Richard, but I suggested that we wait and discuss it with you."

Once Lily had filled him in on the specific charges, Richard dabbed his mouth with his napkin. "The sentencing judge has the option of sending him to prison for either four, six, or ten years."

Shana said, "But he won't serve that many years."

"Probably not," Lily answered. "If he gets the lowest term, he could be released in less than two years."

"Why are there all these options?" the girl asked. "I thought a judge could send people to prison for as long as he wanted, then the parole board made the decision when they were released. Isn't that why Curazon was released, because the parole board had its head up its ass?"

"Not really," Richard said. "He served his time. His particular crime fell under the determinate-sentencing law. In that case the parole board didn't determine his release date. It was preset by law."

Shana asked, "What's the determinate-sentencing law?"

"Every state has different laws, Shana," Richard explained. "Here in California we have what's called the 'determine-sentencing law.' Only a handful of crimes have indeterminate terms, such as first- and second-degree murder, for example. An indeterminate term would be twelve years to life. In this case the parole board would come into play in deciding when the person gained release. The greatest majority of crimes fall under the guidelines I mentioned first."

"I'm confused."

Lily said, "I can't begin to tell you how

confused people get interpreting some of our laws. Isn't that right, Richard?"

He nodded, but wanted Lily to continue. Motioning for the waiter to bring them a dessert menu, he ordered coffee for himself. Shana and Lily asked for tea. Then they all took a moment to select a dessert. Lily wanted to make things as clear as possible. Her daughter's desire to become an attorney was fueling a portion of her interest, yet sadly, her mother knew she was also attempting to prepare herself. If worse came to worst, and the authorities decided to prosecute her on the crime her father had almost certainly committed, she had every right to know what kind of punishment she might be facing.

"Okay," Lily continued, "a determinate term is where the judge has to decide between three different sentences."

"How does he decide?" Shana asked. "Does he just pick one or the other?"

"Of course not," Lily explained. "The Judicial Council in San Francisco provides certain guidelines or rules that every judge and court must follow. These are called circumstances in mitigation and aggravation."

"I know what those words mean," she said, "but I need you to explain what they mean in relationship to a court case."

"Once a defendant has been judged

guilty," Lily told her, "either by a judge or a jury, or even if he enters into what we call a negotiated disposition, just a less offensive term for a plea agreement . . ."

The waiter arrived with their desserts, and Lily stopped to take a bite of her cheese-cake. "To explain this in as simplistic a fashion as possible," she said, "circum-stances in mitigation could mean that the de-fendant stole a bottle of milk or some other type of food product because his baby was starving, that he had never committed a crime before, and he was sorry for what he did."

"Remorse, right?"

"Precisely," Lily said, having to remind herself that Shana was a college student and not a child any longer. She found it uncanny how both of their minds appeared to track in almost an identical fashion. Most people marveled at the similarities in their physical appearance. Lily thought the fact that their thinking and ability to comprehend fell along the same level was far more unique. "One of the guidelines the court provides poses the question of whether or not the crime was an isolated incident, not likely to reoccur. Such could be applied to the case I just made up, as our fictional offender would more than likely get a job and be able to provide for his family after his case was resolved."

"Why do you think that would happen?"

"Intervention," her mother explained. "Meaning, once this guy came into contact with the authorities, even if he still couldn't obtain employment, someone in the system would hopefully assist him in applying for some other form of state assistance so he wouldn't have to commit another crime."

"That makes sense," Shana said, nodding thoughtfully.

"Now," Lily continued, "let's backtrack for a moment. Since the court has decided that circumstances in mitigation applied, the law would charge the judge with imposing the lesser of the three terms for whatever crime this person had committed. Am I clear?"

Shana's jaw dropped. "They'd send someone to prison for stealing a bottle of milk?"

"Probably not," her mother said. "Remember, I'm only using these scenarios so you can grasp the overall concept. Stealing a bottle of milk would be classified as a misdemeanor theft, and people don't go to prison for theft. They can go to jail, but they can't be sentenced to prison. That is, unless they used a gun. Then they would have committed an armed robbery."

Shana was stunned. "Even if all they took was a bottle of milk?"

"Absolutely," Lily said. "A robbery is a robbery. Like I said, people take years to fully understand the complexity of our laws. There's also what's classified as a strong-armed robbery. That means you either rob someone by hitting them, or by any means of force, even if you simply threaten them and never follow through on your threat."

"I've got it," Shana said, crossing her legs under the table. "Tell me more."

Lily was getting hoarse from talking. She stopped and drank some of her tea. "So," she went on, "mitigating circumstances just means that the person who committed the crime might not be such a bad person. On the other hand, an example of what would influence a judge to impose an aggravated or longer term would be an offender with a lengthy criminal history, who also showed no remorse, or who had been proven to have been under the influence of drugs or alcohol at the time he committed the crime."

"What about the middle term?" Shana asked. "What would make a judge go in that direction?"

Lily pushed her dessert plate aside, happy to share the knowledge she possessed with her daughter. "Envision the scales of justice."

Shana's face lit up. She held her palms out on both sides of her body. "I get it," she said. "A judge would select the middle term if all these factors you just described were more or less evenly balanced, right?"

"Exactly," her mother said, smiling at Richard. "There's no doubt that you'll pass your law school entrance exam."

"You really think so?"

"For sure," Richard agreed. "Of course, with Lily as your mother, I wouldn't have expected anything less."

"Can you have breakfast with us to-morrow morning?" Lily asked, feeling as if they hadn't had a chance to simply visit with one another due to the nature of their dinner conversation. "There's a great break-fast place in Summerland. I'm certain it was there when you were growing up, Rich, but I don't remember the name." Summerland was a small town only a few miles away, yet far more casual and beachy than Montecito. The rich and famous, however, still showed up there from time to time. People claimed Hillary and Bill Clinton had even shopped for homes in Summerland several years back.

"As long as I can get to the courthouse by ten," Richard said. "Is eight too early?"

"Eight is perfect," Lily told him. She was

still uncertain how she was going to proceed in regard to Shana's school and living situation. She knew she would have to check into the office for a few hours the next day, if for nothing else than to touch base and bring some paperwork home to work on over the weekend.

They proceeded to toss around the merits of various law schools. Shana wanted to make arrangements to see Greg as well, but since she didn't know where she was going to be living, she asked his father for his phone number and jotted down her e-mail address. Like most of the college kids today, she seldom went anywhere without her computer.

"I wasn't putting Greg down about his job," Richard said, slightly defensive. "He's working hard. He probably told you I pitched a fit when he told me he didn't want to be a lawyer. In retrospect, I think he would have made a mistake if he'd gone into law."

"Why's that?" Shana asked, tilting her head to one side.

"At this point in history," he told her, "I think the world needs more marine biologists than it does attorneys."

Shana took a bite of her chocolate cake, then placed her fork back on the table. "Do you think I'm making a mistake as well?"

"No," Richard answered. "I think people have different aptitudes and interests. I didn't mean to imply that being an attorney isn't a worthwhile way to earn a living."

"Shana will be wonderful," Lily said, placing her arm around her daughter. They were sitting together, with Richard on the opposite side of the table. The interior of the restaurant was similar to a cave or a wine cellar. The stone walls gave it a damp, chilly feeling, even with several logs burning in the fireplace. Above the bar there were three circular stained-glass wall hangings, each one depicting a different season. Lily spotted autumn, spring, and summer. For some reason, perhaps space constraints, the one for winter had been positioned on the wall next to their booth. "We were talking this afternoon, Rich," she continued. "I believe Shana has what it takes to become a fabulous legislator. I'd like to see her writing laws someday, or at least working toward cleaning up some of the convoluted language and outdated statutes."

"The problem is, Lily," he said, "that when anyone makes an attempt to improve things, we generally end up with what turns out to be nothing more than some politician's catchy campaign slogans. We're still dealing with the three-strikes-and-you're-out bill. Wasn't it supposed to put an end to recidivism? I personally thought it was absurd. Where are we going to warehouse all these prisoners? We need more rehabilitation programs, not more ridiculous laws."

"I concur to some degree," Lily said. "I forgot to mention, Shana, that there were some outlandish instances where offenders received life sentences for stealing something as trivial as a candy bar."

Shana asked, "How did that happen?"

"It was their third felony conviction, and that's what 'three strikes and you're out' means." Lily paused. "The problem is, we're not talking about baseball. These are human lives."

"If the crime they committed was a felony," Shana argued, "then they must have taken the candy bar during a robbery. Isn't that the way you explained the analogy of the guy stealing milk for his kid? So what if the person they robbed didn't have a lot of valuables? That law doesn't sound absurd to me. A robbery is a serious crime. No one can predict what kind of property the person has on them, unless it's a bank or they've already been inside their house." She stopped and stared out over the restaurant, for her thoughts had returned to the missing picture.

"I'd hire you," Richard blurted out, placing his hands on the edge of the table. "Next summer you can intern in my office if you're interested. It's hard to find young people with your kind of reasoning ability."

"Really?" Shana said, excited. "You realize I'm only in my second year of college."

"Trust me," he said, asking the waiter for a check, "I could use you right now. That was a valid job offer I just made. And it has nothing to do with my friendship with your mother."

Shana leaned back in her seat, flattered by his offer. Lily was sad their evening together was about to come to an end. For the past hour and a half they had enjoyed themselves. Richard was the proverbial charmer, and Shana had grown into a polished young lady. Seeing her in jeans and sweatshirts most of the time, Lily reflected on how stunning she looked in the clingy black dress, her hair slicked away from her face in a French twist, the top portion exploding in what resembled a flower arrangement of shiny red curls. She didn't wear eye makeup, only a touch of mascara, but she loved lipstick. When they had first walked into the restaurant, people had stared at them as if they were celebrities. Lily had no doubt that it was Shana who generated the attention. She didn't mind being in her daughter's shadow. The only thing she regretted was coming to the realization that her only child was maturing so quickly.

"Let me pay for this," Lily said, picking the check up off the table. "You drove all this way."

"In my book," Richard said, smiling rakishly, "ladies don't pay. Besides, I can think of a dozen men who would give their right arm to have dinner with two gorgeous and intelligent women."

"Don't lay it on too thick," Lily said, shifting her eyes to her daughter. "Let's set the record straight. I'm buying breakfast tomorrow. And whether you realize it or not, women have a tendency not to believe a man when he heaps on too many compliments."

"At school," Shana laughed, a wispy strand of hair tumbling onto her forehead, "my friends and I think guys who drool all over us are just saying things to get in our pants."

"Listen to your friends," he said, a fatherly expression on his face.

As Richard escorted them to their car, he recalled his dinner with Joyce at the Indian restaurant. She hadn't moved her things out of his house yet, but she'd called the office that morning and apologized for the way she had behaved, claiming she didn't want them to end their relationship as enemies. Rather than take a chance on her having another tantrum, though, he had no intention of returning to the house until he was certain she was gone. While Joyce had been at her office that morning, he'd sent June over to pick up some of his clothes. After the nerve-racking pace of the previous week, he'd booked himself into the resort for the weekend. Of course, he didn't want to say anything in front of Shana, but he hoped to entice Lily to come back to his bungalow later that night. This would also give him a chance to speak to her privately about what he had learned about Marco Curazon. He was also somewhat reluctant for Lily and her daughter to stay in the guest house alone, one of the reasons he had rented such a large place for the weekend.

Shana realized she'd left her purse in the restaurant and hurried back inside, leaving Richard and Lily waiting for the valet. He pressed a key into her hands, and a card with directions to his bungalow. "Come over later," he whispered. "We can talk privately."

"I can't," Lily said, sensing he wanted to do more than talk. "Not when Shana is here."

"Listen to me," Richard said, seizing her arm. "Didn't you tell me some of her friends attend the university here in Santa Barbara?"

"She has several girlfriends that go to school here," Lily said. "What are you suggesting?"

"She's a young girl, Lily," he told her, wanting to accomplish his objective without being blatant about it, reluctant to frighten Shana any more than she already was. "Maybe it would be good for her to be with someone her own age, you know. She could stay at one of their houses tonight. That way we'd have some private time together."

Lily glanced at her watch. It was nine-thirty, and she felt odd asking Shana to try to find one of her friends and impose herself on them. Seeing her walking toward them, she whispered to Richard, "I'll ask her in the car after we leave, then buzz you back and let you know."

"What are you guys talking about?" Shana asked, stepping up beside them.

"Nothing," her mother said. "Just the resort."

"Your mother says you have some friends in this area." Richard decided to take control. "They tell me Thursday is the in-night to go out dancing. Greg comes up here every now and then to surf and visit some of his friends. He claims the clubs are too crowded on Friday and Saturday nights."

"Are you serious?" Shana asked, tilting

her head to one side. "You really want to take my mom and me out dancing?"

Great, Richard thought facetiously. He had talked himself into a corner. "Not exactly," he said. "I mean, I'd love to take you both dancing one of these days, but that wasn't my intention. I was trying to suggest that you might want do something with people in your own age group."

Shana fell silent, her eyes shifting to Lily's face, then back to Richard's. "Ronnie came up and stayed with me about a month ago," she said, popping a mint into her mouth. "I didn't do much but sit around all day today and worry."

"Everything is going to be fine."

"Yeah," Shana said, shuffling her feet around on the gravel driveway. "I've got Ronnie's phone numbers in my purse, as well as a few other people. I guess I could call around and see if anything's going on."

Both Richard and Lily offered her their cell phones at the same exact moment. Shana had intended to pretend she didn't know what was going on between them, but she couldn't stop herself from laughing. "People your age are funny," she said. "I'm the kid, remember? It's okay. You have every right to tell me to get lost. Where are you staying, Richard?"

"Here," he said, chagrined at how easily

she had figured out the situation, maybe not about his concern for them to stay at the cottage, but his secondary objective, which was to get Lily alone. "It was close to your mother's place, and I haven't been here in a long time."

"So you're registered under Fowler, right?" Shana asked, winking as she climbed into the driver's seat of her mother's car.

"What are you doing?" Lily exclaimed, chasing after her. "I don't want you to go home alone. Richard was just making a suggestion."

"I probably know more people in this town than you do, Mom," Shana said, holding the cell phone up to the window. "I'll check in with you in about fifteen minutes. I'll probably spend the night with Ronnie." Before Lily could stop her, she turned the key in the ignition and sped off.

22

Richard and Lily walked up a fairly steep hill to his bungalow, both of them lost in their thoughts. The valet had offered to take them in a golf cart, but they decided to walk. Each of the bungalows at the ranch had been given a name. "Magnolia, huh?" Lily said, squinting to read the little wooden sign in the dark. "I love magnolia trees."

"Good," Richard said. "Then I picked the right place."

The resort also had wall-mounted slots where they inserted the names of the guests during their stay. That is, if the guest wanted his name displayed. Many people who visited the ranch possessed the type of fame that made them constantly dodge exposure, and recently the owner had required that all employees sign a confidentiality agreement swearing they wouldn't reveal the names of guests who were either on the property or who had stayed there on previous occasions. The only people they excluded were long-dead notables, whose publicity shots they proudly displayed on the walls. The establishment's pride was the legendary bungalow John and Jackie Kennedy had stayed in on their honeymoon. They named it the "Kennedy Suite," while the remainder of the bungalows were named after trees, plants, or flowers.

Richard Fowler might not be a recognizable name throughout the universe, but he had asked that his name not be placed on the door. All he needed was his dish-throwing former girlfriend to come storming into the bungalow.

"I don't feel right," Lily said while he was unlocking the door.

"Why?" he asked, glancing over his shoulder. "Because of Shana?"

"Of course," she said, hugging her arms around her chest in the chilly night air. "I don't want my daughter to know my personal affairs."

"At least you used the right word."

"What does that mean?"

Richard stepped inside and flipped on the lights, taking Lily's hand and pulling her into his arms. "Don't you think Shana knows we had an affair?" He kissed her on the forehead. "She even called my office pretending to be your secretary years ago, inviting me over for dinner. She wanted to patch things up between us, remember? She doesn't want you to hide from the world, Lily."

His statements hit too close to home; Lily disentangled herself from his arms. "Don't you understand? I want Shana to feel she can rely on you if this thing with John gets out of hand. Imagine how a girl her age would feel knowing her attorney was sleeping with her mother."

Richard made a sweeping movement with his arm in the direction of the living room and separate bedroom. "It's not like I invited you back to a motel room, Lily," he told her. "This place is almost the same size as your guest house. Shana can come over tomorrow night if you like. We can even have dinner brought in from the restaurant."

"Tomorrow night?" she said, a puzzled look on her face. "You're not going back to Ventura after you make your court appearance tomorrow?"

"No," he said. "I booked this place through Sunday."

Lily turned around in a small circle, her palm pressed to her forehead. "It's not that long of a drive, Richard. Don't tell me you're going to charge this to your client."

"You know me better than that," he said. "Now that you mentioned it, though, maybe

I should bill him. This isn't one of my favorite clients."

"Henry Middleton, right?"

"God, no," he said, grimacing. "I'm referring to the drug dealer. The last thing I want to talk about tonight is the Middleton case."

"What if someone saw us at the restaurant?" Lily asked, concerned that they might compromise the case. "With everything that's been happening, I actually forgot you were representing him. I'll call Shana now and have her pick me up."

"Stop it, Lily," he said, so frustrated he wanted to pull his hair out. "I just told you we weren't going to discuss the Middleton case. We're not acting in collusion. Can't we enjoy what's left of the evening?"

"Whatever," Lily said, wandering around the bungalow. It appeared to have everything a person could ever need, with the special touches and warmth of a home. There was a dining room table, a kitchen, and lovely but comfortable furnishings in the detached living room, along with dozens of gadgets such as TVs, a video and DVD player, and what appeared to be a high-quality stereo system. Lily stepped through French doors into the bedroom, appreciating the fact that the room could be closed off from the rest of the cottage. Some people liked to sleep in an open space or have one room flow freely into the other. Lily preferred to sleep in a smaller room. If she awoke during the night, she didn't want to have to stumble around trying to find the bathroom only to end up on the other side of the house.

The bed itself was covered with a green linen comforter. White robes with the resort's logo emblazoned on the front were folded neatly on each side of the king-size bed, a note indicating that they could be purchased as a souvenir and were not included with the room. On the end tables were cherub candle holders containing vanilla-scented candles. The housekeeping staff must have already performed their evening duties, as the bed was turned down. Placed on an angle at the foot of the bed was a wicker tray containing bath salts, exotic oils, and a small gold box of Godiva chocolates, along with a single white orchid in a China vase.

Glancing at Lily out of the corner of his eye, Richard slipped his jacket off his shoulders, walking into the bedroom to hang it up in the closet. Lily backed into the shadows, marveling at how a man of his height could carry himself with such grace and agility. His footsteps hardly made a sound, and his arms and legs appeared to move in perfect synchronization.

"I have some fabulous wine," he said, having ordered it in advance. "One of the reasons I didn't order wine with our dinner is I didn't want Shana to feel slighted. I know she's under drinking age." He looked at her and smiled. "Another reason is this is a special French Bordeaux, bottled in 1984. I was shocked that they even had it when I called. But then, the ranch is renowned for its wine cellar."

"I'll pass on the wine, Richard," she told him. "I'm not interested in drinking right now."

He uncorked the wine, then poured two glasses. "I understand how you feel about alcohol because of John," he told her, "but let's not go overboard. My philosophy has always been that anything is all right if it's done in moderation. Doctors say a glass of wine now and then is healthy, even good for your circulation."

Richard was beginning to suspect that his plans of rekindling their romance might fizzle out, and wondered how long it would be before she asked him to drive her home. What a bitch that would be, he thought, turning away so she wouldn't be able to detect his disappointment.

"Just when I was beginning to feel comfortable in my new position, John had to call me and tell me he'd killed someone." Lily gazed at him from across the room. Since the rape she had become too conservative, too rigid. When the phone rang, she started to rush over to answer it, then realized that the call might be for Richard.

"Great," Richard said, turning his back as he listened to the caller. "Do you want to speak to your mother?" He paused, then added, "We haven't spent much time together over the past six years. We're just talking about the days when we used to work together in Ventura. You know, the kind of things folks our age do."

Lily walked over to take the phone from him, but he had already disconnected. "She's spending the night with her friend."

"Ronnie?" Lily asked, having met her when she'd attended high school with Shana in Camarillo. Since then Ronnie's family had relocated to Goleta, an area not far from the university. "Are they going out to one of those dance clubs you mentioned? I didn't think that was such a good idea, by the way. This might have been a safe city while you were growing up, Rich, but Santa Barbara has changed. It's almost like that area they renovated in Miami. What's it called? South Beach, I believe. I've got a case on my desk right now that occurred downtown near State Street where most of the nightclubs are located."

"Sorry," Richard said, hanging his head. "She didn't mention taking me up on my suggestion to go to a dance club, Lily. She just said she was going to crash at her friend's house, then drive home in the morning."

Lily rubbed her forehead. "Did you remind her what time she has to be home?"

"From what I saw tonight, Shana is responsible enough to remember what time we're getting together for breakfast." He arched an eyebrow, giving her a look that said she was being overprotective and worrisome. "She knows we're going to try to figure out how we can protect her from being implicated in the accident. Don't you think this is a meeting she wouldn't want to miss?"

"You're right," Lily said, sitting in an overstuffed chair with a matching ottoman. She leaned her head back against the plush cushion and closed her eyes. When she opened them, Richard was standing over her with a wineglass. She brought it briefly to her lips, then set it down on the end table. Removing her jacket, she tossed it on the opposite chair. Underneath, she was wearing an off-the-shoulder white sweater. She kicked her shoes off, resting her feet on the ottoman.

Richard leaned back against the bar, passed the wineglass under his nose, then took a swallow. The bottle of wine had cost him almost three hundred dollars, and she'd taken one sip, then set it aside as if it were club soda. "No matter how many problems come our way," he told her, "a person still has to extract some enjoyment from life. If not, what's the purpose of living?"

"Punishment," Lily said. "I work, I eat, I sleep, only to get up and do it all over again. I feel like a broken record. I'm certain I'm going to keep spinning around in the same circles until something inside me explodes. It's not as if it hasn't happened before."

"In that respect," Richard answered, "I'd classify you more along the lines of a hurricane than a broken record." He was trying his best to set the right mood, wanting desperately to hold her, make love to her, attempt to recapture the magic they had once shared. It wasn't merely to satisfy his physical desires. Joyce would have gladly engaged in sex with him several times a day if he had encouraged her. The woman had been an eager and accomplished sex

344

partner, but he wasn't in love with her.

For sex to be sublime and meaningful, Richard believed the participants had to possess an all-consuming desire to not only please their partners but be comfortable enough to allow them to reciprocate. Men were generally eager to accept, whereas many women, especially those raised in strict religious households such as Lily, grew up thinking pleasure was a sin. Before the rape they had been about to embark on what he considered a once-in-a-lifetime relationship. Then everything had come to a screeching halt.

Richard stared at Lily with longing. He wanted to take her to a point that transcended sex, merge with her to the degree that he could not only please her and convince her she was loved, but could manage to reach inside and extract the bitterness and hurt buried deep inside her.

With Lily, although he wasn't certain if she even discussed the situation with her therapist, the rape had reopened a wound so deep he had not been surprised that she'd killed someone. As a child she had been sexually abused by her grandfather. The night she had removed her father's shotgun from its dusty resting place in the garage, then driven to Oxnard to gun down Bobby

Hernandez, Lily had been attempting to rid the world of two demons — both the man who had raped her and her daughter, as well as the ghost of her long-dead grandfather.

Richard adjusted the dimmer switch on the light, bathing the room in a soft glow. Then he walked over to the stereo, selecting a collection of Billie Holiday's greatest hits from the CDs already in the bungalow. The legendary jazz singer's sultry voice drifted out of the recessed speakers, her voice so intimate and clear, it was as if Billie Holiday herself had crept into the room to give them a private performance.

"Dance with me," he said, walking over and pulling Lily to her feet.

They held each other, swaying back and forth to the music. "Have we ever danced?"

"No," he said, his breath brushing across her cheek. "I'm not very good."

"Neither am I," Lily whispered, trembling with emotion. "Tall girls don't get asked to dance that often, particularly redheaded tall girls. In high school I was a wallflower."

"Don't you know that tall guys *love* to dance with tall girls?" As soon as the words were spoken, Richard placed his hand on her buttocks and pulled her closer. "When a girl is too short, things don't match up as well."

She didn't understand until she felt his erection. Then she tilted her head up, her nerve endings tingling with sensation. Richard kissed her, his hands softly caressing her neck, then drifting down to her bare shoulders. He tugged on her sweater until her breasts were exposed and in his hands. She unbuttoned his pants, unzipped him, then pushed his slacks to the floor.

"Bedroom," Richard said, pointing. "I'd rather make love to you than dance."

"No." Lily was swept away with desire. The wine, the bungalow, the music, and the man had suddenly caused her inhibitions to disappear. "Over there."

He finally realized she was referring to the chair she'd been sitting in earlier. He started removing what was left of his clothing as fast as he possibly could. Lily disappeared into the other room, picking up the wicker basket with the scented oils and carrying it with her to the bathroom. When she came back out, she found a book of matches and quickly lit the candles on either side of the bed.

Richard was sprawled out in the chair waiting for her, the rest of his clothing in a heap on the floor. "Don't you know how beautiful you are?" His eyes feasted on the sensuous curves of her body, the softness of her luminous skin, the way her curly red hair bounded and moved, wild and exotic.

She stroked his abdomen, her fingers trailing through his pubic hair. Although his stomach wasn't as solid as it had been years before, he was far from flabby. "You're beautiful, too," she said, boldly placing both of her hands around his penis. A few moments later she straddled him, tossing her long hair to one side, moaning as he cupped one of her breasts in his hands, then placed the nipple in his mouth. With her free hand she reached over and turned out the light, wanting the room dark so she could enjoy his body at the same time she touched his soul. The area between her legs was pulsating, aching, wet. She could feel him pushing the crotch of her panties to one side, then stroking her with his fingers.

"God," she exclaimed, bending down to kiss him, probing the inside of his mouth with her tongue. She tasted fermented grapes from the wine, inhaled his lime-scented cologne, kissed his face, his chest, his stomach, delighting in the salty taste of his skin on her tongue.

Richard whispered, "Change places with me."

Lily was floating in another dimension, ready to walk off the edge of the world for him. She staggered in the direction of the bedroom when he caught her by the hand, then lightly pushed her back down onto the chair, spreading her legs and burying his head between them.

"Stop, don't, please." She tried to sit up. "It's too soon. I'm shy."

"Let me love you," Richard said, firmly pushing her back to a reclining position. "You weren't shy the first night we were together. Don't tell me you have to get drunk in order to let me make love to you."

As her passion took over, her body bowed upward, her head falling back into the soft cushions of the chair. She laced her fingers through his hair, wanting it to go on forever. Although the pleasure began in her genitals, she felt it moving like an electrical current — behind her forehead, down her arms. Her toes contracted in muscle spasms when she suddenly released a cry of pleasure so intense she felt as if she had become embedded in the chair. For a few moments she was unable to move, her body limp and satiated. Then she sat up, clasping his face in her hands as she kissed him.

"We can come back to this chair later," Lily told him, leading him into the bedroom with an impish grin on her face. "Since you flew me to heaven, I have to see if I can do the same for you."

"I love you, Lily," he said, falling serious. "I'll let you fly me anywhere you want. I want this night to be special."

Lily stood by the bed in the candlelight, tears of joy glistening in her eyes. "I want this to be our new beginning," she told him, her voice small and childlike. "But I have to know the past isn't going to come back and destroy me. How can I let myself love you, only to lose you like before?"

Richard engulfed her in his arms, pressing her head down on his shoulder. "I'm not going to leave you this time," he said. "I promise, Lily. We would have been together sooner if you hadn't shut me out."

"I was scared," she told him, dropping her head. "Now I'm afraid for Shana."

"Look at me," he said, lifting her chin. "I'm going to take care of you and Shana. All I'm asking is that you have faith in me, give me a chance."

Lily reached up and traced the outline of his lips with her fingers. She tossed the comforter on the floor, stretching out on her back on the bed, her arms reaching out to him. He stared at her for a long time, waiting for her to say she loved him, trusted him, knew he would do everything humanly possible to prevent anyone from ever hurting her again. Considering all she had been through, he told himself, her vulnerability and willingness to surrender herself to him were more than he could have ever expected.

"Come to me," Lily whispered, letting her arms fall back on the bed.

23

John Forrester woke up a few minutes past nine on Friday morning, his head pounding and his throat parched. He hadn't shaved in two days. Empty beer cans and fast-food wrappers littered the top of the coffee table. Since his arrest he had sworn off Jack Daniel's. As many alcoholics did, however, he mistakenly believed that beer was less harmful than other forms of alcohol.

Among the clutter on the coffee table were several hundred-dollar bills, the proceeds of his trip to the pawnshop that afternoon, minus the few items he had purchased at the grocery store. He'd pawned his watch, his wedding ring, his camera, his VCR. At least he still had his television. Five times since his arrest he had called the real estate office where he worked to see if the check he'd been waiting for had arrived. The amount was insignificant, only a few thousand dollars. On the last real estate deal he'd closed, he had kicked in more than half his commission, or the transaction would never have been completed. Today he had traveled by foot or by bus. The manager at the Prudential real estate office where he was affiliated hadn't heard the news of his arrest, and already she was threatening to give his desk space to another agent. How could he work when he didn't have a car? Regardless of whether or not he was convicted, he had to be able to provide himself with food and other essentials during the trial.

John wished he had the courage to kill himself. How could he, though, when he was terrified of what awaited him on the other side? He glanced over at a photograph of Shana and Lily on the mantel, both of them with bright smiles on their faces.

Lily had taken his daughter from him, the only reason he had left for living. She had tricked him, posting his bail, then snatching Shana right out from under him. "How could you refuse to help me?" he shouted, shaking his fists at her image. Fueled with desperation and rage, he grabbed the photo off the mantel, removed it from the frame, then used his Swiss Army knife to slice Lily's face out of the picture. Picking up his cigarette lighter off the coffee table, he touched the flame to the edge of the paper, holding it in his hands over an ashtray until there was nothing left but a smoldering pile of ashes.

This time, he decided, Lily wasn't going

to walk all over him. Picking up the portable phone off the coffee table, he read Fred Jameson's number off a scrap of paper as he punched in the numbers. After identifying himself, he said, "You left a message saying you wanted to speak to me."

"Right," Jameson said. "Where are you now, Forrester?"

"What difference does it make?"

"Just curious," the detective told him, sensing he had a hothead on his hands. "I've been trying to get in touch with you. A detective by the name of Hope Carruthers contacted me about this murder you claim your ex-wife committed. I'm not sure you're aware of it, but that crime occurred in our jurisdiction, not Los Angeles. They just kicked it over to us."

John didn't give a shit about jurisdiction. Striking out at Lily was something altogether different. He fired up another cigarette. "Are you going to reopen the case?"

Jameson had slept only a few hours the night before. They were putting the finishing touches on a case that was scheduled to go to trial in two weeks, a domestic violence homicide. Harold Bachman had battered his wife during their entire fifteen-year marriage, some of her injuries so severe she had required hospitalization. When the poor woman had finally decided to put a stop to the vicious cycle of violence and contacted a divorce attorney, her husband had pumped three bullets into her head as she walked to her car in the parking lot of the law firm.

"We'd like to get a formal statement from you," Jameson told him, sipping on his sixth cup of coffee since he had arrived at the station that morning. "I doubt if we can spare the time for another two weeks. What I'd like to do now, though, is schedule a date for you to come into the police station."

"Two or three weeks!" John exclaimed, flicking his ashes. "I don't know if those people in L.A. told you, but I've got some problems of my own right now."

Fred Jameson tossed his legs onto his desk. "Your problems are our problems, pal," he told him. "A witness with a vehicular homicide hanging over his head doesn't carry a lot of weight in the courtroom. There's also the problem of finding and reviewing the evidence. Reopening a six-year-old crime presents a lot of problems."

John crushed an empty beer can in his hand. "You're not going to do anything about it, are you? You're going to let her get away with it. Why? Because she's like a member of your little cop family."

"If you want us to nail your ex-wife," Jameson said, "watch your mouth, Forrester. I'm not in the greatest mood today, but I can assure you of one thing, I'd arrest the fucking chief if he killed someone. You can throw your code of silence baloney out the window."

"Fine," John said, stubbing out his cigarette. "But I'm afraid if you wait too long, I might be in jail."

"We'll come to you, then," the detective told him. "For the time being, why don't you start by filling me in on what you know? And don't waste my time with a bunch of hooey. Carruthers and Osborne sent me a tape of your interview with them, so there's no reason to go over old ground." He paused, gulping down the remainder of his coffee. "This isn't grade school where you can get another kid suspended by running to the principal and tattling. What kind of proof do you have that Lily Forrester killed Bobby Hernandez?"

John leaned back on the sofa, shutting his eyes as he tried to bring forth details he might have forgotten the morning he had spoken to the Los Angeles detectives. While he was thinking, he heard a beeping sound on the line. He was about to hit the flash button, thinking he had another incoming call, then realized it wasn't the same sound. "Are you recording this phone call?"

"Always," Jameson told him. "We record every call, for your protection as well as ours."

"The night of the rape," he said, speaking slowly now, "Lily asked me to take Shana back to our house in Camarillo. I didn't want to leave Lily alone . . ."

"Where were the police?"

"Lily refused to call them," John told him. "A police report would never have been filed if I hadn't reported it myself the next morning."

Jameson pushed his chair to an upright position, excited at the prospect that there might be a crucial element involved in the crime that no one had considered. The motive was obvious — Lily had killed the man she believed had raped both her and her daughter. What Forrester was telling him could be used to establish that her actions were planned, or what was legally classified as premeditation. This took the crime to a more serious level. "Why would your ex-wife refuse to call the police as soon as the crime occurred? She was a prosecutor. Of all people, she knew how important it was to secure the crime scene and collect evidence before it became contaminated. Not only that, a rape victim should undergo a medical-legal exam immediately following the assault. The most definitive way to establish the identity of the rapist is through DNA evidence found on the victim — hair, sperm, saliva, or any type of bodily secretion."

"Before I took Shana home," John continued, "Lily told me she didn't want our daughter to go through all that poking and prodding, then have to go through the trauma of testifying in court. Basically, she convinced me that the best thing for Shana would be to forget about it so she could go on with her life. She said they might never catch the rapist, and even if they did, he wouldn't serve more than a couple of years in prison. She also told me he —" John stopped, momentarily unable to continue, gripped with the pain of that night, the atrocities committed against his precious daughter.

"Please continue," Jameson said, scribbling notes to himself although he would later have a transcript made of the recording.

"Lily said the rapist hadn't ejaculated, that a siren or something had scared him off."

Jameson cracked his knuckles, thinking through what he had just heard. "What caused her to change her mind and report the crime the next morning?"

"She didn't change her mind," John said. "She stayed out all night. I was worried sick, afraid the rapist had come back and killed her. She didn't even call me to tell me she was okay." He struck himself in the chest with his fist. "I'm the one who called the police."

"Where was your wife?"

"Lily pulled into the driveway around seven or eight the next morning," John told him. "The police were already at the house talking to Shana. When I asked Lily where she'd been all night, she said she'd been so upset, she accidentally took the wrong freeway and ended up lost somewhere in downtown Los Angeles. Then when she finally figured out where she was and started driving back home, she got stuck in rush-hour traffic."

Having reviewed some of the particulars of the Hernandez homicide, Jameson asked, "Did Lily own a shotgun?"

"Yeah," John said, "she had a Browning twelve-gauge semi-automatic. I mean, it wasn't really her gun. It belonged to her father. I remember because when we split up, and she moved to that house she rented in Ventura, I'm the one who packed her stuff. There was a box of ammo as well. Lily's father used to take her deer hunting when she was a kid. The man's been dead for years, but she used to tell me how her father bragged about what a good marksman she was, how she could always hit the bull's eye when they went target shooting. I guess she kept the gun because it belonged to her father. You know, it had sentimental value to her. The reason I say that is Lily was dead-set against guns."

Now the man was finally coughing up the type of information Jameson needed to get the department to reopen the investigation. "Where's this shotgun now?"

John sighed. "I have no idea."

"You haven't seen it since the day you packed it?"

"No," he said. "To tell you the truth, I just now remembered that Lily had that gun. In the months after Shana was raped, I didn't think about anything but my daughter."

Seeing his other phone line blinking, Jameson knew he had to return his attention to the more pressing matters at hand, particularly completing the paperwork on the Bachman homicide. Thus far, Forrester had provided him with some interesting tidbits. He would love to put the screws to Lily. However, he hadn't heard enough as yet to drop what he was doing and try to convince the brass to reopen the case. "Listen, For-rester," he told him. "I'm going to check this out as soon as I free up some time. We'll be in touch."

Before John could say anything else, the detective disconnected. "Damn," he said, tossing the crushed beer can at the wall. Even though Osborne and Carruthers hadn't been willing to give him special treatment for pro-viding them with information regarding Lily and the Hernandez homicide, he thought there was a possibility that Jameson would. After his DWI arrest he'd decided that at least a third of the police officers were only a few steps away from criminals, some of them nothing more than legally sanctioned thugs. No matter what they told him, Lily was one of them. It was only a matter of time before he was convicted and sentenced to prison. Over the past two days he had come close to a level of acceptance of his fate, but he could never accept the loss of his daughter. They were all just using him, treating him like he was a joke or some kind of amusement. He'd be in prison, and Lily would still be prancing around the courtroom as if she'd never done anything wrong. "Not fair," he mumbled aloud, deciding he had to find a way to teach Lily a lesson.

Of course he was devastated over the accident, sorry that the young man had died. But nothing he could do could bring him back. He had to focus on his own life, find a way to survive.

In John's mind, the road that had led him to this point stretched far into the past. Once Lily had graduated from law school, she had decided she no longer needed him. When they had first met, she had reminded him of a gentle, wounded fawn. Looking at his daughter's image in what was left of the photo, he superimposed the youthful face of her mother gazing up in innocence, always eager to please, listen, to do whatever he said. He had picked Lily's clothes, taught her to cook, cared for her like a father. After all he had done, she had walked off and left him.

Knowledge could be a terrible thing, he thought, his bloodshot eyes gazing out over the cluttered room. How could he have imagined that attending college and obtaining her law degree would change Lily so much that she would gain such strength and independence that she no longer needed him? The woman who had talked to him like a dog on the phone the day before was not the woman he had married. The Lily he knew was gone, as dead as the boy he had struck and killed with his car. In her place was a cruel and heartless woman.

Even before the accident, Shana had taken on many of her mother's characteristics, bossing him around, failing to understand that a man was supposed to make the decisions, steer the ship, rule the roost. Even the Bible depicted women as an afterthought. His lips compressed as he wondered how women had come to believe in their own self-importance.

John picked up the phone, flicking the button off and on, trying to figure out what kind of action he could take next. Suddenly a light came on in his head. The cops and D.A.'s might hang together and protect one another, but politicians would accuse their own mother of committing a crime if the result was free publicity. He punched in the area code for Ventura information.

"I'd like the number to the mayor's office."

As soon as Fred Jameson returned from lunch Friday afternoon, Detective Keith O'Malley advised him that the captain was looking for him. "Why?" he asked, scowling. "Don't tell me they're accusing me of falsifying evidence again."

"Hey," O'Malley answered, shrugging, "I'm just the messenger."

Jameson dropped his head and shuffled

off down the corridor, stopping outside Captain Andrew Nelson's office to speak to his secretary. Monica Bell was a pretty blonde in her late twenties who appeared habitually exhausted. She had four young children to support, and the previous year her husband had abandoned her. "Good news or bad news, Monica? One of my kids was up puking all night. With my luck, I'll probably come down with whatever he's got by tomorrow."

"The flu bug is bad this year," she said, picking up a file from her in-basket. "Drink lots of hot water. That's what my grandmother used to tell me. That way you stand a chance of flushing it out of your system before it gets too bad. I have no idea why the captain wants to see you," she added, a tinge of annoyance in her voice. "You guys are all the same, you know. Every time he sends for someone, everyone asks me to tell him what he wants. Why would you think I'd know? I'm just his secretary."

"Can I go in now?"

"Be my guest," she said. "He's waiting."

Andrew Nelson was a fairly small man in his late thirties, with dark hair, a slender frame, a personality that was as dry as the desert. His expertise rested in the fact that he was an excellent administrator and had managed to obtain a master's degree in business as well as computer science. He peered up at the detective from behind wire-rimmed glasses, his computer screen blinking in the background.

"Sit," Nelson said, continuing to shuffle through some paperwork on his desk.

Jameson fidgeted in his chair, thinking the captain was intentionally making him wait. Nelson was a wimp when stacked against the men who had traditionally sat in the captain's chair before him. From what people were telling the detective, though, things were only going to get worse rather than better. A guy either went with the flow, or he would end up looking for a new occupation.

Nelson had made it to the top almost overnight, leapfrogging over men who were far more deserving and experienced. No one doubted he would become chief before he turned forty, if not in Ventura, then with a larger department. People around the office joked that he was the Bill Gates of law enforcement. The majority of men in uniform, the ones who still worked in the trenches, couldn't stand him. No one considered him a bona fide cop, not when he had served only a year in patrol before being promoted to sergeant. "You wanted to see me, sir," Jameson said, wondering how long he was going to ignore him. "I've got some pretty pressing cases on my agenda right now. You know, homicides, that type of thing." Nelson let his sarcasm pass without comment, considering it counterproductive to reprimand him. "A call came in this morning via the mayor's office regarding vital information on a six-year-old homicide."

The detective leaned forward. "Great, I'm in the process —"

"May I finish?" Nelson asked, giving him a stern look before he shifted his eyes to his computer screen, then back again. "John Forrester is listed as the reporting party on the message I received this morning from the mayor's office. He claimed he was willing to testify that his wife, Lilian Forrester, a former district attorney in our jurisdiction now actively employed in Santa Barbara, shot and killed an individual by the name of Bobby Hernandez. Mr. Forrester additionally stated that he informed the Los Angeles authorities of this information, and to date, they've failed to follow through on it. Do you know anything about this?"

Fred Jameson was rocking back and forth. Here he had thought some idiot had filed another grievance against him, and instead the biggest jerk of all time had handed him exactly what he wanted. "I'm already looking into it," he said, his speech rapid-fire. "At first I had trouble locating the files and tracking down the evidence. Yesterday, I hit pay dirt."

"What did you find?"

"Okay," Jameson said, "I feel fairly certain everything we need to take this to the D.A.'s office is intact in the property room. Last night I went down there myself and sorted through all the containers. Some stuff, of course, is on ice at the crime lab. We have sworn depositions of eyewitnesses, forensics, basically the whole ball of wax." He paused to take a breath. "Not only that, I managed to track down the Oxnard detective who originally handled the case. You might have heard of him. His name is Bruce Cunningham."

"I see," Nelson said, tapping his pen on his glass-topped desk. Even if he had at one time worked with Cunningham, he tried to clear his mind of unnecessary details such as the names of former employees. "What problems do you foresee in pursuing this, other than the fact that we have had more than our share of recent homicides?" He had already pondered the opportunities that might present themselves if John Forrester's story was true. When something sensational went down, he served as the department's press liaison. That kind of exposure could be valuable in advancing his career.

Jameson cracked his knuckles. "You do know that John Forrester has been arraigned on a vehicular-manslaughter case in Los Angeles, right?"

The captain maintained the same stoic expression. "No," he said, not liking what he was hearing. "Is the manslaughter in any way related to the Hernandez homicide?"

Jameson made a wavy motion with his hand. "It is and it isn't," he said, waiting for Nelson to nod for him to continue. "One of the investigators in Los Angeles who passed this along, Hope Carruthers, thinks Forrester might simply be trying to manipulate his ex-wife into paying his legal bills."

"Are you saying her husband fabricated the story?"

"Not at all," Jameson said, shaking his head. "I stumbled across a composite drawing of the suspect last night that would blow your mind. I don't have the actual drawing itself. Someone may have accidentally destroyed or misplaced it during the Ventura/Oxnard merger."

The captain frowned. "That's unfortunate," he told him. "It's always better to be able to provide the prosecutor with an original document."

"Yeah," Jameson said, having no desire to listen to a long-winded lecture on the preservation of evidence. "When the case was hot," he went on, "the composite was published in the local paper. I pulled it off the archives from the computer. If you hold the drawing up next to a photo of Lily Forrester from the county personnel files, the facial features are strikingly similar. This lady is shrewd, Captain. Trust me on this one, and not just because she's a district attorney. She's almost six feet tall, and from the composite, she must have disguised herself to look like a man, knowing this would throw everyone off track. Most people would never consider that such a brutal crime could be committed by a female. The autopsy photos are pretty gruesome. Not only did Hernandez have a hole in his chest almost as a big as a football, one of his arms was attached only by a few tendons."

"Your analysis, then, is the gender issue was one of the primary reasons the case was never resolved."

Jameson said, "Precisely."

"Give me the date of the article," Andrew Nelson said, "and we can pull it up right now. I have a direct link to every major newspaper and news agency."

Jameson rubbed his fist over his chin. Bully for him, he thought, tired of listening to people brag about all their links, channels, Web sites, or how they could put their fingers on just about any information they wanted in a matter of minutes. They even had computers in the patrol cars now, linked directly to what they used to call NCIC, the National Crime Information Center. When they weren't conducting police business, officers could park under a tree and surf the Net on their department-issued portable computers. It was a crazy world they were living in, and Jameson was sometimes afraid of where it was all leading.

"You were saying," Nelson said, pulling him out of his thoughts.

"I can't tell you the date off the top of my head," the detective answered. "To tell you the truth, Captain, I wasn't rushing headfirst into this for a variety of reasons." He proceeded to fill his superior in on the McDonald-Lopez homicides, the rape of Lily and her daughter, and how it all appeared to be intertwined. Then he felt he had no choice but to remind him that Lily was the person who had tarnished his career by implying that he'd falsified evidence in the Walter Evans homicide. "I mean," he added, "that Evans mess went down almost five years ago. It's doubtful if anyone even remembers."

Propping his head up with one hand, Nelson took a drink of water as he attempted to think through all the underlying issues. "O'Malley can take over," he said finally. "That way we won't have to deal with anyone claiming that you're pursuing this only because you have a personal vendetta regarding this Forrester woman."

"But that isn't fair," Jameson said. "I've already done a lot of legwork on this thing. Why should O'Malley get an opportunity like this?"

Captain Nelson shot him a black stare. "Law enforcement isn't a game, Jameson, where one person or the other has to compete for scores. No matter who serves as the lead investigator, whatever work you do will be noted."

He wasn't thrilled, but it was better than nothing. "So we're going forward, right?"

"I don't see why not," Andrew Nelson said smugly, leaning back in his chair. "A murder is a murder, and this one is intriguing and complex enough to draw national attention." He snapped his chair back to its upright position. "Ventura is not a large city, do you understand?"

"I'm there," Jameson said, standing. "You're saying it's about time we put Ventura on the map."

"Right," Captain Nelson said, a glimmer in his eyes as he glanced over at his computer. "The global map. And you know what? I think this might be the perfect ticket."

24

Lily awakened Friday morning in Richard's arms, feeling more relaxed and content than she could ever remember. Her head was nestled under his shoulder, her right leg tossed over his lower body, and the toes of her left foot were clamped onto the narrow ridge of his heel. She wondered how long he'd been awake. She watched him silently without moving, gazing lovingly at his profile — the regal slant of his nose, his lips, his strong chin. She suspected he was purposely not moving in order not to disturb her, but his eyes were open and focused on the ceiling.

"Good morning, gorgeous," Richard said, smiling as he leaned over and kissed her on the lips, memories of their night of lovemaking fresh in his mind. "You might be slow to convince, but after that you're unstoppable."

Lily cupped her hand over her mouth, grinning as she glanced up at him. "Did I wear you out?"

"I'll survive," he told her, stretching his arms over his head now that she was awake.

"What we need to do is make this a habit, not a one-night marathon."

She playfully punched him in the side. "You're embarrassing me."

"Embarrassing you," Richard said, pulling her on top of him. "I embarrassed myself last night. That's not so easy to do, at least not at my age. Now if I was eighteen, it might be different."

Lily pushed herself up on her arms. "Oh, really?"

"I hate to admit it," he continued, his dark eyes probing hers, "but I haven't been quite as chaste as you. The male biological makeup, you know. It's in our genes."

"Sounds too clinical," Lily told him, stroking his hair off his forehead.

"It's a fact." Richard lifted her off him. "I took a biochemistry class in college, thinking I could solve the mysteries of the universe. I only learned one thing. The purpose of life is to procreate. Men are genetically designed to have sex. Otherwise, the human race would have ceased to exist."

"Why are you talking about other women?" Lily asked. "Are you trying to make me jealous?"

"Nope," he said. "Just attempting to be honest."

"I'm not the jealous type," she told him,

then gave her statement a second thought. "I take that back, okay? What you did in the past doesn't matter, unless you have a disease." When he didn't answer, she assumed his sexual activity had not been irresponsible and that he had undergone routine tests as she did. Even with her rare sexual encounters, she was a stickler for safe sex. "What you do in the future might be a problem, depending on where we go with our relationship."

"I can handle that," Richard answered, stroking her breast. "But only under one condition."

"What's that?"

"You have to promise not to throw things at me."

Lily was puzzled. "Why would you say that?"

"Don't ask."

She kissed his mouth, his chin, his stomach, then began moving down his body before he gently pushed her away.

"I never thought I'd live to say this," he said, propping several pillows behind his head, "at least not to you, anyway. But the only way I could perform right now is if you can arrange an immediate transplant."

The lower halves of their bodies were still covered by the sheet. Lily yanked the sheet off. When she saw his penis, she had to force herself to keep from laughing. The skin was red and inflamed. It reminded her of a hot dog roasted over an open flame. She pointed at her chest. "Did I do that?"

"Unless there was someone else in the bed with us," Richard said, touching his genitals and then grimacing.

"How could someone with your coloring have such sensitive skin?"

"Ah," he said, pulling on a strand of her hair, "it's my sensitive skin, right? It couldn't have anything to do with the fact that we thrashed around in bed until after four this morning. If I'm not mistaken, the last thing I remember is you calling me your 'little pony.' I don't mind you referring to me as a pony," he continued, "but I don't care much for the word *little*."

Lily's lovely face was flushed with the glow of a woman well loved, her red hair drenched in a streak of vibrant sunlight. Her problems suddenly seemed unimportant. "I think I know where the little pony remark came from," she told him. "Shana had a book with that title when she was in kindergarten. I used to read it to her every night. The book even came with a little pony necklace." When she finally stopped laughing, she sat up and pulled the sheet up over her body. "Are you complaining?"

"Of course not," Richard said, climbing out of bed to head to the bathroom. "I'll buy some cream at the drugstore. By tonight I should be ready for an encore."

A few moments later, Richard poked his head out of the bathroom to tell her it was already after seven. Lily was sitting with her legs crossed, a serene, otherworldly look in her eyes, almost as if she were meditating.

"I hate to disturb you," he said. "But we better get moving. You don't want Shana to get to your place before we do. Then you won't be able to keep her from finding out we spent the night together."

"Oh," Lily said, giving him a blank stare, "it doesn't matter if she finds out. I'll probably tell her eventually."

"Boy," Richard said, "did you do a hundred and eighty-degree turn-around here or am I crazy?"

"I'm a woman," Lily told him. "Women change their minds, remember?" Even though she'd given him a light-hearted answer, she felt different. What they had shared was not only pleasurable, but in some way uniquely profound.

The feeling reminded her of a picture on the bedroom wall of her rented cottage, a reproduction of a painting entitled *Embrace*, by an Austrian artist named Egon Schiele. She had become intrigued with not only the sensuous nature of the painting, but because she'd spent hours staring at it during the nights when she couldn't sleep. Coincidentally, the artist had painted it in 1917, the same year her mother had been born. It depicted a man and a woman reclining on what appeared to be a blue sheet, the fabric rippling beneath them like waves in the ocean. Thumbing through art books at the Tecolote Book Shop in Montecito one day, Lily had found the painting in a book compiled by an art historian and nun named Sister Wendy Beckett. The author had explained that those who viewed the *Embrace* were allowed to witness the mystical enigma of what she referred to as a *true embrace*, meaning the couple in the painting were uniting and each was becoming the other.

"Aren't you going to get dressed?"

Lily walked into the bathroom, hugging Richard from behind while he smeared shaving cream on his face. "Thank you," she said, her eyes moist with tears. "I believe last night did change me. I don't know how exactly. I only hope it lasts forever."

Richard said jokingly, "Don't lay it on

too thick, Lily. I haven't forgotten what you and Shana said about guys who pay them too many compliments."

"I'll meet you at the restaurant," Richard said, leaning over and kissing Lily before she got out of the car in front of her guest house. Just as he drove off, she realized she was locked out. The key to her cottage had been on the same ring as her car keys. Now she'd have to wait outside until Shana returned, and her daughter would know she had spent the night with Richard. Lily might have said she didn't mind her knowing they were lovers, but she wasn't prepared to tell her right at that moment.

Lily had hidden a spare key somewhere on the property. Since she had never needed it, she'd forgotten where it was hidden. She suddenly panicked, certain Curazon had found the key, then used it to enter the cottage and steal the portrait of Shana. Her fears were magnified by the fact that the key to Shana and John's duplex had also disappeared from her key ring.

Where had she put it? She couldn't ask the owners to let her in, as they were on vacation in Europe. Finally she raced around to the side yard, whipped off the brown tarp covering the barbecue grill, and pulled a small magnetized box about the size of a matchbook off the top of the inside lid to the cooker. Someone had given the box to her as a Christmas gift one year.

Once she was inside the house, her eyes went to the end table where the missing picture and envelope had been. Now that she had found the key, she tried to regain her earlier sense of well-being.

Why would Curazon replace the key, she asked herself, if he had found it and used it to gain entrance to the house? She couldn't fathom him going to the trouble of making a duplicate, then returning to replace the original in the little box hidden inside the barbecue.

From what she had learned about him following his arrest, Curazon was a seriously disturbed individual. He had been severely abused by his mother as a young boy. Most people didn't realize that rape was a crime of violence, that sex was only the weapon, similar to a gun or a knife. Men raped to punish, inflict pain, gain power over their victim. In Curazon's case, he had raped to alleviate his own emotional pain. He was a sexual predator who acted on impulse, one of the reasons she didn't believe he had removed her key, then replaced it with a duplicate.

Wanting to change her clothes from the night before, Lily rushed to the bedroom and selected a pair of black slacks and a purple knit top. When she heard what sounded like the front door opening, she clutched the knit blouse in her hands, her pulse pounding.

"Mom," Shana called out. "Are you here?"

"I'm getting dressed," she answered, pulling the top over her head and walking out to the living room. "How was your visit?"

Lily's night of bliss with Richard seemed weeks behind her, and the lack of sleep showed on her face. Under her eyes were dark circles, and her naturally curly hair was more unruly than normal.

"Okay, I guess," Shana said, sitting on the sofa, then picking up a package of gum off the table. "You look exhausted, Mom. How long did you stay over there with Richard?"

"We have to hurry." Lily glanced at her watch, wanting to tell her the truth but knowing it wasn't the right time to engage in such an intimate discussion. "We're supposed to meet Richard at the restaurant in less than ten minutes," she added. "I'm also going to have to stop by the office, but you can come with me. All I intend to do is show my face, then download some case files from my computer. Later this afternoon we'll drive over to the university and check things out."

"I don't want to transfer to Santa Barbara," Shana protested, smacking on her chewing gum. "Ronnie even wants to switch to another school, maybe UCLA. Most of the people she introduced me to last night were airheads."

"It can't be that bad."

"Oh, really?" she said. "The ones who aren't potheads are into that silly retro stuff with the big band music and old-fashioned dancing. They bored me to death talking about their stupid costumes."

Lily hadn't expected her to return home in such a bad mood. Her daughter's sour attitude was causing her earlier cheerfulness to take a nosedive. "Aren't the young people in L.A. into the same scene?"

"Who cares?" Shana said, standing. "The only scene I'm into is trying to finish college so I can go to law school. I've only gone out on two dates this past year, Mom. The kids last night are wasting their parents' money."

Lily walked over and hugged her. "That's why I'm so proud of you, sweetheart." When she pulled back, she said, "Let's have a nice breakfast, listen to what Richard has to say, then we'll attempt to solve some of your problems this afternoon."

As they were about to leave, Lily came up with another idea. "Maybe I can find a way to rent you an apartment. We'll pick up an L.A. newspaper this afternoon. We could get lucky and find a college girl around your age who's looking for a roommate."

"We could do that over the Internet," she told her, jangling the key ring. "What about Dad, though? Isn't that why you told me not to stay in L.A.?"

"I was only concerned if you stayed in the duplex," Lily told her. "And besides, if you have a roommate, he won't be able to pressure you into letting him live with you."

Shana removed her lipstick from her backpack, putting it on without a mirror, then blotting her lips on a tissue. "Dad isn't going to put pressure on me over *anything*," she said, her voice firm with conviction. "Right now I don't care if he jumps off a bridge. I can't even stand thinking about him, I hate him so much."

"Don't say that," Lily answered, scowling. "It's one thing to be angry because of what he did, but you shouldn't hate anyone."

"Not even when they kill someone?" Shana shouted, kicking the rear tire of the Audi.

"No," Lily told her. "Hate will eat you up inside. I lost six years of my life because of it."

Shana refused to let it go. "The guy Dad ran over was my age, Mom. He even went to UCLA. Maybe I can get another place like you said, but people are going to find out. If the police don't come after me, people will still know my father killed someone."

"It's a big school," her mother said, placing her hand on one side of her neck. "You're the one who brought that point up to the detectives. I think you're worrying about the wrong things right now."

"Right, sure," Shana said, her eyes blazing with intensity as she paced around in a circle in the driveway. "Why don't you just put me in a nut house? That would solve all my problems. Then I wouldn't have to worry about Dad. I wouldn't have to find another place to live, change schools, stay up all night certain Curazon or some other creep is going to rape me." She walked over and spat the words in her mother's face. "You said I shouldn't be bitter, that I shouldn't hate. Tell me how to do that, Mom! Go on, tell me!"

Lily shook her head, knowing there was nothing she could say to console her. Even though her heart was being wrenched, what her daughter needed was to vent. The only thing she could do was listen and love her. She felt guilty for spending the night with Richard, for experiencing pleasure when her child was suffering such emotional pain. She watched as Shana shoved a pair of sunglasses on her nose, seeing how badly her hands were shaking. The girl was desperately trying to hold herself together, find the necessary strength to continue functioning.

"It's bad enough knowing that my mother killed someone," Shana said, glancing back at Lily as she headed to the passenger side of the car. "At least I know you had a reason."

Lily's mouth fell open. Black spots danced in front of her eyes. The blood drained from her face, and she felt as if she were about to pass out. She knew! There was no doubt now that her daughter knew the truth.

Tossing her backpack into the backseat, Shana said, "Did you think I didn't know? I even know who you killed, that it wasn't the man who raped us. I figured it out a long time ago. You killed the guy whose picture was in the newspaper clipping, the one who murdered the prostitute and butchered those two teenagers."

Lily spun around, starting to rush back into the house.

Shana chased after her, grabbing her by the arm. "Wait," she said. "I might hate Dad, but I don't hate you. I understand what you did. You were protecting me, making certain no one ever hurt me again. You risked everything for me . . . your career, your freedom, even your life."

"I — I was wrong," Lily stammered, choking up with tears. "No one should take the law into their own hands. When I told you I had lived with hatred all these years, I wasn't talking about Marco Curazon. I hated myself, Shana. That's the worst punishment of all. That's why I told you not to hate your father. No matter how many years he serves in prison, he'll spend the rest of his life regretting what he did, reliving the horror of that moment, pleading to God for forgiveness."

"I hope he does," Shana said, kissing her tenderly on the cheek.

The two women seemed frozen in time, locked inside the moment, merged together like the picture on the wall in Lily's bedroom. Daughter became mother and mother became daughter, divinely entwined, yet each with her unique brand of wisdom.

"I just want you to know one thing," Shana continued. "I would have done the same thing you did. Maybe you're right about me not hating Dad, but sometimes people do things that are so awful, they don't deserve to live."

25

"Thanks," John said, picking up an envelope with a check from the receptionist at the real estate firm where he was employed. It was five-thirty on Friday evening, and everyone had already left for the day. The only person remaining in the office was the receptionist, and he had caught her just as she was preparing to leave. "Tell Martha I'll call her next week. My mother's sick. I didn't realize it was so serious when I called in and spoke to her yesterday."

"The flu?" the girl asked, using a tissue to blow her nose.

"No," John lied, "she has cancer. She's not expected to live."

"I'm sorry."

"Thanks," he answered, rushing out the door to cash the check at the bank down the street before it closed.

Exiting the bank, he shoved the money into his brown leather jacket and used his cell phone to call a cab, instructing the driver to take him to an area off Pico Boulevard where there were a number of used-car lots. What he wished he could do was lease a car. That way he wouldn't have to spend what little cash he had. But since his credit was lousy, he assumed it would be a waste of time to even try to get a company to lease him a car. He had approximately twenty-five hundred dollars, and after the phone call he'd made that morning to the mayor's office, extorting additional money from Lily was out of the question.

"Turn around," he suddenly told the cab driver, placing his hand on the back of the front seat. "Take me back to the same place you picked me up."

"Hey, buddy," said the driver, a long-haired man in his early forties. "You want to go back where you came from, that's fine with me. You still got to pay me." He stepped on the brake, turning around and sizing up his passenger. "Let me see the money. I got kids to feed."

"Here," John said, flashing a wad of bills. "I left something in my office, okay? I'm going to pay you to wait while I run in and get what I need."

As they traveled back down the same street, John sat with his hands folded in his lap, gazing out the window at Mother Nature's exquisite display of colors — the deep pinks and vibrant blues, the muted greens, the intriguing shapes of the clouds. He'd never been much of a nature buff, but with the thought of a prison sentence looming over his head, he wondered how many more sunsets he would see.

Using his key to enter the building, he headed toward the back office, where the desk of a highly successful agent named Bryant Montgomery was located. Taking a seat in his chair, he booted up his computer. John hadn't kept up with all the recent advancements in computer technology, but Shana had taught him a great deal since he had entered real estate. He knew Bryant was addicted to buying things over the Internet, particularly stuff at auctions. In addition, he knew the code words he used to access all his files and personal data. One day while Bryant was bidding on an antique mirror for his wife, he had called John over to watch. He couldn't help noticing the man's code, as it was so easy to remember. Bryant used his name, plus the numbers on the outside of the building: 1276. He assumed, like everyone else, he'd picked a code he was certain he wouldn't forget.

Not only did people shop on-line, they paid their bills, shifted information from one computer to another. In less than five minutes, John had a piece of paper with

Bryant's Social Security number, his driver's license number, listings of his various bank account numbers, even his passport number. Just as he was about to leave the office, he realized the car dealership would require some type of photo ID. "Damn it," he said, feeling as if he might as well toss this plan in the trash can. He went to the water cooler and snatched a paper cup out of the holder, filling it with water and guzzling it down.

Through the front windows John saw the taxi waiting at the curb. He'd probably wasted his money having the cab driver sit there with the meter running. Most dealerships stayed open until eight or nine o'clock, yet even if he talked them into letting him take the car without showing them his driver's license, they wouldn't be able to process a lease this late in the day. He wanted the car tonight. The only solution was to take off, possibly hide out in Las Vegas, see how long he could survive before the police caught up to him. Why should he care if Lily forfeited the bail money when he failed to appear in court? And leaving town might even benefit Shana. In most instances the police considered it evidence of guilt when a person fled. Even if he never saw his daughter again, at least he could feel he'd done something *worthwhile* in her behalf.

Lily and Richard were seated on the enclosed patio to the rear of his bungalow at San Ysidro Ranch at seven-thirty Friday evening. He had tracked down his son, Greg, at his apartment in San Diego. Wanting the two young people to feel as if they could speak freely, he had insisted that Shana use the phone in the bedroom, closing the glass-paneled French doors.

Lily said, "I can't come back later, you know."

"I understand," he said, swirling his brandy in the glass. "We were up late last night, anyway. You and Shana had a difficult day. We could all benefit from a good night's sleep."

Richard had arranged for them to dine in the room, as he'd suggested the night before. She had called to cancel, but he had persisted, reminding her that she and Shana would have to eat somewhere and he was persuasive enough to get them to drive over. Since Lily lived alone and the kitchen in the guest house wasn't that well equipped, she seldom cooked, outside of making herself a bowl of soup or heating up something in the microwave.

Shana had been withdrawn, saying only a few words during the time they were eating.

Richard had tried his best to salvage the evening. He'd told jokes, stories, then finally come up with the idea of attempting to get Greg on the phone. Regardless of his efforts, the evening had not been enjoyable. The three of them seemed to share the same ominous feeling — that they were in some type of holding pattern.

Richard was concerned about Lily, but his concern for her daughter was even more pronounced, particularly since her mother had told him the details of their conversation that morning. How tragic, he thought, that a decent, bright girl such as Shana had to carry such a tremendous burden — the knowledge that both of her parents had caused another person to lose his life.

"We made some progress this afternoon," Lily told him, setting her coffee cup down on the table beside her. "Shana found several ads on the Internet. You know, girls looking for roommates near the campus in Los Angeles."

"Tell her to be careful," he said, scowling. "Some of those girls might turn out to be dirty old men. Besides, didn't you tell me you wanted her to transfer to the university here so you could spend more time with her?"

"My primary goal at the moment is to get these problems off her back." She paused, trying to recall the details of their afternoon. "At least one good thing happened today."

"What's that?"

"When we stopped by my office," Lily told him, managing a weak smile, "Matt Kingsley, the young attorney serving as my co-counsel on the Middleton case, took Shana for a ride in his Ferrari while I was downloading files to my laptop. She thought he was better-looking than Brad Pitt."

"How old is this guy? Is he married?"

"Twenty-eight and single," Lily said, shifting her eyes to him. "I don't know if he has a steady girlfriend or not. We've never talked about his personal life. To be honest, I prefer it that way. He seemed enthralled with Shana, though."

"I don't know if I would encourage that situation," Richard said, leaning forward over his knees. "Just because the guy works with you doesn't mean you can trust him with your daughter. The way you've described him, he sounds like trouble."

"Matt's a good guy," she said, laughing at his fatherly demeanor. "Anyway, I wasn't suggesting that she should date him. Seeing her smile was nice, that's all."

"Hey," Richard said, shrugging, "you're her mother."

He looked up at the night sky. The moon was out, the temperature brisk; the smell of burning firewood filled the air. The evening took him back to the Christmas he had spent with his family only a few weeks after his father had passed away. Everything had been perfect — the food, the tree, the brightly wrapped presents. Under the shadow of his father's death, however, it had been impossible to feel festive. "Speaking of Middleton, how much time have you spent with Betsy?"

"I dropped by the hospital this afternoon," Richard said, taking a sip of his brandy. "It's a tragic situation. I understand what you meant the other day. Keeping her alive at this stage seems almost cruel."

"But you still believe Henry is innocent?"

"Yes, I do," Richard said. "You should know me well enough to know I would never agree to represent a man I believed had poisoned his own child."

"If Henry didn't poison her," Lily asked, "who did?"

"I wish I knew," Richard answered pensively. "It was either a maniac, her mother, or another family member. How can we be certain someone didn't put strychnine in that candy at the plant?"

"Don't you think we pursued that angle? We almost demanded a recall, but after testing hundreds of batches of the stuff, we couldn't get the government to support us."

"There're too many possibilities," Richard said. "We may never find out who committed this crime. Just because Henry isn't the most ethical businessman doesn't mean he was ruthless enough to poison his child to save his business."

"We have a witness who saw him buying the candy."

"She must have mistaken him for someone else."

"She identified Middleton," Lily shot out. "Not only that, she remembered the car — a red Ford Explorer. She even stated that a woman resembling Carolyn Middleton and several other children remained outside in the car while Henry went inside to purchase the candy."

"Greg bought a car recently."

Lily did a double take, thinking Richard was purposely changing the subject because he didn't want to admit that Middleton was guilty. She then reminded herself that this was not a man who wasted his energy on small talk. "Now you're going to tell me he bought a Ford Explorer, right?"

"Yeah," he said, smirking. "It's not red, though, and it's an older model than the one the Middletons and God knows how many other families own." Before she could respond, he held up a finger. "The key word in that sentence was *families*, Lily. Your witness identified a popular family car and a common everyday occurrence with people with children. How many times a day, in some part of the county, do a man, woman, and a couple of children drive up to a convenience store in a red Ford Explorer? And in many instances either the husband or the wife enters the market, leaving the rest of the family outside in the car."

"I can buy that," Lily said, thinking they were holding their pretrial conference under fairly strange conditions. Since they were both occupied with other things, talking about the case seemed practical, as long as neither one of them crossed the line. "There are other factors, Richard. Our entire case doesn't rest on this one witness. Don't come to court with that in mind, or you're going to lose."

"Just hear me out," Richard said, his commanding courtroom demeanor taking hold. "The woman didn't write down the license plate. Unless she left the register, there's no way she could have gotten a good enough look at the people inside the car to make a positive ID of either Carolyn Middleton or the children. Regarding Henry, how many cases of mistaken identity do you think have occurred in the criminal justice system over the past twenty years? A hundred, a thousand, maybe ten thousand. We don't really know, do we? Why? Because a large number of people are serving time in prison for crimes they didn't commit. As sad as it is for people in our profession, innocent people are also put to death. You, of all people, should understand the point I'm attempting to make."

"I don't think I need you to remind me," Lily snapped, thinking he was hitting below the belt. "Here I have to carry all this guilt because I shot the wrong man, and the man I should have killed is still terrorizing us."

"The police are looking for Curazon," Richard told her, thinking he had picked the wrong time to argue his viewpoints on the Middleton case. "If it will give you some peace of mind, I can sleep on the sofa at your place tonight."

"No," Lily said, shaking her head. "I called the Santa Barbara P.D. and asked them to have a unit watch my place. Besides, I don't want Shana —" She stopped and sucked in a breath. "You should have told me as soon as you heard that Curazon was carrying around a picture of Shana."

"I didn't want to alarm you," he explained. "This thing with the picture may only be a coincidence. For all we know,

Curazon could have shown the guy an actual photograph of some woman he's been dating. You know the psychological profile of men who commit these types of crimes. It isn't uncommon for them to seek out relationships with women who resemble their former victims."

"None of this stuff with Curazon is a coincidence," Lily said, adamant. "It all fits, don't you see? He had to have been inside the guest house. The key to the duplex disappeared, along with the envelope with Shana's address on it. That's why I don't want her to go back there."

Richard ran his hands through his hair. "I thought you said there were no signs of forced entry. I've searched for months for things I've misplaced. Then one day they just turn up. The more emphasis you place on the Curazon situation, the less strength you're going to have to help Shana during this ordeal she's facing with her father and the accident."

Lily scooted her chair even closer to him. "I got into a screaming match with John yesterday," she said, nervously scratching her shoulder. "He believes I'm the one who told Shana not to talk to him. Then when I told him I expected him to be out of the duplex by Monday, he started threatening to turn me in to the police again."

"You've already told me," Richard said. "You didn't answer my question, Lily. How do you think Curazon managed to get inside your place? Did you change the locks when you moved in?"

"No," she told him. "I could have accidentally left the door unlocked one day. He could have found my spare key, for that matter." She saw him grimace, and impulsively shouted, "Okay, I was an idiot to keep a key hidden on the property."

He pointed toward the window, reminding her that if she didn't want her daughter to overhear their conversation, she would have to lower her voice.

"I realize most criminals know people hide spare keys," Lily whispered, rubbing her forehead. Why did she do such foolish things? Hadn't she learned the worst lesson any woman could learn when it came to personal safety? She did stupid things because she was habitually preoccupied. When they had worked together, she'd seen Richard in the same state — times when he'd fallen into such a deep state of concentration that she'd practically had to kick him to get his attention. "Curazon may have crawled through an open window," she continued. "I felt safe there, don't you see? I let my guard down.

Now I'll have to get a security system installed right away. The only problem is, I can't do it without getting permission from the owners."

"Why would they care?" he rationalized. "All you're doing is improving their property. You'll be paying the monthly expense."

"My landlords area way in Europe until next month," Lily said, a sudden breeze lifting her hair off the nape of her neck. "What makes it so terrifying is the man Shana saw prowling around outside the duplex the night of the hit-and-run. It had to have been Curazon, Richard. Thank God I called the police that night. They must have pulled up just in time to scare him off."

"Well," he said, "at least she's with you now."

Lily rolled her neck around to relieve the tension. "Maybe this is what he's been waiting for."

"What do you mean?" he asked, swallowing the few drops of brandy left in his glass.

"How could you forget?" Lily's eyes glazed over with fright, memories from the past surrounding her. "We were together when he raped us."

She glanced at the bedside clock. It was al-

most eleven o'clock. Lily started to retrieve her briefcase from the living room to go over a few cases, but she couldn't muster up the energy and instead removed her clothing and climbed under the covers, thinking that tonight sleep might come. Almost euphoric knowing her daughter was asleep in the new four-poster bed across the hall and the evening had gone so well, she turned off the light. It then dawned on her that she had not checked the doors, a chore John had always handled before their separation.

With her terry-cloth robe wrapped loosely around her, she padded barefoot into the kitchen, deciding to check the kitchen door first. It was a quiet neighborhood: no cars, no barking dogs, just blissful stillness.

Entering the kitchen, she saw the drapes billowing in the slight breeze, being sucked through the open sliding-glass door. She chastised herself for not locking it but felt the area was so safe, it probably wasn't even necessary. As she pushed the drapes aside and started pulling the door in the track, a funny feeling came over her, a sense of something amiss. Holding her breath in order to hear better, she heard a squeak, like the sound of a basketball player's sneakers on the court.

It all happened at once: the noise behind her, her heart beating so fast it hurt, her robe pushed up from the floor over her face with lightning speed. As she struggled to scream and free her-

self, her feet slid out from under her, but she did not fall. What must be an arm was placed directly over her mouth. Trying to sink her teeth into the arm, she bit a mouthful of terry-cloth instead. She was nude from the waist down and felt the cold night air against her lower body. Her bladder emptied, splashing against the tile floor.

She tried to move her arms, but they were trapped across her chest inside the robe. Kicking out furiously, her foot connected with what must be a kitchen chair, and it screeched across the floor, landing with a loud thud against the wall.

The backs of her calves and her feet were burning, and she knew she was being dragged down the hall — toward where her daughter slept. Shana, she thought. Oh God, no, Shana! The only sound she emitted was a muffled, inhuman groan of sheer agony coming from her stomach through her vocal cords to her nasal passages. Her mouth would not move. Her feet struck something. The wall? No longer kicking — no longer struggling, she was praying: " . . . as I walk through the Valley of Death . . ." She couldn't remember the words. Flashes of the past were meshed with the present. Not Shana, not her child — she had to protect her child.

"Mom." She heard her voice, first questioning and childlike, and then the terror of her sickening high-pitched scream reverberated in

Lily's head. She heard something heavy crash into the wall, body against body, the sound heard on a football field when the players collided. He had her. He had her daughter.

In another moment they were on the bed in Lily's bedroom. When he removed his arm, the robe fell away and she could see him in the light from the bathroom. Shana was next to her and he was over them both. Light reflected off the steel of the knife he held only inches away from Lily's throat. His other hand was on Shana's neck. Lily grabbed his arm, and with the abnormal strength of terror she almost succeeded in twisting his arm backward, turning the knife toward him, seeing in her mind the blade entering his body where his heart beat. But he was too strong and with eyes wild with excitement, darting back and forth, his tongue protruding from his mouth, he forced the blade sideways into her open mouth, the sharp edges nicking the tender edges of her lips. She bit down on the blade with her teeth, her tongue touching something crusty and vile. His face was only inches away, his breath rancid with beer. "Taste it," he said, a look of pleasure on his face. "It's her blood."

"Lily!" Richard shouted, leaping out of his chair. She had been sitting there silently, staring off into space when she suddenly struck out at him, shattering the wineglass in his hand.

"My God," she exclaimed, "you're bleeding. What happened?"

"I don't know," he said, wrapping his hand in a white napkin, the crimson blood soaking through almost instantly. "You were just sitting there when you began flinging your arms around."

"I'm sorry," Lily said, forcing back the memories. "Is it bad?"

Richard let her take his hand and look at the wound. A sliver of broken glass was embedded in his palm. "I feel terrible," she said. "Do you have a pair of tweezers?"

With his left hand Richard quickly plucked out the piece of glass, then held the napkin pressed tightly against the wound to stop the flow of blood. "It's nothing, Lily," he told her. "In a few minutes it will probably stop bleeding."

"Let me see it again," Lily protested, still fighting off the terrifying images from the night of the rape.

"No," he said, taking another look at it. "It's not that deep. I'll be fine. You and Shana need to go home, try to get some rest."

Lily glanced in through the window and saw that Shana was still talking to Greg. They were both pleased when they observed the animated expression on her face and heard her laughing. Entering the bungalow, Lily tiptoed over and closed the French doors; her daughter was so preoccupied, she didn't notice.

"Come on, Richard." Lily grabbed a piece of the hotel's stationery and dashed off a note to Shana, telling her that they had gone for a drive and would return shortly. Leaving the note on the dining room table, she told Richard, "There's a Von's down in the village. That's a nasty cut and I don't want it to get infected. We'll take my car and pick up some bandages and disinfectant."

Richard protested. "You're making a big deal out of nothing, Lily."

She placed her hands on her hips. "Would you rather go to the emergency room?"

"No," he said, shuffling behind her and grudgingly climbing into the passenger seat of the Audi.

"Sign here, Mr. Montgomery," Norm Reynolds said, sliding a lease agreement on a metallic blue Buick LeSabre across his desk. An African American in his mid-twenties, Reynolds was a good-looking young man, dressed in a brown turtleneck sweater and matching slacks. He was excited that he'd managed to close another deal in time to make the weekly stats, even if he did have to stay past the dealership's nine o'clock closing time. There was still time to go home, shower, then swing by and pick up his girlfriend. He'd already called her and told her, bragging that he would be posted on the board as salesman of the week come Monday. She was home primping for their big night out on the town.

John quickly forged the name Bryant Montgomery in the spots where Reynolds had affixed small red tags, then handed the stack of papers back to him. "What do we do next? I've got something important on the burner. One of my biggest clients is arriving at LAX tonight. I can't afford to leave him waiting at the gate. He's looking at homes in the two-million-dollar range."

Reynolds stood, deciding he would have to check out the real estate profession. From the financial information Mr. Montgomery had provided, the man was raking in a pile of bread. He'd listed his income as thirty thousand per month. "What kind of commission would you make if this guy bought a house in that price range, if you don't mind me asking?"

"Oh," John said, "I'd estimate around forty grand. My client is a high-level executive with Microsoft. Need I say more?"

"Real estate sounds like my kind of game,"

the young man said, quickly stapling all the forms together. "How long would it take me to get a license?"

"I'd be happy to tell you all about it," John told him. "But like I said, I've got to get to the airport. Being Friday night and all, I could get stuck in traffic. My client might get pissed and decide to take his business elsewhere."

"We'll get you out of here," Reynolds assured him, circling around to the front of the desk. For some reason, when people bought cars they wanted them immediately. He might not be selling million-dollar estates like this Montgomery guy, but a person couldn't just walk in off the street and expect to drive off in a new car in the time it took to pick out a pair of tennis shoes. "All I need now is a copy of your driver's license and a check for the deposit," he told him, "and then you'll be out the door. You already called your insurance man, right?" As soon as John nodded, he continued. "Are you going to leave your other car here on the lot and come back for it in the morning? If so, make certain it's inside the gate."

"My wife dropped me off," John lied, relieved the man hadn't seen him pulling up in a cab. "This car is a surprise gift for my wife's birthday." He remembered how jealous he'd been when Lily had given Shana the Mustang for her high school graduation, realizing why he had fabricated that particular story. He reached into his pocket as if he were going for his wallet, then came up with the folded-over stack of hundreds. "What in the hell —" he exclaimed, making a show of patting down all his pockets, then looking around as if he thought his wallet might have fallen out on the floor. "Someone must have picked my pocket when I was walking around at the shopping center a few hours ago. I had several checks in there as well."

Reynolds glanced at the rolled-up bills on the desk. "Why would a thief snatch your wallet and not go after your cash? Did you carry your wallet and money in the same pocket?"

"No," John said, brushing his palm over the top of his head. "I usually carry my wallet in my back pocket." He swept the bills up, quickly putting them away before one fell under the desk. "I'll give you the six hundred for the deposit in cash. My driver's license number is on the lease application, so you've already verified I have a valid license."

Reynolds was beginning to get antsy, afraid he was going to ruin his own plans for the evening. He couldn't afford to blow his job, however. "I'm not supposed to let you take the car without a photo ID."

"Look," John told him, noting a slight tremor in his hand, making him even more uneasy. "I've not only got this big customer coming in, the whole family is counting on me bringing home the car for my wife's birthday. You've seen my credit history," he said. His need for a drink was getting stronger with each passing moment. "You've got enough to write a book on me. Want a photo ID, take a damn picture of me with one of those fancy computer cameras everyone owns these days."

"Take the car, okay?" Reynolds said, not wanting to lose the deal. "Just get in touch with our leasing agent as soon as you get another license."

"You're a good man," John said, shaking his hand.

26

"Now that I've talked your ear off," Shana said, adjusting the pillows behind her head, "why don't you tell me about your job at Sea World?"

"It's not the money they pay me," Greg Fowler told her. "I just resent the fact that the dolphins I work with have to spend their lives performing stunts. They belong in the ocean with other dolphins."

"Now, wait a minute," Shana argued, "if we didn't have zoos and places like Sea World, people would lose interest in certain forms of animal life, even stop giving money to institutions to preserve them. Sea World might be a tourist attraction, Greg, but it's also a place to protect your precious dolphins and a lot of other sea life that might never survive in some of our polluted waters."

"Dolphins are special," he said. "Last summer I interned at a place in Hawaii where people with physical and emotional disabilities flew in from all over the world to work with the dolphins."

Shana unwrapped a piece of gum and placed it in her mouth. "Don't you mean they *swam* with the dolphins? I've never heard of anyone *working* with them, unless they're feeding them or cleaning the tank the way you do." She stopped and laughed. "Dolphins don't have jobs at this place, do they? If they do, they'll have to give them a paycheck."

"You're making fun of me. I'm trying to tell you something."

"Sorry," she said, twirling a strand of her hair around her finger. "I'm being awful to everyone lately. Don't ask me why, because I'm not going to tell you. Just finish the rest of your story."

"Let me explain," he continued. "Some dolphins can sense where a person's physical weakness is, almost like an underwater doctor. If someone who is disabled or sick swims with them, the dolphins will actually provide support for the part of that person's body that's been weakened either by illness or injury. I've seen children who were miraculously healed, even some who had spinal cord injuries."

"That's incredible," Shana said. "The way I feel about people right now, maybe I should go to Hawaii and swim with your dolphins."

"Not unless I can go with you."

Shana's ear had gone numb from their lengthy phone call, even though she had shifted from one ear to the other several times. "I better go now," she told him. "My mother's probably chomping at the bit right now. And you can imagine how much this phone call is going to cost your dad."

"Don't worry," Greg reassured her, "Dad's got plenty of money. The problem is, he can't find anything worth spending it on, and he certainly isn't going to give it to me. He's tough, you know, thinks everyone has to make their own way."

"Hey," she replied, thinking of how hard her mother had struggled, "at least he's able to pay for your education. A lot of my friends have had to drop out of school. Next semester I'm going to get a job and see if I can't take care of my own expenses."

Telling Greg she was looking forward to seeing him in the near future, Shana hung up and went outside to find her mother. When she discovered the note on the dining room table, she was certain Richard and Lily had snuck over to her mother's guest cottage to have sex. She went back to the bedroom and curled up on the bed, quickly falling asleep.

★ ★ ★

En route to the duplex, John stopped off at the liquor store and bought a fifth of Jack Daniel's, then walked next door to the newsstand to pick up a Las Vegas newspaper, wanting to check out the classified section and see what kinds of jobs were listed. He subscribed to the *L.A. Times*, but he'd been too distraught to read it that morning. Something compelled him to pick the paper up off the stand, sensing there might be something inside regarding the accident. When he found what he feared — the article about the death of the young man he had killed, his name in print for all to see — he staggered backward, dropping his head and ducking back into the car.

At least the article didn't contain a picture of him. It did state, however, that he had been arraigned on charges of vehicular manslaughter. What choice did he have now but to flee, attempt to establish a new identity? He was no longer John Forrester, loving father. His family name was now publicly vilified. Even if they failed to convict him, he knew his life would never be the same.

While driving to the duplex, John remembered a recent segment on *Prime Time Live*, or one of the other news programs of that nature, emphasizing how easy it was for a person to obtain various forms of false identification, even credit cards. On his way out of town, he decided to drive by the location they had mentioned, an area known as MacArthur Park, located at Seventh Avenue and Alvarado, hoping he had enough money to pay for what he needed.

The shock of seeing the article caused him to unscrew the bottle of Jack Daniel's and take a swig before he reached his front door, wadding up the paper bag and tossing it into a trash barrel. Swiping his mouth with the back of his hand, once he was in the house, he placed the bottle on the coffee table and headed to the kitchen to check his voice mail, hoping Shana had called him. When he heard only the nasal voice of a woman inquiring about one of his listings, he smashed his fist into the wall. All he wanted was to say goodbye, tell Shana he was sorry, tell her how much he loved her. How could his life have sunk to such a disgusting level? It was as if Hell had risen up out of the ground and swallowed him.

He had hoped to be able to keep the Buick for at least thirty days, thinking the real estate agent whose identity he had stolen wouldn't find out until the first payment. He had promised the car salesman, however, that he would bring in some type of photo ID the next day. Maybe he could have one of those guys on the street make him up a dummy license, then send a copy of it in the mail. With the new seal the state of California imprinted on each license, it was impossible to simply print one up on a computer. If he couldn't take care of the problem, he'd be forced into ditching the car after he reached Vegas. At least the public defender had advised him that his next court appearance wasn't scheduled for another three weeks.

John headed to the front door to retrieve his luggage from the detached garage, grabbing the bottle of Jack Daniel's off the table. The shakes were getting progressively worse. He had to make them stop, and the only solution was to feed his body what it craved. Once he threw some of his clothing and personal items into a suitcase, he would make a pot of coffee to try to offset the effects of the alcohol before embarking on such a long drive.

As he stood in front of his garage, a car drove past full of young people, loud music blasting through the open windows. He imagined families inside the houses on the block, laughing, loving, enjoying one another. He would never live a normal life again, never see his daughter step onto the stage to receive her diploma.

He hesitated before hoisting up the door to the garage. Inside were the remnants of the life he had once lived with Lily. Tables, chairs, lamps, items that had been in their home in Camarillo. This time when he tipped the bottle to his mouth, he guzzled it down as if it were water.

John ducked inside when he spotted one of his neighbors out walking her dog, quickly closing the garage door behind him. Beverly Murdock was a white-haired busybody, and he was in no mood to deal with her. A small window was situated in the rear of the garage, vaguely illuminating the interior. Before he had a chance to turn on the lights, he suddenly froze, hearing a noise in the far left corner of the structure. A neighborhood cat must have managed to sneak inside when he came out a few weeks back to retrieve his toolbox.

He was feeling along the wall for the light switch when he heard another noise — a strange wheezing sound. Whipping out his pocket knife, he flicked open the blade, fearing the sound had been made by a rabid raccoon or some other type of wild animal. He never locked the garage, almost hoping someone would break in and save him the trouble of hauling the junk inside away. Outside of a few pieces of cheap luggage, there was nothing of real value worth stealing.

He waited and listened, holding his breath. With the alcohol now coursing through his bloodstream, he decided to open the garage door rather than continue groping around in the dark for the light switch.

Just as he reached for the handle to lift the door, John heard something rushing toward him at tremendous speed, like a raging bull. Boxes and furniture tumbled over. The next thing he knew, he was pinned face first against the wall, held in place by the maniacal force of his attacker. "Booze, huh?" the man hissed, yanking the bottle out of John's hand and slamming it against the wall.

A dagger of white-hot pain entered John's back as he frantically struggled against his attacker. As he slashed out blindly with his pocket knife, the man seized his arm in an iron grip, a guttural, inhuman sound erupting from his throat.

John screamed in agony as he felt his wrist being bent backward until the bones emitted a loud, sickening crack.

"You thought you were gonna cut me with that pussy knife," his attacker snarled in his ear, closing the knife and slipping it in his pocket. "You're a joke, man. That knife's not good for nothing but cleaning your fingernails."

John felt warm liquid gushing down his back, knowing instantly that it was blood. The man had stabbed him. He had to force each word out of his mouth. "Money . . . I . . . have . . . money."

The man waved the Bowie knife in front of his face, a streak of light reflecting off the shiny surface of the blade. "This what a knife looks like, asshole," he said, his words spoken with a Latin accent. He plucked out the roll of cash and stuffed it into the waistband of his sweat pants.

The man had said something about booze. John thought of Antonio Vasquez. Had one of his relatives decided to seek revenge? His eyes closed, the weight of his body fell limp in the man's arms. The man's voice and the words he spoke pulled him back.

"You're her daddy, ain't you?" he said. "Is she in the house? That's who I want, old man. I want that pretty little daughter of yours. You, I don't want. You just a man in the wrong place at the wrong time."

John released an involuntary grunt with each thrust of the knife. He no longer felt the pain, only the pressure of the blade as it passed into his flesh. He had been driving Shana's car. Vasquez's family must believe she had killed their son. He suddenly saw himself inside a sun-filled room. Shana was a little girl again, her eyes filled with love and innocence as she gazed up at him. "Take me to the park, Daddy," the vision said, her hand tugging on his sleeve. "You promised, remember?"

Shana's image vanished with the light, replaced with the face of the beautiful young boy he had driven off and left to die. He felt himself diving into the same fathomless pool of swirling darkness he had glimpsed that night of the hit-and-run. He mouthed the same exact words Lily had the night Curazon had dragged her down the hall toward the bedroom where Shana was sleeping: "Please, God, not my daughter."

27

Lily had been mistaken about Von's being open. Determined to treat Richard's injured hand so it wouldn't become infected, they ended up driving to Goleta, a small city just north of Santa Barbara. When they returned to San Ysidro Ranch it was almost midnight, and Shana had fallen asleep on the bed. "Don't wake her," Richard whispered, peering over Lily's shoulder. "There's two sofas in the living room. Stay here tonight."

"That's ridiculous, Richard," she told him. "I can't let you sleep on the sofa, particularly not after I caused you to cut your hand. That wound was worse than I thought. I'm worried now that we should have taken you to the E.R., let the doctor put in a few stitches."

"God, Lily," he said, "you really are a mother hen."

"Let me wake Shana," she said. "It's time we got out of your hair."

"Stay here tonight," he insisted. "I saw some extra blankets and pillows in the closet."

"Are you sure?" Lily asked, glancing at the two sofas. One was large enough to sleep on, but the other one was only a love seat. "You won't be comfortable, Richard. I can curl up on the love seat, but your legs are too long."

"Your daughter needs her rest," Richard told her, walking over and closing the French doors leading to the bedroom. "I wouldn't care if I had to sleep on the floor. Knowing you're both safe is all the comfort I need right now."

Shana's eyes sprang open Saturday morning. For a few moments she was disoriented, thinking she was in her bedroom in North Hollywood. When she realized she had spent the night in Richard's bungalow at San Ysidro Ranch, she tried to sit up, then flopped back on the bed, her body shivering as if she were covered by a sheet of ice.

The French doors leading to the outer room were closed. Her mother and Richard must have gone back to her place to be alone, she decided, thinking they would sneak back in before she woke up. As she climbed under the covers to get warm, her stomach began gurgling with hunger. Outside of her phone conversation with Greg, much of the previous evening had passed in a fog, and she couldn't remember what she'd eaten for dinner. Since she had slept in her clothes, she got up and walked out into the living area to see if she could find anything to eat.

"Good morning," Lily said, surprised they had slept so long. The clock on the wall read nine-fifteen. "How long have you been up?"

"I don't know," Shana said. "Why didn't you wake me so we could go home?"

"Richard cut his hand," her mother explained. "We went to the store to get some bandages and disinfectant. When we got back, you were sawing logs."

Hearing the two women talking, Richard lifted his head off the sofa. His injured hand had become sandwiched between the cushions during the night. When he pulled it out, he grimaced in pain. A few drops of blood had seeped through the gauze bandage.

"God . . . your hand!" Shana exclaimed. "How did you get hurt?"

"I broke a glass," Richard told her, yawning. "It just smarts a little, that's all. Your mother put all kinds of bandages on it." He followed her eyes to a small bloodstain on the fabric. "Good thing she did. Don't worry. A little cold water should get that off."

"Didn't you go to a doctor?"

"Nah," he said, shaking his head. "Really, it's nothing."

"It was my fault," Lily told her. "I knocked his hand while he was holding a wineglass."

Shana wasn't certain they were telling the truth. She felt a strange feeling in the pit of her stomach, but this time it wasn't hunger. "I don't understand, Mom," she said, shaking her head. "Your place is only a five-minute drive from here. Why did I end up with the bed? Richard hurt his hand. This is just stupid."

"Richard refused to let me wake you."

"I want to get out of here," the girl suddenly exploded. "And I don't mean this hotel . . . ranch . . . whatever you call it. I want to get out of this damn town. I'm tired of sitting around waiting for someone to figure out what I should do. Just get me a car and stop treating me like a child."

Lily frowned, folding up the blanket and stepping into her shoes. "Fine," she said, standing and picking up her handbag. She started to apologize to Richard for her daughter's rude behavior, but he gave her a look that said that nothing was required.

Lily heard the phone ringing inside the guest cottage while she was still turning the key in the lock. Racing across the room to answer it, she knocked over one of the kitchen chairs. Shana had sulked during the short drive home. She followed her mother inside, then headed to the bathroom and slammed the door.

"I'm sorry," Lily said, pressing down on her left ear to hear better, "what did you say your name was? We must have a bad connection."

"Detective Keith O'Malley," he answered. "Ventura P.D. Homicide."

"How did you get my home phone number?" As soon as Lily said it, she realized how foolish she sounded. The police could get any number they wanted, even if it was unlisted. "If you're calling regarding one of the cases I'm handling, you'll have to get in touch with my associate, Matt Kingsley. You can reach him at the D.A.'s office Monday morning."

"What we need to speak to you about doesn't have anything to do with your job," O'Malley told her. "We'd like to talk to you at the station this afternoon."

"Today's Saturday," she answered. "What is this about?"

"We'd rather not discuss it over the phone, Ms. Forrester."

Lily slapped back against the wall, her heart doing a tap dance inside her chest. John had called the police, told them she'd killed Hernandez. Nothing else made sense.

"Can't this wait until Monday?" Lily asked, pausing as Shana marched out of the bathroom, picked up her portable computer, and carried it outside to the patio.

"You're either coming here," O'Malley said gruffly, "or we'll have the sheriff in Santa Barbara pick you up and bring you down here. It's your decision."

"I'll come there," Lily told them, her hand on her throat. "What time?"

"One o'clock."

After all these years, the ceiling had finally caved in. Lily slid halfway down the wall, then rushed to the medicine cabinet in the bathroom, rummaging through the bottles. After she'd killed Bobby Hernandez, she had numbed herself with tranquilizers. Without them she would have never been able to continue to function. Each day she had driven to the courthouse, terrified the police were going to discover what she'd done and lead her out in handcuffs.

Finding nothing stronger than Tylenol, Lily stared at her own reflection in the mirror. Valium wasn't the answer. She had to send Shana to Los Angeles immediately. The same sense of urgency her daughter had felt at Richard's bungalow that morning took hold. Retrieving her purse from the kitchen table, she removed a handful of bills, what was left of the money she'd collected when she'd posted John's bail.

Shana was staring at her computer screen at the round table on the porch. Lily took a seat beside her. "You were right," she said. "You need to go back to school. Is there anyone you can stay with while you check out some of those ads for roommates?"

"I could probably stay with Jennifer," her daughter told her, removing her reading glasses. "We'd have to sleep in the same bed, though. They have a big family, Mother. She has five brothers."

"Tell her you'll pay rent until you get a new place." Lily handed her the three hundred-dollar bills.

Shana stared at the money in her hands. "I don't have a car, remember?"

"You can take the Audi," Lily told her. "Call your friend, verify that you can stay with her, then take off for Los Angeles. If you call some of those ads, you might be able to line up an apartment right away. At least you won't have to miss any more of your classes."

"Are you certain, Mother?" Shana looked away, ashamed at the way she had acted earlier. "I don't have to take your car. Why don't I just use the Honda until they give me my car back? It still runs, doesn't it?"

"No!" Lily said, rising several inches in her seat. She cursed herself for not having disposed of the Honda years ago. Covered with a canvas tarp, it was parked to one side of the guest house. Manny Hernandez's description of the car was one of the factors that had caused Cunningham to suspect she had killed the man's brother. No matter how many years had transpired since the crime, the authorities could always trace a car through the VIN number. With infrared scanning and other new developments in forensic science, a criminal could never be certain he had removed all evidence of his crime. Lily had considered giving the car to a wrecking yard, but since the Honda was in fairly good condition, she knew they would just turn around and sell it. If she had insisted that it be demolished, she would have raised suspicions. "I don't want you to drive the Honda," she said. "You might break down on the freeway. Next week I'll take it in for a tune-up."

"I'm sorry I acted like a bitch this morning," Shana told her. "I don't feel right taking your car. Dad has caused enough problems for you."

"Please," Lily said, touching her arm, "do what I say. We're both going stir crazy. I'm glad you got to spend some time with Richard, though. At least you know he'll be there if you ever need an attorney."

"What's going to happen, Mom?"

Lily pulled her daughter into her arms. "Everything's going to be fine," she told her, gently stroking her hair.

Shana stood, then placed a hand on top of her head. "I feel strange," she said. "You're acting just like Dad did the night of the accident. He told me he was moving away. I knew he was drinking, so I didn't pay any attention to him. When I went to sleep, I had nightmares. I thought he was going to kill himself or something."

Lily looked up at her. "Your father would never kill himself," she said, her face shifting into hard lines. "He's not the type."

"What does that mean?"

"Forget it," she said. "After you leave, I'll go to my office and see if I can catch up on my work. I want you to take my cell phone. Make certain you keep it on all the time. I'll call you as soon as I buy another one. That way we'll always be able to reach each other. Just don't forget to recharge it every night."

"What about the duplex?" Shana asked, letting out a long sigh. "If we're giving it up, I'll have to move all my things out."

"Your father should be moved out by

Monday. Don't worry about the furniture. I'll hire a moving company to pick it up and put it in storage. If you make several trips, you can probably move most of your clothes and whatever miscellaneous things you have in the duplex in the Audi. Get some of Jennifer's brothers to help you."

Lily and Shana stood side by side, gazing out over the lawn. "Maybe I was wrong not to talk to Dad," the girl said, placing her head on her mother's shoulder. "Should I call him when I get to the city?"

"That's something you're going to have to decide for yourself," Lily told her. "I loved your father very much during the early years of our marriage. I'm not really certain why we drifted so far apart."

Lily went inside the house, leaving the screen door standing open behind her. Under the circumstances, she had made the most magnanimous statement of her life.

"Check out of your hotel," Lily said, calling Richard the moment Shana pulled out of the driveway.

"What do you mean?"

"I sent Shana back to Los Angeles," she told him, slouched in her chair at the kitchen table. On the butcher block table was a gray fireproof storage box. It resembled a

430

small safe with its sturdy locking mechanism, but since a thief could merely pick the box up and walk off with it, the primary function was to safeguard important documents in case of a fire. "She's going to pay rent at her friend's house until she finds another place to live. That way she can go back to her classes at UCLA on Monday."

"I was going to suggest something along those lines," Richard said. "Things seem even worse when a person has too much time on their hands. What's this about me checking out of the hotel?"

"Now that Shana's gone," Lily said, fingering the pink slip on the Honda, "you can stay here with me. Why waste the money? Besides, I need you. A homicide detective from Ventura called. They want me to report to the police station by one o'clock today. They even threatened to send the sheriff over here if I didn't come in voluntarily. John must have called after the argument we had the other day, somehow talked them into reopening the Hernandez case."

"I'll be right over," Richard said. "You're not going to Ventura alone."

"You can't go with me." Lily felt as if she were about to step into the eye of a hurricane with nothing to anchor her to the ground. Her impulsive actions had caused

431

enough pain. Richard had forfeited his dream of becoming a judge; Cunningham had given up the job he loved. John had become an alcoholic. It didn't matter how many people Bobby Hernandez had killed. Even the fact that she had believed he was the man who had raped her and her daughter couldn't justify her actions. This time Lily knew she was on her own. For six years she had been pleading with God to forgive her. Perhaps she had finally reached the crossroads. She could either redeem herself, or thrust herself back into another bottomless pool of agony.

"I'm not going with you just because I care about you," Richard told her. "I'm going as your attorney. If the police file charges, I can always have Marty Schwartz represent you."

"Your partner?"

"My associate," he said. "He's a fine attorney."

After Shana had left, Lily had thrown herself on the bed and cried. She picked up a bottle of eye drops off the table, tipped her head back, and squirted them in her eyes. "Don't you see?" she said. "This is what we feared all along, that you'd be called to testify against me. I won't allow you to perjure yourself, Richard. And I can't let this continue to the point where the police figure out that you knew I killed Hernandez and failed to report it. What good is it going to do if we both go to prison? How can I allow you to destroy Greg's life as well as your own?"

"Hang up the phone," Richard shouted. "Now, Lily!"

"Why?"

"I'll be over there in five minutes."

"But, Richard —"

"Damn it," he said, "do what I say."

Lily hit the disconnect button. She didn't have to worry about stepping into the eye of the hurricane. The way it appeared, she was already inside it.

28

Pulling into her driveway, Richard slammed his gearshift into park and flung open the door to his Lexus. Lily was waiting behind the screen door, dressed in a pair of jeans and a pink turtleneck sweater. He almost yanked the door off the hinges in his haste to get to her, crushing her in his arms. After a few moments he released her, hurrying past her into the cottage. Lily remained near the door, her arms dangling at her sides. In some unknown way, he seemed to have extracted the panic and despair she had felt earlier. She took a few steps forward, then stopped.

"Don't say anything," he said, ripping the cushions off the sofa, the chairs, checking the light fixtures, then picking up her phone off the kitchen table and dismantling it. "Do you have more than one phone?"

"Yes," Lily said, pointing, "in my bedroom."

Richard hurried into her bedroom, then returned a few moments later. "Let's talk outside."

Lily followed him onto the porch. He kept walking, however, wanting to conduct their conversation as far away from the guest cottage as possible. She was barefoot; the gravel in the driveway cut into the heels of her feet. Richard continued until he reached the yard to the left of the main house, only stopping when he saw a grouping of lawn furniture. On each of the four corners of the swimming pool, there were statues of various Roman gods and goddesses. Lily remained on the grass. She had always respected her landlord's property.

Richard glanced over his shoulder. "The owners are out of town, right?"

"Yes," she said, a question mark on her face. "Can't you tell me what's going on?"

Richard took a seat in one of the cushioned lawn chairs, motioning for Lily to do the same. Reluctantly she walked over and sat down. "The police may have bugged your house," he told her. "I never considered anything along those lines until they contacted you today."

"You're becoming more paranoid than me," Lily answered, flicking the ends of her fingernails. "It's ludicrous to think the Ventura police convinced a judge to issue a court order to bug my place, Rich. The only way they could legally step foot inside that cottage would be if they had proof that there was a body or a bomb inside."

Squinting from the glare, Richard pulled his sunglasses out of his pocket and slipped them on. Even though it had been overcast that morning, the sun was out now, and the temperature had skyrocketed. His shirt was damp with perspiration. "You're probably right," he said. "You have to realize, though, that your position places you on a different level. You're not the run-of-the-mill criminal, Lily. And don't forget, Fred Jameson isn't one of your biggest fans. From what I've heard, he believes you ruined his chances of getting promoted. Didn't you accuse him of falsifying evidence in the Walter Evans homicide?"

"All I did was review the case for the appellate judge," Lily told him, defensive. "He might have ended up with a notation in his personnel jacket. He wasn't officially reprimanded. I called it the way I saw it. That's what I got paid to do."

"Wasn't the conviction overturned?"

"Yeah," Lily said, "but it didn't pivot around anything related to Jameson. That case was rife with errors, from the street cops all the way to the judge." She stared out over the pool before continuing. "Jameson didn't call me, anyway. The person I spoke to identified himself as Keith O'Malley. What time is it?"

He glanced at his watch. "Eleven-fifteen."

"Did you check out of the ranch?"

"No," he said, standing and following her back across the yard. "I rushed straight over here. I'll have to go back and get my things if you want me to stay here tonight."

"I'll leave you my key," Lily told him. She saw he was about to speak, and she knew exactly what he was going to say. "You're not going with me, Richard. It's not even up for discussion." She shot him a firm look, then added, "If you want to do something to help me, loan me your car. I let Shana take the Audi back to Los Angeles. I don't think it would be wise for me to pull up at the police station in the same car I was driving when I shot Hernandez."

"God, woman, why would you keep the car?" Richard exclaimed. "There might still be evidence inside it."

Richard and Lily shared a number of common traits, but like most individuals, they reacted differently under stress. She liked to have everything under her thumb just as much as he did, yet she was more of a trooper, whereas Richard could become overly excitable. She couldn't blame him, however, for wanting to protect himself. "I kept the Honda for the same reason you just mentioned," she told him. "I'm not certain the top forensic team in the world could find anything in that car after this long. At the same time, technology is moving at such lightning speeds that we can't be sure." She gave him a sour look. "Three months from now, the entire science of forensics may have changed. It's time the Honda disappears, don't you think?"

"Absolutely," he told her, scowling. "And please, don't tell me you're going to sell it. That wouldn't make any sense."

Lily managed a weak smile. "Why do you think I still have the damn thing? If you have a suggestion, I'm more than willing to listen."

Richard shook his head. "I don't want you to handle this," he insisted. "While you're in Ventura, I'll find a wrecking yard, then drive the car over."

"No good," she said, a breeze whipping her hair off her face. "The police will want to impound the car if they've decided to re-open the case. How could I ask you to dispose of evidence for me?"

"You didn't ask, remember?" Richard smiled. "I offered."

"No," she protested, explaining why she had ruled out the wrecking yard as an option. "Maybe it would be safer for me to keep it. If they ask about the car, I'll just tell them I don't have it."

"Lily," he said, holding onto her arm, "listen."

"Okay, okay," she said, jerking away, "I'm listening."

"This is what I'm going to do," Richard told her, his agitation gone now that he had formulated a plan. "After you leave for Ventura, I'll go to a hardware store and buy some tools. Then I'll come back here and remove all the VIN numbers on the car, both on the engine and the frame, leaving only the license plate. That way I won't get stopped by the police. As soon as it gets dark, I'll drive it up in the mountains behind the ranch, find an isolated spot, then push the car over the cliff. When I go out to the hardware store, I'll make a preliminary run up there to check out the area. If I pick the right spot, they may never find the car. Even if they do, they won't be able to identify it or manage to trace it back to you."

This was Richard Fowler the prosecutor, Lily thought, calling to mind the chalkboard he had kept in his office in Ventura — how he used to map out each and every detail, assembling the events of the crime piece by piece until he finally came up with a picture he was certain would convince a jury to deliver a guilty verdict.

"How are you going to get back here?"

"I have two feet," Richard said. He patted the small roll around his midsection. "And a little exercise won't kill me. All I have to do is walk down the hill, then I'll stop by the Plow & Angel, have a few drinks, and catch a cab back here to your place."

Lily started to protest, then stopped herself. He wanted to do this; she could read it on his face. This was his way of reassuring her that whatever happened in the future, he was in too deep to walk away.

Richard had loaned Lily his cell phone, and on the forty-five-minute drive to Ventura, her thoughts turned to Bruce Cunningham. She called and asked the operator for the number to the company the police had told her he worked for — Jineco Equipment Corporation. She had located the company's Web page several months back and had thought of sending the former detective an e-mail, wanting to tell him that she was okay and had taken another job as a prosecutor. "They have a toll-free number," the operator said. "Do you want me to give it to you?"

"Yes," she answered, repeating it several

times so she wouldn't forget, then quickly punched the numbers into the dial pad. As soon as a female voice came on the line, she gave her name and asked to speak to Bruce Cunningham.

"I was wondering when you were going to get around to calling me," Cunningham said, his deep voice resounding in her ear.

Lily smiled, feeling as if she had reconnected with a powerful force. "How is your family? You know, the wife and kids."

"Fine," he said. "The youngest went off to college this year."

"Your job?"

"Great," he said, pausing for several moments. "What's going on? You didn't call me just to shoot the breeze, did you? A fellow claiming to be a detective called here a few days back, asking questions about the Hernandez homicide. Said his name was Fred Jameson. Do you know him?"

The phone slid out of Lily's hands. Richard had tried to warn her that Jameson might be involved, but knowing that he had already gone to the trouble to track Bruce Cunningham meant the police were not merely mulling over reopening the Hernandez case, as she had hoped.

She parked along the side of the freeway, bending down to pick up the phone off the floorboard, assuming Cunningham had been disconnected. About to hit the redial button, she glanced at the LCD display, then brought the phone back to her ear.

"I've been waiting for them to outlaw driving with those damn phones," Cunningham said before Lily began speaking. "How many people do you think have been killed because some bozo was driving down the road talking on his phone, not paying attention? At the very least, they should make it mandatory that people wear a headset, or that they have one of those speaker phones installed in their cars. What do you think, Forrester?"

"You haven't changed, Bruce," she said, swallowing hard before continuing. "What did you tell Jameson when he called?"

"About you or about the case in general?"

"All of the above," Lily said, seeing the sign for the Victoria Boulevard exit only a short distance away.

"I didn't tell him anything that would incriminate you," the former detective said, carefully measuring his words. "All I said was Hernandez was a rotten apple, and I didn't think the man merited a waste of the taxpayers' money to put his killer behind bars."

"A detective named O'Malley called and insisted that I come down today," Lily told him, the muscles in her neck and back tightening. "I'm about to pull into the parking lot of the police department right now."

"When you think about it," Cunningham said wisely, "you might be better getting this out in the open rather than spending the rest of your life waiting for it to jump out and bite you."

With the stress she was under, Lily wondered if Cunningham was suggesting that she clear her conscience and confess. By accepting whatever punishment the state imposed, would she finally free not only herself but the individuals she'd held captive by involving them in her crime? She had already confessed to Cunningham six years before. He had taken it upon himself to withhold the information she had given him. She had not pleaded with him, or coerced him in anyway. Unlike the impulsive act Lily had committed, Cunningham had carefully weighed the circumstances and arrived at his decision that sending Lily to prison would not constitute an act of justice.

Bruce Cunningham had sacrificed both his moral and professional integrity in order that a daughter would not lose her mother at the time when she needed her the most; the state would not forfeit a brilliant and dedicated attorney; and the death of a man who had killed brutally and without provocation on two separate occasions would not be avenged.

After parking the car, Lily began walking toward the front entrance of the police station, the heat of the midday sun and the intensity of emotion causing her to feel as if her feet were made of cement. If the Ventura D.A.'s office accepted the case for prosecution, Cunningham would be subpoenaed to testify, in addition to the two people who were the closest to her heart — her daughter and Richard Fowler. How would she feel if Shana, Richard, and Cunningham were forced to stand in the witness box with their hands on the Bible, listening to the bailiff pose the age-old question echoing inside her head? "Do you solemnly swear to tell the truth, the whole truth, and nothing but the truth, so help you God?"

29

At one-fifteen Saturday afternoon Lily was ushered into an interview room at the Ventura Police Department by Detective Keith O'Malley. A tall, good-looking man in his late thirties, he had blond hair and a ruddy complexion. Fred Jameson was already seated at the table.

"Did you have a pleasant drive?" Jameson asked, smirking. "I love that stretch of freeway, the way it runs parallel to the ocean. I used to fantasize about owning a beach house one day.

There's this one area. What's it called? You know what I'm talking about, Lily. Lots of trees, sort of juts out into the ocean."

So this is how he wanted to play it, Lily thought, slowly lowering herself into the chair. "There's several areas like the one you described," she said, setting her purse down on the table. "Did you call me down here to talk about real estate?"

O'Malley was standing behind Lily. He made the time-out sign with his hand, wanting to remind Jameson that Captain

Nelson had placed him in charge of the investigation.

Jameson ignored him. "This place, well," he continued, "it reminds me of a cheaper version of that fancy section in Malibu where all the movie stars have their homes. Of course, on a detective's salary, the only kind of oceanfront real estate I'll ever be able to afford would be next to that sewage plant in Channel Islands. Now, if someone hadn't falsely accused —"

"Knock it off, Fred," O'Malley barked. He set a tape recorder in the center of the table. He then proceeded to read Lily her Miranda rights. Once he was finished, he pulled out a chair and took a seat at the head of the table.

"The area in Malibu is called the Colony," Lily said, fixing him with a steely gaze. "When people used to mention it when I was a kid, I thought they were referring to an ant colony. Maybe you should check it out, Fred. You might fit in perfectly."

Keith O'Malley placed his large hands on the table. "We're here to discuss the homicide of Bobby Hernandez." He stated the date and time and, as a safeguard, asked Lily once more if she was waiving her right to have an attorney present during questioning.

"I am an attorney," Lily told him, one corner of her mouth curling into a smile.

"That's not the question," O'Malley said, pulling his collar away from his neck.

"Yes," she said, leaning forward. "I waive my right to an attorney."

The detective pulled out a piece of paper, questions he and Jameson had prepared over the past two days. "Did you know Bobby Hernandez?"

"No."

"You do know who I am referring to?"

"Not necessarily," Lily answered, crossing her arms over her chest. "Bobby Hernandez is a common name."

"Cut the crap," Jameson interjected. "You know the guy we're talking about, damn it. This isn't a courtroom. It's not like you're on the witness stand."

"Didn't you read me my rights?" Lily asked, pointing at the tape recorder. "You're recording this conversation. And you just informed me that whatever I say can be used against me in a court of law."

"May I handle this, Fred?" O'Malley said, beads of perspiration popping out on his forehead.

"Handle your partner, O'Malley," Lily said, her temper surfacing. "He's already wasted enough of my time today. I agreed to speak to you without an attorney. Return the courtesy by conducting yourself in a professional manner."

Jameson left the room to cool down. Not only did he have a personal agenda when it came to Lily, he'd never gone head to head with a district attorney, and certainly not one as cunning and strong-willed as Lily Forrester.

O'Malley waited until he heard the door close behind the other man, then turned back to Lily. "Bobby Hernandez was identified as one of the five gang members who killed Carmen Lopez and Peter McDonald. Since you prosecuted that case, Ms. Forrester, I'm certain you recall Mr. Hernandez."

"Now that you've clarified yourself," Lily told him, "the answer to your question is yes."

"Fine," he said. "How did it come to light that Hernandez had participated in the McDonald-Lopez killings?"

"Aren't we going over old ground here, detective?"

"To some degree," O'Malley said, pausing to look over his notes. They had a serious problem on their hands. The records on the McDonald-Lopez case were complete, the majority accessible by means of the department's computer system. The Patricia Barnes and Bobby Hernandez murders, however, had been investigated by the now defunct Oxnard police department. The two detectives didn't want to tip their hand and let Lily know that they weren't as yet certain what percentage of the evidence and records relating to these interlocking crimes had been lost or accidentally destroyed during the consolidation of the two police departments. They needed information and they needed it fast. A conference was scheduled the following week at the district attorney's office. Ironically, Lily was one of the three individuals who could fill in the missing blanks. The challenge was to tap into her memory without revealing that they were using her as a source for information.

Richard Fowler had been involved in the combined investigations, but Jameson had been dead set against approaching him. Fowler was a highly respected defense attorney, and according to Jameson, his friendship with Lily had extended beyond the office. When Lily had shown up alone for their one o'clock meeting, the two detectives had released a collective sigh of relief. They were both expecting Fowler to have already signed on as her attorney. From the attorney's statements regarding Marco

Curazon, even if Lily brought in another attorney to represent her, Richard Fowler was firmly entrenched in her corner.

Overall, Bruce Cunningham held the greatest wealth of information. The former Oxnard detective had investigated both the Hernandez and Barnes homicides. His reluctance to cooperate might be frustrating, but O'Malley didn't consider it spiteful. Cunningham had relocated to Nebraska and was no longer involved in law enforcement. His analysis was simple — the man didn't want to be bothered.

"The Barnes homicide wasn't handled by our department," O'Malley continued, clearing his throat. "Can you explain how Mr. Hernandez came to be identified as her killer?"

Lily stared at him for a long time. "Why are you asking me this question? Are you implying I had anything to do with the death of Patricia Barnes?"

"Of course not," O'Malley said, shaking his head. "We're just attempting to put together the overall picture. Mr. Hernandez was never arrested in the McDonald-Lopez case, correct?"

"Correct," Lily answered.

"He was never arrested because by the time his involvement came to light,"

O'Malley continued, "he was already dead. Is this true?"

"Yes."

"Then Mr. Hernandez killed Patricia Barnes after he killed Peter McDonald and Carmen Lopez, right?"

"Yes."

"How was it determined that Hernandez killed Barnes?"

"You have the files," Lily snapped. "Why are you asking me something you already know?"

"Rather than talking in circles," O'Malley told her, speaking softly, "why don't I explain where we stand. Your former husband claims you murdered Bobby Hernandez because you mistook him for the man who raped you and your daughter. There's also evidence —"

"You're aware John's been arraigned on vehicular-manslaughter charges in Los Angeles?" Lily told him. "I don't think a jury would view him as a credible witness."

"I'm aware of the circumstances," O'Malley said. "The truth of the matter is, his statement correlates with the evidence or you wouldn't be sitting here."

"Exactly what evidence are you referring to, detective?"

"You know I can't discuss that with you."

451

Lily rubbed the side of her nose. "I thought we were going to put our cards on the table."

"May I continue, please?" O'Malley said, attempting to maintain control of the conversation. "Bobby Hernandez might not have been charged with the murder of Peter McDonald and Carmen Lopez, but he was arrested for the kidnapping and rape of Patricia Barnes. You were supervisor over the sex crimes unit at that time. Why was Hernandez released?"

"We had no choice," Lily told him, rubbing her sweaty palms on her slacks. "Barnes was a prostitute. It isn't uncommon for a prostitute to claim they were raped when a customer fails to pay. We had to dump the case against Hernandez because Barnes failed to show up in court. We continued the case three times. Finally I had no choice but to dismiss and release him."

Jameson stepped back into the room carrying a tray with a pitcher of ice water, several glasses, and his oversized coffee mug. He could tell that O'Malley had made progress during his absence when Lily immediately reached for a glass and filled it with water. When she brought the glass to her mouth, he detected a light tremor in her hand. He quietly took his seat, not wanting

452

to interrupt his partner's momentum.

"Patricia Barnes didn't appear in court because she'd been murdered," O'Malley continued. "Is that correct?"

"Yes," Lily told him, her eyes focused on a spot over his head. "Hernandez murdered her after she reported the rape. Her status as a prostitute caused the Oxnard P.D. to drag their heels, so an arrest warrant wasn't issued for quite some time. As soon as the case landed on my desk, I insisted that we move forward with it. Hernandez must have picked Barnes up off the street after she went to the police with the original rape complaint, killed her, then buried her in a remote area on the outskirts of town." She stopped and took another drink of water. "The Oxnard P.D. found the victim's purse near the grave. The crime lab positively identified Hernandez's fingerprints from the plastic surface of the purse. This is the point where the two cases began to converge."

"You mean McDonald-Lopez and the Barnes homicide, correct?"

"Yes," Lily said, sucking in a deep breath.

O'Malley waited a few moments and then continued: "We know Bobby Hernandez and Marco Curazon resembled one another. We also know you left the office the

453

night you and your daughter were raped with Mr. Hernandez's file in your possession, as we've already confirmed this information with Clinton Silverstein."

Lily jerked her head back as if she'd been slapped. Whatever was done was done, she told herself, looking down at her hands. She couldn't resent Clinton for telling the truth. For all she knew, the attorney hadn't been aware at the time that his statements would be used to incriminate her.

O'Malley stood, deciding to turn up the heat now that Lily was unnerved. "You had a mug shot of Bobby Hernandez at your house," he said forcefully. "You had his address. You were certain that this was the man who had just brutalized you and your daughter. Your ex-husband told us that you insisted that he take the girl back to his house, telling him that you would drive over as soon as you collected some of your things." The detective walked toward the opposite side of the room, then spun back around and faced her. "You were already planning your crime, weren't you? Isn't that why you talked the girl's father into not reporting the rape? Why would a district attorney not report a crime, especially one committed against her child? You'd already made up your mind that you were going to execute

Bobby Hernandez. You only sent your daughter home with her father so you could get in your car, drive to Oxnard, and pump the man full of lead."

Lily remained silent, her hands locked on the arms of the chair.

O'Malley circled her like a shark, pointing and gesturing, his voice loud and accusing. "This wasn't an act of self-defense. You and your daughter were raped sometime before midnight. Hernandez wasn't killed until the following morning. Sure, you were traumatized. If someone had raped my daughter or another member of my family, I might want to blow their brains out, too." He stopped, grabbed his chair and turned it around backward, then straddled it only inches away from Lily. "The difference between you and me, Lily, is no matter how outraged I became, I wouldn't act on those impulses. And you did, didn't you?"

Lily spontaneously placed her hand over one ear. She was locked inside the horror of that morning in Oxnard. O'Malley's voice reverberated inside her head like the blast from her father's shotgun. She saw the gaping hole in the center of Hernandez's chest, the blood pumping out. Bile rose in her throat. She coughed, then managed to swallow it. She remembered vomiting on the ground before leaping back in the Honda and fleeing.

"You know what constitutes first-degree murder, right?" O'Malley was back on his feet, relentless now that he sensed Lily's fear, certain that if he pushed just a little harder, she would crack and confess. "I'm certain you know what the term 'lying in wait' means, Lily. Both premeditation and lying in wait are elements used to prove that special circumstances existed during the commission of a crime. That means you committed an act that could merit the death penalty."

"You made certain Hernandez got the death penalty," Jameson said. "The only problem, Lily, is the man never went before a jury."

Lily's eyes narrowed, her inherent sense of self-preservation returning. "You don't have an arrest warrant, do you?"

The room fell silent.

"Not at the moment," O'Malley finally answered, his face flushing. Lily had picked herself off the floor and, for all practical purposes, kicked him in the balls. It was one thing to speculate and intimidate a suspect, but to get a court to issue an arrest warrant on a case of this severity, they needed documented proof.

"We can arrange a meeting with the district attorney," Jameson said, "see if they might consider accepting a guilty plea on a less serious offense. The first step toward that direction is to come clean. You've been sitting on this for six years, Lily. That's not going to sit well with a judge. Know what I mean?"

"I know everything," Lily said, standing and glaring at the detectives. "Next time, don't call me until you have an arrest warrant, or I'll have my attorney sue you for harassment."

Shana was sitting Indian-style on the bed in Jennifer Abernathy's room, the portable telephone in her lap and the stereo blasting. "Can you turn the music down?" she asked. "I want to call my dad again."

"Yeah, no problem," said Jennifer, a small, slender girl with brown hair and hazel eyes. Seated at her desk, she was engrossed in a fashion magazine, flipping through the pages and staring at the images. "Should I bleach my hair this color?" she said, holding the magazine up so Shana could see the picture. "What do you think?" She glanced in the mirror across the room. "Blonde hair would make my face look too fat, wouldn't it?"

Although not clinically anorexic, Jennifer was convinced she had to starve herself to be attractive. At five-six, she weighed one hundred and twenty and considered herself fat. Shana walked over and turned the stereo down herself, then tried to reach her father at the duplex. When the answering service picked up, she decided not to leave another message. She'd called five times since she had arrived at Jennifer's house, and on each occasion she had left her friend's number. Her mother's statement before she had left Santa Barbara had disturbed her, made her feel bad that she'd refused to speak to her father. "I want to get some of my things," Shana told her. "You don't have to go with me."

"I said I'd help you," the girl said. "Weren't we going to wait until tomorrow when my brother gets off work? That way we can use his pickup."

Because the two girls had been friends since junior high, Shana had found it impossible not to tell her about her father and the accident. "I'm only going to get a few clothes for now. I'm worried about my dad, Jen."

"Why?" the girl asked. "You said you didn't want to see him the last time I talked to you."

"I changed my mind," Shana answered, finding a box of tissues on the end table and blowing her nose. She changed the subject, not wanting to express her concern that her father might have killed himself. "I thought I was over this stupid cold. Now it's coming back again."

"It's probably an allergy," Jennifer said, touching up the polish on her toes. "That's why it's so hot today. When the Santa Ana winds start blowing, all I want to do is guzzle water. I bet it's nice and cool in Santa Barbara, being near the ocean and all."

"Are you coming?" Shana said, in the wrong frame of mind to discuss weather. "I've been wearing the same clothes for the past two days."

"Sure," Jennifer said. "We'll take my mom's van. It's probably better than the truck anyway. At least if it rains, your stuff won't get wet."

30

The green Ford van pulled into the driveway of the duplex on Maplewood Drive at seven-fifteen Saturday evening. When the two girls opened the door and went inside, Shana was appalled at the filth and clutter. "My father's not only a drunk," she said, angrily kicking an empty beer can across the floor, "he's a pig. He probably doesn't care about leaving the place clean, since my mother put up the damn deposit."

"It's okay," Jennifer said, patting her friend on the shoulder. She glanced down at the coffee table and saw the picture of Shana that was singed around the edges. "Look," she said, holding up what was left of the snapshot, "someone ripped your mother out of the picture I took at our graduation. Do you think your dad got mad and set fire to it?"

Shana had already started down the hall to her bedroom. When she came to her father's room, the hairs prickled on the back of her neck. Drawers were pulled out, clothes were tossed everywhere, a lamp was toppled. She quickly checked her own room, finding it in the same state of disorder. "Jen," she called out. "Hurry, come here."

"Gee," Jennifer said, stepping up beside her, "maybe we should call the police."

"That's the last thing I need," Shana said. "The last time my mother called the cops, I was certain they were going to arrest me." She bent down and picked up some of her underwear off the floor, more despondent than ever. "Dad was probably drinking. And Mom pressured him. She told him he had to be moved out by Monday, or the landlord would throw everything out in the street."

"Your mom was going to let them throw your stuff out?"

"Of course not," Shana told her. "You don't understand how booze fries a person's brain. My father's desperate for money. He could have taken the clothes from the drawers because he was going to try and sell the furniture. I'm so embarrassed." She placed her hand over her mouth. "Please, promise me you won't tell anyone. Not just about this, but all the things I told you about my dad and the accident."

"You know I'd never do that," Jennifer told her. "Look, this place gives me the creeps. Since we're not going to call the

461

cops, let's get your stuff together and split."

Shana found a cloth laundry bag in a corner, then began filling it with jeans, T-shirts, blouses, underwear, several pairs of shoes. After dragging the bag into the living room, she told Jennifer that there might be some empty boxes in the garage. "I want to take as much as I can," she said. "I don't want to come back here tomorrow."

Before they went to get the boxes, Shana picked up the phone and dialed the number for her father's voice mail, wanting to see if he had received her messages. She listened to two calls from people inquiring about various real estate properties, then heard a male voice identifying himself as Detective Mark Osborne, asking that her father contact him as soon as he received the message. According to the recording, the call had come in Friday night.

Quickly checking her own voice mail, Shana discovered that Hope Carruthers had left a message in her box that morning as well. She rushed into the other room, finding Jennifer stacking some of her school books by the front door. "Th-that guy . . ." she stammered, "the one my father hit with the car . . . Antonio Vasquez . . . he was in one of our classes."

Because of their friendship, the two girls

were enrolled in several of the same courses. "Which class?"

"Philosophy 265."

"I don't remember him," Jennifer said. "But it's a gigantic class."

Shana wasn't aware that she was holding a tennis shoe in her hand. "The police asked me if he was in any of my classes. They thought I'd been dating him, that we got into a fight and it was me instead of my father who was driving that night."

"From the way it looks," Jennifer said, walking over and hugging her, "the police have already picked up your father. You have to stop freaking out. The world isn't coming to an end. You've always been tough. I'm the whiner, remember?" She pried the tennis shoe out of her hand, setting it down on the table beside the phone.

"No," Shana said, crying now, "don't you understand? My dad was going to leave me here to take the blame. He's probably left town. I started to feel sorry for him. I tried to call him, see him, tell him I would always love him. He doesn't care about me. He doesn't even care if they arrest me. The only person he cares about is himself."

Hope Carruthers suspected it might turn out to be a slow watch, even though the night was just beginning. Since Osborne held rank over the majority of the officers in their division, his shift ended at eight o'clock every Saturday, giving him a chance to take his wife out to dinner and an occasional movie.

Neither Shana nor John Forrester had responded to their phone messages. Fearing Forrester was the type to skip town, Hope decided to swing by his residence and see if anyone was home. Spotting a young woman carrying what appeared to be a box outside to a black Audi, she caught Osborne on his cell phone as he was heading home from the office.

"I think you should get your butt over here to the Forrester place."

"What's going on?"

Hope was in an unmarked car, parked several houses down from the duplex. She had made a preliminary drive-by, then circled the block and returned. Picking up a pair of binoculars, she peered through them as she spoke. "There's a short dark-haired girl putting some boxes in what appears to be Lily Forrester's black Audi, the car she was driving when the patrol units stopped her the first time to bring her daughter in for questioning." She paused, adjusting the binoculars to a higher magnification. "I see

Shana now. She's carrying a green sack . . . looks like it might be a duffel bag or something. The garage door is open."

"I'm five minutes away," Osborne said. "Keep your eyes on the house, and I'll have dispatch get a backup unit rolling your way. Do you see the father?"

"No," Hope said. "But he could be inside the house."

"Wait for the patrol unit."

"I'm going in," she told him. "It's possible that Forrester and his daughter are attempting to flee. All I see are the girls right now. Even if Forrester's inside the house, he doesn't seem like the type of man who would pull a gun on me."

"Am I mistaken?" Osborne said caustically. "Didn't you get shot not too long ago? Seems like that would make a normal person exercise a little more caution. Of course, you're a woman and women just aren't that smart."

"At least I don't talk out the head of my dick." Hope turned off the phone as she cranked the engine and then slammed on the brakes in front of the duplex. Just to be safe, she reached across her chest and removed her service revolver from her shoulder holster, flicking off the safety and holding the gun with the muzzle pointed toward the ground.

★ ★ ★

"I can't believe you don't have a garage opener," Jennifer Abernathy said, puffing as she tried to lift the heavy door.

"This is an old house," Shana told her, walking over to help her. They had found one box on the back porch. It hadn't been that large, however, and Shana was determined to pack as much of her stuff as she possibly could.

Jennifer said, "Something stinks. Can't you smell it?"

Shana caught a whiff of something unpleasant. "It's probably fertilizer," she said, glancing at the adjacent yard. "The lady that lives next door is out here every day, planting and snipping."

Both girls jumped when Hope walked up behind them. By the time the detective had determined that John Forrester wasn't inside the residence, Osborne and the patrol unit had arrived. Her fellow officers at the precinct had dubbed Hope as the resident "nose," not that she possessed the kind of second sense that many in her line of work did, meaning they could tell in advance when something was about to go down. In Hope's case, the meaning was literal. A Frenchwoman had once told her that her highly refined sense of smell could earn her a great deal of money in the perfume industry in her country. But what Hope smelled inside the garage was far from pleasant. It was the unmistakable odor of death.

"Let's talk over here," she said, anxiously leading Shana and her friend to the street.

"Are you girls going somewhere?" Osborne asked, the two uniformed officers taking up positions on either side of the two young women.

"I'm just moving some of my clothes out," Shana told them. "I didn't get the message that you wanted to talk to me until I came home about an hour ago. I've been staying with my mother in Santa Barbara. I have no idea where my father went."

Advising the patrol officers to detain the girls on the opposite side of the house, the detectives returned to the garage. Osborne yanked his service revolver from its holster on the chance that someone might be hiding inside. Hope flicked on her flashlight, seeing several pools of blood near the front entrance. "Get the crime-scene unit and more officers out here right away," she said, panning the walls and spotting what appeared to be bloody handprints on the wall near the light switch. "There's a dead body in here somewhere."

Osborne asked, "What about the girls?"

She knew better than to touch the light switch. Hope used her eyes like a camera, rapidly sending images and data back to her brain, wanting to make certain these images were firmly set in her memory. The first impression of a crime scene was crucial. The technicians would photograph and collect the various evidence, but things might be inadvertently moved or damaged. Preparing herself for the day she would be called to testify, she wanted to make certain she remembered the scene as she had found it. "I didn't see any blood on the girl's clothing," she said, continuing to pan the flashlight across the garage. "Check them again. If they look clean, get them out of here. We have to find the body." Osborne stood with the revolver pointed upward until he felt certain that whatever was inside the garage was no longer alive. "I'll have one of the patrol units take the Forrester girl to the station and stash her somewhere. Should we take her friend into custody as well?"

"It's your call," Hope told him. "I think she was just helping Shana move her things."

A short time later, Officer Joe Sisely had jotted down Jennifer Abernathy's name, address, and driver's license number and sent her on her way. He waited until the girl drove off to tell Shana that Detective Osborne had instructed him to take her to the station. Shana was terrified. She struggled when the officer tried to get her into the backseat.

"I'm going to have to handcuff you if you keep fighting me," Sisely told her, placing his hand on top of her head as he helped her into the backseat of the patrol car.

Shana stared at the screen separating her from the police officer. She felt like a stray dog en route to the pound, caged and panicked. Peering out the rear window, she saw several more police units and a white van pulling up in front of the duplex. She began gasping for air, certain now that the awful odor her friend had smelled had not been fertilizer. Unable to accept what her reason was telling her, Shana fainted, her head striking the back of the seat of the police car with a thud.

31

Mark Osborne and Hope Carruthers discovered John Forrester's mutilated body underneath a piece of plastic in the rear section of the garage. Because of the proximity to the window and the fact that it had been exceptionally warm that day, the glass pane had magnified the heat. In a cooler climate, it would have taken a longer period of time before a body began emitting an odor.

John's stomach was swollen with gastric fluids. What Jennifer Abernathy had smelled near the entrance had not been decayed flesh but human excrement. At the moment of death the bowels and bladder had spontaneously emptied.

The blood near the front of the garage had spread, some being partially absorbed into the concrete, leaving a few rather sizable pools which had already started to coagulate.

While Osborne checked out the crime scene, careful not to contaminate the evidence anymore than it had already been contaminated by the two girls, Hope rushed to her car to make the necessary notifications. They didn't want the medical examiner to respond until they had secured the crime scene and the department's forensic technicians had started the tedious process of collecting and identifying evidence.

Errors made at the crime scene were where many investigations failed, ultimately leaving a prosecutor without the necessary evidence to convict the killer. Both Osborne and Hope were determined that mistakes wouldn't be made. They assigned a team of officers to rope off the area, then charged them with checking the credentials of every law enforcement officer who was allowed entrance.

Some people mistakenly thought the medical examiner was in charge of everything related to the crime scene. In reality, their responsibility was to study and analyze the body of the victim, then correlate their findings with the evidence technicians. When members of the press questioned why an M.E. was not allowed access to the scene as soon as the police determined that a homicide had been committed, the reason was simple. The victim's body was merely an object to be protected for later examination and dissection, and outside of photographs and outlines related to its position when discovered, it was to be left undisturbed until the M.E. and police official in charge agreed it was time to transport it to the morgue. Once the body was identified and stored, the chief pathologist would schedule the autopsy.

In less than an hour, John Forrester, for whatever his strengths and weaknesses, had now became no more than a name, a number, a memory, a mystery — just another corpse at the morgue.

Hope massaged her forehead, surrounded by the odors and images of death, kneeling as she stared at the multiple stab wounds in Forrester's back and lower torso. "What happened here, Mark?"

"Did you hear about Shana Forrester?"

"No," she said, looking up. "Don't tell me you think she did this? The accident, yeah, I can see how something like that might have occurred, even though I personally think her father got drunk and ran over the boy. This —" She motioned toward the body, shaking her head back and forth. "Not this, Mark. You'll never convince me that the girl butchered her father this way. Look at the size and number of wounds the killer inflicted. We're looking at the work of a psychopath. Whoever did this was either completely out of control or they enjoyed it."

"Anything's possible," Osborne said, sipping a cup of coffee one of the other officers had brought to him. "Just thought you should know that the girl passed out in the backseat of the patrol car on the way to the station."

"Is she okay?"

"They took her to the hospital to be checked," he told her. "She only fainted."

Hope stepped aside to let another officer pass. "I'd faint too if someone told me my father had been murdered. God, Mark, she was only inches away from finding the body."

Osborne compressed his lips, looking up at the night sky before he turned back to his partner. "Shana Forrester fainted only a few minutes after the patrol officer drove off," he said. "At first the officer thought she had been knocked unconscious when he hit the brakes and she smacked her head against the back of his seat. The doctor who examined her said she got that bump on her forehead after she'd already fainted."

Hope grimaced at the growing influx of officers and equipment. They needed to keep their attention focused on what was going on around them. "Why are we talking about a bump on Shana Forrester's forehead?"

"She didn't know her father was dead."

"I'm lost," she said, stopping to point out the area they had decided to rope off to two officers. "You still haven't told me what you're getting at, Mark."

"Why would she faint?" Osborne said, pausing for emphasis. "It wasn't as if she hadn't been brought in for questioning before, or she's some five-year-old kid that was scared out of her wits because she had to ride in the back of a police car. Of course, if she had just killed her father and you happened to come along, that would make her little fainting episode a lot more significant. What do you think?"

Hope sighed, wishing she'd never transferred into homicide. "I guess you better send a unit over to pick up her girlfriend," she told him. "We could be looking at more than one killer, isn't that what you're saying? That could explain why there are so many stab wounds."

"Exactly."

Richard and Lily were staring at each other across the kitchen table. Both of them were exhausted — Lily from the grueling interview at the police department that afternoon, Richard from disposing of the Honda. He had hobbled in the door about an hour after she'd returned from Ventura, his legs cramping from walking the seven miles down the mountain to San Ysidro Ranch. He had been smart enough to have the cab driver drop him off several blocks from Lily's guest cottage in case anyone became suspicious.

"I have to be in court in Ventura by ten tomorrow morning," he told her. "If you're not awake, I'll just slip out and lock the door behind me. What are you going to do about a car now?"

"I'll have Kingsley pick me up," Lily said, wanting to block out the events of the day. "Until Ventura officially files charges against me in Hernandez's death, I'm going to do everything I can to get my cases cleared up. Brennan may decide to put another prosecutor on the Middleton case. Kingsley's come a long way, but I still don't think he has enough trial experience to handle it alone."

Hearing the phone ringing in the other room, she said, "That's probably Shana. I gave her my cell phone and told her to stay in touch."

When Lily returned a few moments later, her face was ashen. She opened her mouth to speak, then closed it, bracing herself against the counter. Richard pushed himself to his feet, knowing by the look on her face that something was wrong.

"John's dead!" she told him. "He was murdered . . . stabbed . . . the police found him in the garage of the duplex."

"No," he exclaimed. "Don't tell me Shana found him."

"They didn't say," Lily answered, rushing into the other room to get dressed. Richard followed her, leaning in the doorway as she dropped her robe to the floor and started throwing on the same clothes she had worn to the police department that afternoon. "I'm assuming they found his body only a few hours ago. The detective who interviewed Shana about the hit-and-run called. I should have asked him for more details. When he said they were holding Shana at the police station, I hung up. I have to get to her, Richard. The only person who could have done this is Curazon. John must have walked in and surprised him while he was inside the duplex waiting for Shana."

Richard seized her by the shoulders. "Slow down," he said forcefully. "Did Osborne specifically say they were holding Shana? That means she's under arrest, Lily, that they think there's a possibility that she killed John."

"Let go of me," Lily said, wrenching away.

"How could you even say such a thing? Shana would never kill her father. Curazon is the maniac who keeps destroying our lives. Why couldn't I have shot him instead of Hernandez? Give me the keys to your car."

"I'm going with you," he told her. "You can't drive when you're this upset. And I refuse to let either you or Shana talk to the police again without an attorney."

Lily grabbed her purse and rushed out the door. She was in such a panic, Richard had to chase after her, or she would have driven off and left him in a swirling cloud of dust.

Lily and Richard were huddled in a corridor outside an interview room at the Burbank precinct of the Los Angeles Police Department. Mark Osborne and Hope Carruthers had kept them waiting in the reception area for twenty-five minutes. "I demand to see my daughter now," Lily shouted almost the moment the two detectives appeared. "How could you make me wait all this time?"

"We understand how upset you must be," Hope said, lightly touching Lily's arm. "Try to see things from our perspective. We're investigating what appears to be a homicide. Until a few moments ago we were tied up at the crime scene. Your daughter is fine. She doesn't know about her father yet. We thought it would be better to wait until you arrived."

Mark Osborne was quietly monitoring Lily's reaction. He had caught a glimpse of her temper the first day he'd interviewed Shana regarding the hit-and-run accident. What he saw now, however, made him believe Lily might be capable of committing the crime her husband had told them about. The more immediate question was — had she killed her former husband as well? While en route to the station from the crime scene, Hope had contacted the Ventura P.D. and reached Fred Jameson at his home. According to the detective, they anticipated having an arrest warrant issued for Lily Forrester by the following week. Osborne pulled Richard aside, wanting to figure out how he fit into the picture before they broke the news to the girl.

"Are you a relative?"

"No," Richard said, introducing himself, "I'm an attorney. Unless Shana Forrester is under arrest, just consider me a friend of the family."

Osborne's shoulder twitched with nervous energy. Jameson had warned him about Fowler. He could understand that Lily was upset at the news of her ex-

478

husband and the father of her child's murder. She couldn't be that distraught, however, not if she'd taken the time to bring along a well-known criminal defense attorney.

When Mark Osborne removed a toothpick from his pocket, slowly unwrapped it and placed it in his mouth, Richard realized the gruff-looking detective was toying with him. "Let's not beat around the bush," he said. "Why are you stalling, refusing to let Lily speak to her daughter after a tragedy like this? Is the girl a suspect?"

Osborne's face was as unreadable as stone. "In which case?"

Hope cleared her throat, hoping she could get Osborne's attention. Shana had been sitting in a glass-enclosed interview room for almost three hours. She didn't consider the fact that the girl had fainted in the back of the police car that significant, any more than the coincidence that she had shared a class with Antonio Vasquez. The only person she considered a possible suspect was Lily Forrester.

"Let me ask you something," Richard said. "Have you ever heard the expression that there's a time and a place for everything?"

"Yeah," Osborne said, shifting the toothpick to the other side of his mouth. "I also have another dead body on my hands, Fowler. This causes a bit of a problem, since this latest victim had already been arraigned on charges of vehicular manslaughter. Ventura P.D. advised us only a short time ago that your lady friend over there is about to be arrested for a man she killed six years ago. John Forrester, the guy on the way to the county morgue, happens to be the same person who brought this Hernandez case back to light. Are you following me?"

Richard took his own advice, knowing it was his turn to listen.

Osborne continued, "What I need to know, Fowler, is if I'm talking to Lily and Shana Forrester's family friend, as you described yourself, or their attorney. Then we can get down to business."

Richard didn't take well to being bullied. "Lily's a good woman, Osborne," he said, feeling as if he wanted to slug the man. "I don't give a shit how many dead bodies you have on your hands. Let the woman see her daughter, for God's sake. Otherwise, you're going to have to throw me in jail."

32

By the time they left the Burbank precinct and got back on the 101 freeway, it was twelve-fifteen Sunday morning. Richard had fortified himself with several cups of coffee, and Shana and Lily were riding in the backseat of his Lexus.

"I didn't want Dad to die," Shana sobbed, a wad of tissues resting in her lap. "I should have called him sooner. I said I hated him . . . that I never wanted to see him again."

"Please, darling," Lily told her, "you didn't cause this to happen."

"I loved him," Shana said. "He didn't mean to hit that boy with his car."

Both women fell silent.

As Richard approached the exit leading to his house, he glanced into the backseat and saw that Lily had fallen asleep, her head resting on Shana's shoulder. Between the interview Lily had endured earlier that day at the Ventura Police Department, the hours she'd spent on the road, and the energy she had expended trying to comfort her daughter, her need for sleep had finally taken over. He thought of renting a hotel room, not certain it was safe for him to continue driving. They still had another hour on the road before they reached Santa Barbara. Deciding the best solution was for them to spend the night at his house, he was relieved when he turned onto his street and saw that Joyce's car wasn't in the driveway.

Shana became alarmed. "Where are we? Why are you stopping here?"

"This is my house," Richard whispered. "You and your mother are going to stay with me. Wait until I unlock the door and turn on some lights, then I'll come back for you."

A few moments later, Richard returned to the car and swept Lily up in his arms, depositing her in what was considered the maid's room downstairs rather than try to carry her to the guest room upstairs without waking her.

He found Shana standing in the kitchen. "I can't sleep," she told him, trailing her fingers across the granite counter top. "Marco Curazon had to be the one who killed my dad. What if he went over there intending to kill me?"

"How about a cup of hot chocolate?" Richard said. "Warm milk is supposed to relax you, help you to sleep."

"I guess," Shana said, lifting her

shoulders, then dropping them.

Once Richard had heated up the hot chocolate in the microwave and poured himself a Diet Coke, he suggested they would be more comfortable talking in his library. The room had high ceilings and floor-to-ceiling bookcases. Two brown leather chairs were arranged in a small grouping in one corner of the spacious room. A beautiful cherry desk stood in front of a leaded-glass window shaped in the form of an arch. "This looks like the Oval Office or something," Shana said, sitting in one of the leather chairs.

"I'm a long way from being the president," Richard said, taking a seat in the chair across from her. "Before I show you where you'll be sleeping tonight," he continued, "I'd like to tell you a story that might make you feel better. Just tell me to shut up when you're ready to go to bed."

"No," Shana said, sipping her cocoa, "I told you I can't sleep."

"I overheard what you said to your mother in the car," he continued. "Whether you know it or not, for almost two years Greg and I didn't speak to each other."

"When was this?" she asked. "He didn't say anything about you guys having a problem when I talked to him the other night."

"Well," Richard explained, "I guess both of us would rather forget it. The only reason I'm bringing this up is because I believe it might help you cope with some of the feelings you expressed in the car about your father. Something could have happened to me during that time period. I don't know who would have felt worse, myself or Greg."

"Was it because Greg didn't want to be an attorney?"

"No," he said, resting his head against the back of the chair. "The summer after he graduated from high school, he got involved with the wrong crowd. He stopped surfing and started hanging out at these nightclubs in Los Angeles, staying out all hours of the night. He was working for me at the time, and I admit that's not always the best situation."

"What happened?"

"He got arrested for possession of marijuana," Richard said. "He later told me the drugs had belonged to his friend. Whether that's true or not, I don't know, and at this point I don't care. Rather than come to me and admit he had a problem, he got some low-life bail bondsman to spring him from jail. One of his other friends used Greg's key, came into my house while I was at work, and filled out all the paperwork right here in my library, listing this house as a guarantee, then forging my name on the document. When Greg failed to show up for court several weeks later, I ended up with a lien on my property." He stopped and made a gesture with his hands. "I came this close to losing my home over a few thousand dollars. I threw Greg out of the house, then told him I never wanted to see him again. I was angry and hurt. I obviously didn't mean the things I said. That's why Greg is behind on completing his master's program. He lived on the beach in Hawaii for two years."

"I'm ready to go to bed," Shana said, tears streaming down her face again. "My dad is dead. Greg is still alive."

Richard walked over and embraced her. "Instead of the bad times, try to remember all the good times. Your father knew you loved him. How many girls your age would live with their dad? According to your mother, you seldom even dated."

"I needed him," Shana said, her voice cracking. "Mom was too busy. I got scared being alone."

"You could have lived in the dorm." Richard showed her to the guest room, started to leave, then turned back around. "What happened to your father shouldn't have happened to anyone, Shana. He did use you, though. He clung to you, turned you into a substitute wife, forced you to put up with his drinking, failures, and weaknesses. You're not the weak one. He transferred his weakness to you. He sucked you dry, manipulated you in a subtle but effective way."

"I'm scared," Shana said, resting her back against the door frame. "I know it was Curazon. He didn't have a reason to kill my dad, don't you see? He was looking for me. What if they don't catch him? I won't be safe no matter where I go."

"Let's hope it was him," Richard told her. "If the police find out he's responsible, they'll make an all-out effort to apprehend him."

"They better."

"They will, Shana," Richard said, his eyes filled with conviction. "And when they do, this time he'll go away forever."

By eleven o'clock Monday morning, Bruce Cunningham was standing in the detective bureau at the Ventura Police Department with Fred Jameson and Keith O'Malley. Both men had been flabbergasted that an individual considered a legend in local law enforcement circles had, for all practical purposes, fallen out of the sky and landed right on their doorstep. Cunningham told the detectives that he'd been sent to Los Angeles to attend a Karcher convention by his company, Jineco Equipment Corporation. Since he'd arrived several days early to meet with an important customer in their area, he had decided to drop by and see what he could do to help the two investigators put together the Hernandez homicide — one of the few cases in his career he had not resolved.

A giant of a man in more ways than his reputation, Bruce Cunningham's brown hair had strands of gray in it, but his eyes were as alert and cunning as ever. He was wearing a white shirt with the sleeves rolled up to his elbows, his tie was slightly askew, and his lightweight tan jacket was tossed casually over one shoulder.

"Talk about being at the right place at the right time," Jameson told him, slapping him on the back. "We were about to walk out the door to drive to the D.A.'s office. Since you investigated this case, you can help us sort through the evidence and get everything in order." He pointed to a stack of boxes in one corner of the detective bureau. "We've got several other homicides going on right now. We can use all the help we can get." He paused before continuing. "I don't know if we can get the city to approve a consulting fee. I mean, we can try to talk the captain into covering your hotel, gas, and food. How does that sound?"

"Sounds okay for now," Cunningham told them, whipping his tie off and stuffing it in his pocket. At least Sharon wouldn't have to worry about forfeiting the fancy vacation he'd promised her. On the financial side, things were going very well at his new job in Omaha. Business was thriving; he'd been able to save enough to put his entire brood through college. He might miss the excitement of police work now and then, but overall, he was happy being back in his hometown.

"Tell you what," O'Malley said, checking his watch to make certain they weren't going to be late for their appointment, "why don't you start on the evidence boxes while we're at the D.A.'s office? I'll have the front desk issue you an ID badge, then you'll be all set. You can come and go anytime you want while you're in town."

Cunningham's rugged face lit up with childlike delight as he shuffled off in the direction of the evidence boxes. Sometimes things worked out even better than a guy expected. In this case, the situation was damn well perfect.

★ ★ ★

Carolyn Middleton opened her large Luis Vuitton purse at one-fifteen Monday afternoon. It was designed in the shape of a shopping bag, and she carefully placed a rolled-up wash rag inside before she left for her obligatory daily visit to her daughter's hospital room. She generally arrived at the hospital after lunch, then left by three, in order to pick up the children at school. Since all she was going to do was sit in a metal chair for the next two hours, she popped several pills in her mouth, then stopped at the bar in the living room on her way out and washed them down with rum. Before she reached her car, she pulled a container of breath spray from the pocket of her white cashmere sweater and squirted it in her mouth. The drive to Saint Francis Hospital took approximately ten minutes. The pills wouldn't cut in for thirty.

Henry didn't understand. No one understood. Her mother might, but she'd been dead for eight years. Her mind drifted back to her childhood, recalling her eleven-year-old cousin Naomi, the one with the strange illness. Even before Betsy had been diagnosed with Aicardi syndrome, Carolyn had suspected that her daughter had the same illness that had caused her cousin's death.

She somehow made her way from her home to the hospital without any conscious recollection. She had been doing that a lot lately. She wasn't certain if it was the muscle relaxants she'd been taking, or if she also suffered from a mild form of the same genetically inherited illness. Out of fear, she had never been tested.

Carolyn passed the nursing station and exchanged a few words with one of the nuns. When she entered Betsy's room a few moments later, she didn't move the chair next to the bed as she normally did. Instead she positioned it so she could look out the window at the coastline. She'd spent enough days staring at her daughter's contorted face and frail body.

After her aunt's husband had died, Agatha and her daughter, Naomi, had moved in with Carolyn's parents at their farm in east Texas. From that day forward, no matter what Carolyn did, no one in the family paid attention to her. Naomi had such substantial needs that Carolyn seemed unimportant, almost as if she had become lost within the confines of their combined families.

She recalled the day her mother had scolded her, telling her what an awful girl she was and how she would never grow up and find happiness because she didn't care about people less fortunate than herself. All Carolyn had done was leave Naomi behind one day. Her eleven-year-old cousin always followed her into a wooded area near the lake where she and her girlfriends met each day after school to smoke cigarettes, talk about boys, and share secrets. Carolyn was thirteen then, and her parents were strict Baptists, refusing to allow her to attend the dances they held at her school. Every time she left the house, her mother made her take Naomi with her, even though she knew the other girls didn't want her around. Her friends said Naomi was retarded because she had to attend a special school. They were also frightened on the occasions when they had been present during one of Naomi's seizures.

Wanting to discourage her cousin from tagging along with her, Carolyn had told her they were going to play hide-and-seek. Then once her friends had gone home, she had left her cousin waiting in her hiding place. She didn't tell her parents what she had done until they started looking for Naomi at dinnertime. The police searched all night, finally finding her cousin at dawn. The poor girl had spent the night shivering and terrified.

Surfacing from her thoughts, Carolyn

Middleton walked down the corridor and asked Sister Mary Luke if Dr. Logan was on the hospital grounds. "No," the nun replied. "I'm not certain when he'll be coming in today. Would you like me to page him?"

"No," Carolyn said, quickly heading back down the corridor.

33

Since Richard had two cars, Lily borrowed his Lexus and drove to Santa Barbara Monday afternoon, knowing she had no choice but to meet with the chief D.A., Allan Brennan, to advise him that her former husband had not only been murdered, but that she might be arrested and charged with the Hernandez homicide. Attempting to keep something of this magnitude under wraps was an exercise in futility, particularly now that John had been killed.

The police officers, district attorney, judges, the mayor — basically any public official who would agree to taking such an old case to trial — weren't seeking justice for Bobby Hernandez, at least not in Lily's eyes. The man was a multiple murderer, and this was fact, not speculation. His crime partner in the McDonald-Lopez killings had cratered under the shrewd and relentless tactics that had made Bruce Cunningham a legend in law enforcement circles, providing him with a moment-by-moment description of what had transpired during this despicable and senseless crime. Hernandez's guilt had also been confirmed by means of the fingerprints left on the murder weapon, a gun his brother, Manny, was attempting to throw into the ocean when he was killed by the Oxnard police in a shoot-out.

In addition to orchestrating the slaughter of Peter McDonald and Carmen Lopez, Hernandez's fingerprints had also been found on the plastic purse which belonged to another of his victims — Patricia Barnes — a woman he had buried in a shallow grave.

The only purpose of prosecuting Lily for the death of Hernandez, as far as she could discern, was to generate media attention. The authorities were using her as a vehicle, knowing the sensationalism of a D.A. charged with murder would afford them the kind of recognition and fame it had so many other prosecutors, judges, police officers, and witnesses, stretching all the way back to crimes such as the Lindbergh kidnapping. People thought the public's fascination with crime and the judicial system was a recent development brought about by Court TV and televised trials, an assumption that was far from the truth. The only difference in today's world versus the past was in how people received their information. In the past, information about newsworthy or intriguing crimes had been filtered through the perspectives of radio, television, and print journalists. Now people could watch and arrive at their own judgments. News via the Internet had taken the world to even another level. Men and women could now program their office computers so that every time a new piece of information came up regarding something in the news that they found interesting, they would be instantly alerted, just as a TV station did when it broke into regular programming. The thirst for entertainment, news, and excitement had reached a pinnacle in the history of mankind.

Matt Kingsley saw Lily sitting at her desk as he walked past the door to her office. "I didn't think you were going to come in today. Is your daughter still in town? She's gorgeous, Lily." Rather than wait for her to answer, he rattled on, "She seems older than nineteen. Don't get me wrong, it's not that she looks older. She just strikes me as more mature. I've dated women in their late twenties who act like they're eighteen."

Lily's glasses were perched low on her nose, her hair was tied up in a knot on top of her head, and she was wearing one of

Richard's white dress shirts under her jacket. On her way in that morning, Richard had learned more details related to John's murder, cautioning her not to go anywhere near her cottage. "I'm only going to be in the office an hour at best," she told him. "You can call me, but only if it's urgent. As soon as I finish here, I intend to ask Brennan for a leave of absence."

"He'll go through the roof, Lily," Kingsley told her, smacking a file against his thigh. "The man's been riding herd on me every day. You know I don't have the experience to handle both your caseload as well as my own. Things have been going fairly —"

Lily cut him off. "My ex-husband was murdered last night."

Kingsley took a few steps backward in shock. "God, I don't know what to say."

"I doubt if God had anything to do with it," Lily answered, lowering her eyes as she signed her name on several documents on her desk. "John was stabbed five times in the garage of the duplex he shared with my daughter in North Hollywood. I'm just thankful Shana wasn't there at the time."

"Do they have any idea who killed him?"

Lily slowly raised her eyes, placing the stack of papers back on her desk. "The way my luck's been running, they'll probably accuse me. I'm beginning to think I have only two roles in life — victim or suspect."

"You don't mean that, do you?"

"My daughter is waiting for me in Ventura right now," she told him, evading his question. "Fill me in on the Middleton case."

"Nothing much has happened since I last spoke to you," Kingsley told her. "I've been checking in with the hospital on a regular basis. I called this morning, and they said Betsy's condition appears to be unchanged." He stopped, trying to think of anything else he needed to bring to her attention. Lily had dark circles under her eyes, but she always looked somewhat ragged, as if she never got a decent night's sleep. "Ron Spencer called Friday. He accepted our offer to settle the Hatteras matter."

"That's one out of the way," Lily said, exhaling in relief. "Under the circumstances, I'm not going to be able to handle the Middleton trial. Brennan will probably reassign it." She saw his face fall, then added, "I'm not saying he'll remove you from the case, Matt, just that you'll have to work with someone other than me. Didn't you just say that you don't feel competent handling the more complex cases?"

"I wasn't referring to Middleton," he told her. "You know how hard I've worked.

497

Brennan might bring in some stuffy old fart like Charles Dayton, and before you know it, all I'll be doing is carrying his briefcase and serving as his errand boy." He saw Lily stand, the chastising way she was looking at him. "Forgive me . . . you must think I'm the most self-centered person on earth to be talking about myself when your husband has just been murdered."

"Ex-husband," Lily corrected him, stepping past him and disappearing down the corridor.

Dr. Christopher Logan had spent the entire weekend reviewing Betsy Middleton's charts. In addition, he had searched the Internet and called several research hospitals, attempting to come up with any information he might have missed related to Aicardi syndrome. The one thing he had been able to confirm and document was that Betsy's seizures had occurred more frequently when her mother was present.

Glancing through Betsy's lab reports in his office during his lunch break, Logan noticed that it had been several months since tests to detect strychnine had been performed. Some of the procedures related to the girl's internal organs were painful, and although there were many physicians who would view Betsy's level-five coma as an opportunity to perform any tests or procedures possible to obtain more knowledge on such a rare disease, Logan refused to use patients as research subjects.

The treatment of individuals in deep comas fell into the same conundrum surrounding the abortion issue: at what point did an unborn fetus become a human being, and when did the laws of mankind become responsible for its protection? Rising from behind his desk and slipping his arms in his white jacket, Dr. Logan decided that with Betsy's trial date quickly approaching, he was justified in ordering another series of tests.

Deep in thought, Logan followed the path up the hill behind the hospital to the transitional care unit. No one was behind the nurses' station on Betsy's floor. He assumed that since the occupancy rate was extremely low right now in that particular section of the hospital, and it was the lunch hour, the staff was probably busy attending to patients. Deciding to check on the girl himself, he opened the door to her room.

Carolyn Middleton was standing with her back turned. When she heard someone behind her, she spun around as if he had startled her.

He spotted a syringe in her right hand.

"Dr. Logan," she said, her eyes enormous. "I was —"

Carolyn's arm dropped to her side as she attempted to conceal the syringe behind her back. Logan rushed toward her, seizing her arm and forcefully prying her fingers off the needle. A nonviolent person by nature, he experienced a rush of rage. He didn't realize he was hurting her until she cried out in pain. He quickly turned his attention to Betsy, ripping the IV from the girl's arm, certain now that her mother had just administered another dose of strychnine, injecting the poison directly into the tube leading into her vein.

"It . . . was . . . Henry," Carolyn stammered, backing up until she was trapped in a corner on the opposite side of the room.

Dr. Logan hit the call button, then shouted into the microphone for a nurse. The next thing he knew, Betsy was in the throes of a violent seizure. He was reaching for the straps to keep her from harming herself when her frail body suddenly rose several inches in the air, then fell limp and lifeless onto the mattress. He started to call for a cardiac cart, but he knew it was too late. Both the machines monitoring her heart and her brain waves were flat.

"Are you happy?" Christopher Logan snarled, bending down to pick up the syringe off the floor.

"Is she —"

"Yes," Logan said, holding up the syringe in his clenched fist. "You finally killed her. And you're not going to blame it on your husband, not when I have the proof right here in my hand."

Because Richard had a mandatory court appearance that morning, he had sent his office manager, June Overland, to his home to stay with Shana until her mother returned from Santa Barbara. The girl had slept until almost noon, and Lily had only peeked in the guest bedroom to check on her before leaving.

Having retrieved her cell phone from Shana's backpack, Lily called Richard's house as she was driving back to Ventura. "Is she awake?"

"Yes," June said, "would you like to speak to her? She's in the other room watching television."

"How is she?"

"Quiet, you know," June whispered, cupping her hand over her mouth. "I tried to get her to let me make her some lunch. She says she isn't hungry."

Sitting on a brown leather sofa in Richard's family room, Shana was facing the television. From the distant look in her eyes, it was obvious she wasn't paying attention. June walked in and told her that her mother wanted to speak to her.

As soon as Shana came on the phone, Lily asked her if she wanted her to pick her up and take her out for lunch.

"I'm not hungry," Shana told her. "When can we bury Dad?"

Lily wasn't prepared for her question. "I'm not certain, honey," she told her, her voice quavering. "It depends on when the police release the body."

"They're going to cut him up, aren't they? You know, do an autopsy."

"Please, wait until I get to the house and we'll talk about everything," Lily told her, wishing she had never left her alone that morning. "I'm in the car right now."

With the remote in her outstretched hand, Shana turned off the TV, wishing she had a button that would turn off the world just as easily. "I called Jennifer. The police went to her house and took a statement from her. They were asking her the same kind of questions they asked me last night. They wanted to know where we were over the weekend, why I didn't stay at the house with Dad, basically the third-degree. They even asked me if Jennifer and I killed him. They said they thought I got mad because he ran over that kid and I thought they were going to blame it on me."

Lily tried to remain silent. She told herself she would have to find out if the medical examiner had determined a time of death. Her assumption was John had been killed the same day his body was discovered, but she now realized she could be mistaken.

"Jennifer's mother is going nuts," Shana continued. "She doesn't want Jennifer to see me or talk to me. Someone killed my dad. I can't go to school. I'm staying in a strange house, and now my best friend isn't even allowed to talk to me. Maybe I should just go out and shoot myself."

"I'll be there in ten minutes," her mother said, a sharp edge in her voice. "I don't care if the world comes to an end, I don't ever want to hear you make a statement like that again."

As soon as she disconnected, Lily punched in the numbers to her voice mail. She heard Keith O'Malley's message, followed by Kingsley advising her of the circumstances surrounding Betsy Middleton's death. O'Malley's call was a blow in itself. Coupled with the news about Betsy, it almost caused Lily to drive head-on into another vehicle. She steered the Audi to the side of the road and turned off the engine.

Lily started to call Richard, then stopped, wanting to hurl the stupid phone out the window. People shouldn't hear this type of stuff while they were driving. No wonder Cunningham had climbed on his soapbox.

As cars whizzed past her on the freeway, Lily recalled visiting a pet store several months back, thinking she might buy a dog. She'd seen a round plastic container about the size of a basketball being propelled across the floor by the efforts of a hamster. At the time she had laughed, but she now felt as if she were inside an identical plastic ball. It was as if God had played a trick, and human beings were no different than hamsters. The scenery changed, the clock ticked, but no matter how fast she pedaled, Lily kept returning to the same exact spot.

34

Lily, Shana, and Richard were seated at the round table in his kitchen by three o'clock Monday afternoon. The Ventura police were now in possession of a warrant for Lily's arrest for the murder of Bobby Hernandez.

She had wanted to keep the news from Shana as long as possible. Richard had not agreed. They had reached a point, he told her, where there could be no more secrets between any of them. Too many of the crimes overlapped one another. If they weren't careful, they would ensnare themselves with their own lies.

Three of the four individuals who knew the truth were seated at the table. John was now dead. Richard had told them that as of that moment, he would be officially representing Lily. Should Shana require legal representation, he would bring in his partner, Marty Schwartz. He proceeded to caution Shana about what she said, not only to the police but to everyone she came in contact with.

"How can Richard represent you, Mom?"

Shana asked, tapping her fingernails on the table. "Won't that be a problem? You just admitted that you told him the truth right before you confessed to that detective who moved to Omaha."

"That doesn't have anything to do with me representing her," Richard told her. "No matter what I know, Shana, I'm going to do everything in my power to protect both you and your mother. No one will ever replace your father, but I want you to know that I'm here for you."

"Thanks," the girl said, reaching over and touching his hand. "It's nice to know someone cares."

"The good thing about having me as your mother's attorney," Richard continued, trying to keep his own emotions in check, "is she doesn't have to worry about legal fees."

A weak smile appeared on Shana's face. "That works for me."

"The only time the situation might become sticky is if the prosecution subpoenas me to testify as a witness," Richard continued. "Right now, there's no reason to believe they know I'm involved. Just because your mother and I were friends and worked in the same office doesn't mean I can't represent her."

Shana walked over to the sink to get a glass of water. "Most people don't stay in their attorney's house, though, right?"

Richard was pleased to see the girl's mind working. Grief was a devastating emotion. Sometimes even a distraction as disturbing as the one they were facing was better than sinking into a pit of despair. "I have a pullout sofa at the office," he said. "You and your mother can stay here as long as you want. I'll send someone to Santa Barbara to pick up your things, Lily. I don't want either of you staying at the cottage. This house has a good security system, and I'll never be more than a phone call away."

Shana asked, "What about *my* stuff?"

"You'll have to wait until the police clear the crime scene."

"I can't deal with this," Lily suddenly erupted, standing and shoving her chair back to the table. "I want to plead guilty. Even Cunningham said it was time I put this behind me."

"Why would you plead guilty?" Shana shouted angrily. "They'll send you to prison. Then I won't have anyone."

"Pleading guilty doesn't make sense, Lily," Richard told her. "Just because the police managed to get a warrant doesn't mean they can bring in a conviction. They could show the jury a film of you committing the crime, and I'd still place my money on an acquittal. You and Shana were raped, for God's sake. You're a mother, an educated professional who has devoted her life to the community. Hernandez was a monster."

"Don't you understand?" Lily said, slamming her fist down on the table. "I've lived a lie for over six years! I want to wipe the slate clean. I don't want them to let me off just because I killed someone to avenge my daughter's rape, or because I happened to kill a man who turned out to be a murderer. What if Hernandez had been an innocent person who just had the misfortune of resembling the man who raped us? Would that be okay? Should they let me go then as well? Every criminal has an excuse, some way to justify his behavior. I'm ready to pay my dues."

"No!" Shana shouted. "You don't deserve to go to prison. The guy you killed was worse than Curazon. Richard just said a jury won't convict you. Listen to him, Mother. Stop talking like an idiot. You shot that guy to protect me. Don't you know how you make me feel when you say these things?"

"Richard will negotiate a settlement with

the D.A.'s office," Lily explained, walking over and putting her arm around her daughter. "The case will be resolved in a meeting, not a courtroom. That means it won't turn into a media circus, where you and I will both be hurt."

"I don't care if they put us on television," Shana said, wiping away a tear, her body shaking. "Please, Mother, promise me you won't do this . . . go in there and tell them you killed him."

"Remember, sweetheart," Lily said softly, "we were talking the other day about how criminals don't spend enough time in prison?" A sense of peace had settled over Lily now that she'd made her decision. "Because of how long ago the crime occurred and the mitigating circumstances Richard just mentioned, the D.A.'s office will probably let me plead guilty to involuntary manslaughter. They might even give me a suspended sentence, structure a punishment where I wouldn't have to go to prison at all. They even have work-release programs."

"When did you talk to Cunningham?" Richard asked, his eyes tracking Shana as she stormed out of the room.

"I'm not really certain," Lily answered. "I haven't had enough sleep. That's why I want

509

to get this resolved. Shana may be upset now, but when it's all said and done, I believe it will be a relief for everyone."

Richard and Lily's ears pricked, hearing the sound of a car engine, then tires squealing on his asphalt driveway. "What in the —"

They both raced over to the window, thinking it had to be the police, that someone had told them where Lily was staying and they had come to arrest her.

One of Richard's prized possessions was no longer parked in the driveway. Shana had found his keys on the hall table and had taken off in his 1965 black Corvette convertible.

Now that they had talked a judge into signing a warrant for the arrest of Lily Forrester, Fred Jameson and Keith O'Malley felt fairly certain that their suspect would surrender. When they returned from the D.A.'s office, they found Bruce Cunningham had moved all the evidence boxes into the conference room.

"It's great having you on board," Jameson said, cracking his knuckles. Cunningham had started to organize the various files and evidence in neat stacks on top of the conference table. "The D.A. wants us to get him everything he'll need to prepare the pleading by Wednesday. That only gives us two days."

Keith O'Malley had brought along a stack of yellow notepads and tossed several onto the conference table so the three men could begin making notes. Then Jameson would be charged with the responsibility of dictating the litany of facts, evidence, witnesses, and chronological events which made up the body of the case. This document would be presented to the district attorney, who would perform an analysis of the overall crime and decide which laws should be presented to the court at the time charges were filed at Lily's arraignment.

"Here's what I'd like to go over first," Jameson said, pulling down one finger at a time. "The composite drawing of the suspect, the one that looks like Lily Forrester dressed up like a man. The interview Cunningham taped with Manny Hernandez before our guys killed him when he was attempting to dispose of the gun used in the McDonald-Lopez killings, along with a current name and address of the neighbor who saw the whole thing from her window."

"I didn't find any tapes or recorded statements," Cunningham said, bending down to pull some items out of another evidence box.

"What do you mean?" Jameson asked, glancing through the notes he had made several days before when he'd searched through the boxes. "I put it back in the same box. Did you check the box marked number twenty-three?"

"I checked all of them," the former detective told him, a disappointed look on his face. "Gosh, don't tell me something that important was lost in the merger."

"No, I saw it the other day," Jameson said, searching his memory. "The original of the composite disappeared. All we have is a copy from the newspaper. That makes Manny's statement crucial. He's the person who provided the description of the killer that we used for the composite. In addition, Manny described the car, the stocking cap the killer was wearing, his facial features. I also taped a phone call to John Forrester." He slapped his forehead. "That tape can't possibly be gone."

"Maybe you left it on your desk," Cunningham suggested, scrunching up his nose. "There aren't any tapes in these boxes. Are you sure you brought everything up?"

Jameson stood as he flipped through a list of the evidence, too wound up to sit down. "There should be thirty-two boxes."

Cunningham counted them to be certain.

"All present and accounted for."

"This is insane," Jameson continued, linking eyes with the former detective. "I know I put that tape of your interview with Manny in the box. The conversation with John Forrester is even more valuable than the tape of Manny Hernandez. At least Forrester wasn't a gangster."

"Shit happens," Cunningham said, taking a seat at the counsel table. "What kind of information did Forrester give you on this missing tape?"

"He said he distinctly recalled that Lily owned a shotgun," Fred Jameson told him. "And he said it was the same make and caliber as the one used to kill Hernandez. He also said Lily didn't come home until around seven or eight the morning of the murder, when she had told him she was coming straight to his house after the rape."

"From what I can see here," Cunningham said, scratching the side of his face, "you guys have sort of gotten ahead of yourself on this thing. John Forrester is dead now, as well as Manny Hernandez. Those tape-recorded statements might have value, but to get a conviction, you need a flesh-and-blood witness." He paused before continuing. "You'll never track down the neighbor you mentioned. Even if you managed to flush out new witnesses, they probably wouldn't agree to testify. That was one of the problems I ran into when I was trying to put this case together years ago. People are scared. The three guys who were partners with the Hernandez brothers in the Mc-Donald-Lopez killings might be in prison right now, but they'll be released eventually. One of them turned state's evidence. He could be back on the street already."

"I think Lily killed her husband," O'Malley told them. "She killed him to keep him from testifying."

"That's not our case, knucklehead," Jameson snapped. "We're trying to put the Hernandez case together."

"Some information came in on the Forrester killing while you guys were gone," Cunningham told them, thinking any man who didn't care about apprehending a murderer, regardless of jurisdiction, just wasn't a cop. Of course, these types of *game cops,* as he called them, were one of the reasons he'd retired from law enforcement. "Seems the lab in L.A. matched the fingerprints of a man named Marco Curazon from those lifted from the crime scene in John Forrester's garage." He gave both men a scalding glance. "You do know who Curazon is, don't you?"

Jameson was pacing back and forth. "Curazon is the rapist, right? The one who raped Lily Forrester and her daughter. That attorney, Richard Fowler, mentioned that he'd recently been paroled from prison. He wanted us to track him down . . . thought he might be stalking the girl."

"There you go," Cunningham said, standing and stretching his aching back. "My guess is, Curazon could have been waiting inside John Forrester's garage. John went out there for some reason, and the guy went nuts and stabbed him. This Osborne fellow in Los Angeles said they found a Swiss Army knife on the floor of the garage. The wounds on the body could never have been made by a knife that small. That means Forrester may have tried to defend himself, which could have explained why Curazon got mad and stuck him five times." He yawned, tired from the airplane ride. "What do I know, though? I just came down here to give you guys a hand."

"Damn," Fred Jameson said. "This doesn't mean we can't move forward, though. The Hernandez killing has nothing to do with the death of John Forrester."

"You got a hard-on for Lily Forrester, Jameson?" Cunningham asked. "When you called me, I told you this Hernandez guy was scum."

"Captain Nelson insisted that we pursue it," Jameson explained, defensive. "Forrester called the mayor's office and raised a stink, saying we were letting a murderer go free. When we dived back into this, Bruce, we were counting on John Forrester's testimony."

"That about does it for me," Cunningham said, removing his jacket from the back of the chair.

"You're not going to stick around?" Jameson asked. "Are you leaving town?"

"Not necessarily," Bruce Cunningham said, his footsteps heavy as he strode toward the conference room door. "Since you guys are so busy trying to play pin the tail on the donkey, I thought I'd hang around a few more days and see if I can't round up that Curazon fellow." Just before he stepped through the doorway, he stopped and turned around. "Bad guys versus good guys, remember? The first thing a man's got to do is figure out what team he's playing on, and then he needs to decide what kind of prize he wants to find at the bottom of the Cracker Jack box. If a cop wants to become famous, all he has to do is get himself killed. Then they'll put your name on a plaque out there in the lobby. Big deal, huh? The problem with police work is there aren't any prizes at the bottom of the box."

"No one said we wanted to be famous," Jameson said, tossing a rolled-up ball of paper into the trash can. "You know what? I think half of those stories people tell about you aren't true, Cunningham. How are you going to track down Curazon in only a few days?"

"He's gone," O'Malley said, his eyes glued on the spot where Cunningham had been standing only seconds before.

Shana stopped at a Subway shop and bought a sandwich and a Coke, carrying it back to eat in Richard's Corvette. She wolfed down the sandwich, knowing she needed strength to follow through on her plan. Glancing at her watch, she panicked when she saw it was already four-fifteen. Sucking the soda from a straw, she tried to wash down a piece of bread that had become lodged in her throat. Opening the car door, she coughed several times, and the piece of bread popped out onto the ground.

Now that she had eaten, Shana gunned the engine on the car, heading to the Target store a few blocks down from the government center. Before she went inside, she checked her wallet, afraid she didn't have enough money. Then she saw the hundred-dollar bills her mother had given her. Locking the car, she got out and headed across the parking lot.

A young man in his late teens walked up to her. "Flowers? I got a dozen roses for twenty bucks."

Shana dropped her head and continued walking.

"Come on," he said, holding a paper-wrapped bouquet of white roses close to her face. "You can give them to your mother. Fifteen, okay? I'll sell them to you for fifteen."

"Get away from me," Shana snarled, the scent of the roses making her feel as if she were going to vomit again. Suddenly she stopped walking, locked inside a horrific vision. Curazon was shoving her legs apart. She heard the guttural sounds he had made as he plunged inside her body, heard her own high-pitched scream. She placed her hands over her eyes, wanting to block out the images.

There was no way to stop them.

Curazon was hovering over her, his teeth bared as he spat obscenities at her, his eyes wild with rage and power. Since the rape, she couldn't go to the dentist unless he gave her a sedative. The moment the hygienist pushed the chair back and the dentist leaned down close to her face, Curazon's hideous face would appear.

But it was primarily the smell of the roses that brought back the full force of the terror. During the many years she'd spent in therapy, she had gone over that night again and again, finally arriving at a specific sequence of events. She must have first awakened when she heard noises on the other side of the house, then momentarily fallen back to sleep, the scent of roses floating in through the open window above her bed. The next time she awakened, she heard a loud banging sound and her mother's muffled cries for help as Curazon dragged her down the hallway. Shana forced herself to continue walking, finally reaching the entrance to the store.

"Ten bucks, okay?"

Shana reached over and snatched the flowers out of the panhandler's hand, then hurled them into the parking lot. "I don't want any damn roses," she said, the automatic door almost striking her in the face. "When a person says no, next time maybe you'll listen."

35

Paul Butler, the chief deputy district attorney of Ventura County, was seated behind his desk in his large corner office on the third floor of the government center complex in Ventura, his eyes bloodshot from staring at columns of figures. Julia Benson, his assistant, called him over the intercom, advising him that he had a visitor waiting in the reception area. "I'm working on the budget, Julia," he said. "I asked you not to interrupt me."

"It's Lily Forrester's daughter."

At sixty-one, Butler was a small, balding man. Scheduled to retire in three months, he was counting the days. His plan had been to talk his wife into selling the house they'd lived in during their twenty-seven years of marriage in exchange for a condominium in a community with a golf course. The previous year he'd undergone hip-replacement surgery. This year he had developed a problem with his right knee, making it painful for him to walk an eighteen-hole course. What he wanted was to be able to scoot around in his own golf cart, jump on the greens anytime he wanted, and make a last-ditch attempt to improve his golf game. He didn't feel he was asking too much. During his marriage his wife had never worked, and he'd always been an excellent provider. At the moment he wasn't a happy camper. His oldest daughter had thrown a wrench in his retirement plans.

"Paul," Julia said again, "didn't you hear me?"

"I heard you," Butler snapped, turning the volume up on the intercom. "Why would Lily Forrester's daughter want to see me?"

"She won't say."

"Let someone else handle it." Butler spun his chair around, gazing out the window as the sun began to set over the Ventura foothills. He had heard that Lily's husband had been murdered, but only after he'd given prosecutor Frank Pearlman permission to file charges against her on the Hernandez matter. He'd only made such a decision due to pressure from the mayor's office. In his opinion, trying a case that old wasn't worth the effort. He didn't really give a hoot. Since the problem would fall into the hands of his successor, why should he become embroiled in a confrontation with the woman's daughter?

"The girl's insistent," Julia told him. "She claims it's a life-or-death situation."

"Jesus," Butler exclaimed, "did someone make certain she didn't slip through with a gun or some other kind of weapon?" While he was up to his eyeballs in work, trying to tie up loose ends for his impending retirement, his oldest daughter had suddenly shown up on his doorstep with her three kids. He loved his grandchildren, but his daughter had spoiled them rotten. She thought she could buy her way out of the fact that she'd walked out on their father. The last thing Butler wanted this late in the day was to have to deal with another hysterical female.

"Everyone goes through the metal detector downstairs," Julia said in her clipped New England accent. "The girl is carrying a Target sack, and one of those bags designed for portable computers. Security looked through them both. I don't think there's any reason for anyone to do a body search." Her next statement held a ring of sarcasm. "You may be important, Paul, but you're not the president."

Butler had nothing against women, but lately they seemed to think they could walk all over him. "I'm tired," he said, placing the palm of his hand on his forehead. "Don't I still have a right to make my own decisions?"

"I spoke to her in the lobby," Julia Bender told him. "Lily and I were friends, Paul. This young woman was raped, and now some maniac has murdered her father. It's over my head, so I don't even want to mention these so-called murder charges. Just give the girl a few minutes of your time, and I promise I'll keep everyone out of your hair until you finish the budget."

"Fine," Butler said grudgingly. "Send her in."

At five-fifteen, Shana was buzzed through the security doors. At forty-three, Julia had short brown hair and pale green eyes. She was dressed in a white silk blouse and a black skirt. "I'm sorry about your father," she said, escorting the girl down the carpeted corridor. "This must be a terrible time for you. Please express my sympathies to your mother. Tell her I said to call me if there's anything I can do."

"Thanks," Shana told her, accepting the card she pressed into her hand.

Julia opened the door to the deputy district attorney's office, then quietly retreated.

"So you're the big boss around here," Shana said, taking a seat in one of the chairs in front of his desk. Her face was void of makeup, and she was wearing a pair of Levi's and a sweatshirt. She crossed her legs, swinging one foot back and forth, purposely wanting to draw Butler's attention to the bulky hiking boots she'd purchased during her shopping trip to Target, the type of boots she recalled seeing her mother wearing the morning after the rape.

"What can I do for you?" Butler asked, placing his hands behind his neck as he leaned back in his chair. "Shana, right?"

"Yeah," she said. "Do you know my mother?"

"Yes, I do," Butler answered. "I know your mother quite well."

"Not that well," Shana told him, reaching into her computer case and pulling out a copy of the composite drawing she'd found in the newspaper archives. "Not if you're going to put her in prison for something she didn't do."

Butler straightened up in his chair. His glasses slid down on his nose as he peered up at her. "We're only doing our job," he said. "I realize this —"

Shana threw up her hands. "If you say what I think you're going to say, I'm going to scream. Everyone keeps saying they know what a terrible time this is for me. That's a crock of shit, okay? My father was murdered. The man who raped me has already been released from prison. He's probably trying to find me right now so he can kill me or rape me again."

Butler reached for the button on the speaker phone, deciding he would have to call security and have the girl removed. She looked fairly young, but she was at least five-ten, if not taller, and she appeared to be in excellent physical condition. He was older and smaller; therefore, there was a chance she could overpower him. He cursed Julia for talking him into seeing her. Although he didn't feel the situation called for such a drastic measure as hitting the panic button under his desk, the atmosphere inside the room had become heavy and oppressive. Lily's daughter seemed to be emitting some type of tremendous energy, and the look in her eyes was menacing.

Just then Shana leaped to her feet, reaching into the sack and pulling out a blue knit cap. While Butler watched, having no idea what she was going to do next, she stuffed her long red hair inside the cap, then rushed toward his desk.

"Call security!" Butler hit the intercom with one hand and the panic button with the other, then shoved his chair back from the desk in order to put as much space as possible between himself and the girl.

"I'm not going to hurt you," Shana said, slapping the paper down on his desk. "This is the drawing of the person they said killed Bobby Hernandez. Look at it. Tell me what you see."

Two uniformed officers burst through the door. Julia Bender stood in the outer office, her arms locked around her chest. A blond-haired officer grabbed Shana's right arm, yanked it behind her back, then reached for her left arm. A taller African American officer handed him a pair of handcuffs.

"You can't do this to me," Shana yelled, struggling until she felt the handcuffs cutting into her wrists. "I don't have a gun. I wasn't going to shoot him or attack him."

"Your actions were threatening," Butler told her, trying to catch his breath. Removing a handkerchief from his pocket, he mopped the perspiration off his brow, wondering if he was going to survive the next three months until his retirement party.

"Aren't you even going to look at the drawing?"

"Get her computer out of my office," Butler instructed the officers. "Have someone check and make certain there isn't a bomb in there . . . some type of explosives."

"No problem," the dark-skinned officer said, picking up Shana's case and leaving the room.

Now that the situation appeared to be under control, Butler finally picked up the composite drawing Shana had placed on his desk, bringing it close to his face. It didn't take him long to detect the resemblance — the long neck, the nose, the almond shape of the eyes, the pronounced cheekbones.

The officer holding Shana asked, "What do you want us to do with her, sir?"

"Give me a minute," Butler barked, using his index finger to adjust his glasses. He continued to study the image, shifting his eyes back and forth from the paper to the girl. "Are you trying to claim this is you?"

"Yes," Shana said, her wrists smarting from the handcuffs. "Why do you think I came here? My mother didn't kill that man. I killed him."

"Calm down," the district attorney told her. "You don't have to try to get my attention. Trust me, you have everyone's attention in this room."

"Can't you take these things off my wrists?" Shana asked, her teeth clenched. "They're too tight."

The officer waited until Butler nodded, then removed a key from his belt and unlocked the handcuffs. Julia Bender tiptoed in and stood in the back of the room. Attorneys and other office personnel had heard the ruckus and gathered in the outer office, watching the drama unfold through the open doorway.

"My mother had Hernandez's picture," Shana said, rubbing her wrists. "She'd just signed his release from jail the night we were raped. My father lied when he said my mother didn't come home until the next morning. I took her car and drove over to the address on the man's booking sheet. He looked exactly like the man who raped us. I found my granddaddy's shotgun in the garage. I waited until he came out of his house the next morning, then I shot him."

"Where's the shotgun?"

"In the ocean," Shana lied, fixing her eyes on a spot over the district attorney's head. "I was thirteen. He held a knife to my throat while he made my mother suck him."

Butler sat at rapt attention. The threatening demeanor Shana had displayed earlier had disappeared, replaced by a childlike vulnerability. The transformation was mesmerizing. Although Shana's back was turned to the people huddled around the open doorway, a cloak of silence fell over the room.

Her voice became low and small, yet she spoke slowly and distinctly, making her recitation even more chilling. The sound of phones ringing in the background was the only distraction, and after a few moments it became obvious that no one was going to answer them. Julia darted out of the room, called the switchboard, then returned.

"Mom tried to protect me," Shana said. "She said she'd do anything if he wouldn't hurt me. He said he didn't want her because she was old. He smelled putrid . . . his breath, his underarms, his clothes. I was praying, certain he was going to kill us." She paused, the bitter young woman reappearing. "He's not even locked up anymore," she shouted. "For all I know, he's the person who stabbed my father. I don't care if you send me to jail. At least I'd be safer than I would be out there." She gestured toward the window, to the parking lot where she knew Curazon had first began concocting his vile fantasies, watching her mother from the windows of the jail.

In all his years as a district attorney, Paul Butler had never found himself in such an emotionally charged situation. Even though he had sat in scores of courtrooms and listened to hundreds of victims, Shana Forrester had managed to draw him inside her soul. Butler's hands trembled on the composite drawing as Shana slowly removed the knit cap from her head, her red hair spilling out onto her shoulders.

"Leave us alone," the district attorney said. "Close the door, Julia. Tell the people out there to go back to work."

As soon as the room had cleared and they were alone, Butler asked her to sit down. Shana did what he said, folding her hands in her lap. "You're going to put me in jail, aren't you?"

Butler's life's work had been devoted to making certain the criminals who victimized innocent people were safely locked behind bars. Experiencing the pain of this young woman made him question what he had really accomplished. "How old are you?"

"Nineteen."

"Your mother was an extraordinary prosecutor," he told her, "as well as an exceptional supervisor." Around the time Lily and her daughter were raped, the governor had offered her a superior court judgeship. Lily had decided to relocate to Los Angeles, and Butler had given her a recommendation for the job she had later accepted with the appellate court. The McDonald-Lopez case came to mind. The gruesome images of the two slain teenagers would always haunt him. Bobby Hernandez had been the ringleader, if his memory served him correct; then the man had gone on to kill another woman.

"Do you work?" he asked. "Go to college?"

"Before my father was killed, I was in my sophomore year at UCLA. I planned on going to law school like my mother." Shana felt her dream drifting away, but she had gone too far to turn back. "I guess girls my age have silly dreams. I wanted to be like Sandra Day O'Connor, maybe work my way up to the Supreme Court."

"There's nothing silly about wanting to reach high in life," Butler said, remembering how he had aspired to the same goal. "I'm not certain the Supreme Court is all it's cracked up to be. I've spoken to a few of the justices, and they say it's pretty tedious work, similar to what your mother did with the appellate court, even though she wasn't a judge. You know, lots of paperwork and no action."

From the explosiveness of only a short time ago, a long silence ensued, neither of them feeling the need to speak.

"What are we going to do?" Shana asked, shattering the silence. "I won't make a scene if you have to call the police officers again. I know what I did was wrong."

"I'm sure you do," Butler said, pondering the moral and ethical complexity she had brought to his doorstep. "The problem is, Shana, I'm not convinced you killed this man. I'm sure your mother told you some of the things you said today, or you read about them in the paper."

"So you think I'm lying?"

"I don't really know," Butler said honestly. "You may have imagined that you killed this man, and no doubt you wanted him to suffer for what you went through. Those type of feelings are normal. What we're dealing with is a lack of credibility."

"Why?" Shana asked, compressing in her seat.

"Because you were only thirteen," Butler said, glancing at the composite drawing again. "You do resemble the person in this drawing. Today, though, not six years ago. Even with the knit cap, this is simply not the face of a thirteen-year-old girl." He read some of the text attached to the newspaper article. "This individual was described as a male, and his height was listed as approximately six feet."

"I was five-eight when I was thirteen," she cried. "I can show you pictures. I can't let my mom go to prison." Most of what she had told him had been true. Lily had pulled the trigger, yet in her mind Shana had been standing right behind her. She started to beg, then stopped herself. She had pleaded with Marco Curazon. She wanted to be strong, fight reason with reason. "You may not believe me. That still doesn't mean you're not going to have a problem. I know how things work. I've watched all those trials on TV, listened to my mom talk about her cases. I'm going to confess, then my mother will confess to protect me. The jury will be so confused, they won't know what to think." She paused, then another thought came to mind. "The jurors will sympathize with my mother and me. They won't care what happens to Hernandez. He killed three people."

"You might be wrong, Shana," Butler told her, sorry he had to be the bearer of bad news. "Mr. Hernandez, no matter how evil he might have been, will not be on trial. What he did doesn't matter. The only way it would be pertinent to your case is if he had been the man who raped you and your mother. You just admitted to me that he wasn't the rapist, that he only looked like this Marco Curazon. Isn't that correct?" Shana felt as if her head were about to explode. Her chest expanded and contracted. She felt dizzy and light-headed, afraid she was going to faint again as she had in the back of the police car. She chewed on a fingernail, thinking of her father, the hateful things she'd said prior to his death. Her mother had made an irreversible mistake when she had shot Hernandez; then her father had driven while intoxicated, causing a young man to lose his life. Was it possible that she had made a serious mistake herself, revealed information that would later be used to put her mother in prison?

She remembered her uncle's funeral several years before, the only funeral she had ever attended. An elderly lady from the church had told her that dying was nothing to be afraid of, that a grave was similar to trading your old house in for a new one. The woman had quoted a statement from the Bible: "In my father's house, there are many mansions."

"I want the police to let me bury my dad," Shana blurted out. "With everything that's going on, I need to plan my father's funeral."

"Julia," Paul Butler said over the intercom, "see if you can get Chief Easterly with the LAPD on the line. I need an update on the Forrester homicide ASAP. Start at the top and work your way down." Once he stopped speaking, he told Shana, "We're going to try to solve at least one of your problems. You and your mother can begin making the necessary arrangements for your father's burial right away. I'll do whatever I can to expedite the release of his body. Will that make you feel better?"

"Yes," she said, "but —"

"You did a lot of talking earlier," Butler interrupted, arching an eyebrow. "I think it's time you listen to what I have to say. I'm certain the police in L.A. are doing everything they can to find the person who killed your father. I'll also make sure our local police department does everything possible to track down the man who raped you. Regarding the Hernandez homicide, from this point on, I would suggest that you only discuss this situation with an attorney."

36

Lily and Richard were frantic. They'd been driving around since Shana had left the house, believing she was somewhere in the Ventura area. Richard steered the Lexus into the parking lot of his law office, wanting to pick up the 9mm Luger he kept locked in the bottom drawer of his office. He also needed the home phone number for Curazon's parole officer. When Richard had first heard the rapist was carrying around what appeared to be a photo of Shana Forrester, the parole officer had informed him that they had already checked the man's known associates, relatives, and any establishment she was known to frequent. Now that John had been murdered, the time had come to do more than merely knock on doors and ask questions.

Returning to the car, Richard slid the Luger under his seat.

"What are you doing?" Lily asked, having seen the outline of a gun in his hand.

"Trying to keep us alive," he told her. "Curazon uses knives because one of his buddies probably taught him that his chances of getting caught with a concealed weapon were less likely than if he packed a firearm. Either that, or he gets a kick out of cutting people."

"Thanks," Lily said facetiously. "We have no idea where Shana is, and you feel the need to remind me that Curazon likes knives. Don't you think I know that by now? Shit, Richard, he used a knife when he raped us."

Richard reached over and pulled her into his arms. "I love you," he said impulsively. "When this is over, I'm going to marry you."

"Do you realize what you just said?" Lily asked, jerking her head back. "And I don't mean the comment about Curazon."

Richard returned to his side of the car, placing his hands on the steering wheel. "I don't know why I said that," he told her, feeling foolish. "I haven't given much thought to getting married again. Not that I don't love you —"

"It's okay," Lily said, lowering her eyes. "People say things they don't mean when they're under stress. You were just trying to make me feel better."

"No," Richard said. "I meant it, Lily. We're going to get through this somehow. Then we're going to do what we should have done six years ago. Shana needs a father.

Greg adores her. Yeah," he said, almost as if he were talking to himself, "I can see it. You know, the marriage and all. I already have the practice. You could become my partner. Then when Shana gets her law degree, she could —"

"Please, stop," Lily said, choking back tears, "you're making things even more difficult for me. I refuse to back down on what I said, no matter how much you and Shana pressure me. If you won't agree to approach the D.A. tomorrow and negotiate a settlement in my behalf, I'll talk to them myself."

"Damn it," he said. "I won't allow you to plead guilty. All that stuff you told Shana was bullshit. The court isn't going to place you in a work-release program. They're going to charge you with murder, Lily. Since when do murderers get work release? You didn't steal the guy's car or hit him over the head. You killed him."

"That's why I can't let this go on," Lily said, shivering at the road ahead of her. "I have to get this off my chest. It's been buried inside me for so long. Even if we did get married, I'd make your life miserable. Why do you think I didn't call you all these years? I even felt guilty that we had that one night together now. I don't deserve to be happy."

"You have every right to be happy,"

Richard insisted. "And I deserve to spend my life with the woman I love, the woman I've wanted since the first day I saw her. Shana has a right to have a family, people who care about her. Hernandez has no rights whatsoever, do you hear me? None. Zilch. Nothing. He forfeited his rights when he murdered those people."

Lily shook her head. "We've gone through all this —"

Richard started the car, then opened and shut both of his fists to release the tension, like a fighter about to slip his hands in his gloves before he entered the ring. "If there is such a thing as Hell," he said, "Hernandez has no rights there, either."

When Richard and Lily finally gave up and returned to his house, the Corvette was parked in the driveway. "Thank God," Lily exclaimed, about to leap out of the car.

"Wait," Richard said, flashing his high beams to illuminate the interior of the car. As soon as they confirmed it was Shana, her mother exited the car and they rushed into each other's arms.

"I'm sorry, Mom," Shana said, sobbing. "I wanted to help you."

"You didn't help me by running off with

Richard's car," Lily said, glancing back at him. "We've been worried sick about you. The most important thing is that you're okay."

An hour later, Richard carried an empty pizza box to the trash can, then poured himself another gin and tonic. Although he'd been famished by the time they reached the house, after listening to Shana explain what had transpired at the D.A.'s office, he had almost lost his appetite. He knew the girl's intentions had been good, but he feared the end results might be disastrous. Shana had gone upstairs to the guest room, and Lily was waiting for him in the library. He started to bring the bottle of gin with him, then changed his mind and placed it back in the liquor cabinet. It had been years since he'd felt the need to numb himself with alcohol. The most memorable had been the night at the Elephant Bar over six years ago, the first time he had slept with Lily. Although they had both sobered up before he had taken her to his house, he had been drinking heavily that night in an attempt to accept the fact that Butler had demoted him.

"Of all people," Richard said, striding back into the library, "Shana had to go straight to Paul Butler. Don't forget, Lily. You got my job as supervisor over the sex crimes division because Butler refused to stand up for me when I walked in and caught Judge Fisher snorting cocaine." He stopped and took another sip of his drink. "You can rule out any attempt to settle this thing outside of the courtroom now that your kid has practically handed them your head on a platter."

"You're overreacting," Lily said, seated on the floor near the fireplace.

"The press will go wild over this story," he continued, wearing out the carpet in front of her. "Your daughter practically reenacted the crime. She not only dressed up to re-semble the composite drawing, she even told him she shot the wrong man. Why in holy hell would she think she could get away with something like this?"

Lily rubbed her hand back and forth on the carpet. "The truth was going to come out eventually. This is my problem. I've told you ten times how I'm going to handle it. All Shana did was make it more difficult for me to negotiate a settlement. Whatever the D.A. offers me, I'll accept."

Richard marched over and slammed the door to the library. He jabbed his thumb to-ward his chest. "I pushed the car over the cliff, remember? For six years I willfully suppressed evidence in a homicide. It's fine and dandy that you want to bare your soul and redeem yourself. What about me, huh? I could be disbarred, and that's only the tip of the iceberg. What if they decide to prosecute me as well? What about Greg? This is the kind of recklessness that got you into this mess."

"I thought you wanted to marry me," Lily said. "Why would you want to marry the kind of reckless, uncaring idiot you just described?"

"Forgive me," he said, squatting on the floor beside her. "I'm frustrated and angry, that's all. I shouldn't have taken it out on you. Under the circumstances, I would have probably gone over there and shot Hernandez myself."

"Don't worry," she told him, "I'll tell them I'm the one who disposed of the Honda. The car may not even come up once I enter a guilty plea. And Shana is the only one who knows I confessed to you. Even Cunningham doesn't know."

He captured her face in his hands, forcing her to look at him. "Who's going to look after your daughter if you go to prison? Why won't you let me take this to a jury and see if I can get you acquitted?"

"Shana's an adult," Lily said, knocking his hands away. "She'll be okay. I refuse to allow her to perjure herself."

Richard stood, seeing a glimmer of light at the end of the tunnel. "Well," he said, smiling briefly, "I guess one good thing came out of this fiasco."

"What's that?"

"You don't have to worry about Shana perjuring herself," he said. "After today, she's the last person they'll want to put on the witness stand."

Lily's face brightened. "They'll think she's going to say she did it again, right? They'll be afraid that she'll plant enough doubt in the jurors' minds that they'll either deadlock or acquit."

"Exactly," he said, extending his hand to help her up. "This time you're going to do things the right way. The D.A. can file any charges he wants. The court will have no justification for holding you without bail, and I have ample funds to get you out. You're going to plead not guilty just like every other defendant who walks into a courtroom."

She remained on the floor, sorting through her thoughts, weighing her options. For years she had worked in the criminal justice system. Her sojourn to the other side of the law had consisted of only a few minutes, the time it took to depress the trigger on her father's shotgun. With John dead, she was beginning to think Richard was right. Could she finally free herself of the past by placing her fate in the hands of a jury? As the accused party, she was protected by the Fifth Amendment from being forced to testify and incriminate herself. Therefore, she wouldn't be committing another crime by getting up on the stand and lying. "Can we win?"

"Of course," Richard said, kissing her on the forehead. "You have a great attorney."

Lily received the call from Matt Kingsley regarding Betsy Middleton's death at approximately ten o'clock Tuesday morning. She had just gotten off the phone with a funeral home, attempting to make the preliminary arrangements for John's burial, even though they would not be allowed to set a date and time for the services until the L.A. authorities released his body. After notifying Richard at the office, she called Dr. Christopher Logan at Saint Francis Hospital, wanting to get the details from him directly since he'd walked in and found Carolyn injecting the strychnine into Betsy's IV.

Shana was still sleeping upstairs, and Richard's large home seemed as if it were filled with a dozen lost souls, her own included. She might have been estranged from John at the time he was killed, but the night before she had lain awake in Richard's guest room, mourning the death of the man she had married. Now she had to come to terms with another death. At least she had some comfort in knowing that Betsy was no longer suffering.

"I don't understand," Lily said when Logan came on the phone. "Was this a case of Munchausen by proxy? Do you think Carolyn Middleton had been poisoning her all along?"

"No," Dr. Logan explained. "From what I ascertained from talking to Henry and other family members, Carolyn had a cousin who suffered from Aicardi syndrome. The disease wasn't identified until the mid 1960s, so they probably treated her cousin for some other type of seizure disorder."

"But you think Carolyn has been poisoning her for sometime?"

"Just since the Halloween incident," he replied. "Then when the poison failed to kill her, Carolyn continued to dose her without our knowledge. I feel partly responsible, as I didn't continue checking her blood and tissue for strychnine, particularly not near the end."

"It's not your fault," Lily told him. "I was certain it was Henry."

"Well," Logan continued, "I'm not a police officer or a prosecutor. All I can do is make an educated guess, and it seems likely that Henry knew Carolyn had poisoned her. I don't believe he assisted her in any way, nor do I believe that he did anything other than buy the candy without advance knowledge of what she intended. And I also feel fairly certain he wasn't aware that Carolyn was continuing to give her doses·of strychnine. This is supported by the fact that Betsy seldom had a seizure when her father was in the room."

"You never mentioned this before now," Lily said, still unable to accept that Henry was innocent. "Also, where did Carolyn buy the strychnine? We have a witness who saw Henry carrying a Coke bottle filled with a strange liquid after paying a visit to the exterminating company next door to one of his warehouses only a few days before the crime. And don't forget the women who saw Henry buying the candy."

"Regarding your witness and the Coke bottle," Logan responded, "it was probably just what it appeared to be. And Carolyn might not have even bought the strychnine. For all we know, she found it in the gardening shed. Their gardener could have easily kept a supply on hand to kill gophers, mice, or some other type of pest. I'm certain they locked up any chemicals on the property, but Carolyn would have had a key."

"Henry was acting strange, though," Lily protested. "And don't forget his business was in trouble. Maybe he only conspired with her?"

"I don't believe so," Logan said. "I think Carolyn told him to buy the candy because she wanted to make certain that she had something to hold over his head. After she placed the strychnine inside the straw candy and Betsy ate it, Henry must have figured out what Carolyn had done. By then he decided it was too late to help his daughter. Carolyn probably threatened to tell the police he was responsible, convincing him that the problems with the business would be viewed as a motive since the girl had a large life insurance policy."

Lily said, "I feel awful."

"I know," Logan said, sighing. "I only began studying her case file again a few days before I walked in and found Carolyn with the syringe in her hands. I wish I had been more alert. The fact that the symptoms of her illness were similar to strychnine poisoning is what threw me for a loop." He paused, catching his breath. "I've learned a lesson I won't ever forget. Like a lot of people here at the hospital, I became very attached to Betsy."

"I guess we've all learned a lesson," Lily said, knowing that by focusing so intently on Henry, she might have overlooked signs that would have pointed toward the child's mother. She was grateful that the prosecution hadn't continued, or Henry might have been convicted. "If he knew, why didn't he come forward? It's hard to believe he would be willing to go to prison for something he didn't do."

"She was his wife," Logan told her. "He must have loved her. It isn't easy having a disabled child. Many times both parents feel responsible, as if by bringing the child into the world, they're to blame for setting them up for a lifetime of hardship. The other Middleton children are well cared for and appear normal in every respect. You should know this from your investigation. Friends and family members have only glowing things to say about how dedicated Carolyn was in caring for Betsy. I think her husband's need to reward her was what drove Henry to become such a successful businessman."

"All the goodies still weren't enough," Lily said. "Is that what you're trying to say?"

"I believe these types of situations reach a much deeper level," Logan explained, his soft voice reassuring and analytical. "A person could have all the riches in the world, and it wouldn't compensate them for the helplessness and despair that's inherent in caring for a child with an incurable illness. I think Carolyn had difficulty enjoying anything, let alone her wealth."

"But you said Betsy could have lived a somewhat normal life."

"I'm a physician," he said. "What I consider normal is not what the average person considers normal. Betsy required constant assistance, medication, schooling, surveillance. You witnessed one of her seizures. They're frightening. If severe enough or if the child is unattended at the time of a seizure, they can cause death."

"I'm certain Betsy appreciates all you've done," Lily told him, slowly replacing the phone in the cradle. She asked herself why she'd spoken of the child in the present tense. But what did she know, what did anyone really know until they stepped over the line and passed into the dimension beyond life? Maybe the little girl did appreciate what Logan had done — that the truth had finally been revealed. Betsy's frail body had struggled against her mother's repeated attempts to end her life. Had her spirit lingered on earth for the specific purpose of telling her story?

Lily's eyes filled with tears. John's life seemed like the leather-bound book sitting on the corner of Richard's desk, a collection of pages, now only memories. Her former husband hadn't been an evil, worthless man, just a weak man. In comparison, Betsy Middleton had been a brave and courageous warrior. She might have lived only eight short years. Nonetheless, Lily felt certain that her book would be much larger, the cover not made out of leather but of gold.

37

Gasping for breath in an intense state of excitement, he rapidly thumbed through the pictures, his chest rising and falling. He had not showered in over a week, but the stench of his body didn't bother him. After years in the joint, he was immune to just about everything. He touched the edge of a photo album, his eyes zeroing in on a particular image. His head fell back, his mouth opened, and a look of pleasure spread across his face. "There's my girl," he said. "That's the one I remember, not that other redheaded bitch."

Yanking the photo out from behind its plastic casing, he placed it in his duffel bag with the other souvenirs he had collected. Rummaging through another drawer, he pulled out a pair of white panties and added them to his growing collection. The next thing he pulled out was a china doll, its frilly dress torn in several places. Around the doll's neck was a red ribbon and a small heart-shaped pendant. He could imagine her tiny fingers reaching out to touch the pendant, the smile on her face, how happy she must have been when her mother gave it to her. She'd been a pretty girl, a smart girl, a girl whose parents had given her everything she had ever wanted.

She should have grown up the way he had, he thought with bitterness, having to steal to buy his brothers and sisters food, his mother beating him relentlessly until his back had become permanently scarred.

Switches — that was what his mother used to beat him with — big, skinny sticks torn from the tree out back. First it was the closet, the dark stinking closet. He had sat in there for hours and cried, beating the door until his hands were bloody and raw. But when she opened the door, it was worse because she had the switches. Over the commode . . . she made him bend over the open, reeking toilet with his shirt off. And she whipped and whipped him, screaming that she wouldn't stop until he quit crying. She had been a liar. Even when he quit crying, she never stopped. She didn't stop until blood dripped from his back onto the filthy, cracked linoleum. Then she made him mop it up, scrub and scrub until it was clean.

He could still smell the awful stuff she had put on her hair. The stuff to make it red. It smelled so awful that his eyes would burn. He had loved her long black hair that hung all the way to her hips — before the switches and the beatings. He used to braid it for her. He'd stand behind her on *a stool and gather it gently in his hands.*

After she made her hair red, she started staying out all night and sleeping all day. She stopped making them food. Sometimes she'd walk in the door with a sack and they thought it was food, but it wasn't. She'd throw a few dollar bills on the table and leave every night. He'd walk alone to the store and try to buy enough for them all to eat, but he never had enough money.

Mark Osborne had taken Tuesday off, as his mother was ill in San Diego. Hope Carruthers was eager to make at least some progress toward resolving the Forrester homicide by the time the detective returned to work the next day. This was her first major homicide investigation, and she wanted to prove that she could handle such a difficult assignment.

Due to the pressure from various high-placed officials, the crime lab in Los Angeles had pushed the Forrester homicide to the top of their list of priorities. The medical examiner's officer, however, didn't care whose body they had on ice. They could perform only so many autopsies in one day. In a city the size of Los Angeles, if the medical examiner's office succumbed to demands from anyone other than their own director, the end results would be worthless in a court of law.

"The fingerprints," Hope said, speaking to the expert at the lab. "Surely you've done a work-up on those by now. The killer left at least one complete set of prints that could be seen with the naked eye. My guess is he left prints all over that garage."

"Hold on," Chan Lee said, "I think I do have something for you."

Hope tapped her fingernails on her desk while she was waiting. At least the hit-and-run had been cleared. Whoever had killed Forrester had put one case to bed. John Forrester had been tanked to the gills the night of his death, so in that respect alone, Hope had ruled out Shana Forrester as a suspect. Then the night before, a young couple had appeared at the station after seeing Forrester's picture in the newspaper, advising that they had seen him the night of the accident at the Ralph's supermarket only a few blocks from the Baskin-Robbins where the accident had occurred.

"Detective Carruthers," Lee said, coming back on the line, "we do have a positive match on the fingerprint samples. The man's name is Marco Curazon. He's in the system as a recent parolee. Would you like me to give you his federal ID number?"

"Yes," she said, scribbling it down on a yellow pad. "Let us know as soon as anything else develops."

Hope immediately put in a call to the number she had for Lily Forrester, but all she got was her voice mail. She tried contacting her at the D.A.'s office in Santa Barbara and was told that she'd requested a leave of absence. Lily and her daughter's suspicion that Marco Curazon had been stalking them had not been a figment of their imagination. Unfortunately, no one had been able to do anything about it until Curazon committed another crime, a situation that occurred all too frequently.

Hope assumed that John must have surprised Curazon while he was hiding out in the garage. She had no doubt that his intended victim had been Shana. The girl had narrowly escaped another meeting with her attacker. From the number and ferocity of the stab wounds inflicted on her father, Curazon's appetite for violence had surpassed the crime of rape.

She called central dispatch, instructing them to enter Curazon into the national system, emphasizing that he was armed and dangerous. They would also notify the parole authorities, although the only assistance they generally provided at this stage were possible leads garnered from other parolees.

Hope placed her head in her hands. She was concerned that Lily and her daughter had stopped answering their phone because they were attempting to avoid the media. Typing in the address she had for Lily into her computer, she printed out the directions and grabbed her cell phone, deciding to drive to Santa Barbara herself.

As the detective made her way out of the building, her tendency to favor her left leg was more pronounced than most days. When the weather changed, the steel plate the doctors had inserted to repair the damage from the gunshot wound expanded, making walking even short distances extremely painful. She refused to take pills beyond aspirin. She'd seen too many injured officers become addicted to either painkillers or alcohol, some even resorting to street drugs. Her own role as a victim caused her to identify with Shana Forrester. She knew if Osborne had been on duty, he would have insisted that she merely contact the local authorities in Santa Barbara. In that respect, Hope was glad he wasn't around. The Santa Barbara police would be notified to be on the lookout for Curazon by the dispatchers, but she personally wanted to tell Shana that they had identified the man who had murdered her father.

Once Hope was in her police unit and on the freeway, she couldn't stop thinking of the night of the crime, how Osborne had left a nineteen-year-old girl alone in an interview room for three hours, only to walk in and tell her that her father had been murdered. She admired the detective as an investigator, and had learned a great deal in the short time they had worked together, yet in some areas his personality bordered on cruelty. Perhaps, she told herself, his insensitivity had grown out of years of working homicide. She was determined that she would never become hardened to the feelings of others simply because she had chosen to enter law enforcement.

Hitting a wall of rush-hour traffic, she decided what the hell, and slapped her light on top of the unmarked car, watching as the speedometer hit eighty, then ninety, slowing down only when she reached the outskirts of Santa Barbara. Just as she'd roared past Ventura, the sky had opened up and it had started pouring. She'd heard on the news that they were expecting a major storm sometime that evening. It looked as if it had arrived earlier than predicted.

Lightning zigzagged across the sky, followed immediately by a loud clap of thunder. Her father had been a simple, wise man. He'd owned and operated his own landscape business. She'd grown up in El Paso in a comfortable home, and her father had managed to put all five of his children through college, a substantial feat that had never been accomplished by anyone else in the Cortez family. She remembered when she was a child and how terrified she used to be when it thundered. Her father would lovingly pull her onto his lap, telling her that thunder was only the sound the gods made when they went bowling.

Flicking on her dome light, Hope checked for the exit leading to Lily's house. The area she lived in was heavily wooded, and there were very few streetlights. She circled around for at least fifteen minutes, then suddenly stopped and backed up, realizing she had driven past the address twice without noticing. The rain was coming down in solid sheets. Pulling into the driveway, she saw lights burning in the rear of a large Tudor mansion. The house didn't appear to have a garage, therefore, Hope assumed that they must have converted it into a guest cottage. Two cars were parked in the driveway, both of them covered. On the opposite side of the house, closer to the guest house, she saw another car, but with the rain it was difficult to make out the model. The car looked new, so she assumed it was Lily's and not that of a caretaker.

Hope pulled into the driveway and parked. She wondered if she had an umbrella in the trunk. Rubbing her hands together to warm them, she gazed at the big house, thinking it must be worth at least a million if not more. She knew Lily was divorced, and even though a prosecutor's salary was slightly higher than a detective's, she wondered how she could afford such an expensive home. Retrieving the newspaper she had tossed in the backseat that morning, she stepped out, placing the paper over her head rather than try to find an umbrella.

The rain was coming down so hard now that even the walkway leading to the front of the house had turned into a slippery mess of mud. She almost fell several times, and wondered why there weren't more lights along the walkway. A strange sensation came over her. She stopped and turned around, seeing something moving near the guest cottage. She reminded herself that she wasn't in Los Angeles. Santa Barbara wasn't that populated, at least not in this particular area. She could have seen a coyote, or a possum, some type of wild animal. Foxes were fairly common in the area, someone had told her once.

Turning back toward the front of the house, she heard another noise. Opening her purse, she pulled out her gun and released the safety, letting the newspaper flutter off in the wind.

It all happened in what seemed like seconds. Curazon charged her like a linebacker, knocking her to the ground. Her gun flew out of her hand. He sat on her chest, pinning her hands over her head. She screamed, staring up at the same horrid image Shana Forrester had seen the night she was raped.

38

Detectives Jameson and O'Malley walked out the front entrance of the Ventura county government center at approximately four o'clock Tuesday afternoon, a signed warrant for the arrest of Lily Forrester in their hands. "Are you certain you want to drive to Santa Barbara tonight in this rain?" O'Malley asked, standing under the overhang for the building. "Forrester may not even be at her place. Since she's not answering her home phone, Fred, why go on a wild goose chase? A stretch of the 101 freeway just outside of Santa Barbara washed out last year."

"You really are over the hill," Jameson said, scowling as they hurried to their car, both of them huddling under the same umbrella. "Do you know how long I've waited to bust this broad, O'Malley? I'd drive five hundred miles to see the look on her face when we slap a pair of handcuffs on her."

"What do you think about her daughter strolling into Butler's office and trying to convince him she killed Hernandez?"

Jameson snorted. "Proves my point,

561

doesn't it? Not only did Lily do the deed, if you ask me, both her and her daughter are psycho. Butler had to call security on the girl. He was sure she was going to attack him."

Locating their unmarked Chrysler in the parking lot, they ducked inside, then continued their conversation. "Frank Pearlman thinks it might be a major problem," O'Malley told him. "We've got to track down some of those witnesses you promised him, as well as that tape you made of your conversation with John Forrester. Pearlman is afraid of putting the kid on the stand."

"We'll find it," Jameson said. "Just because Cunningham couldn't find some of the evidence doesn't mean it doesn't exist. I know the tape is there, because I saw it. Besides, I called from the department phone. All the calls are recorded. It just takes a long time to find what you need. As soon as we track down Lily, we can start picking through the evidence boxes again."

When they finally made their way to Santa Barbara, not only had the storm increased in strength, Jameson turned too fast and they got stuck in a ditch about a block from Lily's residence.

"You're the biggest jackass I've ever met," O'Malley said, getting out to push the car.

"I told you we should have waited until to-morrow morning."

"Just push," Jameson said, grunting. "I thought this was supposed to be a fancy neighborhood. There's potholes in the street, no lights, and I feel like I'm lost in some kind of maze."

O'Malley stopped, opened the trunk, and removed a rag to wipe his hands. He pulled his jacket away from his body, his clothes soaked. "This car isn't going to budge," he told his partner. "You're going to have to get a tow truck out here."

"Call the local P.D.," Jameson said, "tell them to send a truck from their yard and pull the car out. According to my directions, the house is only a block away. By the time we pop Lily, we'll be ready to head back to Ventura and book her into the jail."

Keith O'Malley shined his flashlight in Jameson's face. "You son of a bitch," he shouted over the rain. "You purposely planned it so she'd have to spend the night in jail."

Jameson smiled. "I'm really God, right? I planned the storm and everything."

"No, idiot," O'Malley said, deciding he never wanted to work with Jameson again. "That's why you forced me into coming up here this late."

A gust of wind swept down from the canyons, and Jameson's umbrella disappeared. He pulled his jacket closed around his body and continued walking.

The storm had given Hope a momentary reprieve.

She had been certain Curazon was going to kill her when he first attacked her, but the torrents of rain had caused his knife to fall out of his waistband. He released one of her hands, feeling on the ground, thinking he would either find his blade or her gun. Because he had moved several inches forward, Hope raised her right knee and slammed it into his groin. Curazon's abdominal muscles contracted from the pain. He seized a handful of her hair. Hope managed to shove him off her and scramble to her feet. While Curazon was shouting profanities and rolling from side to side on the soggy grass, a flash of lightning illuminated the sky, and she suddenly saw her gun on the stone pathway a few feet away.

Hope picked up her service revolver and trained it at Curazon, her arms aching from the struggle. "Don't move," Hope shouted, her finger resting on the trigger. "Right now I'd just love to shoot you."

A beam of light came from behind her.

Hope didn't take her eyes off her prisoner, believing it was only another streak of lightning.

"Who in the hell are you?" Jameson said, his flashlight pointed at her face.

Hope jerked her head around. "LAPD homicide," she said, thinking he was a neighbor who had heard her cries for help. "Call the Santa Barbara police and have them send someone out here right away. This man is under arrest for homicide and assault on a police officer."

"Well, if this don't beat all," Keith O'Malley said, shoving Jameson aside, then removing his handcuffs. As he walked toward Hope, he reassured her by holding his shield out in front of him. "Ventura P.D. homicide," he told her. "What's your name, officer?"

"Detective —" Hope lowered her arms, too weak to finish her sentence. Her blouse was ripped, both her shoes were gone, her hair was dangling into her face in wet clumps, and the pain in her leg was so severe, she was certain she was going to collapse at any moment. Once O'Malley had Curazon in handcuffs and had rolled him over onto his stomach, she remembered her father and found a renewed sense of strength. "Detective Esperanza Cortez

Carruthers," she told him proudly.

"That's a mouthful," he answered. "I'm Detective O'Malley. I think we spoke on the phone a few times." He reached over and nudged Curazon with his foot. "And who is this sack of shit?"

"Marco Curazon," she said, sitting down on the porch step. "His fingerprints match those found in the garage at John Forrester's residence. He's also the man who raped Shana and Lily Forrester six years ago."

"Where's Lily?" Jameson asked, reaching for the soggy arrest warrant in his pocket.

O'Malley looked at Carruthers and shook his head. "You're not only a prick, Fred, you don't have the reasoning abilities of a fly. If Lily Forrester had been here tonight, she'd be dead."

39

The courtroom was packed, every seat taken. Reporters and other spectators had been allowed to stand along the back wall, as long as they didn't cause a disruption. Lily was seated at the counsel table with Richard, waiting for the municipal court judge to render her ruling at the preliminary hearing.

In a felony case, the prelim could best be described as a mini-trial, where both sides were allowed to present evidence and call witnesses if they felt it was to their advantage. There was no jury, however, and the burden of proof was far less than it would be during the actual trial. All the state needed to establish in the lower court was that a crime had been committed, and that there was sufficient evidence to hold the defendant, Lilian Forrester, to answer in superior court.

Lily was dressed in a navy blue suit, her hair secured in a knot at the base of her neck. She was wearing her reading glasses and only a touch of lipstick. Her face was pale and drawn, but when Richard glanced over at her, he felt she had never looked more beautiful. He touched her hand under the table, then whispered in her ear, "It's going to be over any minute now. Stay strong."

Shana was seated in the row behind the counsel table, as was Richard's son, Greg. She reached forward and placed a hand on her mother's shoulder. Lily gave her a weak smile, then turned her eyes back to the front of the courtroom. What happened today was insignificant, her mother had told her before they'd left the house that morning to drive to the courthouse. They no longer had to live in fear. Marco Curazon would either receive the death penalty, or he would spend the remainder of his life in prison without the possibility of parole. The D.A.'s office in Los Angeles had assured Shana and Lily that they had more than enough evidence to make the charges against Curazon stick. He would never taste freedom again.

On the left side of the room, Fred Jameson and Keith O'Malley were conferring with Frank Pearlman. At forty-two, the prosecutor was a short, wiry man with bushy hair, a beard, and small dark eyes. He had a look of disgust on his face when he finished speaking to the two detectives. They had promised him evidence and then failed to deliver. With the knowledge he possessed about the victim in the case, Bobby Hernandez, his feelings about the outcome of the case were ambiguous.

"I still don't know what happened to the evidence," Jameson mumbled under his breath. "How could the central system have erased a whole day's worth of tapes? Nothing like this has ever happened before. It's insane."

"It's a little late to discuss it now, don't you think?" O'Malley told him.

"All rise," the bailiff said. "Division Eleven of the Municipal Court of Ventura County is now in session, Judge Francine Parks presiding."

Judge Parks took her seat on the bench. She was an attractive woman in her late forties, with brown hair trimmed just below her ears, an olive complexion, and lovely eyes. She peered out over the courtroom, then moved the microphone closer to her mouth. "In the state versus Lilian Forrester, case number A4873468," she said, "the court finds there is insufficient evidence to hold this defendant to answer in superior court." She paused and linked eyes with Lily, then tapped her gavel lightly. "This court is hereby adjourned."

Richard and Lily were already on their feet. Shana and her mother embraced each other, tears streaming down both their cheeks. Greg shook his father's hand. "Good job," he said, smiling broadly.

Lily threw her arms around Richard. "You were right," she said. "I did have a great attorney."

Now that the court was no longer in session, reporters rushed over and snapped Lily's picture. Seeing the crush of people in the aisle, the two bailiffs came around from the side and escorted Lily, Shana, Richard, and Greg Fowler out of the courtroom, where another group of individuals had assembled. "This is a madhouse," Lily said, clinging to Richard's arm. When the bailiffs finally cleared a path for them to the front steps of the courthouse, she suddenly stopped, unable to believe her eyes.

Bruce Cunningham was standing in the parking lot. If he hadn't been such a large man with such distinctive features, Lily wouldn't have recognized him. For a moment she thought she was hallucinating from stress. They had tried to reach him several times in Omaha, but the company he worked for had consistently told them he was too busy to take their phone calls. Lily had been convinced that the detective had been avoiding her, so she had asked Richard to stop calling him.

Lily pointed toward the parking lot. "That's Bruce Cunningham."

"Where?" Richard asked, following her line of vision.

Cunningham's gruff face spread in a smile; then he raised his hand and waved. Lily broke away from Richard, Shana, and Greg, shoving aside the throngs of people to get to him. By the time she reached the area of the parking lot where he had been standing, the detective was gone. Lily found herself standing in a vacant parking spot. She lifted her face to the warmth of the sun. A few moments later she was surrounded by a circle of love as Shana, Richard, and Greg walked up beside her.

Author's Notes

Many individuals played an important role in this novel becoming reality: my agent, Peter Miller, at PMA Literary and Film Management; Delin Cormeny, also with PMA; my new editor at Hyperion, Maureen O'Brien; my special angel and friend, Michaela Hamilton; Dr. Christopher Geiler for his medical expertise; my heavenly muses, too numerous to mention by name. You know who you are and how extremely grateful I am for all you have beamed my way.

I owe a special debt of gratitude to my mother, Ethel LaVerne Taylor, a woman so enchanting and mystical that she saw my books in a store window before I even published my first novel in 1993; to my sisters and brothers: Sharon, Linda, and Bill; and to my various children and their spouses: Forrest Blake and Jeannie; Chessly and James Nesci; Hoyt and Barbara Skyrme, Nancy Beth and Amy Rosenberg; my heroic adopted daughter, Janelle Garcia, please know I cherish each and every one of you.

To my precious grandchildren: Rachel,

Jimmy, and the adorable little girl born almost on the same exact day I finished the novel: Camille Skyrme.

The employees of Thorndike Press hope you have enjoyed this Large Print book. All our Large Print titles are designed for easy reading, and all our books are made to last. Other Thorndike Press Large Print books are available at your library, through selected bookstores, or directly from us.

For information about titles, please call:

(800) 223-1244
(800) 223-6121

To share your comments, please write:

Publisher
Thorndike Press
P.O. Box 159
Thorndike, Maine 04986